THE REVENGE OF DEAD HORSE CANYON

Sweet Medicine Spirits - *Novavose*

I0590390

Book III of the Dead Horse Canyon Saga by

Marcha Fox & Pete Risingsun

Kalliope Rising Press

Naples, New York

Kalliope Rising Press
Naples, New York 14512

Sweet Medicine's Prophecy in Chapter 23 derived from "The Cheyenne Indians: Their History and Ways of Life," Volume II by George Bird Grinnell. Used with permission from World Wisdom Inc.

KalliopeRisingPress.com

First Printing 2025
Printed in U.S.A.

Editorial assistance provided by: Dawn Greenfield Ireland / Artistic Origins degreenfield.com/Services

Cover and interior design by Kalliope Rising Press

Front Cover Photo Credits: Bear Butte with Buffalo by John Brueski, Shutterstock 483013729
Bison Head by art_rich, Shutterstock 130395841
Back Cover Photo Credit: Prayer Cloths at Bear Butte State Park, Richard345, Shutterstock 2167160593

ISBN: 979-8-9923393-0-7

EBOOKS: 979-8-9923393-1-4

BISAC: FIC59090 Indigenous/Mystery/Detective

PRAISE FOR BOOK I:

The Curse of Dead Horse Canyon:

Cheyenne Spirits

"Exceptional. The intricate plot and dramatic storyline create a breathtaking and intense story." -- Readers' Favorite

PRAISE FOR BOOK II:

Return to Dead Horse Canyon:

Grandfather Spirits

"The depth of ethnology packed into both novels is meticulously researched and beautifully detailed. Fox and Risingsun are a dream team with this saga." -- Readers' Favorite

OTHER BOOKS

This Series with Pete Risingsun

The Curse of Dead Horse Canyon: Cheyenne Spirits (Book 1)
Return to Dead Horse Canyon: Grandfather Spirits (Book 2)

Website: Dead-Horse-Canyon.com

Science Fiction by Marcha Fox

Beyond the Hidden Sky*
A Dark of Endless Days*
A Psilent Place Below*
Refractions of Frozen Time*
The Star Trails Compendium
The Sapphiran Agenda (Short Story)*
The Terra Debacle: Prisoners at Area 51*

Website: StarTrailsSaga.com

*Available as audiobooks

Family History

The Family History Fun Factor

Astrology

Whobeda's Guide to Basic Astrology
The Dark Side of Eclipses

Website: Valkyrieastrology.com

DEDICATION

To the memory of

Father Peter John Powell

Scholar, Ethno-historian, Author, and Anglican Priest

July 2, 1928 - December 15, 2022

Award Winning Author

of

"Sweet Medicine" Volumes 1 and 2, as well as "People of the Sacred Mountain," Books 1 and 2, and many others.

Father Powell, a dear friend of author, Pete Risingsun, chronicled Cheyenne ceremonies and history so it could be preserved and used extensively in these stories.

We are grateful for his dedication to the Cheyenne people and his incredible volume of work on their behalf.

Biographical Information

https://www.newberry.org/news/father-peter-j-powell-1928-2022

https://aihschgo.org/in-memoriam-father-powell/

BOOK THREE

In their first ancient days of despair, Maheo sent his People the Sacred Arrows (Mahuts) that, for some of them at least, remain the soul of Cheyenne tribal existence.

Since then, in nearly every generation the Cheyennes have known that someone must return to Nowah'wus; someone must represent the People on the windblown sides of the Sacred Mountain. For power in abundance awaits the Cheyennes there; strength like the power flowing from Mahuts themselves.

Blessed by the Sacred Arrows, the Sacred Buffalo Hat, and the strength that pours from Nowah'wus, the Sacred Mountain, all will be well for Maheo's People, even in the strange new days that lie ahead.

—"Sweet Medicine", Volume 1, p. 428

DRAMATIS PERSONAE

Bryan Reynolds - Systems Administrator, Denver Employees
Federal Credit Union (DEFCU) (deceased)
Sara Reynolds - Bryan's wife
Charlie Littlewolf - Bryan's closest friend
Joe White Wolf - Charlie's uncle, Medicine Man
Will Montgomery - Sara's father
Connie Montgomery - Will's wife, Sara's step-mother
Jason LaGrange - NSA operative
Bernard Keller - CEO, BG Security Services (BKSS)
Eddie Johannsen - BKSS Task Force Lead (deceased)
Eaglefeathers - Charlie's grandfather (deceased)
Liz Hudson - Sara's neighbor
Jim Hudson - Liz's husband, Col., U.S.A.F., ret.
Angela Bentley - Bob's wife, Sara's neighbor
Bob Bentley - Angela's husband; U.S. Fed. Dist. Judge
Gerald Bentley - Bob's brother; CEO, Lone Star Operations
Ida Schwartz - Sara's neighbor, RV Park/Marina owner
Mike Fernandez - Falcon Ridge P.D.
Kyle Bishop, M.D. - Belton Reg. Med. Ctr.
Virgil Steinbrenner - Elite Management Partners Inc. (EMPI)
Program Manager (deceased)
Steve Urbanowsky - Captain, Falcon Ridge P.D.
David Tompkins - Manager, DEFCU
Patrice Renard - Proprietor, Cosmic Portals
"Big Dick" Duncan - LSO Toolpusher
Trey Maguire - LSO General Manager
Guy Allison - FBI, Denver Field Office
Ingrid Thorson –PURF party planner
Thomas Martin - U.S. Army Corps of Engineers
Myron Bentley - LSO founder, lobbyist
Ice - Northern Cheyenne Medicine Man
Naomi Iron Shirt - Secretary of the Interior

I will tie another one to it...*

*Old Cheyenne saying for when there's more to the story

PROLOGUE

ELITE MANAGEMENT PARTNERS INC. (EMPI)
Denver, Colorado
August 3, Friday
9:43 a.m. MDT

Jason LaGrange scowled at the start-up costs for his business plan. As ludicrous as it seemed, that seven-figure windfall wasn't enough. Staffing, servers, software, hardware, and subscriptions required for surveillance alone could take as much as half.

He swiveled his chair toward the window, pondering other options. A Small Business Administration loan, perhaps? Except it probably wouldn't fly for a mercenary business.

He jeered with disdain. Then again, maybe it would, given the current administration.

His annual combined salaries from the NSA and EMPI were over six figures, first number not a *one*, but insufficient to amass that kind of cash in a timely manner. Besides, his job with EMPI would end as soon as they brought in that guy from the Army Corps of Engineers to oversee PURF to completion.

His NSA assignment started out as Bernie Keller's handler for what should have been a no-brainer security contract. A Top *(Dirty Little)* Secret job that Keller's team botched from Day One.

Could that bunch of yahoos even tie their own shoelaces?

Especially team lead, Eddie Johannsen.

What an arrogant SOB.

Not researching the targets, a simple task given their resources, set them on a path to self-destruction. Using excessive force was a serious violation, except it morphed to acceptable once they stumbled upon Bryan Reynolds' hacking escapades.

An unbelievable stroke of luck.

Luck that failed, however, when Johannsen's behavior at the wreck site aired on network TV, courtesy of the vehicle's dash cam.

He chuckled, remembering the GPS tracker's erratic path as Johannsen's truck careened over the side of the same canyon where this debacle began.

Reynolds' widow miraculously survived the initial wreck. Now she was exposing what her husband unearthed, causing troublesome headaches for corrupt higher-ups and their lobbyist cohorts.

That national broadcast flipped to Keller's benefit, however, when those with much to lose hired his band of wannabes to finish her off, once and for all.

The job that ultimately became Jason's $1.7 million windfall.

Having infiltrated the team for a closer look, he did his best to help. Handing over that designer poison formulated in some U.S.S.R. spy hidey-hole should have made the job a done deal.

Until Johannsen messed that up, too.

He scowled.

Maybe, maybe not.

Perhaps the stuff degraded, being organic and decades old, based on the fact it took a few days before the toxic effects manifested. During the interim, the target survived long enough to attempt another TV appearance.

Security footage from NBC's Manhattan studio indicated she'd succumbed, but was resuscitated and transported to a Brooklyn ER quickly enough to save her life. According to the hospital's database, she'd defied death yet again.

Who was Sara Reynolds, anyway? Wonder Woman?

A window washer working the upper half of the Marriott City Center across the street, one of Denver's iconic monoliths, caught his eye. Suspended on a scaffolding a few hundred feet above the sidewalk, he chuckled at the vision of the guy dropping the squeegee on some unsuspecting pedestrian on his way to a four-martini corporate lunch.

Ka-bam! Lights out!

Life was like that.

Things blasted out of the blue, sometimes good, sometimes not.

Just like the wreck in Dead Horse Canyon that started it all.

Still, it wasn't over. And wouldn't be as long as Sara Reynolds was alive.

Keller's second payment was due when she was proved dead. Some believed she was. The official FBI record was still open though it implied as much with her status "assumed dead," based on hospital release papers that stated, "referred to Hospice."

Really? *Assumed*?

The ones who wanted her silenced were less trusting, withholding the second payment until Keller produced the death certificate. Not likely to happen with him in jail on conspiracy charges, even if she was.

Jason could forge one easily enough, but of all the personas he'd assumed throughout his career, a liar wasn't one. In his line of work, trust by those he worked for, whether informers or clients, was essential. With the caveat, however, that when immersed in a particular role such actions didn't constitute a lie as opposed to an improvised script.

His eyebrows lowered with his thoughts.

If he finished the job, the second payment would be his.

Another million bucks!

Perfect!

All he had to do was inform the client he was Keller's duly appointed representative, which would be a cinch.

Then convince them this time the job would get done right.

My mind is a place I can't escape your ghost.
—*"Wrecked" lyrics by Imagine Dragon*

1. CARS

MONTGOMERY RESIDENCE
BOULDER, COLORADO
August 4, Saturday
3:17 p.m. MDT

Since being poisoned, Sara felt as if she were trapped in a cadaver. And perhaps she was, her spirit evicted from the *Other Side* and forced to reoccupy this veritable corpse.

All her mother told her was that she had to go back. Not so much as a hint why. Or that she'd be stuck like *this*. At least she slept a lot, to pass the time. Whether or not time was in her favor was another story.

She had but one hope to ever be normal again.

But, as with life in general, there were no guarantees.

Her shoulders drooped as she turned her attention to her window where tiny vehicles streamed along Boulder's Diagonal Highway a half-mile away. A peaceful, hypnotic scene she'd contemplated from her second-story bedroom much of her life.

Just not from a wheelchair.

Nor filtered through the recently acquired blur, as if viewing the world through a dirty window.

Was she losing her sight, too?

Panic flashed, forcing her to dismiss the terrifying thought and refocus on the steady flow of anonymous traffic. Each driver pursuing their own destination amid troubles, triumphs, and tragedies. Yet, from this perspective, just another car.

With her no more than just another house.

7

The doctor's words as she left the hospital that she was lucky to be alive didn't help. Four months ago she was happily married to the love of her life. Now she was a paraplegic widow.

What was lucky about that?

Movement on the sidewalk snagged her attention. A brightly attired female jogger pranced past the front of the house. Ear-buds in place, her blissful expression radiated the euphoric blast of a runner's high.

Her heart sank. Another feeling once familiar that would forever be archived as distant memory. Now her body knew nothing but pain. Except her legs which, for all intents and purposes, no longer existed.

How much of life had evaporated? Deprived of those little things that made it worth living:

Carefree hikes.

Skiing with Bryan.

De-stressing with a quick run.

Shopping with Connie.

Enjoying a tasty meal without funky overtones.

How many more simple pleasures once taken for granted, gone forever?

Without them, what was left to live for?

When her mother lost her ability to walk, crippled by Lou Gehrig's disease, the thought of ever being in a similar situation never crossed her mind.

An ironic, but oddly enough, positive result of her mother's disabilities was that they'd necessitated upgrading the house years before. Her father designed and fabricated a lift mechanism from the master bedroom's walk-in closet to the laundry room below, so her mother wouldn't be trapped upstairs.

After over a decade, her wheelchair was retrieved from the attic.

Did sitting in the same wheeled prison every waking moment make it easier?

Or worse?

Her mom lived an active life, her favorite horseback riding. She played tennis and golf. Taught Sara to ski when she was a mere toddler. She learned to walk at ten months, mobility ever since never questioned.

She smiled, remembering. That purple snowsuit with the embroidered bunny on back. Was it memory? Or was she too young to remember? More likely it was home videos featuring her fearless escapades skimming down Vail's beginner slope.

Even when she broke her ankle hiking, she had a walking cast. Never before was the simple task impossible.

Why did Mom tell me I had to come back? Why? Some masochistic directive to understand what she went through?

She cringed at the undeserved accusation.

Ellen Montgomery didn't have a mean bone in her body. Like everything else she did, it was with love.

Even though as a child or teen it wasn't apparent at the time.

Things she didn't understand at ten she did at sixteen. Thirty-three certainly qualified as an adult. No doubt there were still things she wouldn't understand until she got even older.

Years of living couldn't be taught in a classroom.

Why Charlie's culture wisely respected their elders.

She straightened her back, hopeful he and White Wolf would arrive soon. Her last chance, one her sanity clung to. Medicine men were no strangers to miracles.

Would she be one of them?

Her New York City doctors were skeptical. As a physical therapist she knew that look. Hopeless cases produced a unique, homogenous blend of sadness, anger, frustration, and defeat.

As healers, they'd failed.

As a physical therapist she always had compassion for her patients. Now her heart ached with genuine empathy.

Especially young men and women. Her throat closed as she thought of those she'd worked with who'd suffered horrific injuries while serving their country. An entire lifetime of limitation ahead.

How did they cope?

Their courage was something she lacked, yet understood like never before. How did they do it? She didn't even have enough nerve to look in the mirror. Her complexion was broken out worse than it ever was as a teen and she could tell by Connie's forced smiles that her appearance was beyond frightening. She didn't even want to think about her hair.

Even her senses of smell and taste were off, a persistent fetid odor that overruled anything pleasant.

Did she smell like that, too?

Could Charlie and his uncle accomplish what modern medicine could not?

Or would she be a tortured soul in a damaged, debilitated body for the rest of her life?

Why would she be sent back with such limitations? Remnants of a faded memory whispered that at one time she knew, but details of her mother's edict vanished upon awakening from the coma.

Her phone chirped.

The text she'd been waiting for.

They'd leave within a few days.

She responded with a smiling emoji.

One didn't exist for how she really felt. One that said she was hanging on by her fingernails with him her only chance.

She set down the phone, eyes back on the highway, hoping to defy the grim odds.

WHITE WOLF'S RANCH
NORTHERN CHEYENNE RESERVATION
BUSBY, MONTANA
August 4, Saturday
8:38 p.m. MDT

YELLOW WEED RUSTLED in the late summer breeze as it had for thousands of years on the Northern Cheyenne Reservation. After putting up the horses for the night, Charlie and White Wolf conversed outside the barn discussing the upcoming trip to Colorado.

"We should take my pickup. It gets better mileage," Charlie proposed, then flinched. "It just needs a quart of oil every time I fill the tank."

His uncle folded his arms. "Yes. It sends smoke signals. I suspect it's pleading for a new head gasket."

"With over three hundred thousand miles it is tired." He frowned. "But your Explorer's transmission slips. Like it's trying to make up its mind."

White Wolf nodded. "True. It, too, is wearing out. Not good for steep grades."

"So it is decided." Charlie looked him straight in the eye. "I will buy you a new one."

White Wolf's eyes narrowed. "*Vonėstséá'e-mo?* Are you crazy? That would take much money. You don't have a job. How would you pay for it?"

"I *had* a job, uncle. A good one." He grinned. "I got a bonus for finding that oil deposit. We will ask *Maheo* to lead us to a better ride for a fair price."

"No." White Wolf shook his head. "We do not ask *Maheo* for material things."

"Uncle. You need a reliable vehicle for your sacred duties." Charlie held out his hands, palms up, pleading with him. "A hundred years ago would you not have asked *Maheo* for a good horse? What if we break down on the way? Sara got home yesterday. She expects us soon. You can only be gone two days. A major breakdown would delay us much longer."

"Yes. Two days is how long Rufus Littlesun can cover my medicine man duties. We must return on time."

"You serve our people on the reservation, which is 690 square miles. Roads are bad. Especially in winter, when our people need the most help. How will we get to the Sacred Mountain safely? It is over three hours away!"

White Wolf's forehead furrowed like the hills sweeping the surrounding prairie.

Charlie bit his lip. Arguing with his uncle was wrong. "I am sorry. I did not mean to be disrespectful."

The elder huffed out a breath as acceptance flashed across the man's face like a heliacal rising star kissing the horizon. "You are correct, nephew. It is needed for *Maheo's* sacred work. We will pray for one that serves him well."

And thus they turned their backs to the setting sun, blessed themselves with the earth, then petitioned *Maheo* to direct them to the needed transportation.

FAIRFIELD CHEVROLET
Billings, Montana
August 6, Monday
10:08 a.m. MDT

AFTER MORE PRAYER and fasting the day before, a vision appeared in Charlie's mind. Intuition led him to Billings, where he followed directions infused to his intuition by an invisible spirit helper.

Spotting a GM dealership, he cruised past dozens of vehicles representing numerous new models in a variety of colors. A banner indicated *Pre-owned Vehicles*, prompting him to pull into the adjacent driveway, then park on the end of a row populated with what appeared to be used cars and trucks.

He turned off the ignition and looked up.

His old truck was nose to nose with the brush guard of a white Chevy Tahoe.

Exactly as seen in his mind's eye.

A luggage rack adorned its roof, another requirement for transporting tipi and sweat lodge poles as well as supplies to the Sacred Mountain.

The only thing missing was a blue Cheyenne flag on the doors.

He grinned, gratitude swelling like a ripening ear of corn as he got out of his truck and approached the Tahoe.

Néá eše, Maheo. *Néá eše.*

His financial criteria, like his hunting rifle, was thirty-thirty: below $30,000 and 30,000 miles.

A lot to ask, but a medicine man's prayers tended to be answered.

A man exited the showroom and strode his way, wearing a used car salesman's grin on his dimpled, round, native face. Charlie's smile was more than just friendly--this would be far easier than expected.

"What can I help you with today, brother?" the man asked, extending his hand. "Wally Whitehorse."

"Charlie Littlewolf," he said, shaking his hand. He patted the SUV's front fender. "I'm looking to buy this for our medicine man. What can you tell me about it?"

"Good choice, brother. This beauty came in off a lease last Friday. Owner got transferred out of the country. We haven't even completed the paperwork yet."

Charlie opened the door and climbed inside. Even though a few years old it still had hints of that enticing new car odor. Then again, just about anything smelled better than his aging Ranger.

No key was apparent. He turned to the salesman with a mystified look.

The man pointed. "In the console. As long as it's in the car, it will start when you push the button." He reached in front of him and demonstrated. The car sprang to life, emitting a powerful purr.

The odometer lit up: 26,854.6 miles.

"How much?" Ready to start negotiating, he held his breath.

"Haven't set the price yet." The salesman gnawed his lip. "You say it's for your medicine man?"

"Yes. Joe White Wolf, on the rez."

"Let me check with my manager," he said, then sauntered back to the showroom.

While he waited, Charlie ran his fingers over the leather console, then eyed the dash. It wasn't new, but seemed so, and exactly what he was looking for.

Compared to his old truck, it felt like a limousine.

The salesman returned. "We have a full inventory of this model. The boss said I can cut you a deal. Blue Book, which we'd get at auction. Sound okay?"

Charlie bit back a smile. "What would that come to?"

The guy pulled out his phone and brought up an app. "$29,500."

"Is that honestly the best you can do?"

"Actually, it is." He laughed. "Brother, you think I don't know? Cheating a medicine man is a real bad idea. We won't make a dime on this one. You live on the rez, right?"

"Yes. Outside Busby."

"We have a really sweet snow plow package for this model."

Charlie's eyes lit up. Being isolated during Montana's harsh winters was too common. With that they could get to anyone who needed help, even clear the roads.

"How much?"

"For you, bro, two thousand. Dealer pricing."

Slightly over his intended budget, but too good to pass up. The assistance it could provide was priceless.

He straightened and held out his hand. "Okay. Let's do it."

The man pumped his hand, corners of his mouth reaching for his ears. "Do you have something to trade?"

"No. I still need my truck and White Wolf has a teenage son waiting to inherit his."

"I get that. What kind of financing do you have in mind?"

"Cash."

The guy's eyes widened, though tinged with a hint of disappointment. "Seriously?"

"Yes." Charlie couldn't restrain a chuckle at the man's quizzical look. "Got a bonus at work."

"Wow. Good for you, brother. Alright, let's go inside and do the paperwork. When do you want to pick her up?"

2. GIFTS

WHITE WOLF'S RANCH
NORTHERN CHEYENNE RESERVATION
BUSBY, MONTANA
August 7, Tuesday
4:18 a.m. MDT

A cool predawn breeze whispered through the skeletal structure of White Wolf's sweat lodge. It was the third morning Charlie knelt within, seeking guidance. If words did not come, no one would know the difference.

His pulse quickened, a reminder this was not an option. It was something he was supposed to do.

There were prayers and there were honor songs. Two branches of the same tree from which to beckon spiritual assistance.

During the ceremonies they planned, singing honor songs for badger, eagle, buffalo, and wolf would suffice. Prayers were easier—pour out your righteous desires, packaged with gratitude and respect.

While praying came from the heart, singing came from the soul. Whether it was the resonance associated with the sound or a different part of the brain he didn't know.

What he *did* know was he needed to make an honor song for Sara. Why, he wasn't sure, unless it were the means by which to connect with her soul.

Since Bryan's untimely death, together they'd slid along the icy road of grief. Charlie lost his best friend, she lost her beloved husband. Both were bound to him such that his sudden and violent departure wrenched part of their own spirits away.

Yet, rather than mourn, Sara put her own life in danger trying to complete his last request. If she'd gone on with her life as most women would, she wouldn't be paralyzed.

That level of devotion, dedication, and courage deserved an honor song.

Time was short.

In less than an hour he and White Wolf would leave to pick up the new Tahoe. Upon their return, what time remained would be consumed with preparations for the trip to Colorado the following day.

It was now or never.

"*Maheo*," he prayed, pleading with sincerity that brought a lump to his throat. "Please. Help me with this sacred task. Bless me with words to make an honor song for my white brother's wife."

WHITE WOLF'S RANCH
BUSBY, MONTANA
August 7, Tuesday
7:03 a.m. MDT

GIFT GIVING WAS a joyful Cheyenne tradition. For this special excursion, several were needed. As a medicine man's wife, Star was no stranger to such, which could arise quickly. As she cleaned up the kitchen after breakfast, her thoughts turned to her latest assignment.

Most items took hours, even days or weeks, to create by hand. She, with her native sisters, spent Montana's dark, frigid winters crafting star quilts and all varieties of beadwork and needlecraft that were tucked away for just such occasions.

She smiled, remembering when a grateful recipient asked why the Cheyenne were so generous when many were so very poor. She explained that giving brought a feeling you couldn't get any other way.

Truly, it never failed to bring a profound sense of joy. The bigger the sacrifice, the greater the blessing.

White Wolf tasked her to gather gifts for Sara and her step-mother, Connie. Since she met both when they brought Littlewolf home, that was easy. Littlewolf mentioned that her father would be there and possibly another woman close to the family.

As soon as the dishes were done, she checked her inventory in the basement, finding she had everything needed for the gifts, but only one set of prayer cloths remained.

She gasped. How did she miss that?

Having none on-hand was unacceptable. She shuddered, remembering that time White Wolf was on his way to perform such a ceremony, only to realize there weren't any on hand.

Back then the cloths were kept in his medicine room. She didn't go in there, so didn't realize they'd all been used. He admitted it was his fault for not telling her, but after that he let her keep them with her cache of gifts—making it entirely her responsibility.

She gathered the last set, placed them in a paper bag, then took them into the living room where the ceremonial items were being gathered. Fortunately, the Lame Deer Trading Post always had fabric in the sacred colors so she could replenish her supply.

She hadn't planned on driving the eighteen miles into town, but this would work out perfectly. She wanted her gift for Sara to be extra special, one that showed how much she cared. For some reason she felt so close to her, as much as to any of her Cheyenne sisters.

Most of what she had in mind was complete, but she needed a few things to personalize it. She could pick that up along with the fabric, maybe run by the thrift shop, too.

She grabbed her bag, then called out the back door to her sons, Winter Hawk and Risingsun, occupied with shucking corn.

"I'm going into Lame Deer to pick up a few things. I won't be long."

With that, she stepped out the front door—

—stopped dead standing on the porch, mouth agape.

The Explorer was gone.

She exhaled hard, plans unraveling like a dropped stitch while knitting a sweater.

How could she forget?

White Wolf and Littlewolf were picking up their new truck in Billings. Littlewolf's old pickup would have to do.

Once behind the wheel, it took a few hefty jerks to adjust the seat so she could reach the pedals.

Her left foot collided with something on the floor.

An extra pedal.

She groaned.

As if a clutch weren't bad enough, the shift lever was on the floor, not the steering column. She hadn't driven a manual transmission since her teens.

Her happy mood crashed as memories hailed a sorrowful twinge from the past. Her brother died in that pickup when an elk crossed his path a few days before her high school graduation.

Tear-glazed eyes peered past the dusty windshield to send him a virtual hug, then her thoughts rejoined her dilemma.

A simple errand on the reservation would be okay. But driving Highway 212, stuttering along while fumbling with the clutch, gas, and gear shift? That road was nicknamed the "death highway" for a reason.

What-ifs crowded her mind, diluting her intent.

The men left at six-thirty so they'd arrive at the dealership when it opened at eight. It would probably take a half hour or more to get everything done, so they'd probably be back around ten o'clock.

Soon enough.

There were plenty of things to do in the meantime.

Like see what she already had on-hand to make Sara's extra special.

WHITE WOLF'S RANCH
BUSBY, MONTANA
August 8, Wednesday
4:08 a.m. MDT

MORNING STAR PEOPLE were no strangers to predawn hours. Thus, on the day of departure Charlie awoke at 4:00 a.m., took a quick shower, then pulled on his fringed and beaded buckskin shirt and matching leggings. He slipped his feet into a pair of fully beaded moccasins, then packed some casual clothes in a backpack for the drive home.

He straightened his shirt, alive with anticipation. How Sara felt would determine whether they'd perform the healing ceremony that day or the next. If today, they'd be ready.

Satisfied he was good to go, he stopped by his teenage cousins' bedroom to wake them up. In Cheyenne culture, they were his brothers, sharing the same grandparents.

"Get up, you two," he said, grabbing their toes through the blankets.

Protests spiced with adolescent giggles intensified as Charlie's efforts to get them up and moving morphed to good-natured rough-housing. Victory arrived when both boys thumped to the floor. Charlie yanked away their blankets, morning chill courtesy of the open basement window sufficient to finish the job.

Once assured they wouldn't sneak back to bed, he hastened upstairs, beckoned by the aroma of freshly brewed coffee.

Star was at the stove preparing a breakfast fit for royalty. As soon as the biscuits came out of the oven, everyone gathered around the picnic-style table. White Wolf blessed the food, then Risingsun took out the food offering.

Charlie savored every bite of scrambled eggs, deer tenderloin steak, fried potatoes and several freshly baked biscuits, which he washed down with a glass of milk.

After living on his own for so long, it was a true luxury to live in a household where cold, rudimentary meals were a thing of the past. The best part of his tenure at LSO besides his paycheck was their chow hall. Food security was something too many of his people lacked, his gratitude laced with sadness for those less fortunate, hoping to be in a position to help them someday.

As soon as Star finished eating, she returned to the kitchen to make steak sandwiches for their trip, which she packed along with a container of dried fruit to snack on along the way.

When the men were done, she sent Risingsun down to her storage area in the basement to fetch several strips of red trade cloth, which she plaited into her husband's braids while Winter Hawk did the same for Charlie.

By then, both bore the unmistakable appearance of two proper Cheyenne men ready to conduct sacred ceremonies on behalf of *Maheo*.

"You both look wonderful," she said, kissing White Wolf on the cheek.

"*Néá'eše* for that fabulous breakfast," Charlie said. "I may not have to eat again before we get home."

White Wolf checked everything assembled on the couch one final time. Anything forgotten could be catastrophic, sacred items not available at Walmart in Boulder or anywhere else.

After that White Wolf went through his medicine bundle's contents while Charlie loaded the buffalo skull, sacred red pipe, sweetgrass braids, prayer cloths, and man sage into a cardboard box. Other than the spring water and soil from Eaglefeathers Creek on the porch, everything was there.

Satisfied, he picked up the box took it outside to their new SUV, White Wolf and his sons right behind.

Constellations blazed overhead, waning crescent Moon preceding the Sun's appearance in the pre-dawn eastern sky.

Charlie set down the box, dug the key fob out of his pocket, and pressed the appropriate button. Parking lights strobed the ground as the rear hatch hummed open to a soft chorus of *ooohs* and *aahhhs*. Grinning, he set the box inside.

His grin morphed to a scowl, disappointed his uncle didn't seem more excited. Rather, it was almost as if he were afraid of it. White Wolf declined driving home from Billings and already instructed Charlie to drive to Boulder, justified by his familiarity with the route.

Charlie didn't mind, only hoped he'd soon feel comfortable with his new ride. ‚

He certainly wouldn't hesitate if it were a horse.

Star's arms were loaded with gifts gathered the day before.

"Open the back door for me, Winter Hawk," she told her older son, then gave each bundle an affectionate hug before placing them inside.

"Now remember," she said, pointing, "This shawl is for Sara, the other two for Connie and their friend. This quilt is for Sara, that one for her father."

"Thank you, wife," White Wolf said. "Such gifts are the Cheyenne way of showing our desire to bless their lives."

"What are we going to name it?" Risingsun asked.

Star turned toward her son, questions in her eyes. "Name what?"

"The new truck!"

White Wolf looked at Charlie, who passed. "No. It's yours, uncle. You should name it."

Furthermore, the last time he named something it hadn't ended well. His throat burned as he remembered naming the borehole, offending Badger, which brought catastrophic results.

White Wolf smiled, probably reading his mind. He worked his lips pensively. "We shall call it *Hó'nehe amàho'héhe.*"

Star laughed. "*Wolf car* is not very original, husband."

"But it fits," Risingsun said with a shrug.

"Especially since it's white," Winter Hawk added.

Charlie hesitated. "That is a bit long. Since it is a Tahoe, how about *Tah-Hó'nehe*?"

Everyone looked to White Wolf for approval. "I agree. *Tah-Hó'nehe* it is."

Winter Hawk retrieved the four gallon jugs of spring water from the porch two at a time, then returned for two five-gallon buckets of soil. He held one out to Charlie, who took it and turned to place it inside.

He could almost hear the rear compartment scream as the first bucket neared the spotless carpeted interior.

He froze.

White Wolf held up a hand.

"Risingsun, get a few old towels from the stack we use for sweats. We will keep it clean as long as we can."

The thirteen-year-old ran inside and returned to spread them in the cargo area. Charlie placed the containers upon them, flicking away a few renegade specks.

The rear hatch closed with a soft thud. They lined up facing the coming dawn for a prayer for safety, then hugs ensued all around. Star and the boys stepped back as Charlie offered the key fob to his uncle, just in case.

White Wolf ignored him and climbed into the passenger seat where he pulled on his seatbelt.

Charlie's jaw flexed as he got settled behind the wheel, buckled up, then started the engine. The dash lit up like a Christmas pow-wow. Eyes sparkling with new car euphoria, he brought up the GPS screen and typed in Sara's address from her text. After that, he paired his cell phone with it as well, having figured out the process the day before, in case any texts arrived during the trip.

White Wolf watched the entire process with narrowed eyes. Whether he was impressed or intimidated was impossible to tell.

"We should smudge it with sweetgrass or sage," he finally commented. "It smells funny."

Charlie stifled a laugh, but didn't respond.

One final wave, then he followed the dusty ranch road to Highway 212, headlights shoving darkness aside with a swath far brighter than his truck ever did. A mile later he turned left onto Highway 314, which led south to Sheridan.

The vehicle's response to his foot's pressure on the accelerator was exhilarating. No more slogging through gears, gradually achieving highway speed. Driving home from Billings he'd been far more conservative, getting accustomed to its size, handling, and response. Already it felt comfortable, speed occulted by its smooth, quiet ride.

He glanced down at the digital speedometer—a glaring eighty-one miles per hour.

Oops.

He backed off the gas, glancing at his uncle who was definitely not smiling.

Attention no sooner back on the highway, the headlights caught a small herd of deer in the middle of the two-lane road.

"Ohohyaa," he muttered through clenched teeth.

Tires squealed as he stomped the brakes and slid to a stop.

Startled animals stared into the light, a cluster of does with a lone eight-point buck.

He tapped the horn with a shaky hand.

After a thoughtful pause, the animals finished their stroll to the other side of the road.

Once certain there were no stragglers, he exhaled hard, then slowly accelerated, setting the cruise control when he reached fifty-five.

"Why don't you find a radio station with some good Indian music?" he suggested, wishful thinking to distract from the lecture that was sure to come.

His uncle's lower lip protruded as he scrutinized the lights dancing on the dash.

"Not now, Littlewolf. We need to talk."

Thus the first lesson that the child learned was one of self-control--self-effacement in the presence of its elders. It remembered this all through life. --George Bird Grinnell in "The Cheyenne Indians: Their History and Lifeways"

3. DEJA-VU

EN ROUTE BOULDER
August 8, Wednesday
5:23 a.m. MDT

The remainder of Charlie's elevated mood dropped like a dead cottonwood in a winter storm.

"What think you of their message?" White Wolf asked.

Charlie inhaled slowly through his nose. "Slow down. I was going too fast."

"Yes. What else?"

His eyes fixed on the edge of light sweeping the pavement ahead. "Pay attention. I should have known they were there before they appeared. My eyes have seen things as they were in the past. Now I must focus on the present."

"Yes. What else?"

"Expect the unexpected. Rosebud Creek follows this road. Many wildlife are in the area, especially at this hour."

"Very good. But there is more."

Pink shades of dawn silhouetted random buttes and pine-studded hills to his left as he ran out of ideas for what White Wolf was implying. They passed a sign to the Rosebud Battlefield, a short time later the Tongue River Reservoir State Park.

The tiny town of Decker with its *"Welcome to Wyoming"* sign sped by on the right. Several more minutes of silence until his uncle spoke.

"Patience, nephew. *Patience!* You cannot move forward as quickly as you want. You have learned very quickly, but there are

24

no shortcuts to where you must go. The Cheyenne way only goes as fast as you can manage *safely*."

With no valid argument otherwise, Charlie nodded agreement.

"Your spirit helpers abandon you when your will pushes them away," White Wolf went on. "*Maheo's* work is done according to his time. We are only his servants, Littlewolf. Without him, we are powerless."

Sufficiently humbled, Charlie was relieved to see Sheridan's lights complementing the sunrise. He snaked his way from the highway through a variety of intersections along the back roads toward a familiar destination.

Past trips along this route clear back to his childhood established another tradition, the Common Cents Travel Plaza.

"If you agree, I'd like to top off the tank and get another cup of coffee," he said.

"Yes. Having my feet on solid ground will be much appreciated."

He stifled a smirk that would surely be perceived as disrespectful as he pulled into the vast parking lot and drove around back to the gas pumps.

Overhead lights were still on, even though it was now light enough to see. As he filled the tank it seemed like years since he was there with Sara. As sick as he felt, he'd wanted to pump the gas for her, but she refused.

Once inside the store and deli to pay, goosebumps tickled his arms. His first eerie encounter with the past occurred in that very place during that same trip. At least now he understood what happened and was learning to control the unexpected gift from his accident.

He was still full from breakfast, giving the food stations little appeal. As planned, he and White Wolf got large cups of coffee, but another caution flared as they neared the door.

The flimsy plastic lids on the to-go cups were scant protection from dousing steaming brew all over *Tah-Hó'nehe's* pristine interior.

He veered away from the exit toward the sales counter, ignoring his uncle's puzzled look. He grabbed two super-sized stainless-steel containers with secure plastic lids from a display rack, paid, then stepped outside to transfer their drinks to safer quarters and ditch the to-go cups in the trash.

Getting settled back in the car, again he felt White Wolf's critical stare.

"You must respect your position as one chosen to serve *Maheo* with as much dedication as you give this truck," he said. "It is big, beautiful, and powerful, but can also be deadly. Time and experience will guide you how best to use it. It is the same with your abilities. They, too, are powerful, but must be used only as directed by *Maheo*."

" *Néá'eše,* White Wolf." He nodded, having to admit that was a wise comparison. "I will remember that," he promised. While often painful, the medicine man's comments were nonetheless wise and, he had to admit, fully deserved.

Upon leaving Common Cents, he wound through the outskirts of Sheridan to Interstate 90 South.

"I am glad you are driving, Littlewolf. I surely would have gotten lost by now."

Charlie tapped the GPS screen to which White Wolf grunted.

They eased onto Interstate 25 outside of Buffalo, which they followed to Casper. Along the way his phone chirped, a text from Sara popping up on the car's media screen.

Hi, Charlie. I'm so glad you'll be here soon. Would you mind picking up Patrice on your way?

Charlie voice commanded back, *No problem. Send her address.*

White Wolf looked from Charlie to the dash, then back to him as if the media screen were a snake ready to strike.

The address arrived. Charlie transferred it to the navigation system, biting back a smile at his uncle's ongoing reaction to another technological feat.

He lowered the visor when blasted by the sun skirting the Laramie Mountains. Soon Wyoming was in the rearview mirror, their arrival in Boulder another two and a half hours later.

While Charlie looked forward to seeing Sara, especially helping her get well, he was just as pleased at the prospect of meeting Patrice.

The psychic connection with her months before had buzzed through him like a close lightning strike, sparking some elusive recognition. Maybe meeting face to face would reveal more.

Upon arriving in Boulder, the navigation system guided them to a small shopping center where the address matched that of *Cosmic Portals*, its windows decorated with colorful space-themed artwork.

It was after lunch, but a few patrons sat at tables while others lined up at the counter where a college-age girl with short blond hair took orders.

No one paid much attention to their ceremonial dress at their previous stop, but Charlie felt all eyes upon them as they got in line to find out if they were in the right place.

"You two look absolutely magnificent!"

Charlie turned toward the vaguely familiar voice. There stood a stately women whose long, multi-colored skirt, impressive array of turquoise jewelry and waist-length platinum hair created a startling image.

The hair stood up on his arms as soulful eyes met his, evoking a jolt of recognition that went straight to his heart. There was no doubt they'd met before. Which indeed they had, albeit through a telepathic conversation.

What was more intimate than a soul-to-soul connection?

"It's so wonderful to meet you at last," she said, linking arms with them both. "You must be worn out after that long drive. Can I get you something to eat?"

Charlie was hungry, but hesitated. What if Sara expected them to eat there?

"Don't worry," Patrice said. "I told Connie I'd feed you lunch. She has a nice dinner planned."

Charlie smiled, certain she'd read his mind.

She led them to a booth in the corner and waved a young Asian man over, who handed them menus.

"Order anything you want. This is on me," she said.

The girl at the counter signaled for her, so she excused herself and strolled in her direction, purple-streaked platinum hair trailing down her back.

Charlie shivered as a strong flash of déjà-vu flashed her image from positive to negative. Silver hair darkened to black, purple streaks now white. Gooseflesh surged as a river of past-life memories flooded his mind.

Eons before she'd been their medicine woman, preparing healing herbs and blessing them in a multitude of ways. But his heart witnessed she'd been far more.

Many lifetimes before she'd been his mother.

His perception returned to the present when the waiter returned. Each ordered a bowl of broccoli cheese soup. Moments later Patrice returned and slid into the booth next to White Wolf.

Tear-glazed eyes met his.

"I have wondered where you were," she said softly, voice heavy with emotion. "I didn't think I'd see you this time."

The words settled in his soul as gentle and unstoppable as morning dew as identical sentiments surged, again raising the hair on his arms. His throat closed, wishing he'd shared such affection with his *Diné* mother who, as far as he could tell, never liked him.

White Wolf broke the silence. "We were once family. How blessed we are to meet again."

MONTGOMERY RESIDENCE
BOULDER
August 8, Wednesday
2:45 p.m. MDT

SARA SLUMPED FORWARD in the wheelchair, holding her head. "What time are they supposed to get here?"

"They're leaving Patrice's now," Connie replied, entering the living room from the kitchen. "It shouldn't be long."

Sara held her head. "I feel awful. I don't know if I can handle whatever they have in mind."

"Of course you can, honey." Her step-mother's tone was as perky as her bobbed auburn hair. She placed a reassuring hand on her shoulder. "It will be fine. You know we're here for you."

A knock at the front door beckoned Connie in that direction, Sara wheeling up behind. The last time she saw Charlie he was physically debilitated, confused, and fearful, to say nothing of cranky. She grimaced with the realization now she was the one out of sorts.

During the trip to the reservation he and everyone else became aware of his strange abilities. His pronouncement they were being followed, much less that the grandfather spirits would intervene, was unnerving enough. Then the offender's truck had a blowout that ended his pursuit, leaving everyone speechless.

More recently, his vision of red-eyed black snakes occupying her toilet seat alerted them to where she'd encountered the poison, which no doubt contained snake venom. Would those same abilities coupled with his medicine man uncle's be sufficient to restore her health and ability to walk?

Her throat constricted. *If not, then what?*

Connie opened the door and beckoned everyone inside. A rush of emotion-laden greetings followed.

Sara's eyes met Connie's in disbelief when Will strode over, hand extended, to greet the astrologer he'd been so skeptical about.

"So you're Patrice. I've heard quite a bit about you. I'm Will, Connie's husband and Sara's father. It's truly a pleasure to meet you."

"Likewise," she replied, enigmatic look unreadable.

Was he that impressed when her readings proved accurate?

Patrice turned to Sara, eyes brimming with moisture as she stooped down to give her an affection hug.

"It's so good to be here, sweetie. Thanks so much for including me."

Sara returned the embrace, affections warming to the woman who'd given her a multitude of profound insights during the difficult journey since Bryan's murder.

"I'm so glad you're here. This is perfect."

Patrice straightened beside her, holding her hand. "Here are the people you really want to see," she said. "Feast your eyes on these two!"

Charlie and his Uncle Joe both wore traditional fringed deerskin embellished with beadwork, including their moccasins, braided hair entwined with strips of red cloth. Before Bryan's death, she barely thought of Charlie as a Native American, only as her husband's best friend. Since then, his heritage had become deeply entrenched in his persona.

Most impressive, however, was that Charlie projected strength, health, and confidence. Nothing like his debilitated condition when they dropped him off at White Wolf's ranch.

His hand rested on her shoulder, sending a shiver down her spine.

"We'll have you out of that wheelchair in no time," he said. "You met Uncle Joe when you drove me to the rez. As White Wolf, he's a medicine man and healer. We're here to get you well as soon as possible."

"Thank you so much for coming," she said, shifting her eyes to White Wolf. The Cheyenne elder's high cheekbones, weathered features, and eyes dark as night were the same as she remembered, yet far more imposing than when he was simply Uncle Joe in jeans and a flannel shirt. "It's wonderful to see how much you helped Charlie."

His response was a solemn nod.

Sara smiled, eyes back on Charlie. "I'm so glad you and Patrice finally met."

The pair exchanged an affectionate look. "You have no idea," he said.

"Can I get you something to drink?" Connie asked, leading them into the parlor. "Iced tea? A cup of coffee?"

"No, thank you," Charlie said. "Patrice took good care of us already."

Sara slouched as the adrenaline surge ebbed, eyelids and smile both sagging.

Charlie leaned forward, hand on her shoulder. "Do you need to rest, Sara? We're not in a hurry."

"No." She exhaled hard. "I feel like this all the time. I'm more interested in how you can help me."

"What exactly would you like us to do?"

Her pleading look shifted between him and his uncle. "Help me walk again. I want a normal life." Her voice trembled. "Heal me from the poison. I can't see or think straight. I hurt day and night." She forced out a shaky laugh. "Ironically, the only thing that doesn't hurt is my legs."

"Do you doubt we can do that?" Charlie asked.

She bit her lip, determined not to cry. "No. It goes against my medical training as a physical therapist. But I know you can. When we talked on the phone I knew you were telling the truth. You've never said anything you didn't mean. So I believed you. I trust you."

Charlie nodded with the hint of a smile. "Good."

Connie gestured toward the couch. "Please, have a seat. Make yourselves comfortable."

Patrice pushed Sara next to the wing chair by the fireplace, where she took a seat, while their two other guests sat on the sofa by the picture window. Will brought in a kitchen chair for himself and placed it on Sara's other side. With everyone else settled, Connie sat in the high-backed chair on the other side of the couch.

"Today we will tell you what to expect and answer any questions," White Wolf stated. "We'll have the ceremonies tomorrow morning. Is seven too early?"

Sara winced.

"Okay, how about nine?" Charlie suggested. "We'll arrive an hour before that to get everything ready, but you don't need to be there."

She nodded. "Okay."

"Our ceremonies are usually done outside," Charlie said. "How private is your yard?"

"The backyard is fenced," Will answered. "We're on a corner, so we only have neighbors on one side and those behind us. They're all gone working hours during the week. Would you like to see it?"

"Yes. That would be helpful."

Will escorted them out through the kitchen door while the others waited. When they returned they explained their plan for the following day.

The healing ceremony, conducted in the Cheyenne language, would come first. When told that they'd all pray along Connie looked puzzled. "How can we do that when we don't understand what you're saying?"

White Wolf smiled. "Pray along with what's in your heart. Concentrate on your feelings for Sara. How much you want her to be healthy again."

Will regarded his daughter beside him with soft, loving eyes. "That much I can definitely do."

Sara turned, eyes connecting with his. Her throat burned at the pain behind them. All of her recent misfortunes affected him, too.

"I love you, Dad," she whispered.

"Love is a powerful force," Patrice said. "Its energy can achieve miracles."

"Indeed it can," White Wolf continued. "First, we will sing four songs. They call upon *Maheo* and our spirit helpers to be here with us. One will be an honor song Littlewolf made for Sara."

Sara blinked hard. "You wrote a song? For me?"

Charlie's eyes met hers as he nodded.

"Singing connects more easily to the spirit," Patrice commented. "It's easier to put your heart into a song. I can be a real cry baby singing along to one of my favorites."

"Me, too," Connie added. "Sometimes just hearing one. Like in the grocery store. It can be pretty embarrassing."

All eyes turned to Sara when she coughed out a laugh. "I might not have had that wreck on I-70 if it weren't for that Sarah McLachlan song."

"Which one?" Connie asked.

She hesitated, emotions rising at the thought. "*A-Angel.*"

"Oh, honey," Connie replied. "I do, too. It reminds me of your mom. It makes me cry, too." Her hand covered her mouth as she turned to White Wolf. "I'm so very sorry. I apologize. I know, I talk too much."

Will laughed.

She gave him a look, then added, "I'm truly sorry. Please continue."

White Wolf acknowledged her apology with a nod. "Crying is common in our ceremonies. It shows our reverence, humility, and sincerity to *Maheo*. Many of our most solemn ceremonies involve a lot of weeping by grown men."

"They say to cry is not being weak, but shows you've been strong for too long," Patrice said.

"Indeed," Will added quietly.

White Wolf continued, describing what else would happen prior to administering bitter root tea, then the concoction's effects.

Sara wrinkled her nose, stomach churning at the thought. "That does *not* sound very appetizing."

"It's not," Charlie answered. "It's really quite nasty. But it works."

Her eyes narrowed. "How nasty?" She shaded her eyes against the glare from the window that washed his features to a silhouette.

"It will make you vomit. But it's what helped me get well, along with a couple sweats."

Sara nose scrunched up. "Nice. Like when I was a kid and got a stomach bug. Or ate too much Halloween candy. *Ewwww.*"

"I'll have a bowl on hand for you to barf into," Connie said, then got up and adjusted the blinds.

"No need," White Wolf said. "We brought containers for that. Throwing up is required. The vomit contains the poison, which is dangerous, so we'll take it back with us. We'll dispose of it in a safe place where it will never harm another person."

After that he explained the prayer cloth ceremony.

"How long before I feel like myself again?" Sara asked.

White Wolf hesitated, eyes fixed on hers. "You should feel your energy shift to a healing condition right away. However, you will need much rest over several days. You'll probably sleep for the first fourteen to sixteen hours, then on and off for three or four days. Maybe longer."

"You know we'll take care of you," Connie assured her, blowing her a kiss.

"During that time drink plenty of the spring water we brought as well as teas from the herbs we will give you," Charlie added. "Be sure to get lots of fresh air and sunshine. That will help eliminate more poison. Face east, like we will tomorrow. When you are stronger, it would be good for you to do a sweat, maybe more than one. That will further rid your body of anything harmful."

A crease formed between Connie's brows. "What's a sweat?"

"It's a special ceremony held in a small domed hut," White Wolf explained. "Rocks are heated in a fire outside, then brought in where water is sprinkled on them to create steam. We place sweetgrass on the hot stones, make prayers, and sing."

"Oh. I get it." She nodded, green eyes reflecting understanding. "Like a sauna with humidity and music."

"Actually, it's another sacred ceremony that cleanses mind, spirit, and body," Charlie added for clarification.

Will pursed his lips, eyes revealing thinly veiled doubts. "So you've done this several times?"

"Many times," White Wolf assured him. "Our ceremonies and medicines have been used for centuries."

"What exactly is this bitter root? What's in it that makes it effective? Has any research or chemical analysis been done on it?"

"Bitter root has been used by my people for generations. It comes from the root of a cactus. It is dried and stored until needed. Then it is simmered in water for several hours. We have many years of what you would call empirical data on its effects." The medicine man smirked. "But it is not approved by your FDA. We believe it has a more trustworthy source—*Maheo*."

"Is *Maheo* your name for God?" Connie asked.

Sara gave her an appreciative look, her questions helping everyone understand better.

"Yes," White Wolf replied with a nod. "He sent Sweet Medicine to teach the Cheyennes our way of life."

Will peered over the top of his glasses. "How do we know it won't make Sara worse? Damage organs that have already been stressed and possibly compromised?"

"I understand your concern," White Wolf said. "Medicine keepers for generations have perfected how to use it to cleanse the body of bad spirits. Our prayers assure its effects are good."

Will's stiff posture reeked doubts.

"Bitter root eliminated the hydrogen sulfide I inhaled during the blowout," Charlie said.

"Was that the only treatment you had?" Will asked.

Charlie shook his head. "No. I had first aid immediately at the drill site. Then I was in the local hospital, followed by hyperbaric treatments in another clinic. But I was still very sick."

Sara bit her lip. She wasn't surprised at her father's reaction, somewhat expecting it, but not wanting him to offend them after traveling so far to help her. Conventional medicine had failed, leaving Charlie and White Wolf her only hope.

"It's okay, Dad," she said, hand resting on his arm. "Charlie was still very sick when we took him home. As you can see, he's doing fine now. I don't think anything could make me worse. I've studied herbal medicine enough to trust it. Many pharmaceuticals are derived from plants or they create a synthetic version they can patent." She shrugged as she held out her hands. "What do I have to lose? The doctors did all they could. I'm willing to try anything." She forced a smile. "Even barf in front of everyone."

Will started to speak, then compressed his lips and said no more.

"Can I assist in some way?" Patrice asked.

Charlie gave her a warm smile. "Yes. It is important for those who care about Sara's health to be involved, not just watching. We are all *Maheo's* spirit helpers. Sara will need help sitting on the ground. You, Connie, and Will can all help her in that way."

"Connie and Will can also help Sara during the prayer cloth ceremony," White Wolf said.

"There's more besides the bitter root?" Sara asked.

"Yes," White Wolf replied. "It is done with pieces of cloth, each in one of the sacred colors. First, I bless them with sweetgrass. Then I wave them over you in a special way. They can remove any remaining evil spirits clinging to you. Does anyone have any other questions or concerns?"

Will exhaled through his nose, lips compressed.

Everyone else shrugged or shook their head.

Connie tossed a concerned look in her husband's direction, then said, "It's nearly six. Is everyone ready to eat? The pot roast and mashed potatoes are ready whenever you are. And of course you're welcome to spend the night."

"It smells delicious," Charlie said. "*Néá'eše*. Thank you so much. But after we eat, we must drive out to my cabin. That takes over two hours and it's best we arrive before dark. I need to pick up a few things to take back to Montana while White Wolf prepares the bitter root. We'll be back first thing in the morning."

*Your religion was written on tablets of stone by the iron finger of an angry God, lest you
might forget it. The red man could never remember nor comprehend it.
—Seath'tl "Seattle", 1854*

4. EXPECTATIONS

RANIER OFFICE BUILDING
WASHINGTON, DC
August 8, Wednesday
5:40 p.m. EDT

"Have a nice evening, Myron. I'll lock up. "

Ingrid Thorsen, Myron Bentley's executive assistant,
smiled as the door closed behind him. Beyond the ninth
story window overlooking the Washington mall her reflection
wore a victorious grin. Surely she'd snagged the opportunity of a
lifetime.

Her appearance was that of a woman far younger than her
sixty years. It didn't take much for her experienced stylist to
convince the encroaching gray to resume its once natural blond.
She was tall, still slender, and carried herself with a sophisticated
air, making her a welcome addition to elite parties that were far
above her station.

Her salary was generous, given her job as executive assistant
to a former U.S. Senator-turned-lobbyist, but far from enough to
maintain her life-style. That's where her monthly five-figure
alimony checks from her billionaire ex came in. In truth, she didn't
need to work, but enjoyed the social aspects of interacting with
Foggy Bottom's upper class.

Coordinating the PURF open house, scheduled for late
October, was a dream come true. Her surgically augmented breasts
rose with pride that she had such a once-in-a-lifetime opportunity.
With the facility no longer Top Secret, such a fete was not only

possible, but required. A superb event planner, she adored doing so, and best of all, this would assure her attendance. While others eschewed the headaches associated with planning such an occasion, especially with only two and a half months to do so, the rewards would be stellar.

Her smile downgraded from ecstatic to wry. It also provided a means to redeem herself. Be remembered for something positive.

Recommending her jail bird son-in-law for that security job was a monumental *faux pas*. She should have stood firm instead of caving to her daughter's pleading.

Oh, well. There's too much to do to lament that gaff any further.

Invitations needed to go out soon, which meant compiling the guest list. She turned to her computer, protecting her custom-manicured nails as she created a spreadsheet with the invitees names and addresses along with a mail-merge function. Cells for additional contact information, payment status, and an RSVP column, were all included.

After that, she imported the list of PURF's two thousand primary residents, chosen via a stealthily-skewed lottery. The facility was being completed in three phases, so this represented a third of its future occupants. Others would be chosen as work was completed on the other two, contingent on Congressional approval.

Next came the Executive Branch, the House, and Senate, all easily imported. Cabinet members whose respective agencies were involved took a bit of research, likewise CEOs and key personnel from the contractor community, and relevant agency directors. Naturally, significant others were included as well.

By the end of the day, the majority of names were in place with a plan for filling in the blanks. As many as ten thousand might attend, which meant caviar by the barrel and Champagne by the tanker load. She grinned, congratulating herself for what she'd already accomplished.

She had one problem, typical for any government-sponsored activity: Funding. Unfortunately, the money originally allocated was given out as bonuses by the previous project manager.

Thus, she'd have to charge $500 a plate.

Another easy challenge, given powers of persuasion perfected when she worked sales for Tiffany's.

All a matter of presentation.

It was a privilege to be invited to such an exclusive event, making that amount trivial to true socialites. To complain would be far below them. People of that station dropped more than that on a bottle of reserve wine or aged brandy.

She tapped her fingernails on her desk, thinking. Increasing it would give the event even more status. Cut out any riff-raff from the contractor ranks, plus provide padding, should expenses run higher than expected. She could certainly find something to spend any excess on.

Like that pair of shoes with matching handbag she admired the other day to go with the formal she'd already picked out.

She giggled. *Why not?*

$1,500 per plate or $2,500 per couple was far more reasonable for such an elite event.

Fortunately, expenses such as the venue and transportation, were minimal or non-existent.

Transportation was via the underground maglev network. Local guests simply had to find their way to the New Greenbrier to get onboard. Those who'd never experienced its high-speed, levitated ride would find it a bonus as opposed to inconvenience, certainly preferable to commercial air travel, even first class. Those from outside the area would require limousine transportation to the nearest hub, which she would arrange.

She rested her chin on her fist, thoughts drifting to one contractor who wouldn't be on the list.

What did Bernie do, anyway?

Her daughter didn't know and said he refused to talk about it. Apparently, it was bad enough he was hauled off by the FBI and currently awaiting trial in a New Mexico jail on felony conspiracy charges with it likely he'd wind up back in prison.

Oh, well. As long as it didn't splash on her, it wasn't her problem. Her daughter was planning to leave him, anyway. Having grown up with a luxurious lifestyle, his current questionable business endeavor, much less another stint at Leavenworth, weren't making the grade.

EN ROUTE FALCON RIDGE
August 8, Wednesday
4:30 p.m. MDT

CHARLIE'S EYES WERE on the road, but his thoughts splintered as if struck by a battle ax. He'd never seen anyone look so bad. In fact, he'd seen dead people who looked better. Sara's hair was thin and dull with hints of grey, not the curly chestnut mane he remembered. Dark circles rimmed her eyes, her pale skin blotched with angry patches of red.

The horrifying vision of scattering her ashes against a backdrop of autumn color slammed him again, his chest imploding.

He felt White Wolf's eyes upon him from the opposite seat. "It was wrong, what you said."

He glanced over, recoiling from the elder's iron-hard glare.

"Do you not remember, Littlewolf?"

"I am trying."

What did I say?

Oh. *That.*

He prefaced his response with a gut-wrenching moan, wishing he could not only see the past, but go there.

"I told her we'd make her healthy again. That she wouldn't need the wheelchair."

"Yes. That was the will of your heart, Littlewolf. You must learn to think before you speak. Narrow ground lies between belief and arrogance. Her health and future are fixed by *Maheo's* will. We do not make promises without sure knowledge of his approval."

Charlie's stomach lurched within darkened halls of regret.

"I planted false hope."

"Yes. Very damaging. Careless statements make you appear over-confident or a liar. That is not the Cheyenne way. That is *Vehoe's* way, broken promises."

"Can I fix it?"

"You must be honest. Explain it may take many ceremonies. A sweat, possibly several, as it was for you. The poison in you was mostly in your lungs. Poison is in her entire body. Damaged nerves may take more than I can do. It may take Sweet Medicine spirits for her to walk again."

The void in Charlie's chest deepened as he left Boulder via Highway 36. He planned to take the back roads, which were less distracting to say nothing of less stressful than dodging eighteen-wheelers on the Interstate.

Not only was there less traffic, but his mind resonated with rural landscapes versus the static encompassing cities. His grip on the wheel relaxed as he turned onto Highway 119 heading west, leaving the metro far behind. Only then did he relax enough to resume the conversation and force out the questions to which he feared the answers.

"Do you think she can recover?" he asked, unconsciously holding his breath.

White Wolf exhaled, perhaps for him. "If it is *Maheo's* will. She has many scars. In body and spirit. Some will heal, others need sweats. Some may be too deep to mend."

"Yes. How does one recover from losing someone you loved? When they leave, they take part of you with them."

The elder's *harrumph* was punctuated by silence.

The road contorted, yielding to the mountains, which fed Charlie's soul, having spent much of his life in their midst. He slowed down, thoughtful again, embraced by looming peaks and random fourteeners dusted with early snow.

The navigation system guided him to Nederland, then eventually south through a tangle of mountain roads. Bryan came to mind as he turned onto Two Brothers Road to Idaho Springs. From there Old 70, then finally the Interstate, which he'd so far avoided.

Remain on the current road to Interstate 70. . .

He smiled at the robotic female voice. He still faltered sometimes along the path between modern technology and his roots. When he was on the rez, he didn't miss it at all. Yet, when surrounded by it in the city, it likewise felt normal.

Balancing the two at once, however, was disorienting. No wonder White Wolf was wary of *Tah-Hó'nehe*. Had their ancestors felt the same when they transitioned from bows and arrows to rifles? From horses to pickup trucks?

It seemed impossible that the white man introduced his people to horses brought from Europe. What would they have done without them?

He shuddered as he remembered tales of their culture and language being annihilated by government boarding schools.

Yet, they survived, cultural hybrids clinging to the past while reaching toward an uncertain future.

Who would ultimately win this modern game of cowboys and Indians?

"You care very deeply for her."

His reverie halted, face flushing.

Being unable to hide anything from a medicine man made him squirm since his days with Eaglefeathers. He smiled to himself, realizing he was developing similar abilities.

"Yes," he admitted. "It is my duty to look after my brother's widow."

White Wolf's response was a knowing smile.

Once on I-70 West the route was comfortably familiar. He relaxed, mind switching to what needed to be gathered from his cabin. Most of what was there, except maybe his old recliner, which wouldn't fit in the cargo area.

"I never left Montana before," White Wolf said. "This is my first visit to where my father spent his final years."

"It is beautiful country, " Charlie said. "There is much sacred ground. Eaglefeathers was its protector. Making sure it was not violated any further since miners were finally driven off over a hundred years ago."

"Harrumph. It puzzles me, nephew, why you helped *Vehoes* drill for oil."

Charlie cringed at the veiled accusation.

"Yes. I, too, wonder. I prayed before taking the job, uncle, but did not receive an answer. Not yes, not no. Only silence. I thought maybe oil was another of Earth Mother's resources for our benefit. Like water. I'm still not sure. Without it, we would not be riding in *Tah-Hó'nehe*, but still living like our ancestors."

"Who had a very good life. Too many of our people and brothers in other tribes are living far worse than our ancestors."

"That is true."

"The accident opened your eyes."

Charlie nodded agreement, silence resuming. Pine forests clung to steep inclines, Interstate dodging the highest peaks with no hint of what lay beyond the next bend. Vast drop-offs were well-protected by guardrails, unlike the narrow county road at Dead Horse Canyon.

"This would be very dangerous in winter," White Wolf said. "Roads on the rez are bad enough and they are mostly flat."

"They do a good job keeping it cleared, close it when they can't, but yes. It is good we have a vehicle that can handle the worst."

The concrete face of the Eisenhower Tunnel loomed ahead, a familiar landmark halfway to their destination. White Wolf stiffened and gripped the seat as they were swallowed within its depths.

"It is odd to be inside the earth," he commented. "I sense its power. Anger. As if we do not belong."

"Yes. I wonder what Sweet Medicine felt inside the Sacred Mountain?"

"We do not know. Only what he was taught."

Charlie smiled when White Wolf started singing the Badger Song, one of their *nésema-noototse*, spirit calling songs.

You are the earth mother messenger
We are calling you to take our prayers
to the sacred mountain for Maheo.

Charlie joined in, repeating the words in Cheyenne until they exited the other side. He pulled down the visor against the glare of the westering sun, corner of his lip creeping upward as White Wolf exhaled hard.

An hour later they passed the shopping center that comprised the bulk of Falcon Ridge. They were on the final stretch.

Thoughts shifted to critters from squirrels to raccoons that may have commandeered his home during his absence.

So much had happened.

His accident; Sara driving him to the rez; his own recovery; the lessons he received so far. Time stretched endlessly without change, that in moments condensed a lifetime into a single fateful moment.

"It is beautiful country," White Wolf commented, breaking his thoughts.

"Yes. There is much I miss when I'm on the rez. But I miss the rez when I'm here. It was probably a mistake to stay here as long as I did."

"There are no mistakes. Only detours. There was a reason you were here, Littlewolf, even if you did not know what it was."

He scowled at the road ahead, wondering. His mind tumbled back months, then years. If he'd returned sooner, he would have missed many years spent with Bryan and all his white brother taught him. How close they became. Had he been on the rez, he would have missed that. Perhaps not even known when he died. And not been motivated by grief to return to his roots.

He bolted back to the present when a lone squirrel sat defiantly in the road, chattering at the unwelcome vehicle.

Charlie braked, less dramatically this time, then leaned forward and hugged the steering wheel. "What think you of our feisty little friend, uncle?"

White Wolf narrowed his eyes. "He is saying there are things you have not told me about your time here."

He drove around the unexpected messenger, reminded once more that no secrets were hidden from a medicine man.

"I did not think them important enough to discuss."

"You are feeling guilt. Toward our Earth Mother."

His fingers flexed on the steering wheel. "Yes. Yet I felt the Great Spirit approved."

"It is true. There is always a reason. *Maheo's* ways are not our ways. We must follow and learn his teachings and ceremonies so we live in harmony with all men and all living things. He created the Earth. His instructions rule over all. There is greater good to come. In time, you will know."

Charlie scowled at the prophetic ring of his words, muscles tensing. Eaglefeathers sounded that way at times, too. He still avoided dabbling with the future unless imposed upon him, as it was when he envisioned the source of Sara's illness.

The obscure turnoff to his cabin bore off to the left. The SUV bucked and rocked along the rut-infested dirt road, shadowed to oblivion by vegetation in the fading light.

Tah-Hó'nehe came to a gentle stop.

Nestled among the pines and brush reposed a dilapidated cabin. The surrounding wilderness encroached on his home during his absence. The Earth Mother was in control, whether the white man admitted it or not.

He turned off the engine. Shivered when struck with certain knowledge his time here was over. A sentimental twinge struck his chest like an unfriendly arrow.

The old mining cabin was primitive, but home. A spring-fed well provided running water in the kitchen and bathroom. Solar panels left over from when Bryan remodeled his own place generated enough power for a tiny refrigerator and single light

45

over the kitchen table. The well had since fouled, but worked for the bathroom, thanks to an inline filter Bryan helped install.

The elder's soft voice beside him was as if his home itself were speaking. "Your memories here are deep. Many moons ago, this is where your journey began. In time you will return. Much here connects you to this land. Your ancestors are near. They are watching you. You were never alone."

Awash in nostalgia coupled with White Wolf's words, memory flared. Sitting beneath the bur oak in front of White Wolf's home when he discovered his ability for remote viewing. He'd seen his home, including surveillance devices planted therein. He smirked, picturing some *Vehoe* spying on them while they conversed in Cheyenne.

Leaving them in place would taunt them.

He stepped to the ground, grateful to stretch his legs, even though *Tah-Hó'nehe* was far more comfortable than the sagging springs and spent shock absorbers in his old Ranger. White Wolf joined him, sniffing the pine-scented mountain air.

"What is the elevation?"

"About sixty-six hundred feet."

"What are the highest peaks?"

"There are many the locals call *fourteeners*." He pointed northwest, where a rugged summit was visible beyond the trees. "That is Eagles Peak. Not quite a fourteener, but close."

"It has powerful spirits. This is sacred ground. I now understand why my father was dedicated to its protection." He glanced at the darkening sky. "We have less than an hour. Bitter root must cook many hours. We should start it now."

"I will light the woodstove."

White Wolf frowned. "It is prepared over an open fire." He pointed at the fire pit outside the front door. "*É-tòhé'kèsaéveméá'ha*. It smells very bad, not as roast venison, Littlewolf."

"We will open windows. It is easier to watch inside."

White Wolf didn't argue, just ambled around outside the cabin while Charlie tromped through the overgrowth to the door.

Ancient hinges creaked as he pushed it open, greeted by an accumulation of spider webs. He brushed them away, then paused, giving any critters a chance to exit. Rustling from the direction of the kitchen announced such a departure.

Then silence.

It was dark and frigid, the familiar outcome of deep shade and chilly nights. His hand tugged the string of the single bulb. Light flooded the room's meager furnishings.

Memories surged as a swollen stream. His gifted eyes followed his thoughts, Eaglefeathers appearing at the old woodstove, preparing venison stew. His mouth watered at the familiar aroma.

The old man turned.

Charlie's heart froze.

"I am sorry, grandfather," he said in Cheyenne, voice trembling. "I vow to make it up to you. Please forgive me."

"It is for our people," Eaglefeathers replied. "For them, you must succeed."

He sensed White Wolf beside him.

Had he shared his vision?

"You have many memories here," his uncle said. "There are good spirits watching. They returned when you built the sweat lodge. They have many sorrows you cannot stay."

Charlie nodded, throat too tight to speak.

"Do you have a pot for the bitter root? I'll use some of the spring water we brought."

He released a measured breath through his nose. "Yes. Of course."

After handing him the stew pot from above the stove, he said, "I'll get some wood."

He stepped out the backdoor and retrieved an armful from the pile on the west side. Once the fire caught he went back out to check his canoe.

Nostalgia struck hard when he yanked off the tarp. Memories surged of when he'd built it with Bryan, back when they were carefree teens. Besides that sentimental link, they didn't have one on the ranch. Enough to justify bringing it along to White Wolf.

He grabbed the gunwales and hauled it to the car. Hopefully the two of them could get it on the roof rack. Transporting it in his truck had been a simple one-person task, but it was too heavy to dead lift to the roof by himself.

Where there's a will, there's a way.

He shivered as one of Bryan's favorite sayings echoed from the past, followed by recalling a substantial length of rope coiled up beside the fireplace.

Back inside the noxious stench of bitter root turned his stomach. *Poor Sara. That stuff is nothing short of disgusting.*

White Wolf stood by the fireplace, examining the quiver of arrows that hung above it. An heirloom from Eaglefeathers' father, Rides the Wind, who would have been White Wolf's grandfather.

Charlie joined him, the heavy stone of guilt reminding him it rightfully didn't belong to him. "It will make a fine addition to your medicine room," he said.

White Wolf's gaze met his. "Yes. *Néá eše,*" he said, shaking Charlie's hand.

The stone fetishes guarding the mantel were clothed in cobwebs. He picked up each tiny animal, dusted it off, then placed it in the buckskin bag with the medicine wheel.

"What are those?" White Wolf asked.

"Fetishes. Carved by our Zuni brothers. I got them at a pow-wow when I lived in New Mexico. They represent spirit animals that guard the medicine wheel." He removed the wheel's miniature representation from the bag and held it up. "It is used with prayer and meditation for guidance."

"I forget you are not pure Cheyenne."

Again Charlie's eyes connected with his.

Did it matter?

While his marriage to a *Diné* woman had been a disaster other than their two daughters, his maternal grandmother, his *amasani,* had been as important as Eaglefeathers in teaching him how to live.

While differences in their beliefs and ceremonies caused bitter contention between his parents, their respective tribal values were like multiple poles in a tipi, each reinforcing the strength of the others. Charlie felt richer knowing the traditions of both and seeing how they complemented each other.

While White Wolf checked the bitter root to make sure it didn't boil, Charlie entered his makeshift bedroom struck by another memory.

His metal frame bed was nothing special, but the cedar chest he and Bryan built together was. Like the canoe, it was one of his most cherished possessions. It also contained sacred items, including buffalo robes used to cover the sweat lodge as well as the cardboard box filled with memorabilia and old photos from Bryan that Sara gave him that night they found the missing data.

The chest without question needed to go to Montana.

His attempt to move it was in vain.

"Uncle, if you're not busy, I need your help."

White Wolf appeared in the doorway.

"This chest has buffalo robes and other sacred items. It must go home with us."

They hefted it outside, set it down to make room by shifting the items in the cargo area, then managed to slide it inside.

White Wolf pointed at the canoe.

"You are bringing that as well?"

"Yes. I built it with my white brother."

"The one who was murdered?"

"Yes. We were around Winter Hawk's age. We can take it out on Eaglefeathers or Rosebud Creek."

"Will it fit inside?"

"I was thinking the roof, but with the seats down, it might."

Measurements proved otherwise. "I have some rope to make a pulley."

A growling sound issued from his uncle's throat. "Do not damage my new truck, nephew."

Charlie narrowed his eyes, not sure if he was teasing. "Surely on the ranch it will get a dent or two. Sooner or later."

White Wolf's hearty laugh silenced the sparrows conversing in the pine beside the old fire pit. "Yes. It will," he agreed.

"Bryan called the scratches and dents on his truck travel souvenirs."

"I call them battle scars."

"Yes. We will do our best to avoid mortal wounds."

"Yes, please." He gestured toward colors gathering along the western horizon. "We should do it now, Littlewolf. While it is still light."

"I will get the rope."

First he protected the passenger side by hanging a quilt from the doors.

With the rope looped over the luggage rack on the driver side, he tossed the rest over the roof, then secured a sling around the canoe with a series of knots Bryan taught him. He never could remember what they were called, but never forgot their function. The canoe was currently upright, but his intent was to flip it over so it was bottom up for the ride.

"Do you want to pull the rope? Or make sure it doesn't bump the doors?" Charlie asked.

"I will protect the doors. You are much younger and stronger, Littlewolf."

The rope moaned as the sling took the weight. Unable to see what was happening on the other side, he backed away as he pulled. When he was several feet back, the canoe arrived at the edge of the luggage rack. Now he'd find out if his scheme to flip it over would work.

"Can you push it straight up, uncle, before I pull further? I want it to flip over."

"I will try."

As soon as the gunwales were visible above the rack, Charlie yanked. Much to his surprise, the canoe flipped as planned. As he stood on the sissy bars to secure it, White Wolf came around to watch.

"The spirits helped or that would not have worked," he stated. "It must be *Maheo's* will to have it on the ranch."

Charlie secured the remaining length of rope and jumped to the ground. "It will be fun for the boys. How is the bitter root doing? Do you think we can leave for a while without it boiling?"

"If I add more water and we are gone a short time. Where is it you want to go?"

"My spirit tells me we should pray and smoke the sacred red pipe at Dead Horse Canyon."

"Yes. Our blood is part of this curse in ways we do not understand. Perhaps it will speak to us."

He watched White Wolf pour several more inches of spring water over the bitter root, nose wrinkling as steam wafted from it again. The firebox glowed with steady embers. He added another log, just to be sure, then they left and got into the SUV.

Charlie smiled when the headlights came on automatically. Tires crunched through brush as he turned around and bumped their way back to the road. An hour of dusk remained, prelude to the dark of a moonless night.

The cutout where he parked his old truck was tight, barely enough room for White Wolf to squeeze out the door. A moment to find the hazard lights, then he led him across the road to where he first sought the counsel of the grandfather spirits.

They blessed themselves with the Earth, sat on the ground. Each made a prayer. White Wolf offered the sacred red pipe to the four directions, loaded and lit it, smoke wafting their petitions skyward.

Ancient healers demonstrated an understanding of this concept, that the universe is filled with and made of intelligent energy, which is able to respond to intention.
--Dr. Bradley Nelson, author of "The Emotion Code"

5. BITTER ROOT

LONE STAR OPERATIONS (LSO) WORK SITE
RURAL FALCON RIDGE
August 9, Thursday
7:30 a.m.

Trey Maguire brushed off his hands, elated as the last salvage truck jostled away loaded with blowout debris. For the first time in weeks his neck and shoulder muscles relaxed. The accident investigation couldn't find any reason the blow-out preventer (BOP) failed. One theory suggested by the fault tree analysis was the site's elevation and reduced air pressure could be a factor.

Suggested modifications were implemented which, right or wrong, allowed the crew to get back to work.

The original truck-mounted drill was beyond repair. An exploration rig was on its way from Fort Worth, due the end of the week. Meanwhile, they were getting the base camp set up to avoid commuting from their original outpost, four miles away.

He couldn't help chuckling every time he looked at the towering crane used to erect the derrick. The eighteen-wheeler hauling the heavy lifter was never able to make it around that tight-ass turn.

With no other choice they offloaded the crane, then put it to work retrieving the pickup and its foolhardy driver's body from the ravine. That saved the locals enough money no more was said about blocking the road, much less any involvement with the wreck.

The rig's driver took more than his share of flack for the accident it caused, too. Fortunately, skid marks vindicated him since the poor sucker was traveling at a ridiculously high speed.

After that, they drove it five long miles to the site.

Trey continued to chuckle as he sauntered back to the office trailer, grateful for progress at last. He sat at his desk where he drummed his fingers on its worn surface.

Close examination of the seismic data confirmed multiple deposits in the location Littlewolf identified. With luck, they'd find the main reservoir, set up a production rig—or two or three—and go to town.

How was Littlewolf doing, anyway? Was there a snowball's chance in hell of getting him back?

He pulled out his phone and tried again. As before, the call went directly to phone mail. Rather than hang up this time, he left a message.

"Hey, Littlewolf, this here's Trey. Just wonderin' how ya'll's doin' and if y'all'd like to come on back. Gimme a call."

Why the calls repeatedly went to phone mail left him baffled. Was his phone turned off? Rejecting the calls?

He looked like pounded shit the last time he saw him. Had he recovered? Or not?

If he knew where he was, he'd pay him a visit. Face-to-face, and find out. Maybe he could turn on the Texas charm and convince him to come-on back.

The day after the blowout, Gerald Bentley high-tailed it out of town. He chuckled as he recalled the man crying about "killing Bob's Indian." He never let him know he'd seen Charlie since and that he seemed to be on the mend. However, if he didn't come back, it was a moot point.

Nonetheless, he'd probably still want to know. It would give Gerald good reason to keep his brother at bay, if nothing else. Besides, maybe as LSO's Chief Operations Officer he'd offer some extra cash to get him back.

MONTGOMERY RESIDENCE
BOULDER
August 9, Thursday
8:38 a.m.

CHARLIE UP-ENDED BOTH buckets of soil on a patch of grass bordered by a flower bed abloom with chrysanthemums. He smoothed it to a mound, creating a miniature Sacred Mountain.

White Wolf handed him the buffalo skull. He positioned it facing east toward the flowers, then set the sacred red pipe against it, bowl facing the same direction.

Only words of necessity passed between them since arising, aside from singing the Badger song as they drove through the Eisenhower Tunnel. Between leaving his cabin behind, perhaps forever, and what lay ahead, his heart and mind were heavy.

What could he possibly say to Sara if they failed? Or her family, especially her father?

Buffalo robes covered the ground, pillows added to maintain Sara in a semi-reclined position. Gallon jugs of spring water, two mason jars of bitter root tea with drinking vessels for each, plus an old metal coffee can to catch what she expelled, were in place. He lit the coals in a hibachi, waited a moment, then placed a piece of sweetgrass braid upon them.

As fragrant smoke blessed the site, White Wolf nodded, then folded a black silk scarf into a narrow strip that he tied on as a headband as protection from bad spirits, completing his medicine man regalia.

"Okay," he declared, "We are ready."

Charlie forced a smile as he went inside to convey the news. Sara was still upstairs with Connie, so Patrice went to check. The hum of the elevator announced their arrival moments later. Charlie carried Sara outside while Will brought the wheelchair, women following.

Charlie lowered her onto the buffalo robes where Connie and Patrice arranged the pillows.

"How's that?" Connie asked. "Are you comfortable, honey?"

Sara nodded. The woman kissed her on the head, then she and Patrice joined Will, already seated slightly behind his daughter in what he recognized as an emotional lockdown.

Charlie and White Wolf each used a handful from the mound to bless themselves with the earth, having explained earlier that the sacred motions represented *Maheo* creating the human body and blowing life into it. After that, Charlie picked up the sweetgrass braid to waft its vanilla-like smoke about to bless those present.

"First we will make a prayer," White Wolf said as they stood behind the buffalo skull. The others got up to join them. "I will go first. Do not worry that you cannot understand my words. Speak your own from your heart."

The others closed their eyes and bowed their heads as White Wolf began in Cheyenne.

"*Maheo*, we humbly ask your help and that of your spirit helpers this day for this woman who has been greatly wronged by evil men," he prayed. "Her injuries are severe. Only with your help can she be healed. I will do all that I know, but I have never been asked to heal such serious illness. Please help us."

Charlie's chest ached all the way to his throat as he began.

"*Maheo*, we are powerless without you. As Creator, you know all things and have wisdom we cannot see. It is my desire to help my white brother's woman be healthy again. It is only through you and your spirit helpers that this can be. I vow to complete my fast on the Sacred Mountain as soon as I can. I pray Sweet Medicine spirits be with us to help Sara be healed and walk again."

SARA'S HOPES SWELLED with their words, the sound pleasant albeit foreign, the feeling behind them clear. While the others uttered their respective petitions, hers expressed gratitude for dear friends and family.

The songs that followed brought the same warm feeling, though unspoken fears rumbled as a thunderstorm beyond the horizon.

What if this doesn't work? Why did I have to come back like this?

The singing ended. The mood shifted as White Wolf picked up the small whistle Charlie told her was created from the wing bones of an eagle. He placed it to his lips, a high-pitched cry saturating time and space. The morning sun warming her face yielded to a chill.

It was time.

Her mind raced with multi-faceted fear. *What have I gotten myself into?*

She eyed the bitter root with an emotional mix as murky as its dark, opaque depths. Hope was the only thing that could overcome the revulsion wrenching her stomach to an unwilling knot. In all honesty, its appearance resembled what she'd expect to see in a septic tank.

Charlie poured some into a glass and held it out. Trepidation triggered a flight or fight response as she caught a whiff of its fetid odor.

Again she cursed her lifeless legs—she couldn't run if she wanted to.

Ironically, this was her only hope to do so again.

Dark eyes met hers as she accepted the glass. "It will be okay," he mouthed, but his knowing sympathy negated any calming effect.

She turned her attention to the brew and took a sniff. It smelled like rotting vegetation and sewage. A gorge rose in her throat, morphing to a gag. Stomach juices seeped into her mouth. She motioned for the coffee can. Spit, then wiped her eyes.

Over the lips and through the gums. Look out stomach, here it comes.

Shut up, Bryan, she thought, his presence strong.

"Just hold your nose and drink as much as you can," Charlie advised.

Her face contorted as she pinched her nostrils. Her eyes closed, as if to block what was sure to be a revolting experience. Concentrating on its potential benefits, she gulped it down until violent gagging signaled her stomach would not tolerate another drop.

Charlie took the glass.

Teeth clamped and jaw clenched, she willed the foul liquid to go down and remain in place. Fingers curled into the buffalo robes as she took several deep breaths.

Charlie handed her a glass of spring water. A few eager swallows later, her stomach rumbled, announcing that thunderstorm had arrived.

"*Ewwwww!*" she exclaimed. "That was *so* disgusting! Horrible! *Ugh!* Now what?"

"We wait. It usually takes about twenty minutes."

"Wonderful. After I barf I'm done?"

Charlie's sorry look was not what she was hoping for.

"No. You must do this five times," White Wolf said.

Sara determination sagged as she buried her face in her hands. "Oh. My. God."

Connie and Patrice moved closer, arms around her.

"It's going to be okay, sweetie," Patrice whispered.

"Yes," Connie added. "You've got this."

"We will pray and sing while we wait," White Wolf stated.

Sara leaned back into the pillows, eyes closed, arms tight around her belly. Their petition soothed her soul, even without understanding the words. Singing had a similar effect, until interrupted by her gurgling stomach.

Her eyes flew open when she started to gag. Singing stopped. Charlie held the can while Connie and Patrice rubbed her back.

Every muscle, organ, and cell convulsed, as if to exit her tortured body. She retched and gagged, the monster inside fighting to retain its domain. Besides seeming like far more came up than she drank, the bitter root tasted worse, further tinged with bile.

After an elongated span of trauma-warped time, the dry heaves stopped. She sputtered and spit, gasping for air.

Charlie handed her another glass of water. She rinsed out her mouth, spit in the can.

"*Ugggghhh*!"

Connie handed her a tissue for her eyes, another to blow her nose.

"Are you ready for the next one?" Charlie asked.

She shuddered, still trying to catch her breath. "Okay," she said, voice raspy. "Like Mom would say, let's get this over with."

The next four rounds were no less gut-wrenching, intensity increasing until it felt as if she'd turned inside-out. Singing and praying somewhere far away coupled with two ministering women bore her through.

At last it was over.

She rinsed her mouth and drank another glass of water. Closed her eyes and crossed her hands over her chest while her vital signs settled to their normal sinus rhythm. Tensed muscles relaxed. At length her eyelids slowly lifted.

Four sets of expectant faces welcomed her back from Dante's ninth level of hell.

"Where's Dad?" she asked.

Connie patted her arm. "It's okay, honey. He couldn't handle watching you suffer. I'll tell him it's over."

"How do you feel?" White Wolf asked.

A quick inventory of her senses registered positive change. "Better. That awful headache's gone. Besides feeling like a gorilla punched me in the stomach, the nausea's gone, too."

"So you feel better. Good." Charlie's eyes locked onto hers. "Can you move your legs?"

FBI FIELD OFFICE
DENVER
August 9, Thursday
11:57 a.m.

TWENTY-NINE MILES TO the south, Guy Allison stepped out of his cubicle on the fifth-floor of Denver's FBI Field Office and strode for the coffee pot.

The fiscal year ended in six weeks, closed case paperwork due within a few days. The number of cases he closed, but not necessarily solved, reflected on his annual performance evaluation, upon which raises and promotions hinged. So far his track record this year, as well as previous ones, was less than impressive.

One high profile case stood out. If he closed that one his boss, the Deputy Director, would definitely be pleased. It was one of those nuisance cases riddled with career limiting booby traps you didn't necessarily *want* to solve.

Where plausible deniability was the best option, the Bureau wanted them buried as quickly as possible. Get them out of the public eye with all the other cover-ups the American people didn't need to know about.

Twenty-seven years with the agency taught him the majority of conspiracy theories had a strong basis in fact. He once heard the term itself was invented specifically to obscure the truth. Admitting that officially, however, was another matter. Such admissions loomed with consequences determined far beyond his pay grade.

But for personal financial reasons, it was time to make a few decisions that *were* within his pay grade.

He returned to his cubical with a mug of scorched coffee, finished his soggy tuna sandwich, and wiped his hands on his pants. He set his jaw, then opened the Reynolds case folder on his computer.

Closing the damn thing would generate some much needed kudos.

CATEGORY: Cyber Crimes - Unauthorized Access
SUSPECT: Bryan Reynolds
STATUS: Deceased
SUMMARY: Hacker downloaded classified documents stored on an NGO server owned by Elite Management Partners Inc.,

project management provider for PURF project. BKSS, a private security firm contracted as a deniable asset to the NSA, neutralized the suspect using a private vehicle when the suspect and his wife trespassed on the site.

Allison laughed. Closing that should be a no brainer with the suspect dead.

However, reading on indicated it wasn't that simple.

ACCESSORY: Reynolds' wife, Sara Reynolds

Survived the accident that killed her husband and anonymously released classified data hacked by her spouse to WikiLeaks. President explained PURF's legality in televised Press Conference, removing any need to remain classified.

His head felt as if it had experienced an unfortunate encounter with a battle ax as he read on, refreshing his memory of the details. It could have/should have ended there.

But, just like a woman, Mrs. Reynolds had to whine publicly about the situation, keeping her on FBI radar.

ACCESSORY STATUS UPGRADED TO SUSPECTED DOMESTIC TERRORIST.

Accessory turned whistleblower. Appeared on local and network television claiming excessive force used by PURF security contractors (BKSS) resulted in late husband's death and her own extensive injuries.

Such anti-government actions jeopardize trust in government by inciting public outrage at lawful actions to support her seditious cause.

Currently, her corporate popularity was right up there with Ralph Nader, an infamous consumer advocate from decades before. Powerful people didn't take kindly to some blabbermouth woman jeopardizing their future well-being.

Information she made public struck damning blows to all corporations with lobbyists working with Congress to pass legislation to assure, or better yet, enhance their profits.

Every. Single. One.

Even though lobbying was legal while her husband's hacking was not, the woman hit a nerve when she questioned the morality of using public funds to benefit corporate representatives, much less killing her husband to keep it quiet.

If enough citizens protested and withdrew their votes from their congressional reps, their cushy situation would collapse. Money donated to her GoFundMe account confirmed favorable public sentiment.

If it escalated it could bring unwanted attention to the 2010 Supreme Court decision that legalized corporate campaign donations and facilitated lobbying through which congressmen "earned" such financial rewards.

That, in turn, could trigger renewed scrutiny of that decision and possible reversal.

If it came to that, every corporation, every lobbyist, and every member of Congress would be out for blood. When public interest collided with corporate profits, much less government policy, the result tended to surround the whistleblower with a gas cloud comprised of ammonia and chlorine bleach.

How many had been silenced for exposing government and corporate incestuous relationships?

One of many reasons corporatism was alive and well.

NOTE: During network television appearance suspect collapsed, cause attributed to poisoning.

Murder was not a federal crime, and therefore *not* the FBI's problem.

However, if the suspect was someone from the lobbyist or Congressional population, it constituted corruption, which fit within FBI's responsibilities.

His nose wrinkled as if smelling rotten meat.

If that were the case, identifying who wanted her dead would open a gigantic can of worms.

More likely boa constrictors.

As a government agency, the FBI was banned from uncovering dirt that reflected badly on government figures or policies, more specifically those of the ruling party. Government corruption was so pervasive they spent more time framing and locking up political opponents on bogus charges than going after actual criminals.

As he dug through the notes he was relieved to find justification against digging any further.

The suspect was identified as BKSS employee, Eddie Johannsen, as responsible for the poisoning incident.

There was a multitude of possibilities who actually contracted with BKSS, but as a hired gun, Johannsen probably had no idea who his customer was. Nor did he care. The odds were high it was one or more members of populations Allison didn't dare touch.

Conveniently, Johannsen was fired by BKSS, but had a personal vendetta against Mrs. Reynolds, who exposed him as her husband's murderer on national TV.

Which provided enough motive at the personal level to render whomever requested the hit job irrelevant. Johannsen administered the poison, therefore he was the guilty party.

End of story.

With him also dead, whether she survived or not was moot.

The death rate of individuals associated with this case suggested it was self-destructing.

Curious whether or not she was, indeed, among the fatalities, he dug deeper.

The New York City hospital where she was taken claimed she checked out on her own volition, not in a body bag. The physician's last note in the file stated simply, "referred to hospice."

So what was that supposed mean?

Did she die? Or not?

After all, she was on the list of suspected Domestic Terrorists. If she surfaced again, it could reopen the entire debacle.

He ground his teeth, trying to decide if he should play it safe and get a copy of the death certificate. Which could take weeks.

On the other hand, all things considered, with Johannsen dead and her doctor stating she went home to die, there was sufficient data to believe that she, too, was deceased.

Whoever hired BKSS was none of his concern. It was a safe bet this case would fade into the annals of those like the Silkwood case, which also had a host of untouchable suspects. The only way it could bite him was if she came back from the dead and continued to make trouble.

A bet he was willing to take. Hands poised on the keyboard he typed:

SUBJECT ASSUMED DEAD: CASE CLOSED.

Plenty of other cases resided on his plate. Too many, in fact, most of which fit the agency's priorities far better. Terrorism and cybercrimes like identity theft and other fraudulent practices were of far more interest and importance to the majority of taxpayers who paid his six-figure salary.

Once joining the archives, the Reynolds case would languish with other touchy incidents such as 70s hijacker, D. B. Cooper.

Discussing that one along with JFK, 9-11, and a plethora of others was in the verboten category.

Inside jobs?

No one would say, but their eyes said it all.

The Red Nation shall rise again and it shall be a blessing for a sick world; a world filled with broken promises, selfishness, and separations; a world longing for light again.
—*Crazy Horse*

6. PRAYER CLOTHS

MONTGOMERY RESIDENCE
BOULDER
August 9, Thursday
12:03 p.m.

Sara met Charlie's expectant gaze. "My legs? Uh, I don't know." She concentrated on moving her toes.

Nothing.

Then her ankles. Knees. Thighs.

Her eyes closed.

"No," she breathed, barely audible, as if to soften her disappointment. "I can't."

Charlie rested a hand on her shoulder. "It's okay. Sometimes it takes awhile. You'll probably need a sweat to remove more toxins. We still have the prayer cloth ceremony, too."

She shuddered. "Is it anything like this one?"

"No, no. Not at all. Rest while we get ready. Let me help you into your chair."

Her arms encircled his neck as he hoisted her upright while Patrice retrieved it. "It's right behind you, sweetie," she said.

Charlie eased her down, lingering a moment to share a hug.

She buried her face in his shoulder, disappointment impossible to dismiss. His arms tightened around her. She squeezed back tears, not wanting him to think she didn't appreciate all he and White Wolf had done, much less leave stains on his buckskin shirt. She released her hold and swiped moisture from her eyes, avoiding his gaze.

He hesitated a moment, then turned to gather up the buffalo robes. While he took them to their truck White Wolf prepared for the next ceremony. When Charlie returned he used the embers in the hibachi to reignite the sweetgrass, then set it in the dish beside the skull.

White Wolf instructed everyone to line-up facing east. Charlie wheeled Sara front and center behind the buffalo skull with White Wolf on her right while Patrice, Connie, and her father stood behind.

White Wolf and Charlie each scooped up another handful of earth from the buffalo mound, made the sacred motions, then White Wolf offered another prayer.

As before, she didn't understand the language, yet it was gentle on the ear and embraced her soul. Charlie's petition left a similar impression.

They began to sing.

Goosebumps tickled her arms, the air electrified.

When the fourth song began, Charlie's eyes shifted to her. After he sang alone for a short time, White Wolf quietly translated. Sara's mouth fell open, having entirely forgotten. If they sang it for the healing ceremony, she was too distracted to notice, though she would remember the translation. This time White Wolf sang the words in English, touching her soul.

Ma'heo'o, Creator of life with healing power
We pray with heavy hearts and tears in our eyes.
Evil spirits have poisoned our sister Sara,
Clean the poison from Sara.
Sara's spirit is broken and her legs will not walk.
Ma'heo'o, heal our sister Sara
Ma'heo'o, have pity on Sara
Ma'heo'o, Creator of life with healing power
We pray with humble hearts.
Ma'heo'o, you are the only way we know.

Tears previously restrained dribbled down her cheeks as its message warmed her heart. Stereo sniffling from behind evidenced she wasn't alone.

She never thought of herself as courageous. To not carry out Bryan's request never entered her mind. What did she have to lose? She'd either succeed or join him, which she nearly had. And here she was, in a condition that gave death added appeal.

She sniffed back tears while Charlie broke off another piece of sweetgrass and placed it on the embers. White Wolf picked up the cloths, each a square yard, in red, blue, yellow, white, and black.

He shook them open individually, knotted them together, then passed them through the sweetgrass smoke which, as he'd told them the day before, was to bless and sanctify them to remove any additional evil spirits.

The elder studied Sara, his dark, weathered face deep in thought. "*Maheo* tells me you should stand."

Panic shot through her.

Was he crazy?

Charlie helped her upright. She gripped his arms for support as she straightened her back, arms trembling as she attempted to support her weight.

Will and Connie stepped forward. "We can support her from both sides," her father suggested.

He moved to her right, Connie to her left. They each supported one of her arms, holding her upright.

"That will not work," White Wolf said. "I must be able to circle around her. Let go."

Terrified eyes met the medicine man's.

"I'm right behind you," Charlie assured her.

She let go of Connie with her left hand, ready to collapse to the ground. Much to her surprise, she didn't. Slowly, she let go with the other. Panic flashed when she wobbled, but somehow remained standing.

Fists clenched at her sides, she gradually exhaled.

White Wolf nodded.

Sacred colors fluttered above her head, then rippled toward the ground in poetic motion. Kaleidoscopic flashes of light rustled around her in four stages. He finished by gently swiping the knot along the sides of her face, then a brief touch on top of her head.

Charlie caught her when her legs gave way and eased her into the wheelchair, then held open a plastic bag where White Wolf deposited the cloths, still holding the knot. He set it aside, then he and White Wolf sang again, including Sara's honor song, before closing the ceremony with another prayer.

Charlie crouched down in front of her, dark eyes fixed on hers. "How do you feel?"

She blinked hard, as if awakening from a dream.

The persistent blur that haunted her vision was gone. Colors were bright and true, objects in sharp focus. She held out her hands, which were steady, tremor gone. Charlie's voice no longer sounded far away. A magpie teased from a nearby tree, even the soft purr of traffic on the Diagonal Highway audible. Energy coursed through her, evicting the last of her suite of aches and pains.

She inhaled, surprised she could smell the mums by the fence, that awful odor gone. While the past few hours persisted in a fog, her awareness of where she was and the present moment were clear. Her stomach growled. For the first time since waking up a week ago hunger begged for sustenance without overtones of nausea.

"Sara? How do you feel?" Charlie repeated.

She ran a quick diagnostic assessment, head to toe. "Better. A little tired, but actually, I'm hungry."

"Who else is ready to eat?" Connie asked. "I made a kettle of cabbage soup."

With no dissenters, everyone returned to the house, Patrice pushing Sara in the wheelchair. The two women entered the kitchen while the others sat at the dining room table.

Sara caught her father's eye across from her and smiled. He returned it, but look preoccupied. She could tell the ceremonies troubled him. It was unlike him to be so quiet.

Patrice set down bowls and utensils while Connie placed the steaming pot on a crocheted hotplate.

Will cleared his throat, drawing everyone's attention. "White Wolf, would you please bless the food for us?"

"Of course."

As he prayed, Sara's mind tripped through years past when the only time they blessed the food was Thanksgiving, maybe Christmas, and even that was when her mother was still alive.

Connie ladled generous servings into each person's bowl, then retrieved a loaf of French bread from the oven along with some butter.

Sara savored each spoonful. "This is delicious, Connie. I can't remember the last time anything tasted this good."

When they finished eating, everyone gathered in the living room while White Wolf retrieved something from their SUV.

"We must return home and it's a long drive," Charlie said. "But there is one more thing before we leave."

As if on cue, White Wolf came through the front door, laden with mounds of color that looked as if he'd just returned from a White Sale at Bed, Bath and Beyond.

"It is our tradition to provide gifts to those we serve," the elder said. "My wife, Star, prepared these for each of you. She also sends special caring thoughts to Sara to get well."

He handed a bag to Charlie, who reached inside and removed a crocheted shawl surrounded by fringe in the same colors as the prayer cloths and embroidered with colorful native symbols and animals. He walked over and draped it around Sara's shoulders.

"It's beautiful!" she said, snuggling within its folds. "Thank you so very much. Please tell Star I'll cherish it always."

He then presented Connie and Patrice with shawls as well, but with less ornamentation.

"Oh, my goodness! Thank you! It feels like Christmas," Connie said, pulling it around her. "This is perfect for chilly nights nearly upon us."

White Wolf smiled as he removed a star quilt in shades of purple, turquoise, and magenta from another bag. He opened it up, then draped it around Sara on top of the shawl.

"Wow! It's absolutely stunning!" She hugged it to her, engulfed by the love emanating from it. "What a fabulous gift. Thank you!"

He extracted another one from the final bag, which he presented to Will. The man's jaw dropped.

"T-Thank you," he stammered. "I don't know what to say."

Connie stepped over to examine it, likewise aghast. "I don't, either," she said, eyes wide.

Will chuckled. "Anything that leaves my wife speechless is priceless indeed."

She gave him a mock glare. "It's spring colors are perfect for our bedroom. Sara's colors are, too. How could she have known? They're both absolutely beautiful! Thank you from the depths of our hearts! You've already done so much. I'm overwhelmed by these wonderful gifts on top of it."

"One more thing," Charlie said as he stepped over to place a medicine bag around Sara's neck. She held it up and sniffed. Its herbal scent was pleasant, but entirely different from the one he'd given her when she was recovering from the accident that killed Bryan.

Then everything caught up to her and adrenaline-sponsored energy ebbed. Her eyes drooped as they met his.

"You've had a long, difficult day," he said. "You need lots of rest to allow your body to heal."

"Yes. Suddenly, I'm very tired," she admitted, still hugging the quilt. "Not bad, like before," she emphasized, "Just tired. Sleepy."

Patrice stepped behind her and swiveled the wheelchair toward the laundry room to access the elevator. Before she could move, Charlie scooped Sara up and strode for the stairs.

"First room on the right," Connie instructed, everyone including Sara exchanging startled looks.

He waited while Patrice added the quilt and Connie pulled back the covers. He laid her down gently, adjusting the pillow beneath her head. His eyes drifted from her face to the poster above her bed.

He smiled.

"I remember watching that movie with you and Bryan at your cabin," he said. "I never knew a white woman could be that tough."

Sara nodded agreement. "She's my inspiration. Whenever I want to give up, I think of what Lara Croft would say. Did you know Angelina Jolie did some of her own stunts in the original 'Tomb Raider' movie? Including riding that beam near the end that the stunt woman couldn't do."

"She'd be very proud of you, Sara," he replied. "Now get some rest."

"When will I see you again?"

He glanced over at White Wolf who'd quietly joined them. "I do not know."

Sara hugged the quilt, eyes holding his for another moment before drifting into a peaceful slumber.

NORTHERN CHEYENNE RESERVATION
BUSBY, MONTANA
August 10, Friday
4:45 a.m.

CHARLIE LAY IN BED, draft from the window raising gooseflesh on his arms. He barely slept a wink, too wound up to relax. The drive back was long and exhausting, again with little conversation. Indeed, White Wolf reclined his seat and slept most the way. Lack of scrutiny allowed him to drive faster, their arrival accomplished in six hours instead of seven.

Charlie's thoughts raced with the miles, festering to the point of obsession. It didn't help when that message came up on the media screen from Trey, begging him to come back to work. He felt bad for him, but there was no way he'd ever go back. Working for an oil company was like tanning a hide, lots of hard, smelly work with a great reward at the end.

For which he was grateful, but that part of his life was over. He didn't want to even think about what White Wolf would say if he did. Or what he'd say to Trey, so just deleted it, hoping not to hear from him again.

It seemed even stranger that he was actually at his cabin when he called. But he left his phone in the truck so he wouldn't have to connect it again, not expecting any calls, anyway. At any rate, that phase of his life was over.

But on top of that, what bothered him the most was Sara.

They failed.

While some improvement was gained, Sara still couldn't walk. Her disappointment left a knot in both his chest and gut. His fault for giving her a false impression.

Was he naive believing they could? What went wrong? White Wolf had not seemed confident. Did that limit the result? He knew beyond a doubt that Eaglefeathers could have.

Deep inside he knew he was to blame. His abilities were barely awake, experience limited. Impatience raged to determine what he needed to do.

Movement in the kitchen followed by the aroma of coffee brewing lured him upstairs. He greeted White Wolf with a nod, poured himself a mug.

"You are troubled," White Wolf stated, heading toward the dining table where they sat down on opposite sides.

"Yes. Tell me, uncle. Can we heal her? Or not?"

White Wolf met his pleading eyes over the rim of his cup.

"You forget, Littlewolf. We do not heal her. It is *Maheo's* decision. Perhaps he has different plans."

Charlie's gut knotted some more.

"Or maybe it's not yet the time," his uncle went on. "Perhaps this is to teach you something. What does your heart tell you?"

He hung his head. "I am not worthy of asking so much of *Maheo*."

"That may be true. You must complete your pledges. However, her illness is very serious and deeply rooted. I have worked with *Maheo* to heal many of our people, but never one so damaged in body and spirit. As medicine men, we must know our limits. When we bump into them, we seek counsel from an elder with more experience."

He sat up straighter, knots loosening their grip. "Do you know such a man?"

"Yes. I go to him when I need help. Ice is very good. He is *ma'heónèhetane*. A holy man, close to *Maheo* and the same generation as Eaglefeathers. He will tell you what to do. You must lay down tobacco and ask him when we can meet. To prepare, we must do a sweat. But first, there is ranch work to do."

LATER THAT MORNING, Charlie dug a hole over two feet deep to bury the toxins Sara expelled. It was beside a boulder to mark the spot in a remote part of the ranch, away from both creeks, as well as where neither bison, cattle, elk, deer, or other wildlife grazed. Given its lethal potential, it wouldn't take long for the bad spirits to kill any vegetation as far as a yard away.

When they returned to the house, Charlie understood why White Wolf made such a big deal about leaving. A multitude of unexpected situations arose during their absence.

Rufus Littlesun covered White Wolf's medicine man duties, which were minimal. Household issues, however, took the entire time since their return to resolve.

Things did not go smoothly like when everyone was present. Did mischievous spirits move in as soon as they left?

The water heater went out; Winter Hawk took Charlie's truck for a ride and got stuck in the mud. As if in a jealous fit against his "new ride," the boy's horse, Hobo, threw a shoe.

Both men drove to Billings to replace the water heater since White Wolf still refused to drive *Tah-Hó'nehe*. When they returned he set out to take care of the installation while Charlie and Winter Hawk drove out to haul his Ranger out of the mire.

When they returned, mud-splattered truck in tow, White Wolf was waiting, unable to complete the installation due to needing more plumbing components. That necessitated *another* trip, but fortunately Ashland's hardware store had what they needed.

It didn't take long after that to discover Winter Hawk's initial attempts to get unstuck burned out the clutch. Charlie had to deal with that the next day while his uncle shod Hobo and Spring Thunder, both of whom were overdue.

NORTHERN CHEYENNE RESERVATION
BUSBY, MONTANA
August 11, Saturday
8:45 a.m.

THE NEXT DAY, with everything back in order, they prepared a sweat, not only to seek answers regarding Sara, but to thank *Maheo* that nothing more serious had occurred at home during their trip.

This was also the first chance they'd had to petition *Maheo* for more details since smoking the sacred red pipe at Dead Horse Canyon. The response to their prayers at that location was as vague as it was dramatic, which they hoped to clarify now that things had settled down.

Charlie took a drink, then passed the dipper to White Wolf while Risingsun brought the last round of stones into the sweat lodge. So far no further answers had come.

The strange message he received at Dead Horse Canyon continued to trouble him, no more comfortable with it now than then. While his uncle had smoked the sacred red pipe he'd sensed movement some fifty feet away.

A lone wolf, clearly an alpha, had loped toward them, then sat beside the aspen that prompted him to check Bryan's truck for evidence following his white brother's murder.

A wave of apprehension rippled through him as the wolf gazed into his eyes. Not fear, but intimidation as he perceived the powerful animal's unspoken message. At that point the wolf nodded ever so slightly and assured him, "*Maheo* will guide you."

Then he'd disappeared like morning mist before the sun.

He didn't feel like a leader, never wanted that kind of responsibility. Now it was clear, whether he liked it or not. But why? What was he supposed to do? Solemnity fell upon him, as a weight far beyond his ability to lift, much less carry.

Upon discussing it with White Wolf, he could tell he was not surprised. "*Maheo* has given you great gifts. He expects you to use them."

But how?

Would the sweat bring understanding? What he really wanted to know was what must he do to please *Maheo* enough to help Sara. Or was it *Maheo's* will for her to stay disabled? A painful lesson for them both?

When they smoked at Dead Horse Canyon he pledged to *Maheo* to complete his fast on the Sacred Mountain. That needed to be completed soon, both because progress depended on it as well as the weather soon to turn cold.

Risingsun stacked the last of the stones and took his place by the door. The familiar fragrance of sweetgrass filled the lodge and the fourth and final round began. They sang the Grandfather Song, Badger Song, Wolf Song, and Buffalo Song, then took turns praying.

The sweat lodge dissolved and he found himself again on the rim of Dead Horse Canyon. Sun low in the sky, shadows long. A slight breeze directing the melodious chime of the aspen's golden leaves. A few fluttered to the ground.

A medley of fall colors spread before him, as far as he could see. Maples clothed in red, cottonwoods in yellow, oaks and box elders ablaze in orange. Some shrubs likewise wore splashes of color, evergreens fading to darker winter shades.

Its symbolism rang as thunder through the canyons. For him and the Earth it was a time of change. Time to prepare for winter's cold, then eventual rebirth. The Earth would renew, and deep inside he knew when it did, he'd never be the same again.

The call of a mourning dove rode the breeze. Moments later, a lone female landed high in a nearby oak, feathers harmonizing with its orange leaves.

Sara.

In his mind's eye he saw her sleeping, aura brightening as vitality returned. The bird fluttered to a lower branch where it remained, still and quiet.

The revelation at Patrice's rumbled through him, confirmation of multiple entanglements.

But who was Sara?

What about Bryan? Who was he?

"You don't know?"

He blinked, recognizing the familiar voice. His gaze shifted from the dove to his friend, standing before him.

"Other than being friends and I suppose, brothers, no," he answered. "Should I?"

His response was a knowing smile. "You will."

The dove abandoned the tree to perch on Bryan's shoulder. He beckoned her to his finger. She stepped onboard, cooing. He regarded her with a tender gaze, caressing her with his other hand.

He whispered something to her.

In response she spread her wings and fluttered to the ground, landing in front of Charlie.

He held out his hand. She hopped onto it, tilted her head in silent query. He looked up to question Bryan.

He was gone.

He scowled at the dove, wondering. Was it what he thought? The bird held his gaze, eyes steady and unblinking.

The vision faded.

Back in the sweat lodge White Wolf waited for him to pray.

7. FLASHBACK

NIELSEN RESIDENCE
GEORGETOWN, MARYLAND
August 11, Saturday
4:18 p.m. EDT

The heavy envelope had the look and feel of an invitation. Calvin Nielsen frowned, mystified. Who was getting married? Someone's child or grandchild, perhaps? If so, why would they invite him?

He snorted. Expecting a gift, no doubt. Which lay somewhere beneath the basement of his least concerns.

He lowered himself into his favorite Queen Anne chair and extracted the engraved card from the second envelope. His puzzled look shifted to a grin.

The PURF open house.

How could he forget? Ingrid asked a few days before if he'd be the keynote speaker. No one was more qualified, to be sure. If it weren't for him, that place wouldn't exist. In a fair world, it would have been named the Nielsen Underground Residential Facility. The convention, however, was to credit the congressman responsible for introducing the bill.

How typical.

His mind cycled back four years. Time had flown far faster than expected while seeming as yesterday.

He'd been preparing to attend a black-tie gala at the Watergate, pondering how congressmen were provided with an apocalypse-proof bunker. There he was with his fellows, the ones doing most the work. Determining what legislation could benefit the petroleum industry, actually authoring the bills, yet having no such benefits.

The world was volatile, potential for a violent natural disaster or global war growing each day. If things escalated, how could surviving House Reps and Senators do their job properly without input from the likes of him?

Rebuilding the nation would require continued partnering between government and industry. A synergistic relationship of which he and his cronies were key components.

The lobbying community in Washington D.C. resembled a small town with an official population around ten thousand. Everyone knew each other, perhaps too well, either directly or through no more than a two-or-three-person chain.

Most lobbyists were honest of necessity. Anything less would jeopardize the trust of those over whom they hoped to bear sway. However, in a world where truckloads of money and power flowed like honey—sweet, but sticky—human nature dictated corruption would inevitably creep in.

He watched this flow of cash and influence with a jaded eye for over twenty years. He had a law degree from the University of Chicago, was a corporate attorney for Exxon-Mobil for over a decade, then eventually joined Meridian & McDowell, one of Washington's top lobbyist firms, to work the oil and gas lobby.

Prevailing upon lawmakers on behalf of the petroleum industry depended much on the dominant political party at the time. Republicans were prone to maintaining a strong defense, its cousin, the space program, as well as supporting corporate profits and a strong stock market.

Industries like oil and gas, automobile manufacturing, pharmaceuticals, and energy generation were part of the country's economic backbone. Any disruption had a severe impact on employment and the economy as well as Wall Street.

Traditionally, Democrats, on the other hand, were more given toward social program expansion, which assured more votes from those receiving such benefits. All well and good, except it raised taxes, drove up debt, and often decimated the economy. Corporations beholden to their stockholders had no problem moving abroad as required to maintain profits.

However, since corporate campaign donations had been legalized, liberals spent more time accommodating their donors than their constituents. Luckily, many life-long Democrats failed to notice while the others took what crumbs were cast their way, less affected by rising inflation and taxes than those working for a living.

That was just the way it was. It didn't make any difference to him. His annual salary in the neighborhood of $500,000 remained the same. Except, perhaps, for bonuses during a boom, and increased risk of unemployment during a bust.

Like a bank clerk handling thousands of dollars each day, none of which made any difference to his own account.

What really stuck in his craw were corporate bonuses. When a company did well, which was usually due to favorable legislation, CEOs walked off with obscene rewards orders of magnitude higher than any he was thrown.

Congressmen fared better as well. At the least, they'd receive immense campaign donations for introducing and supporting bills that favored various industries. In addition, there were some who took money or other perquisites under the table, legal or not.

It was impossible to ignore that he did all the work while those on either side of his efforts got all the credit, to say nothing of a sweet piece of taxpayer pie.

He'd done fairly well in the stock market, often from what was technically insider information, though it was usually received in such an indirect manner it was difficult to identify as such. Overhearing the prognosis for legislation that would favor some particular industry was business as usual. He knew when to get in and he knew when to pull out.

But it still was chump change, compared to that received by those for whom he mediated.

Actually, his biggest problem, like so many—including the government itself—was not an income problem so much as a spending problem. Keeping up appearances and all that. To rub elbows with those of high station required appearing as a member of the "club."

The highest echelons of D.C. were snooty. If he didn't look as if he belonged, he'd be shunned. Everything from his Berluti shoes to his Armani suits accented by his Salvatore Ferragamo ties were necessities. The uniform of his trade, yet not an allowable tax deduction.

Indeed, he tried, and the IRS was not amused.

Then again, the auditor was a civil servant earning a salary far below his, which certainly didn't garner any sympathy.

While his salary exceeded that of the average schmuck, it still took him a while to accept it for what it was. In reality, he made more than most congressmen, with the exception of the Speaker of the House. But it didn't take a genius to figure out their net worth far exceeded what they could have accumulated based on salary alone.

All of this weighed heavily on his mind as he prepared in the master bedroom of his luxury townhome for that fateful gala. He remembered examining his tuxedoed image in the full-length mirror of his walk-in closet. He turned, checking all views, noticing the seat of his pants was a tad shiny.

Another expense to take care of, before the holiday season and upcoming inauguration balls.

Sheen aside, he looked good. Damn good. He laughed out loud--the glazed fabric did a nice job of showcasing his museum grade ass. His gym membership, along with his personal trainer, made sure he was in top physical shape for someone in his early sixties. His hair was mostly silver, but still covered his pate, which was more than many his age could say.

He allowed just enough beard growth to maintain the current macho look. Dark brown eyes accented by laugh lines were the *coup de grace.*

As expected, all divorcees and widows within a two-decade radius pursued him like she-wolves after the pack's alpha. He smiled as he adjusted his matching tie and cummerbund, reminding himself that paying for an occasional dinner and a few bottles of reserve wine were cheaper than dealing with an escort service.

That fateful night, however, he was flying solo. His intentions would be encumbered by some superficial, drooling female hanging off his arm. Nonetheless, he added a splash of Creed Aventus, after which he was good to go.

He looked fantastic—and ready to kick Uncle Sam in the crotch.

It was April, the height of cherry blossom time, but cool enough after dark that he grabbed his overcoat, then plodded down the stairs and through the kitchen door to his garage, where he climbed into his Ferrari.

The flick of a finger on the garage door opener, then he backed out into the street, powerful engine disturbing the quiet of the exclusive neighborhood. As the overhead door rumbled closed, he put the car in first gear and headed for the Parkway.

He left his car with the valet, pocketed the tag, and strode inside and across the lobby, where he rode the elevator up to the Moretti ballroom. The hum of conversation mingled with the illusive scent of bitters and whiskey greeted him as he rounded the corner.

A wet bar hugged the paneled wall on one side, sheer full-length draperies the other. They spanned the foyer's curved face, tinted pink by the sun descending toward the Potomac from which a panorama of sparkling lights refracted through its fibers like precious stones.

Their silent, hypnotic motion originated from pleasure craft on the river as well as vehicles and lighting on the Francis Scott Key Bridge and GW Parkway on the river's opposite shore. The lazy blinking of portside red lights of an airplane on descent to Reagan Airport slashed a diagonal path above them all, while those of a more static variety radiated below.

Modern day Camelot, to be sure.

His chest expanded with pride to be part of the highest ranks of society, whether he was counterfeit or not. He checked his overcoat, then scoped out the room for familiar faces. Most held positions like himself, though some were independent or employed by other firms. Nonetheless, they were his peers, the ones who would benefit from his intentions.

If there were two things at which he excelled, they were diplomacy and manipulation. He'd been told he could charm the robes off the Statue of Liberty, which was exactly what he intended to do:

Convince the powers-that-be that he and his compadres were essential, a vital link to America's survival.

He got himself a martini, extra dry, then strutted over to a knot of acquaintances, including fellow oil and gas lobbyist, Myron Bentley. The congressman, for whom the fundraising event was being held, was there at center stage, Texas District 25 U.S. Representative, Joseph Pearson.

Since Calvin's proposal involved new spending, the bill to fund it had to originate and be approved in the House before it could go to the Senate.

To use a term popular with his constituents, Pearson's signature look was that of one who'd been "ridden hard and put up wet."

His thinning, dull hair was fashioned in a sketchy comb-over, his medium build failing to fill out his jacket, which hung off his frame as if he were heading to prom in his father's tux. A glassy-eyed appearance finished his persona, one undoubtedly courtesy of an abundance of alcohol.

There was also something creepy about him that made his skin crawl, as was the case with too many members of the D.C. elite.

Calvin stood by politely, listening. The topic was perfect, the synergistic relationship between government and corporations. He worked a lot with Pearson, keeping him informed of the needs of his constituents in the oil and gas industries, which were essential to that state's economic well-being.

The conversation paused, allowing him to officially join in, shaking hands all around, as he favored each group member with one of his multi-million dollar smiles.

"Since we work together so closely, something comes to mind. You folks have some fancy five-star subterranean hotel setup over in Virginia, in case we have some sort of apocalypse," he directed at Pearson, while purposely maintaining a light, thoughtful tone. "What are you going to do without the likes of us if that happens?"

Pearson laughed. "Good question, Nielsen. I really hadn't thought about that. If everything goes teats-up, I don't know why they'd need us, anyway. What good is government without people to govern?"

"True enough. But there's a good chance many would survive and laws would be more important than ever to prevent anarchy. Our government's structure is a well-oiled machine. We scratch your back, you scratch ours, if you'll pardon the cliché."

"If the entire country went into survival mode, rebuilding the economy would be essential," Myron added. "No offense, but you congressmen aren't exactly in a position to reestablish corporate America. That would involve not only restoring the infrastructure, such as the power grid and transportation, but providing jobs for survivors. You wouldn't even know where to start."

"I agree," another portly fellow added. "Corporate executives have the means to build their own survival quarters or buy into one of those fancy underground communities. Meanwhile, we, as your liaisons, are out in the cold."

"Or heat, depending on the scenario," Calvin added, earning a knowing chuckle from the Texans.

"You both make valid points," Pearson admitted. "Important points with regard to our country's preparedness. I'll be sure to bring that up in our next meeting. As you know, I'm on the House Natural Resources Committee and energy production is within our purview. If the response is favorable, I'll get started on some legislation. I see no reason why this doesn't fit under the umbrella of National Security."

They all raised their drinks in a toast. At the sound of the dinner bell, they strolled toward the dining room, Calvin barely able to restrain a victory shout.

His idea took off like a Roman candle on the 4th of July.

Within two weeks, Pearson recruited a co-sponsor and introduced legislation, which went to his committee. Conveniently, besides American energy production, their domain included mineral lands and mining, fisheries and wildlife, public lands, oceans, Native Americans, irrigation, and reclamation.

Many of those areas would be involved or affected. Not only the energy sector, but mine clean-up work, and the availability of a sufficiently sized parcel of public land.

The plan was for a sprawling facility comprising six thousand individual residential units. Colorado easily fit the requirements, its mineral lands and wildlife issues often discussed within that Committee.

The Committee noted that EPA Superfund activity involved with mine cleanup could be incorporated into the project, thus providing part of the needed budget. Furthermore, once the cleanup work was accomplished, the vacant mines could be used as part of the tunneling. It would be easy to dispose of the spoils since they'd contain more than the usual amount of precious metals.

The U.S. Army Corps of Engineers, a.k.a. USACE, was always happy to find work. They'd handle the bulk of heavy construction, including tunnel extensions from existing ones and basic infrastructure.

It had been awhile since they built a major underground facility and were enthusiastic. Being familiar with Top Secret protocol coupled with experience working with EPA Superfund projects comprised a perfect fit.

It needed to be surreptitious, classifying it above Top Secret. This placed it in the Black Projects category and brought in

Homeland Security. Secrecy was not only justified for National Security, but politically as well.

It was a mid-term election year. If the public found out how much was being spent to benefit non-government officials, much less corporations, it could have a very negative effect. It already promised to be a close election with potential to upset the current Congressional ruling party.

A few bumps slowed it down in the Appropriations Committee. The estimated cost was close to six billion dollars. However, since the project spanned several agencies, the cost was covered, given cuts in other areas.

Unfortunately, they included a few sacred cows: Social Security and Medicare (hopefully Baby Boomers would start to die off as fast as younger ones joined the rolls); Healthcare (Medicaid and CHIP reductions, plus FDA approvals would take even longer); Veterans Affairs (who bought in when convinced the project offered job potential for returning vets); Aid to Families with Dependent Children, Food stamp (SNAP) programs, and other areas that Congress considered "entitlement fluff."

The EPA had to shift funds from other projects, but cutbacks had been the norm the past several years anyway, the agency accustomed to shrinking.

To reduce the impact, the facility would be built in stages so funding could be spread over three or more years, delaying its completion, but assuring passage.

The bipartisan bill soared through the House, then went to the Senate. It passed there as well, with the addition of a few amendments that provided opportunities for contractor participation. These included the oil and gas industry as well as general construction.

They weren't quite earmarks, since they'd been outlawed in 2011, but as a Top Secret project, Requests for Proposals, called RFPs, would be limited to those with a current security clearance or the ability to obtain one.

The Conference Committee developed a version acceptable to both the House and Senate, after which the bill was sent to the president for signature.

POTUS was beyond proud of what lawmakers had accomplished. Knowing the importance of industry in keeping American strong, legislation that would further assure recovery in the event of an apocalypse was well-received. He signed it with a flourish within the ten-day limit and Calvin's dream became law.

With Calvin's and Myron Bentley's help, Pearson examined the list of those from the oil and gas industry who'd worked classified projects, combined with the unspoken caveat of generous campaign contributors.

Lone Star Operations, one with which Myron had ties, was at the top of the list. Myron's executive assistant, Ingrid Thorsen, had a son-in-law who ran a private security operation out of Albuquerque. The Colorado senator found a generous contributor well-suited for the project management and interior finish work contract, Elite Management Partners Incorporated, in which his wife was a major stockholder.

It had been quite a journey.

Calvin grinned as he came back to the present. All thanks to him. It was about time he and all his cronies got what they deserved. Phase one was nearly complete, or would be by the time the open house took place in October.

However, one potentially problematic detail still roiled in his gut. Phase one only constituted space for one third of the originally planned six thousand residents. It was not only troublesome, but suspicious that his name was not among the residents chosen for that first section.

Oversight? Or sinister message?

Upon questioning it, he was assured the next two phases would be more luxurious and worth the wait.

Hopefully, no catastrophes, either courtesy of Mother Nature or Congressional funding, would occur before PURF was complete.

8. WAKE-UP CALLS

ELITE MANAGEMENT PARTNERS INC. (EMPI)
Denver, Colorado
August 12, Sunday
3:43 p.m. MDT

Jason LaGrange scowled. As suspected, Sara Reynolds was alive, but far from well. No surprise she was staying at her father's place if she went home to die. If that were the case, all he'd have to do was wait, then provide a copy of the death certificate.

However, there was no record they'd contacted any hospice providers. Were they handling the situation themselves? Her mother died in a debilitated condition, so the situation was familiar, if not comfortable. There was no evidence they were religious nuts, but there was no telling what went on without indoor surveillance.

BKSS records indicated cameras and microphones had been installed, but there were no apparent feeds. Either they were stand alone units with SD cards that needed to be retrieved, her former FBI father found them, or that bunch of slackers never placed them as reported.

He suspected the last, knowing Keller's group of clowns.

Security footage from the hospital showed her leaving in a wheelchair, which was normal. When she was in one again when they arrived at the private terminal of the Boulder airport, he still didn't suspect its unspoken commentary.

Even when he sent a drone over the property and saw her sitting in one outside, the implications failed to register.

Meanwhile, he hid a doorbell camera beneath the shutter of a street-facing window that alerted him to any activity. When her Indian friend showed up with some older native guy, the truth became evident.

Whether or not she was dying was unknown, but a fly-by with a drone during their visit established she was definitely paralyzed.

Which worked both ways.

Neutralizing an incapacitated target was a cinch. Access was the issue. For days she hadn't left the house. Her step-mother came and went regularly, "daddy" on no discernible schedule. Apparently, he frequently worked from home, a potential complication.

All that aside, once he knew if she had a schedule and favorite spot for sunning herself, he'd find a location for a clear shot, the rest like shooting fish in a barrel.

He pulled up Google maps and examined the Montgomery's upper middleclass neighborhood. Homes were mostly two stories surrounded by generous yards, up to a half-acre or more. They lived on a corner with one neighbor on the west and two within range to the rear. A second story window from either would work, provided no trees were in the way.

Getting inside wasn't a problem, depending on when the residents were home. Collateral damage wasn't a big deal, but the cleaner the job the better.

Something Eddie Johannsen never figured out.

He locked up his office, got in his car, and drove up to Boulder to check things out. He smirked at the *Neighborhood Watch* sign. Adjacent streets were deserted.

He avoided the front of their house, concentrating on those within a one block radius. After memorizing the layout, he parked across the street from the house behind them. *For Sale* glared from a sign next-door.

Perfect.

An interested buyer as opposed to a hit man scoping out his quarry.

A obese woman, probably in her fifties, waddled out of the house directly behind the target's. She paused momentarily, staring.

He chuckled.

Neighborhood Watch in action.

He lowered his window and displayed his most charismatic smile.

"Good afternoon, ma'am. Do you know what they're asking for the house next-door?"

"I'm not sure," she replied, biting her lower lip. "I think around $750,000. They might have dropped it. They moved out a month or two ago and are probably getting anxious. The realtor's number is on the sign."

"Thanks. I'll give them a call."

The woman proceeded to check her mailbox while he noted the number on the sign, then drove away grinning.

Now all he needed to determine was whether the infamous Mrs. Reynolds pursued afternoon sun fests on a schedule.

MONTGOMERY RESIDENCE
BOULDER
August 13, Monday
7:45 a.m.

THE PAST SEVERAL days had been a world of soft, grey flannel: cozy, warm, and timeless. Sara vaguely remembered a multitude of gentle nudges from Connie, beckoning her to drink either spring water or some strange tasting tea—not unpleasant, just unfamiliar.

A persistent herbal scent reminiscent of wildflowers and herbs engulfed her from the medicine bag around her neck. Her only excursions from bed, assisted by Connie, had been to the bathroom, feeling like a toddler in the midst of potty training.

This morning, however, her eyes opened to alertness lacking since waking up in the hospital. Sunlight streamed through the blinds, a gentle but persistent wake-up call. She lay there a moment, mind a muddle of obscured memories, strange, abstract dreams, and a few visitations from Bryan.

Gradually, the past few weeks focused, leading her back to the present. An assessment revealed no pain. Not even the usual aches and pains that lingered since the accident in April. Her mind was alert. Yet, though painless, her body still felt tired. Not achy; more like she'd simply overdone it the day before.

She used her elbows to push herself up to a sitting position, expecting dizziness. None came. Instead, her heart warmed with gratitude at the beautiful array of colors greeting her from the star quilt.

Next, the aroma of toast and bacon caught her senses and she realized she was hungry. *Very* hungry. Soft footsteps approached her door.

It opened slowly.

"Good morning, Connie. What's for breakfast?"

The woman stood there several seconds, holding Sara's morning dose of tea. She set the tea on the nightstand, then gathered Sara into a hug.

"Oh, Sara. I'm so relieved." She sniffled, dabbing her eyes. "You need to text Charlie." She handed her the phone from beside the bed. "He wanted to know as soon as you woke up."

"Okay."

Good morning. I'm awake and hungry. Thank you for helping me. I feel pretty good.

She hit *Send*. "There. Done."

"So how do you feel?" Connie's green eyes remained wide.

"I don't hurt anymore, which is great. That heavy, dark depression is gone. I feel alert, but my body feels tired. I'm hungry, so after having something to eat I think I'll take a nap."

"That's exactly what Charlie said would happen. The worst is over, but your body needs to finish rejuvenating. Now that you're able to eat, it will go faster. But he emphasized no junk food, only organic, for now mostly fruits and veggies. You still have a lot of toxins to get rid of."

"I could really go for some waffles, though. Are they on the no-no list?"

"I'm afraid so, honey. No white flour or sugar."

"Toast?"

"Yes, I have organic gluten-free bread. And organic coffee. Plus all sorts of fruits and berries from the farmer's market. Tomorrow, if your stomach is still settled, you can have eggs."

"Okay. Let's go. I'm starving."

"I can bring it up to you," Connie offered.

"No. I've been here long enough. Help me into my wheelchair. I'd really like to get out of this room. Now that my brain is back, I need to return to the real world, whether or not my legs cooperate."

Connie supported her under the arms and rotated her to the seat. "Do you have any feeling in your legs?"

Efforts to wiggle her toes failed. Running her hands over her thighs, however, delivered a tingling sensation. Her lips crept into a smile. "The skin woke up, but the muscles are still asleep."

"That's wonderful! At least it's some improvement."

"Yes! Very encouraging."

Connie pushed her across the hall to the elevator, then exited through the laundry room into the kitchen. The coffee smelled heavenly.

Connie dropped two slices of bread in the toaster and set a bowl of strawberries before her. "I need to text your dad. And Patrice. This will make their day."

Sara laughed. "Yes. Mine as well. But tell you what." She paused to plop a strawberry in her mouth. "Don't text. Let me call."

Connie handed over her phone.

Her father reacted as expected, his cough a vain attempt to disguise being choked up. Patrice was less surprised, but tied up with a client so their conversation was cut short. As she ended the call, she heard her own cell going off in her bedroom. She cast Connie a pleading look, convincing her to retrieve it.

As expected it was Charlie. She put the call on speaker.

"Welcome back, Sara. How are you feeling?"

Her smiled stretched. It was so good to hear his voice. "Great. No pain, just tired."

"After what you've been through, being tired is to be expected. It will take awhile. You are still mending."

"I'm doing pretty well." She laughed. "I was starving when I woke up."

"Are you still drinking the tea, at least six times a day?"

"Yes."

"And lots of spring water?"

"Yes. Connie said we ran out of what you brought, but water, yes. The reverse osmosis filter takes everything out. We use a TDS meter to make sure. And I'm trying to eat right. But I have to admit, I'm dying for a doughnut. And some ice cream."

"I'm glad you want to eat. That's good. But please, no sugar. If you must have something sweet use organic honey or agave. What about your legs? Any change?"

She wrinkled her nose, wishing she could give him better news. "Well, they're not numb to the touch anymore. But I still can't move them or wiggle my toes, though."

"It takes longer for muscles to recover, but that's a good sign. There's more we can do to get all the toxins out. If you don't feel up to coming to Montana, there's a sweat lodge at my cabin, so we can do it there. Has anyone bothered you since you got back?"

"I don't think so, but I was asleep most the time." She looked at Connie, who shook her head.

"No. Everything's been quiet. Apparently it was all that guy, Johannsen. With him dead, looks like it's over."

"He's dead? The guy in the black truck?"

"Yes. The same guy who was at the cabin for that raid."

"Dead? How? When?"

"It was while I was in the hospital, about a week after we took you back to Montana." She explained how he was going too fast, came around the same bend where hers and Bryan's wreck occurred, and collided with a jack-knifed eighteen-wheeler, then flew over the edge into Dead Horse Canyon. "Talk about poetic justice. Quite a coincidence, right?"

He scoffed.

"I doubt it. No such thing in my world. Keep eating right, drink your tea, and text me when you make it through the day without a nap. Then we'll figure out where and when to do the sweat. Meanwhile, now that you're up, be sure to get plenty of fresh air. Sit out in the Sun as much as you can. It will speed the healing process."

"Okay. I'll get out there this afternoon for sure."

NEW LSO WORK SITE
COLORADO
August 13, Monday
8:30 a.m.

TREY HUNG UP with a grunt. His mouth turned down at the corners in line with his white mustache. It wasn't easy to admit Littlewolf wasn't coming back. He liked that Indian guy and certainly admired his ability to sniff out what lurked below.

However, his calls kept going to voice mail and it was time to take the hint. Either he was out of the area or blocking the calls. Whatever the reason, he could only conclude lack of interest.

After what he'd been through, he couldn't blame him.

He leaned back in his chair and relit the cigar reposing in the ashtray on his desk. It was time to admit defeat and ask Gerald to send up a new petro-geologist and lab tech along with the mud logger to replace Ben, who quit following the accident.

All he could do was cross his fingers that Charlie's replacement wouldn't be as useless as teats on a boar hog, like his predecessor, Dr. Phil.

It wasn't easy to build a good team. Like it was with Littlewolf, Big Dick, and Ben. Once they got rid of Dr. Phil, they were unstoppable.

Practically legendary.

Oil patch superheroes.

At least until that blowout damn near killed their star player.

He slammed the desk with his fist. It sucked, but that's the way it was. No more lying awake at night like a tree full of owls.

The exploration rig would be good to go within a few days and fully equipped to deal with any further blowout conditions. So far, the previous strike had vented enough to reduce the hazard, but there were no guarantees.

Hopefully, that explosive fart the month before, which had taken over a week to burn off, was the extent of the hydrogen sulfide gas with a nice oil reserve waiting below.

The trailer rocked ever so slightly beneath his feet.

He scowled.

There'd been more tremors lately, however. To be expected during a fracking job, but so far all the remaining crew was doing was refitting the old bore hole with new casing.

That fault where the seep surfaced was apparently active.

Not good.

If it shifted enough to block the main reservoir they were screwed.

9. LIBERATION

MONTGOMERY RESIDENCE
BOULDER
August 17, Friday
2:11 p.m.

Sara knew she was definitely on the mend when she was no longer satisfied to relax at her childhood home. Her melancholy playlist that comprised a loop of *Wrecked*, *Angel*, and a few other grief-saturated tear-jerkers had even been replaced with more upbeat music.

The raw grief of losing Bryan was fading with the lyrics of *Wrecked*, even though she still missed him horribly. Her thoughts drifted to Charlie, noting how her feelings for him had not only grown, but shifted.

Were they only together because of their connection with Bryan? Or something more?

She sat in the backyard at her usual time as promised, fingers tapping the wheelchair's arm in time to the Jonas Brothers' latest streaming through her headphones. A stemmed glass of organic Zinfandel that Connie found in Whole Foods sat on the patio table beside her. Charlie probably wouldn't approve, but at least it was organic.

It was nice to be waited on, but too comfortable back in the Boulder Bubble where she grew up. That said, it was time to go home.

Which wasn't simple. Doing so would require a variety of modifications to her two-story townhome. Such was the domain

94

of occupational therapists, with whom she'd worked enough to know exactly what could be done to live a relatively normal life.

Fortunately, affording it wasn't a problem.

Her throat ached at Bryan's foresight that made it possible. As Patrice pointed out, Virgos were beyond a doubt detail oriented. Sometimes to a fault.

Which brought her to his final request.

Considering all that happened, should she drop the corruption issue and resume normal life?

Anger fired her veins.

What was she thinking? They murdered the love of her life and tried to kill her, too.

Three times!

The fact she was even alive was nothing short of a miracle. She shivered at how close she'd come to dying more than once for this cause.

Yet, here she was.

Surely, the message was this was something she was supposed to pursue. Without her taking action, "they" would continue to get away with it.

On the other hand, was it nothing more than an exercise in futility? The proverbial losing battle fighting city hall, or in this case, Capitol Hill? An even bigger obstacle.

Her television appearances stirred things up, but only for a day or so. After that, it dissolved within the simmering cauldron of yesterday's news. If she were going to accomplish anything, it needed to last longer than that.

People needed to be spurred to action. Before her disastrous *Today Show* appearance her GoFundMe account was over $48,000. The biggest donation was only $100, showing there were thousands of people behind her. People didn't donate their hard-earned money to something they didn't believe in.

She laughed—obviously no corporate donors.

Any residual doubts regarding the pursuit of Bryan's request evaporated.

She owed them as well.

Her mind wandered back to when she was on the *Today Show* where Davis Jenkins claimed Bryan's *research*, a.k.a. hacking, was illegal.

That was a valid point, one she'd have to address and refute. It really came down to what other hackers, like Snowden, and those who disseminated the data, such as Assange at WikiLeaks, had done and its legality, if any.

In some cases, leaked information, such as revealing an individual's cover, resulted in their death. That was clearly wrong.

But what about when it was something the public had a right to know? Then what? Corruption, money laundering, crooked elections, and things like that.

There was a fine line between situations that truly related to national security versus covert, questionable activities conducted at taxpayer expense.

From what she understood, she was protected by the First Amendment. Bryan was guilty, but once the documents were released, everyone who disseminated the data was in the clear.

Those involved with PURF deserved to be exposed. Every single elected official. Their constituents deserved to know how their supposed "representatives" were spending their tax dollars.

Something else tickled her mind that Jenkins said. Not on the show, but after.

No, it couldn't be. She'd passed out during the interview.

Was it before?

No.

After.

Mike, her bodyguard, told her father that Jenkins came to visit her in the hospital. And apologized! Admitted to being the devil's advocate. He offered to edit her disastrous appearance and post it to their website with an addendum.

Curious whether he may have done so, she removed her laptop from the wheelchair's storage pocket and turned it on. Once it booted up, she moused to their website to check. She grinned with satisfaction that it was there, pleased with what a nice job they'd done. They'd cleaned it up beautifully, giving it the feel of a blockbuster trailer, a promise of more to come.

She shuddered to think if they hadn't, instead showing her barf all over Jenkins, then pass out on the sound stage floor. She giggled in spite of herself.

That would have gone viral for sure.

A link to her GoFundMe account was there as well. She hadn't checked it since before the show.

She gasped. Over $147,000!

Holy crap on a cracker!

She needed to set up a nonprofit. Will gave her the name of an attorney who would do so, but Friday afternoon was not the time to call. She put a note in her calendar to do so Monday, first thing.

Her understanding was that donations were considered gifts and not taxable up to a certain amount. But what was interesting was that for figures that exceeded that, which varied year to year, the tax liability fell to the donor. That seemed pretty weird, but so was the tax code.

If the money was used to start a business, then it was taxable. But not for personal use.

Or so it appeared.

Having a lawyer or accountant figure it out was definitely called for. The last thing she needed was trouble with the IRS.

One thing for sure, amassing six figure's worth of donations constituted public support. Now that she was confined to a wheelchair, they might be even more sympathetic.

Not that she wanted to exploit her condition. She still couldn't accept she'd be like this the rest of her life.

On a whim, she googled PURF to see what was out there. Several articles showed up, but not as many as expected. They stressed its legality, echoing the president's words when he responded to the initial release.

A Bloomberg article mentioned it wasn't fully funded, but would be included in the proposed budget each year until complete.

Reignited outrage fired through her.

Ya think? Ha! Not if I can help it!

Preventing its completion would be a major coup.

Raison d'être restored, she opened the file with Bryan's research. It was organized, as he always was, but at a very high level. A book or series of podcasts would need to be presented in logical order, each factoid building on the previous one.

The best part was podcasts and blogs could be done from home. It didn't matter if she was confined to a wheelchair.

The email list from her GoFundMe account would get her started with people who were already on her side. More than likely they would share anything she posted.

Which was how things went viral.

Imbued with new enthusiasm, she sorted through a few documents, organized their contents, and jotted down some potential blog and podcast topics.

Satisfied with her renewed commitment and progress, she closed her eyes, yielding to the music and sun caressing her face.

She'd been on this journey for four months, to the day. How life had changed, far beyond anything she ever could have imagined.

MOUNTAIN VIEW DRIVE
BOULDER
August 17, Friday
2:38 p.m.

IT TOOK NO MORE than a phone call spoofing Keller Williams' number in Denver for Jason to snag the lockbox code to the vacant house.

He stepped through the door.

Secured it behind him. As expected, the living room was devoid of furniture.

"Hello?"

An empty-house echo was the only response.

First, a quick walk-through to scope the place out. Pure habit, just in case. Nice house in an upscale neighborhood, but badly in need of improvements. Especially the kitchen, much less the bathrooms.

No wonder it hadn't sold.

Lucky for him, whatever the reason.

He flew up the stairs, two at a time, briefcase in hand. With luck, within a few days that million-dollar-payment would be his.

Two bedrooms faced the Montgomery's backyard. The target in her wheelchair was visible from both, but the angle was better from the master.

He opened the window, wincing when it squeaked. No response from the target, who was wearing headphones.

Another lucky break.

He removed the screen and leaned it against the wall, a slight breeze wafting inside, but not enough to compensate for.

He stared at her a moment, wondering. After all she'd been through, how could her situational awareness be so lax? This was so easy it insulted his skill level.

Easiest million bucks ever.

He set his briefcase on the carpeted floor. Took his phone out of his jacket's inside pocket to snap a quick photo of the target to include with the death certificate. Before and after pictures for wet jobs validated the job's completion as well as who pulled the trigger.

He put the phone back in his pocket and hunkered down to open the briefcase.

Removed his .308.

Attached the barrel to the stock.

Mounted the Vortex scope.

Stood-up, positioned himself at the open window, and lined up the crosshairs for a perfect head shot.

The target lifted a glass of wine to her lips.

He chuckled.

"Here's a buzz for you, honey."

The buffalo was the foundation of their economy and the centerpiece of their cosmology,
and the wholesale slaughter shook their existence at its core.
—Pekka Hämäläinen

10. REVELATIONS

NORTHERN CHEYENNE RESERVATION
MONTANA
August 18, Saturday
9:03 a.m.

It was Charlie's first time performing a healing without White Wolf. It wasn't a difficult one—food poisoning involving a ten-year-old boy.

While his mother was helping a friend with a new baby, he ate some chicken that his sister hadn't cooked well enough. He consumed the leg and thigh, which had still been quite bloody. His sister warned him not to, but he insisted warriors ate raw meat and he would soon be a man.

Nothing that required any special skills to discern.

After explaining there were some things that needed to be cooked thoroughly, something Sweet Medicine taught them, Charlie prepared the room by burning sweetgrass, sang the appropriate songs, then cleared the child's energy. Next, he provided him with a medicine bag, and instructed his mother how to fix some herbal remedies to settle his stomach.

It was at that point intuition kicked in, jolting through him like an electrical shock that raised the hair on the back of his neck.

That was but a part of why he was there.

The boy's sister was jealous of her little brother. Their father made his disappointment clear that she was a girl from her infancy. When her brother was born, she felt even less important.

His eyes met hers, their depths immersed in profound sadness. Her youthful appearance dissolved to the image of a beautiful woman, one who had specific work to do for the Cheyenne people. Gooseflesh spread to his arms as the vision evaporated, leaving prophetic tracks behind.

He reached out and took her hands in his own. "*Maheo* loves you very much," he told her. "You are here for a very important purpose. Someday you will do a great service for your people. Do not ever forget that."

The girl's eyes misted, followed by a smile that transformed her entire being. Her mother wrapped both arms around her daughter and pulled her close.

"*Néá'eše,* brother," the woman said, stroking her daughter's hair. "*Néá'eše.*"

Charlie blinked hard. Delivering that message to one of *Maheo's* chosen daughters was the true reason for his visit. The boy's foolish actions simply got him there.

He accepted the tobacco offering graciously, and walked to his truck, thanking *Maheo* for the sacred opportunity to touch a life.

The key turned in the ignition and his old pickup rumbled to life. He'd taken it instead of *Tah-Hó'nehe,* not wanting to appear arrogant before this particular family, who lived in very humble circumstances. Indeed, he wondered if their ramshackle house would make it through another harsh Montana winter.

Was that why White Wolf resisted the SUV from the start? Would the appearance of wealth have a detrimental effect on his standing with those living in poverty? As a tribal family, the usual reaction was to rejoice in other's successes.

But was their luxurious vehicle too much? Should they have used the money to help their brothers and sisters in favor of a less showy means of transportation? White Wolf continually emphasized setting a good example.

He hung his head, throat tightening. They could build two or three houses, maybe even a new community center for what it cost.

Maybe they should sell it and do just that.

As he drove home his thoughts rambled, gravitating to how much he enjoyed working with children. They were so sweet and full of wonder, and looked at him with such awe. No telling what *Maheo* had in store for them.

It had been over two years since he'd seen his daughters. What did their futures hold? Time passed so quickly, he'd lost track. He made up his mind to visit them, before the year was out. He grunted at the downside. Seeing his ex-wife and her new husband was a far less pleasant prospect, but unavoidable.

Prairie grass was dry this time of year, scrubby vegetation already starting to don its fall wardrobe of yellows and browns with a dash of orange. He sensed his time staying with White Wolf's family was drawing to a close. Where he would go from there, he didn't know. While he felt he belonged on the rez, so far he hadn't given much thought to finding his own place.

Maybe it was time.

Bryan deeded his cabin over to him years before. He could sell it, use the money to get settled on the rez.

The thought impaled his chest as a cold blade in a butcher's hand.

Absolutely not.

There was no way he could do that.

Too many memories.

Good ones.

Furthermore, that entire area was sacred ground.

Selling it would be a betrayal, not only to Bryan, but indirectly to Sara. Maybe he could manage to get a place anyway. If they sold *Tah-Hó'nehe*, part of that could go toward that. Plus he still had about half of his LSO bonus in the bank.

He hadn't had a chance to ponder what he'd seen during the last sweat. He didn't mention it to White Wolf, knowing he'd tell him in due time. For now, it didn't matter.

Meanwhile, he'd been absorbing what it meant to be a healer. The concept was slowly trickling into his conscious mind like a spring feeds a small stream, then a mighty river.

He was surprised how much he remembered from Eaglefeathers. His intuition was sharper than ever, confidence with his new direction growing.

When he saw the sick boy, he immediately sensed what was wrong and what he needed to do, on both the physical and spiritual planes. As if *Maheo* whispered in his ear.

Whether it would always be that easy, he could only hope. Perhaps learning to set aside his will and opinions so he could listen with an open mind was all that was required.

When he and White Wolf healed Sara, at least partially, it had been far more intense. The transfer of energy necessary drained them both, yet was inadequate. Something important was missing, but what?

Could they do more so she'd fully recover?

His heart ached as he thought about her. He missed her. Before the week was out, she'd be ready for a sweat. The thought of seeing her again stirred something he hadn't felt in a long time.

He parked in his usual place beneath the oak in front of the house. Inside, he was greeted by a mouth-watering aroma.

White Wolf was browning venison on the wood stove while Star chopped onions and peppers, beans simmering in a cast iron pot. He greeted him with a nod.

"How's the boy?"

"He'll be fine. Ate some undercooked chicken. I don't think he will again."

"Good." White Wolf returned to his task.

"We should do something to help the family. *Maheo* has a special plan for the boy's sister."

White Wolf turned toward him once more. He smiled.

"Yes. I know."

THAT NIGHT, CONTENT from a satisfying day and shortly after he fell asleep, Charlie found himself in a vivid dream. Of an event from the recent past, something of which he sensed he needed to be aware. The location was an elegant private dining room, filled with some forty men in expensive suits.

The man at the head of the table looked well into his seventies, but nonetheless of powerful stature and good health. His eyes were cold, countenance that of someone who refused to take "No" for an answer. His aura was dark, evil. Beyond greed.

Something about him was familiar, including his deep, resonate voice. Had they met in person?

His mind rumbled—*Where had he seen him before?*

While the gathering appeared to be a celebration, its purpose soon became clear. A group of Washington D.C.'s elite influencers, the ones for whom PURF had been built. Their collective concern the facility might not be completed as initially planned, due to federal budget cuts, which could be influenced by public opinion of their taxpayer funded boondoggle.

To assure they got what they'd been granted, they spawned a ruthless plan to protect their interests by whatever means necessary.

Charlie's view shifted to the room's chandelier.

Why was he seeing this?

Its sparkling orbs morphed into the vision he'd seen a month earlier—Sara's toilet, writhing with red-eyed serpents.

Were these the people who placed a price-tag on her life when her actions threatened their dubious perk? Johannsen but a pawn, their hired gun?

If so, these men did not achieve what they had by quitting. Without a doubt, Johannsen would be replaced.

White Wolf promised that, little by little, he'd understand the truth, followed by what needed to be done and why. As always, the elder was correct. The pieces tumbled into place, infusing his entire being with sure knowledge of a complex mix of fate and fortune entangled in the web of space and time.

One thing was certain: Bryan's last request to Sara and indirectly to him was clearer than ever. Nonetheless, it was far from simple. Corruption so deeply ingrained was beyond the ability of any one person to eliminate. Something of that magnitude would require *Maheo* and the Earth Mother herself.

The vision returned to the elegant room where men dined on gourmet meals replete with imported wine and *hors d'oeuvres.* He peered more closely at the man at the head of the table.

Where had he seen him before?

His identity felt important. He willed the man's age to roll back in time. His white hair darkened, his weathered look reversed by some twenty years.

The vision zoomed in closer. His blood ran cold.

The man's eyes were red.

Charlie bolted awake. The man was Bob Bentley's father.

LA GRANGE'S PENTHOUSE
DENVER
August 18, Saturday
10:03 a.m.

EXECUTING CORRUPT DICTATORS, crooked politicians, or mafia bosses was one thing.

But a woman in a wheelchair?

What had he become?

Jason sat in his favorite chair, pondering his failure the day before.

The scowl hadn't left his face since puking in the toilet of that empty house, breaking down his rifle, then racing home, aghast at what he'd nearly done.

He lifted the steaming mug of Irish coffee to his lips, relieved that at least no one need ever know. His plan to provide evidence of her death to the people who'd contracted Keller was unknown.

Diverse thoughts collided, piling on top of one another like a rear-ender on the interstate.

Now what?

He needed that money.

Blackmail the Lobbyist Opportunity League? He had recordings of their conversation with Keller and traced the burner phone back to Bentley. It would serve those greedy bastards right.

With Johannsen dead no one could identify him as the one who provided the poison that put Sara Reynolds in a wheelchair.

Not that he could have anyway, given the steely-eyed old man with a limp at Lakewood's Centennial Airport didn't exist, like Jason's other personas.

He chuckled, mind drifting back to when he failed to get the lead role in *Hamlet* back in college. He swore he'd prove his acting ability, one way or another. While actors performed on a set, he did so in the world at large.

Where consequences for a poor performance earned a bullet, not a bad review.

High resolution audio surveillance he installed outside their kitchen window revealed the target planned to move out. Her over-protective father was trying to convince her to hire a live-in housekeeper.

He chuckled. Was a Mrs. Doubtfire role in his future?

That would necessitate expanding his props and wardrobe extensively. Furthermore, if anyone were to see his closet, his reputation would definitely be in question. Playing such a role, much less identifying as a woman, was never on his bucket list.

No, the duties that job would entail weren't worth it. Except, perhaps, helping her bathe. He laughed some more, adding another splash of whisky to his cup.

Why would a paraplegic woman who knew her life was probably still in danger sit out in the open like that? Death wish, perhaps? Too cowardly to commit suicide, but not caring whether she lived or died?

She wasn't stupid. Far from it. Naïve, perhaps? With Johannsen dead, did she think she was safe? What was she thinking? Brain damage, perhaps, from the poison?

Was her sense of social justice on par with a vigilante? Was it about government corruption? Or revenge for killing her husband?

All this whistleblower crap couldn't be about the money. Not with that seven-figure life insurance payout she got.

The solution to his own dilemma was such a head-slapper he nearly choked on his last swallow of booze-laced joe.

Such a performance was right up his alley.

All animals except man know that the principle business of life is to enjoy it.
--Pete Risingsun

11. HOMECOMING

SARA'S CONDO
DENVER
August 22, Wednesday
2:04 p.m.

Sara surveyed her condo's new look from her upgraded wheelchair, her mother's abandoned for a new electric model. It was more compact, controlled with a joystick, and had a variety of storage options, including a tray for her laptop. Getting around quicker with less effort further lifted her spirits and spurred her move toward independence.

For the moment all was quiet. She was alone with her thoughts while Will and Connie picked up another bed, kibble, water bowl, and food dish for the condo.

She reached over and scratched the roan pit bull's head, the service dog acquired the previous Saturday as a result of Will's latest full-blown paternal fit. Anticipating resistance like she displayed to hiring a live-in housekeeper, his jaw dropped when she was elated.

"That's a terrific idea, Dad! I can't believe I didn't think of that!"

Little did he realize she always wanted a dog. Clean-freak Bryan forbade it, not only because of the assumed mess and required training, but claiming it would tie them down.

Haha, Bryan. I'll train her to run the Roomba, just for you.
Train, indeed.

The dog was not the one who required instruction. Already she had pages of notes on how to utilize her companion's many talents. She could even answer her phone! She had several more classes to attend over the next week, practice daily, plus take her to the groomer the breeder recommended.

She looked down at the canine, smiling as she remembered finding her. The trainer had a half-dozen candidates that completed basic training. A couple German shepherds, a collie, two Rottweilers, and a pit bull.

It was like meeting her canine soulmate. Their eyes met and it was as if there were a touch of fate involved, because she knew instantly as did Blossom that they belonged together.

Had it been a few years earlier when pit bull terriers were banned in Denver, she wouldn't have been an option. She reached over and scratched her behind the ears, grateful the ruling was no longer in effect.

"We both knew as soon as we met, didn't we, girl?"

The pitty gave her a smile and licked her hand. Yes, they were definitely besties from day one.

After the brief interlude, she returned to her emotional dichotomy. Being back in her condo felt wonderful on one hand, intimidating on the other.

She straightened, curious. That was a new couch. What happened to the old one? The one she and Bryan bought at IKEA. Not that she'd be sitting on it, anyway.

Connie and Will helped rearrange the cabinets so everything would be reachable to her and the dog. A new refrigerator with a bottom freezer was there as well. That part, at least, was settled.

She scowled at the closet disguising the doorway built so her bodyguard had quick access from the adjoining unit. The opening had since been sealed, its storage potential ready at her earliest convenience. It would definitely come in handy to avoid trips upstairs.

Nonetheless, the irony it was used to her detriment turned her stomach. Would Blossom have detected such an intrusion, warning her about the poison deposited on her toilet seat?

Most likely, bolstering her confidence in returning with her new best friend.

As further assurance precluding the closet's previous use, a vertical lift was installed against the back wall that brought her up to her walk-in closet. If she regained use of her legs and didn't need it anymore, or decided to move, it could be easily removed without leaving scars in any actual rooms. A similar one would be installed at the cabin, though first ramps were needed outside along with a paved parking area.

No telling when that would happen. Finding skilled, reliable contractors in rural Falcon Ridge was a major challenge. Bryan did all the work himself, so the need hadn't manifested. Charlie could have done it, but living in Montana nixed that.

The cabin was where she really wanted to be, but no telling how long she'd have to wait. She could just imagine Will's reaction to *that*, dog or otherwise.

At least she wouldn't have to drive around in some ugly van. Friday she'd pick up her new Buick Enclave Avenir with an automatic ramp and rear entry, which facilitated parking anywhere, rather than demanding a handicapped space.

That, too, brought a rush of freedom-fueled ecstasy coupled with caution. Most of her usual errands could be resolved via home delivery services, though being home all the time wasn't the point.

Getting out was essential to resume normal life.

She eyed the lift again, envisioning one to take her to the loft of the A-frame, a good twelve feet from the ground. Placing it next to the stairs on the main floor, then arriving on the landing outside the bedroom door was probably the best place. Nine feet in the condo was bad enough. Her fear of heights kicked in for every descent, even though it was entirely enclosed.

One thing that amazed her the most about the dog was that she had a special bark her phone was set up to recognize as a voice command to call 911. It was nothing short of incredible what her canine companion was trained to do.

Behind her outward acceptance, hope remained that she would eventually walk again. She needed to be more diligent about detoxing. Charlie would have a fit if he knew she indulged in an occasional glass of wine, even though she made sure it was made from organic grapes.

She inhaled deeply, proud of all they'd accomplished, crossing her fingers her condition would be temporary.

Meanwhile, for now she was all set.

No time like the present to get back to work.

She checked her To-Do list, wondering how the accountant she called earlier that week was coming along with how to handle setting up a nonprofit.

She made another note to follow up, then checked the laptop's charge. Strong enough to last several hours, she directed the wheelchair for the patio door, Blossom leading the way.

NORTHERN CHEYENNE RESERVATION
MONTANA
August 22, Wednesday
3:11 p.m.

"IT HAS BEEN TWO weeks since I promised *Maheo* I'd complete my fast at the Sacred Mountain," Charlie said, leaning against the fence post they'd just replaced toward the ranch's south side, in view of Eaglefeathers Butte. "What must I do to prepare?"

White Wolf's dark eyes were unreadable beneath a red bandana sweatband, trademark of his rancher persona as opposed to the black silk version he wore during sacred ceremonies. "Yes. It is growing late in the season. It is already much cooler at night. Frost could come at any time. However, you have a year to fulfill a pledge. This is not the usual time to go to *Novavose*."

Charlie stood firm. "Yes, but I do not want to wait. How soon can we leave?"

His uncle's eyes narrowed. "Are you sure you are ready, Littlewolf? There is much to prepare for your fast. Besides, there is much work ahead for the *Peace Gathering of Indigenous Leaders* in October. It will be here before we know it."

"Of course I will do everything I can to help. And yes, I am ready. It is time. I completed a four day fast alone in Colorado. I know what to expect."

White Wolf grunted, squinting against the sun. "You know what it's like to go without food and water for four days. Do you understand what fasting on *Novavose* tells *Maheo*?"

The import of the simple question hit hard. It seemed simple. But was it?

"It shows I am ready to listen to him," he answered, moving along the fence line to the next post. "Do what he wants, whether or not it's what I want."

"Yes, that is part of it." White Wolf stopped, looking him square in the eye. "It shows you submit your will to the spiritual powers of the universe. But it goes deeper. You show that you accept life as it is and the truth of living and dying. You open yourself to *exhastoz*, cosmic powers, and invite out-of-body spirit selves, the *hematasoomao,* to direct you."

"Like the *maiyun*?"

"Yes. Did you realize when the spirit selves of plants, animals, rocks, or other *maiyun* connect with you it is because they chose you?"

Charlie pondered that a moment before replying. "I hadn't thought about it, but that makes sense," he said. "When I was seeking to know who killed my white brother, an aspen tree who witnessed it told me I should check his wrecked truck for answers."

"And you did?" His uncle's surprised look was almost insulting.

"Yes. And found exactly what we were looking for," he answered, scowling back. "I've had many experiences that I didn't understand at the time. Messages that I recognized as information, but didn't fully appreciate where they came from. In fact, one happened when Winter Hawk and I went on that trail ride."

"Really? What happened?"

"We prayed on Eaglefeathers Butte that *Maheo* honor Black Cloud's curse as it applied to the evil person who killed my white brother. On our way back, I fell off Spring Thunder."

White Wolf laughed. "Yes. I remember that."

"I have not fallen off a horse since I was a child," he said with a crooked smile. "On the ground nearby I found an ancient arrowhead. It told me our prayer was heard. Not long after that, the murderer, *ok kliwus,* and his truck fell into Dead Horse Canyon."

"A *maiyun* no doubt spooked the horse. It is good you hear their voices already." He resumed walking while continuing to explain. "The fasting ceremony is an act of self-purification," he said. "It releases you from being tied to earthly things or foolish desires. It opens your heart, mind, and soul to experience the mysterious and beauty found in *Maheo's* world. I am glad you had those experiences. After your fast you can expect many more."

Goosebumps tickled his arms.

"Yes, *Maheo* has given me special glimpses into that world. I believe that I am ready. And I see why as a young man I was not. Eaglefeathers told me those things, but they made no sense. Now they do. But I do have one concern."

White Wolf's dark eyes drilled into his own. "Only one, Littlewolf?"

He held his gaze as one would a poisonous snake. "No. There are many. But other than *Maheo's* response and what he wants me to do, this is the main one. It's about my promise to Eaglefeathers to fast on Eagles Peak. Will he be disappointed if I go to *Novavose* instead?"

His uncle smiled. "He will be pleased you are finally fulfilling your promise. That location was designated since that was where you both were bound at that time. Now you are here. Eaglefeathers, your father, and I all completed our first ceremonial fast at *Novavose.*"

"Yes, but he chose the exact place he wanted me to go. It feels disrespectful to not do as he said."

"Eagles Peak is sacred ground, but *Novavose* is, too, and of special importance to our people. It is where *Maheo* instructed Sweet Medicine how we should live. Every time another of our people completes a fast it increases its power. It binds us together as brothers. To each other as well as Sweet Medicine."

"That makes sense," Charlie agreed, feeling some relief. "And it is closer, though still a fair distance away."

"Yes. *Novavose* is less than two-hundred miles." A gleam appeared in White Wolf's eyes. "Of course you could fast at Eagles Peak as well. It could certainly use the blessings."

Charlie met his gaze. "Yes. Something draws me to it. Perhaps to thank *Maheo* for my experiences there." He smiled. "Where *maiyun* chose me."

"Okay." White Wolf paused to kick the next post. Satisfied it was solid, he kept walking to the next one. "I will contact the Park Ranger at Bear Butte State Park and ask him to expect us early next week, unless he has some reason for us to delay. You have much to do to get ready in such a short time. If you want me to be your painter and instructor, you know how to ask."

"Of course. I apologize for taking you for granted. I will lay down tobacco whenever you say."

"Tomorrow is fine. We meet with Ice, then, yes?"

"That is correct. I drove out there a few days ago and offered tobacco for his advice about helping Sara walk again. He wanted a few days to think about it."

"He may tell us we should not interfere. Leave her fate with *Maheo*."

"Yes," he agreed, then exhaled hard, hoping that wouldn't be the case.

SARA'S CONDO PARKING LOT
DENVER
August 23, Thursday
2:44 p.m.

JASON LEANED BACK in the harness securing him to the power pole across the parking lot from the target's condo. Disguised as an employee of Xcel Energy, he lifted military grade binoculars to his eyes and focused on her sitting on her patio.

Good. Her schedule hadn't changed, making it easy to predict her actions.

His facial muscles tumbled into a frown. She wasn't alone.

So now the target had a dog. Pit bull, no less. Undoubtedly, a trained service animal.

Which made sense, now that she was out on her own and given her condition.

And situation.

He scowled as previous experiences with K-9 units rumbled through his memory. They often responded to German commands, which saved his ass, literally, more than once.

He liked animals. They generally liked him. In many cases befriending an animal took no more than a friendly greeting accompanied with a few treats. Giving it no reason to feel threatened.

Service animals, however, were different. Their instilled discipline made them unlikely to be deceived. Their bond with their owners made them practically clairvoyant in their ability to sense threats.

He admonished himself—*again*—for going soft. His original plan was simpler. No telling how this would play out. The more variables, the more likelihood of failure.

And dealing with a service dog was definitely a complication, especially if it had K9 training as well.

Furthermore, logistics here in a gated community, his current perch the only place for a clear shot a case in point, were not as favorable as her father's place.

Frustration clawed its way upward from the pit of his stomach.

What was the matter with him, anyway?

Sara Reynolds was a target, nothing more.

It didn't matter if she was a young handicapped woman or a bomb-wielding terrorist. Even Keller's bunch of goons had no qualms about it. As a professional, gender or condition should have no effect on his performance.

A new dilemma arose.

He chuckled.

In reality, it would be easier to take her out than the dog.

Yet, hesitation continued to reign.

Tracking her, prepared for any opportunity, was the best course of action, one way or the other. Assuming she talked to the dog as most pet owners did, he'd put a microphone outside her kitchen window. Her car, too.

Patience and flexibility had always been his superpower.

NORTHERN CHEYENNE RESERVATION
MONTANA
August 24, Friday
7:04 a.m.

CHARLIE AND WHITE WOLF sat on antique wooden chairs across from Ice in his log house behind the old Busby boarding school. He lived with his wife, Standing Dove, who was a friend of Star's. The tipi outside was the repository for his many medicines, hanging in buffalo hide bundles. The cabin's dirt floor was swept clean, packed solid enough to gleam from sunlight streaming through the dusty window beside the front door.

The scent of ancient wood and seasoned earth felt as if they'd gone back in time. The old medicine man's braids were mostly grey, his round face wizened with age and wisdom. They explained the reason for their visit, answered his questions, then waited. His far-away look indicated silent communication with *Maheo*, as if he were peering into another world.

Charlie glanced at White Wolf, who gestured to fold his arms and bow his head. He assumed a similar stance.

He prayed in support of the man's petition, that it would bring answers. His impression was of fog on a spring morning. Trees and brush barely visible, all else obliterated by impenetrable mist.

Were further ministrations on Sara's behalf contrary to *Maheo's* will?

White Wolf told him the future was territory on which he should tread lightly, as if stalking dangerous prey—prey that could consume him, should he make a mistake. Some matters were decided by *Maheo* while others were negotiable. Badger was traditionally involved with prophetic future views.

Which didn't bode well, if Badger was still angry with him for naming the bore hole *Mahahkoe*.

Was Sara's condition one she chose prior to birth? One from which she would learn and grow? Would interfering be wrong?

After what seemed a long wait, Ice cleared his throat. Charlie opened his eyes. Had the elder had a similar vision? Did his eyes penetrate the fog?

"*Maheo* revealed many things," Ice said. "I was instructed not to tell you. You must seek answers through sacred ceremonies. You have much to do in a small time. Destiny is revealed to you by *Maheo* so there is no mistake in understanding what you must do."

The elder's words rang with truth, yet left him befuddled. Why couldn't he tell him? White Wolf nodded as if understanding, adding to his confusion.

"I pledged to fast at *Novavose*," Charlie said. "We plan to leave next week."

Ice replied with a solemn nod. "That is good. Your questions will be answered."

On the way back to the ranch Charlie wanted to ask White Wolf what the old man meant, but it felt like a stupid question. Ice told him *Maheo* would give him answers during sacred ceremonies. If White Wolf knew more than that, he wasn't going to tell him, either.

If nothing else, it validated his determination to get to *Novavose* now, not next year.

What other ceremonies?

And what about Sara? Would he be told during his fast if and how to help her?

They planned to leave Monday for *Novavose*. Besides fasting, the sweat lodge was a ceremony as was the Sun Dance. No doubt Eaglefeathers mentioned them years ago, but at the moment he couldn't recall what they might be.

White Wolf's mysterious smile bespoke neither information nor comfort.

If you fear making anyone mad, then you ultimately probe for the lowest common denominator of human achievement.
—Jimmy Carter

12. ERRANDS

DENVER METRO
August 25, Saturday
11:40 a.m.

Sara knew the only way to get comfortable with the car's hand controls was to drive. Preferably in familiar, uncongested areas. She ran a few errands, picking up things she needed, like all the cosmetics and toiletry items her father and Mike threw out, hoping to eliminate anything toxic, which failed miserably when they missed the actual location.

After taking care of that at a Walgreens, she stopped to get a much-needed haircut. Her hair was a wreck. Since being poisoned clumps had fallen out. What remained was stringy and lifeless, but hopefully as she continued to detox it would grow in as it was before, thick and shiny.

When the stylist finished, she sat looking at herself in the mirror as she ran her fingers through what was left, which was mostly only a few inches long. She wrinkled her nose.

"I'm sorry, ma'am," the girl said. "Don't you like it?"

"The haircut's fine," she reassured her. "I've just never had it this short before. But I've had a health issue and figured it best to get it whacked off so it could grow in fresh."

"That's usually what I recommend," she said. "It should grow back quickly."

"I hope so."

The girl recommended a few products to help, which Sara bought plus gave her a generous tip.

After that, she continued to drive around.

Thoughts of Charlie persisted while she took routes in low traffic areas around Denver. She was feeling well enough that doing that sweat he mentioned had tremendous appeal. Would that be all it required to walk again?

Another thought dawned: Patrice answered a host of questions the past few months. Could she see that in the cosmos?

She bit her lip.

What if the answer was no?

Did she really want to know? Or not?

Sitting at a traffic light she pondered all that Patrice had done the past several months, even participating in the healing ceremony. A few months ago she had no clue astrology could provide so many insights. Furthermore, Patrice was more than an astrologer. She was now a dear, trusted friend.

The light turned green and she pushed the hand control forward, debating where to go next. Remembering Blossom's appointment at the groomer's in less than an hour decided for her.

"Well, girl, now it's time to get you all prettied up," she said, reaching over to pat her in the passenger seat.

Maybe while Blossom was getting her beauty treatment she'd go see Patrice since Cosmic Portals was in the University Hill area, less than a mile away.

"Call Patrice," she commanded her phone. The woman picked up on the first ring.

"Hi, Sara," her cheery voice replied. "How are you doing today?"

"Great! Hey, I'll be in the area and wondered if it would be okay if I dropped by for a few minutes. Are you busy?"

"No, actually, I'm not. I'd love to see you! Someone will watch for you and open the door."

"Perfect!"

"Is there a reason you want to see me, Sara? Or just to visit?"

"Actually, I do have a question. One of those horaries. At least I think I do."

"Great! What's your question? I can run the chart and be ready, since it sounds like you're on a schedule."

Sara hesitated, again pondering whether she really wanted the answer.

"Well, I'm wondering if I'll ever walk again. *But* if the answer's 'No,' I'm not sure I want to know."

"I understand. Listen, sweetie, I'll run the chart and see how it looks. Think about whether you want to know on your way over and we'll take it from there."

"That sounds like a plan. See you in a few."

She hopped on I-25 North, exiting in Boulder a few minutes later. She worked her way across town past the University of Colorado, grateful traffic was light. Pushing the control forward was gradually becoming intuitive, like stepping on the accelerator was before. Being a mechanical system, that was exactly what she was doing. The brakes were delayed by a fraction of a second each time. It freaked her out at first, but was getting used to it.

She pulled into the Puppy Palace parking lot, a spot available right in front. She released the wheelchair's anchors, let Blossom out of her chair, then rolled to the back where she opened the rear hatch and activated the lift.

The afternoon sun was hot as she attached the leash to the dog's special harness, as required by the establishment as well as federal law. The dog gave her a classic side-eye.

She laughed. "I know, girl, I know," she said, scratching her behind the ear. "It's the rules. Sorry. Not all canine clients are as smart and well-behaved as you."

One of the reasons the trainer referred her to this groomer was their handicapped door button. Blossom knew the drill and activated it with her paw, then led the way.

The dark-haired receptionist wore a friendly smile. "Mrs. Reynolds? And I assume this is Blossom?"

"Yes. How long do you think it will take? I thought I'd run a quick errand, if that's okay."

"Of course. It usually takes about an hour. No problem, as long as it doesn't upset your dog to have you gone. Just be aware if you're not back in time, there's a $20 service charge for dog-sitting."

She laughed. "I understand. I'll make sure I'm back on-time. It's only a few blocks away."

"Give me your number and I'll text when she's almost ready, if you like." She held out a note pad.

"Perfect!"

She wrote it down, noticing her dog was giving her another suspicious look, as if understanding the conversation. She leaned forward to place her forehead against the pitty's big head, something she'd done since their first day together.

Sometimes she felt as if the dog could read her mind, but whether or not that was true, the affectionate gesture felt good.

"I'm just going to see Patrice. Mommy will be right back. You be a good girl, okay?"

It wasn't quite a growl, but definitely a comment, accompanied with a snort. The canine looked back as the woman led her to the wash unit in back, side-eye look one of clear canine dissent.

"Thanks so much," Sara said with a wave, then swiveled around and returned to her car.

It took all of two minutes to get to Cosmic Portals. She always smiled at its colorful window entirely covered with zodiac and planetary symbols accompanied by stylized stars. As promised, the coffee shop manager opened the door.

"Go right back," she said. "Patrice is expecting you."

"Thanks!"

She wheeled past the counter where two customers devoured specialty pastries. There was nothing more enticing than their Spiral Galaxies. Their cinnamon aroma beckoned. She paused. Indulged in another whiff, tempted—then nixed the idea for the sake of time.

One more sniff of culinary heaven, another thing she appreciated more than ever, then she wheeled through the beaded curtain. Within the cozy reading room, the pungent scent of ylang ylang replaced that of the pastries, subtly shifting the mood.

Patrice got up, moved the armchair to make room for the wheelchair, then sat down across from her.

"You cut your hair," she said. "It looks cute."

Sara shrugged. "It's okay, I guess. I've never had it this short and it feels weird."

"It will grow back before you know it." Questions beamed from her violet eyes as she tucked a long strand of hair behind her ear. "Well, sweetie, what did you decide?"

Sara's smile was apologetic. "I'm so sorry, Patrice, but I decided I don't want to know. I'm doing fairly well these days, managing this new challenge. We've got the condo all fixed up, plus Blossom, my service dog, is an unbelievable help and companion."

"You got a dog? That's wonderful! Where is she? Aren't they supposed to be with you twenty-four/seven?"

"Usually that's the case, but she's at the groomer over on Williamson. I just need to be back in an hour or less."

Patrice's surprise was evident. "I'm amazed she let you leave."

Sara chuckled. "She didn't like it, that's for sure. But I wasn't sure how your coffee shop patrons would react, so figured I'd take advantage of a few minutes without her."

"Service animals and even those that are well-behaved are always welcome. Next time feel free to bring her along. I'd love to meet her."

"I will. She's a lifesaver. It's absolutely incredible what she can do. Fetch things from the fridge, open and close doors, even help me get dressed and undressed. You should see her help make the bed! It's so cute! And unload groceries. Take things to the trash. Even helps with laundry! I got a front-loading washer so she can transfer everything to the dryer. She even has a special bark to voice activate my phone and call 911. She's truly amazing."

"What breed?"

"She's a pitty. Pit bull."

"It's sad they have such bad reputations, isn't it? All the ones I've known have been wonderful family pets."

"Definitely. Sweetest dog ever. And so smart! I figure if her breed puts the fear of God into anyone who wants to hurt me, that's all the better."

"True. So, you've decided to skip the horary and just take it one day at a time?"

A frown creased her forehead. "Yeah. I apologize for the trouble. I'll be happy to pay for it, of course."

"No, absolutely not. Don't even think about it, sweetie. I didn't put a lot of time into it. Ran the chart and that was about it. Can you share the reason you decided against it?"

Her nose wrinkled, a bit unsure still. "While I hope not being able to walk isn't permanent, I think I'd rather maintain false hope as opposed to none, if you know what I mean."

"I can understand that." Patrice's eyes searched hers for a moment. "You seem to be doing so much better since Charlie and White Wolf were here."

"Yes. At least the brain fog and depression are gone plus my complexion has cleared up. I'm still overwhelmed and discouraged sometimes, but I deal with that by staying busy. Some sensation has come back to my skin, at least, which is encouraging, but I can't wiggle my toes or anything. Yet!"

"That's the spirit! At least that's something."

"Exactly. Nerves take longer to heal. I told that to my PT patients for years. Besides, there may be more Charlie and White Wolf can do, so we'll see. He mentioned one of their sweats. It makes sense that would be an effective way to detox." She forced a smile. "I certainly don't like being disabled, but I can't allow it stop me. I don't need to be able to walk to fight for justice."

"So true. I'll tell you a little secret I've discovered over the years with my clients who have big challenges to overcome," Patrice said. "Once they quit fighting, accept it, and deal with it, the crisis tends to go away. Plus, they seem to build a sort of immunity to similar crises. The Universe backs off once you've learned a lesson. If you don't, you can count on it coming back."

"It sure wouldn't hurt my feelings for this to go away, but for now, it is what it is. *C'est-ça, que ça,* as my mom used to say."

Her phone chirped. She dug it out of her purse. "*Uh oh!* She's done already. I need to go. I'll be in touch, Patrice."

She tucked the phone back in the handbag's outside pocket, then reached back to loop the strap over the side of the wheelchair. It didn't catch, flipping over and dumping everything all over the floor.

An exasperated cry escaped as its contents scattered everywhere, from beneath her feet to under the reading table and possibly beyond.

Billfold. Keys. Notebook. Grocery lists. A bottle of Ibuprofen. Sunglasses. Pens. Business cards. Plus the usual clutter stashed inside, then forgotten.

Patrice got up, laughing. "Don't worry, sweetie. I'll get it."

Sara expelled another impatient breath. "Thank you! Moments like this I definitely want my legs back. But actually, picking things up is something Blossom is trained to do. That'll teach me for leaving her behind."

Patrice knelt down, handed her the wallet, keys, and sunglasses, then scooped everything else up in her hands.

"Here, just dump it inside," Sara said, holding it open. "I'll organize it later."

They exchanged a hug, then Patrice walked her to the door and held it open.

"See you soon," she said with a smile, then disappeared inside when Sara waved upon starting the car.

Seeing Patrice always left her with a good feeling, her smile lasting until, a few blocks later, a tell-tale thump erupted from the rear. The steering wheel vibrated violently, telling her immediately what it was.

How could it be?

Where could she have possibly gotten a flat?

Well, it was what it was. *C'est-ça, que ça.*

She pulled over to the shoulder and retrieved her purse from the passenger seat. She dug through the mess, admonishing herself again for being so clumsy.

Where was her phone?

Panic flared.

Oh, no!

She buried her face in her hands. Probably somewhere at Patrice's.

Panic melted her brain.

Now what?

Then she remembered.

Both hands shifted to her chest to still her runaway heart.

How could she forget?

The Enclave had On*Star. They'd send someone to fix it.

Undoubtedly, she'd be late picking up her dog, but that couldn't be helped. She pushed the Buick's call button and it started to ring.

Movement in the rearview mirror caught her eye. A late model Subaru crossover pulled up behind her. A few seconds later someone tapped on her window. A friendly looking guy with scruffy brown hair, penetrating blue eyes, and a neatly trimmed beard wearing an orange Home Depot vest.

The glass crept down just as someone answered at On*Star.

"This is Brad at On*Star. How can we help you today?"

"Please hold on just a moment," she said.

"Don't bother them," the guy at her window said. "I can change your tire, ma'am."

She debated. No telling how long it would take otherwise.

"Hi, I'm sorry, Brad," she said. "Someone just stopped behind me and offered to change my tire. Thank you, though."

"Okay, ma'am," the On*Star guy said, apparently overhearing the conversation. "Any problems or complications, feel free to call back."

"I will. Thanks!"

She turned back to the window. "Thank you so much! I'm in a bit of a hurry so this is very much appreciated."

"You should probably get out while I jack it up," he recommended, then stopped, apparently noticing she was in a wheelchair.

"Do you need help?" he asked.

"No. I've got this."

She released the wheelchair anchors and exited out the back, engulfed again by late summer heat.

"Wow, it's a hot one today, isn't it?" she remarked.

"It sure is. Do you know how to get to the spare?"

She blinked a few times, trying to think. "I don't. The owner's manual's in the glovebox. Hold on, I'll get it."

"I can do that, ma'am," he offered.

"No, that's okay. It's a bit of a mess in there. I'll do it."

Not so much a mess as the fact her Glock was in there. Definitely not a good idea for him to find it, no matter how nice he was.

In fact, maybe she should get it, just in case. "Nice" people weren't always as they appeared. Like that fake cop, Officer Leonard, who'd helped her after the Lakewood wreck. Weird how both he and her car vanished.

She reached up and opened the passenger door, careful to avoid the sloping embankment beyond the shoulder. She groaned. Reaching the glovebox wasn't going to happen.

Now what? Trust him? Or lie?

She jumped when he spoke behind her. "Let me," he said.

Renewed panic flared.

A thick binder in the door panel caught her eye. "Wait! I think it's right here." Her eyes met his as she handed it over, feeling as if she'd dodged a bullet.

"By the way, I'm Jake." He held out his hand.

She extended her own. "Hi. I'm Sara. Thanks for helping."

"You look pretty uncomfortable. I keep a small ice chest with bottled water in my car. Would you like some?"

She exhaled, trying to relax. Maybe a cold drink would help. "Yes, thank you. I really need to get over to the Puppy Palace to pick up my dog."

"Would you like me to drive you over there to get it?"

"That would be great!"

"What's the best way to get you into my car?"

"It's not that hard," she said, swiveling the wheelchair around and heading back to his passenger side door. "Just lift me up under the arms and rotate me around into the seat butt first."

When he lifted her up their eyes connected, triggering an odd flash of deja-vu.

Where could she have possibly met this guy before?

When she and Will bought dead bolts for the condo a month or so ago perhaps? She dismissed it, though it seemed weird.

"Now help me get my legs inside and I'm good to go. My wheelchair folds up."

"Got it," he said, stashing it in back..

She glanced around the car's interior. It had that new car smell and features of a high-end vehicle. How could a guy working at what was probably a minimum wage job afford it? Married to a woman with money, perhaps?

Then she noticed the Enterprise sticker on the windshield. Most likely a rental.

Odd.

Back at her door he twisted off the cap of a bottle of water and handed it to her, then walked around and got in the driver's seat.

"Thank you," she said, taking a long, sustained swallow.

"You're welcome." He chuckled, adding, "Goodnight, Sara."

"What did you say?" she gasped.

His answer faded into a turbulent sea of black.

Where there were myriads of buffalo the year before, there were now myriads of carcasses. The air was foul with a sickening stench, and the vast plain which only a short twelve months before teemed with animal life was a dead, solitary putrid desert.
—Army Lt. Col. Richard Irving Dodge, 1873

13. MISSING

COSMIC PORTALS
BOULDER
August 25, Saturday
3:20 p.m.

Patrice's phone was dark and still. But clearly someone's was ringing. In her reading room, not the coffee shop.

Under her chair, actually.

She picked it up just as the ringing stopped. The screen was locked, no telling who it was.

No doubt Sara would be back shortly to pick it up. She smiled. Then she could meet her dog. No clients were scheduled, freeing her to visit a bit more.

She set it on her desk, pondering the chart for Sara's question.

A strange horoscope loaded with same-degree aspects that told a convoluted and conditional story. It wasn't absolutely clear one way or the other, indicating a lot of free-will was involved.

Just as well she didn't want to know since it didn't contain a definitive yes or no. Her gut feeling was optimistic, but wouldn't want to instill false hope, even after what Sara said.

The phone rang every few minutes, but the locked screen precluded answering. No doubt Connie or Will looking for her, probably frantic. She needed to call Connie. Let her know the phone was there. Sara was probably looking for it, too, though she should figure out it was there. Maybe she hadn't missed it yet.

She picked up her own and made the call.

"Connie? You sound stressed. Is everything alright?"

"Hi, Patrice. I'm not sure. I can't get in touch with Sara. I'm kind of worried."

"Well, I can help with that. She accidentally dropped her phone at my place. I'm surprised she hasn't been back yet to pick it up."

"Oh! Do you know where she was this afternoon besides your place?"

"Yes. She took her dog to the groomer and came over to chat since she was in the neighborhood. They finished up early so she left in a hurry. In the rush she dropped her purse and everything dumped on the floor. I didn't realize we missed it until it rang, under my chair."

"Oh. Maybe she's still at the groomers. Do you know which one?"

"The one on Williamson. A few blocks from here."

"Okay, great. I'll call to see if she's still there."

Patrice ended the call, puzzled when an ominous feeling crept through her that something was very wrong.

MONTGOMERY RESIDENCE
BOULDER
August 25, Saturday
3:35 p.m.

"WILL! WE'VE GOT A PROBLEM!"

He got up from his desk, concerned by the urgency in Connie's voice, hoping it was as simple as not reaching something on a top shelf.

"What's wrong?" he called down the stairs.

"Sara was supposed to pick up Blossom from the groomer an hour ago," Connie replied, worry lines marring her forehead. "She dropped her phone at Patrice's so doesn't have it. What should we do?"

Deep concern gripped his chest, sure sign his blood pressure just spiked.

"First thing is pick up her dog and her phone," he stated, coming down the stairs as quickly as he dared. "Then see if we can find her. Not having her phone is a serious problem. That's the one way we can track her, to say nothing of getting in touch. C'mon, let's go." He scurried for the kitchen door to the garage. "Let's go, woman! Time's a'wastin'!"

Connie grabbed her tablet and purse from the counter, made sure she had her phone, then followed.

Both settled in the car, garage door humming open. "Do you know which groomer?" he asked.

"Puppy Palace on Williamson." She checked her tablet and relayed the address. Another quick call confirmed Sara still hadn't shown up.

Once there, the establishment was reluctant to release the dog. Will explained the situation to no avail, frustration building. When both he and Connie showed multiple calls and texts from Sara, that finally convinced them who they were. Will provided his driver's license, paid the grooming and dog sitting fee, then signed for picking up the dog.

Blossom was not happy. She greeted them with enthusiasm, but sat down whimpering and wouldn't move, no doubt looking for Sara. They finally coaxed her into the backseat, where she continued to whine. Connie got in back, Will not sure who was comforting whom.

"Where's Patrice's from here?"

Connie gave directions. Halfway there, he spotted Sara's car parked on the shoulder on the opposite side of the road.

"*Uh, oh,*" he mumbled, waiting for oncoming traffic to pass before whipping an illegal U-turn across the four-lane road. He pulled up behind it, noticing the car listed to the side, back passenger tire flat.

"Holy hell," he grumbled. "Why didn't she call?"

"She didn't have her phone, remember?"

"Right. But the car has On*Star, she should have called them. Where could she be? She sure as hell didn't walk anywhere."

"I have no idea," Connie said, wringing her hands. "Maybe one of her friends came by."

"Not likely. She would have gotten the dog and her phone, first thing. This isn't good, Connie. I have a really bad feeling about this."

"What should we do?" she asked, eyes widening with panic.

"I have the second key to her car, but it's at the house. I'll call On*Star, like she should have in the first place, and have them come out and fix the flat. Then we can take it to the house, rather than leave it here."

"What if she comes back?"

"Let's hope she does."

"True. But in the meantime should we call the police?" Connie asked, eyes wide.

He shook his head, forcing himself to stay calm, for her sake if not his own. "They won't do anything until she's missing forty-eight hours."

"Even though she's disabled? And missing from her car?"

"Good point. I suppose it wouldn't hurt. But let's wait until I get the key. They'll want to look inside the car and so forth for any clues. Which I'll do, too, before we call them. Maybe she left a note inside or something."

WOODLAND PLACE
BOULDER, COLORADO
August 26, Sunday
7:35 a.m. MDT

IT WAS THE NEXT morning before Sara's eyes eased open. Shards of sunlight split the blinds, revealing a dimly lit unfamiliar room. It appeared relatively new with modern furnishings, walls adorned with framed paintings of mountain landscapes.

Supine in a recliner, her thoughts spun, awash in confusion. Where was she? How did she get there?

What happened?

She stiffened at the sound of footsteps. The blinds opened, filling the room with light. A man appeared at her feet, face vaguely familiar.

Probably forty-ish, dark hair slicked back, and clean shaven. Wearing a blue shirt with tan pants—the Colorado State Trooper uniform.

Officer Leonard?

How could it be? *Was she dreaming? Or crazy?*

"Are you hungry?" he asked, the smooth, radio-announcer voice oddly familiar.

"What am I doing here?" she asked, doing her best to stifle her anxiety. "Who are you?"

"Don't you remember?" His eyes softened, almost as if he were hurt. "I saved your life that day, outside Lakewood. When you had that wreck, with the logging truck."

Her heart raced, pounding in her ears. Random memories, recent and past, zapped her like an up-ended jigsaw puzzle.

A few snapped into place.

Blossom. *Where was she?*

Patrice.

Flat tire.

Some guy with an orange home store vest stopping to help.

Oh, my God.

"Are you hungry, Sara? There's not much in the fridge, but I can have Door Dash deliver something. What do you feel like? I'm sure you haven't eaten for a while."

Eating was not something that rated any sense of urgency. If anything, the bathroom was far more inviting.

"Where's my dog?" she demanded.

"She's fine. Your parents have her."

Her eyes narrowed. "How do you know that?"

The man shrugged his shoulders. "I watched them."

"Do they know where I am? Are they coming to pick me up?

His response registered somewhere between a laugh and a sneer. "Surely you already know those answers."

"Where's my car?"

"Your father picked it up." He laughed, harder this time. "He couldn't figure out how to drive it without a driver's seat and those hand controls. He finally gave up and had it towed."

"Who are you?" she demanded, glaring. "What do you want?"

"C'mon, Sara. You're smarter than that." Hazel eyes locked on hers and held for several long seconds as he moved to her side and loomed over her. "Really? What do I want? Oh, I'd say somewhere in the neighborhood of a million dollars."

She gaped at him, incredulous. *"What? Are you crazy?"*

"I don't think so. Just to be clear." He hunkered down, eyes level with hers. "You. Have. Been. Kidnapped."

Its confirmation triggered an adrenaline blast, heart tripping staccato beats.

"Do they know?" she asked, hands across her chest.

"Not yet."

"Why not? What are you waiting for?"

"I haven't decided whether you're worth more alive or dead."

NORTHERN CHEYENNE RESERVATION
MONTANA
August 26, Sunday
11:40 a.m.

TAH-HO'NEHE'S CARGO AREA WAS loaded with supplies:
- Bedrolls
- Expansive bundle of man sage
- Sacred paints
- Buffalo robes
- Sweetgrass braids
- Sacred red pipe
- Buffalo rattles

- Buffalo skull
- Eagle bone whistle
- Tobacco
- Tipi
- Cooler with food
- Five gallon jugs for spring water they would fill along the way at Crazy Head Spring.

Even with the third row of seats collapsed, it was getting tight as Charlie unloaded sundry camping items they'd brought from the barn in the collapsible wagon Star used for the garden. Once empty, he folded it up and tucked it in beside the bedrolls.

"Do not hurt my wagon," Star said with a rare frown. "It is not intended for heavy loads."

"We will treat it kindly and with respect," Charlie promised, but she did not appear convinced.

"One more thing," White Wolf said. "It is our tradition that each Cheyenne who visits the Sacred Mountain leave a stone behind."

"What kind?" Winter Hawk asked. "Like what we use in the sweat lodge?"

"Yes," his father agreed. "Which reminds me. We need to bring all our stones for the ceremonial sweat when Littlewolf finishes his fast. We can leave two behind. We have blessed those stones many times. That will leave part of our spirit on the Sacred Mountain. In the future when we pray, we can picture them there. We will find replacements for ours when we return."

Charlie, Winter Hawk, and Risingsun hoofed it up to their sweat lodge on the rise behind the house to fetch the forty-four stones, then distribute them as evenly as possible among the other items in the cargo area and on the back seat floor. Each one weighed between eight and ten pounds, collectively adding the weight equivalent of two men.

"It is good that we have a vehicle that can carry such a load," White Wolf said as they finished. "Our old Explorer's suspension could not handle it. *Néá'eše*, Littlewolf, for providing it for us."

"It is ironic that the money came from violating Grandmother Earth," Charlie replied. "I pray she forgives me."

"There is always a reason. Always a reason. It was part of your journey and return to the red road."

Charlie lowered *Tah-Hó'nehe's* cargo door with a satisfied grunt. The full-size SUV was loaded from the cargo area to the roof rack with what they'd need at *Novavose*. His old pickup, like White Wolf's Explorer, couldn't have handled the load either, by volume or weight. Both vehicles would have been required to handle it all.

Next, the bag with prayer cloths from Sara's ceremony were placed in the backseat so they could hang them at the Sacred Mountain, plus a bundle of offering cloths in the four sacred colors.

When word made its way around the reservation that they were going to *Novavose*, several tribal members brought them to deliver on their behalf. The cloths represented blankets for the spirits in exchange for their help, sometimes for a specific need, others for simply a long life.

Fortunately, Rufus Littlesun agreed to cover White Wolf's medicine man duties again during their absence. The man was so pleased for Charlie's intent he had tears in his eyes as he accepted their tobacco offering.

White Wolf finished tying down their tipi to the roof rack, poles extending from the hood to slightly beyond the back. The tipi was a smaller replica of the only one that survived when Chief American Horse's camp on the Powder River was burned to the ground centuries before by Colonel Joseph Reynolds' troops. He was later court-martialed for the unjustified attack. Young choke cherry trees to build a sweat lodge were there as well.

He turned to Charlie. "The drive usually takes over three hours." He paused, sternness seeping from his dark eyes. Charlie set his jaw, expecting another comment on his driving, relieved when none came.

"If we leave after the midday meal," his uncle went on, "we'll get there before dark. We can set up camp, fix something simple to eat, then start your fast at sunrise." Again, White Wolf's eyes locked on his, but with a far softer message. "Eaglefeathers is singing."

Gooseflesh covered Charlie's arms, assurance the location had his grandfather's approval. "If only he were here."

"He can be."

Charlie straightened, hopeful, yet curious what he could possibly mean.

"Bring his medicine bundle," White Wolf answered, as if it were obvious. "With that, he will be with us. Of course I will take mine as well."

"Of course." He grinned as he retrieved Eaglefeathers' from his room, then set it in the backseat with White Wolf's.

14. ARRIVALS

NORTHERN CHEYENNE RESERVATION
MONTANA
August 26, Sunday
12:23 p.m.

Charlie watched as Star prepared a bounteous spread to send them off. He would not see such a feast again until she brought a similar one when she came out to meet them Friday, when he came down the mountain and broke his fast.

While everyone enjoyed the hearty meal, Winter Hawk picked at his food, unusual for the usually voracious fifteen-year-old. At length, he set down his fork and cast his father a pleading look.

"May I go with you?" he pleaded. "*Please*? I will help with anything you want. Anything!"

White Wolf studied his son. "It would be a good experience for you, son. Wife, what do you think?"

Star looked from her husband to their older son of those still at home, their older three had moved out years before, now with children of their own. Risingsun shared his brother's hopeful expression, as if being the man of the house for a few days suited him as well.

"I agree," Star replied with a nod. "It will be good for us all. Risingsun and I will manage just fine."

Winter Hawk's grin stretched ear to ear.

"Finish your meal, then gather what you need," White Wolf instructed. "Your mother will add some additional food for you."

White Wolf exchanged a look of parental pride with Star while the boy wolfed down the rest of his dinner. The youth excused himself from the table, then dashed off to the basement.

Charlie was pleased, too. His bond cemented with his brother ever since that trail ride. The boy was wise beyond his years. He sensed Eaglefeathers watching over him when the boy assisted with his prayer cloth ceremony when he first arrived.

Even though the old man died a few months before Winter Hawk was born, it was clear he had an abundance of his grandfather's spirit.

They squeezed the extra items in the cargo area and made room for Winter Hawk in the back seat. Ready at last, they lined up facing east while White Wolf made a special prayer that all would go well for Star and Risingsun during their absence and would arrive safely to meet them at *Novavose* on Friday.

Farewell hugs and well-wishes were exchanged, then they climbed into *Tah-Hó'nehe*, waved farewell, and drove down the dirt road toward Busby and Highway 212.

Winter Hawk couldn't contain his excitement. Long before reaching Busby he started singing the Grandfather Song. Littlewolf and White Wolf joined in, pausing when just outside Lame Deer they stopped at Crazy Head Spring, named for a man who mourned at that location for his wife's passing.

They drove along the dirt road, past a few campers, then pulled over and parked. Dry, late summer brush flanking the surrounding trees crunched beneath their feet. They paused a few moments to watch the resident buffalo herd, then stepped over to the stream and filled their containers.

They no sooner got settled back in the SUV when a text popped up on the media panel. Seeing it was from Sara's number Charlie smiled, but it was short lived.

Charlie, this is Will, Sara's father. She's missing and we're worried. Her car broke down and she's nowhere to be found. If you have any insights into her location or safety please let us know. We'll keep you posted if we hear anything or find her.

Its timestamp indicated the day before, only arriving when they got far enough from the ranch for cell phone service. It had probably been there awhile, but no one noticed while they were singing.

Charlie's mood plummeted. "*Ohohyaa.* This is very bad." He glanced over at White Wolf whose solemnity indicated he'd likewise read it.

"We will make a prayer," White Wolf said, getting back out.

They blessed themselves with the earth, and stood facing east. "Littlewolf, pray for us."

Charlie's mind ran amok with concern as he focused on Sara. He closed his eyes.

"*Maheo.* We have great concern for our sister, Sara. We ask that you protect her from harm and help her family find her. We are grateful for traveling to the Sacred Mountain and ask that we arrive safely. I pray for your help that Sara may regain her health and return safely according to your will."

White Wolf nodded approval as they climbed back inside *Tah-Hó'nehe.* "I sense that for the moment she is safe," he said. "But there is potential for considerable danger."

Charlie restarted the car, anxiety replacing his jubilance. "I felt it, too. I wonder where she is and who is the threat?" He considered using his remote viewing ability to check, but for some reason it didn't feel right.

"We will learn more during your fast," White Wolf said. "There is no place we can do her more good than the Sacred Mountain."

BEAR BUTTE STATE PARK
SOUTH DAKOTA
August 26, Sunday
5:43 p.m.

THE DRIVE WAS QUIET after receiving the ominous text. Charlie concentrated on driving as Highway 212 took them southeast across the corner of Wyoming, then into South Dakota. He stopped for gas in Belle Fourche, then continued to Highway 79, where they turned south for *Novavose*.

His neck, and shoulder muscles were as tight as his grip on *Tah-Hó'nehe's* steering wheel, concern for Sara ripping his brain to shreds.

Where was she?

How dangerous was her abductor?

What would he want in exchange for her safe release?

The worry loop continued for over an hour of silent driving, before White Wolf finally spoke.

"You must let it go for now, Littlewolf," he said. "This is where you belong. We will pray for her here, where Sweet Medicine Spirits always respond. We will place her in *Maheo's* care. There is a reason this happened at this time."

Charlie's muscles relaxed ever so slightly, the worry loop less frantic, but still there, until a few hours later when their destination came into view.

Known to the public as Bear Butte, the formation was described geologically as an intrusion of igneous rock—not technically a mountain, being caused by different forces within the Earth Mother.

From over a mile away they could see the scorched 150 acres on its north side caused by a piece of burning debris from a rancher's burn pile. Fortunately, none of the local bison herd was injured and no buildings were destroyed. Charlie and his two passengers lamented the loss of so many trees, which would take years to regrow.

As they got closer, he pulled off on a wide stretch of shoulder so they could get a better look. He stood by the SUV's hood, gazing at the destruction. He dialed back time to when the fire occurred several months before, heart sinking as he watched hungry flames consuming trees and vegetation.

Wanting to see what it looked like before, he went farther back, to the previous summer, then returned to the present. The decimated trees made his chest hurt, concerned for any wildlife that was destroyed as a result. He would pray for it to return as quickly as possible to restore balance to such a sacred site.

They got back in *Tah-Hó'nehe* and continued to the south side where a narrow road crossed a small bridge east of the main parking lot and led to the ceremonial area. It was early enough to set up camp while it was still light.

Charlie parked, noting a few other vehicles. The ground was mostly level other than the slope leading up to the peak. Trees flanked the parking lot, beyond which sprawled an expansive camping area populated with a few tipis and a single modern tent, set up some fifty or more yards apart.

More familiar with the Rocky Mountains where other peaks obstructed the view, Charlie marveled at *Novavose's* solitude, view in other directions unrestricted to the horizon. The elevation of its highest point loomed four thousand four hundred twenty-six feet.

When he was there as a youth it was equally impressive as a natural wonder, but lacked spiritual significance. This time the scene blurred as his eyes feasted upon what his spirit witnessed was a sacred site where Sweet Medicine was taught.

What might the Sweet Medicine Spirits reveal?

It took about an hour to unload their gear, then transport it to the camp site two hundred yards up the trail. Its upward slope along *Novavose's* base made the transfer serious work. The forty-four stones were left behind, to be retrieved when White Wolf and his son set up the sweat lodge.

The area was mostly bare, scruffy vegetation dried and spent as summer yielded to autumn, but far better than burned. He offered a silent prayer of gratitude that this side had been spared, no doubt protected by *maiyun* and other spirits.

Stone tipi circles, remnants from generations past, as well as scattered fire pits, welcomed them, the scene oddly familiar.

Charlie's mind raced as he surveyed the area for the best place for the tipi.

Abruptly, he felt light-headed, similar to how it did when he found the drill site. The elevation was about the same as home, yet it felt as if he were disconnected from his body.

Exertion? Excitement? Or something more?

As if in response, his vision tunneled. Hackles crawled up the back of his neck as their tipi, distinctive with its ancient artwork, appeared a dozen yards away. A sweat lodge lay beyond, a heap of stones engulfed in flames in front of its closed door.

The buffalo hide door moved to the side. A *kâsováahe* in a breechclout exited and picked up a forked branch to retrieve stones for the next round.

The young man stopped.

Their eyes connected.

"*Epêhéva'e tséxho'êhneto*," he said, grinning. "*Nêstaévâhósevó omâtse.*"

Before Charlie could respond, the vision vanished.

Had White Wolf seen it, too?

He turned to ask, finding the man scrutinizing him with a puzzled look.

"What did you see, Littlewolf?" he asked.

"Our tipi and a sweat lodge. A young man, probably around Winter Hawk's age, came out to get stones for the next round. He said, 'It is good that you came. I will see you again.' Then it all disappeared. Who do you think it was?"

"If it was our tipi, probably Eaglefeathers." He smiled. "He accepted our invitation."

The hair stood up on his arms.

"Where was it? Let's set up camp there."

Charlie pointed.

While they did so, Winter Hawk moved the choke cherry trees several paces beyond to where he'd seen the sweat lodge.

After unloading the wagon with the last of their supplies, Winter Hawk took it back down to the parking lot to collect firewood from the pile the park ranger kept stocked for campers.

White Wolf chuckled as his son took off down the hill, bursting with teen energy, unaffected by the work so far. "It is good we brought him along," he said.

"Yes," Charlie agreed. "He has been a big help."

In spite of the generous dinner at home, hauling everything stimulated everyone's appetite. Once the tipi was set up, they built a fire, adjusted the smoke hole according to the wind direction, then heated up a pot of soup.

By the time they sat down to eat outside, it was dark, ascending Grandmother Moon joining her entourage of stars.

Charlie turned to his brother.

"Four planets are watching over us tonight," he said, pointing out the brighter orbs that represented Mars, Saturn, Jupiter and Venus lined up in the darkened sky.

"Wow! How do you know that?" the boy asked.

"My white brother, Bryan, taught me. He would love this view." He swallowed the sudden lump in his throat, missing his brother.

The Moon washed out the glow from Sturgis seven miles to the southwest, the rest of the sky alive with stars. The Milky Way, known to the Cheyenne as *séotséméó'o*, the road of the dead, loomed overhead, so brightly it seemed within reach. Charlie's heart grieved as he pondered loved ones who'd taken that road: Bryan, his father, Eaglefeathers, and *Amasani*.

Were they watching over them, too? He longed to see them again someday, wondering when that might be.

As fasters pause on its heights they hear the ceaseless wind moaning through stunted ponderosa pines with remnants of sacred offering cloths flapping from their lower branches. Rising and falling like the echoes of a great waterfall, the noise of the wind recedes into the infinity stretching beyond the four directions where the Sacred Persons dwell.
— Peter John Powell, "Sweet Medicine," Volume I, p. 19

15. *NOVAVOSE*

BEAR BUTTE STATE PARK
SOUTH DAKOTA
August 27, Monday
4:23 a.m.

The next morning Charlie awoke to a cold blast. He pulled *Amasani's* blanket up around his neck, then opened his eyes when the scent of sun-scorched grass and juniper with a hint of smoke reminded him where he was.

The other bedroll was empty, Winter Hawk still asleep. He got up and stepped outside, greeted by White Wolf and a fire that embraced the campsite in its golden glow. A star embellished sky reigned overhead, eastern horizon barely hinting at approaching dawn.

Behind them to the north the looming shadow of Bear Butte dominated the view. Once again, *Novavose's* majesty and history washed over him. After so much anticipation, at last he was here.

His ancestors' spirits surrounded him in welcome, assurance this was where he belonged. Where family members close to him conducted a ceremonial fast.

Winter Hawk stumbled out of the tipi, rubbing his eyes.

"We need to get started so we're done before sunrise," White Wolf said.

Charlie took off his clothes and donned a breechclout so his body could be painted for the fast. "Let us begin," White Wolf said. "Pray for us, Littlewolf."

Charlie stood, shivering, with Winter Hawk on his left, White Wolf on his right, all facing the eastern sky. They blessed themselves with the earth.

Charlie bowed his head. "*Maheo*, spirit father of all creation. We are grateful to be here in this sacred place to honor your teachings that tell us how to live. I ask for your blessings upon my people.

"The purpose of my fasting ceremony is to honor my grandfather, Eaglefeathers, and grandmother, *Amasani* for their teachings that led me to a spiritual way of life. I am grateful for their wisdom and patience as well as White Wolf for all he has done to help me and for agreeing to be my instructor.

"We are thankful to be here at your sacred mountain to pray with Sweet Medicine spirits. *Maheo*, we ask for your guidance that we may follow your ways and help our people live a peaceful life."

He paused a moment, gathering his other requests for which he desperately needed *Maheo's* help.

"My brother's widow, Sara, has been poisoned by evil men and now stolen from her family," he went on. "She is unable to walk. I am thankful to Ice for telling me to come here to find answers to help her. Our prayer is for you, *Maheo*, to heal her and bring her home. My spirit is happy for your wisdom and guidance."

In spite of the chilly air, his spirit burned as an ember as the blessings received the past few months consumed him with gratitude.

"*Maheo*, I belong with my people and to live on the same land where my grandfather was born, near Eaglefeathers Creek," he said. "I humbly ask for strength and courage to complete this ceremony and be taught what I must do to serve you and my people as directed by Sweet Medicine Spirits."

When he finished praying, White Wolf gestured for him to sit beside the crackling fire where Winter Hawk combed out and re-braided his hair, then wrapped each one with red trade cloth.

That done, White Wolf's eyes met his with chilling solemnity. "Today you begin the first day of your fast here at the Sacred Mountain," he said. "We sacrifice food and water for four days and four nights to receive strength, courage, and wisdom to live the ways of *Maheo*. The Creator's ways are not our ways. We follow his ways to live a long life with good health.

"The Sacred Mountain is home to our prophet, Sweet Medicine. His spirit lives inside the mountain. *Maheo* sent Sweet Medicine to teach us our ceremonial way of life, the healing lodge, *Novavose* fasting, and the Sun Dance.

"The healing lodge or what we call a sweat, is the oldest ceremony, from when we lived at the bottom of Eagle Mountain near the great lakes in the north. The golden eagle gave us the lodge. They asked our protection over their families. We made an honor song for the eagles that we sing inside the lodge."

His look intensified, eyes boring into his. "This fasting ceremony is not easy. The medicine inside your grandfather's bundle will help take you through the four days without food or water. The medicines are man sage, bee balm, sweetgrass, and power weed. Root medicines are bitter root, big medicine root, and bear root.

"They are all found on our homeland. To find them, you must know who to ask. When you ask with your heart for ceremony, they will show you where to find them. Remember to lay down tobacco first.

"On the third day when you are weary and thirsty, your mouth will be very dry," he explained. "Take a piece of big medicine and chew it for a long time. Your mouth will be wet again. Don't spit it out, swallow it."

Charlie nodded, remembering his fast on the rim of Dead Horse Canyon when he used it, but did not know he was supposed to swallow it.

"During this fast you will learn what kind of man you are. Do not become afraid when the Sweet Medicine Spirits come to you. Do not disobey them. Be humble and do what you are told."

The hair on Charlie's arms stood up in cryptic prelude to what lay ahead. Ice's mysterious refusal to tell him what he saw sprang from memory.

What did the elder perceive that he'd been forbidden to convey?

"These earth paints protect you and give you strength to complete your fasting vow," White Wolf continued. "Our paints and medicines are sacred gifts from Grandmother Earth. "The paints are yellow, red, blue, white, green, and black. Do you understand all that I have told you?"

"Yes," Charlie replied as he nodded understanding.

Apparently satisfied, White Wolf gathered the earth paints needed for the fasting ceremony.

Blue. Yellow. Black. White.

He used a branch from the fire to light a sweetgrass braid, smudged the paints, and reached for blue. His index finger hovered above it, then withdrew.

"Son, would you like to help? This is not something we do often. It will be good for you to learn."

Winter Hawk's eyes brightened and a broad smile captured his expression. "I would be very honored to help, Father. What should I do?"

"Give me your hand."

White Wolf took his son's index finger and dipped it in the blue paint. Then he guided it from the top of Charlie's forehead in a line to his ear, then down to the bottom of his chin.

"Now do the same on his other side to create a diamond shape. That symbol identifies Littlewolf as one of the Morning Star people."

Winter Hawk did as instructed, Charlie's bond with his brother warming even more as they shared the sacred ritual.

"Wipe the blue from your finger on this sage, then use yellow to trace a circle over his heart," White Wolf continued. "Start in the center and move outward in a spiral until its solid yellow." White Wolf demonstrated the motion in the air. "That represents the sun and invites *Maheo* to enter his heart."

Next, he returned Winter Hawk's finger to blue, traced the outline of a quarter moon on Charlie's left chest/shoulder, then let the boy fill it in, followed by a blue full moon on his right.

Then came black, made from burnt cottonwood. "Now, we will both paint because there is much to cover. You do his right side, I'll do his left. Carefully dodge the other markings and cover his face, neck, body, and both arms, then from below his knee to his ankle."

While it tickled his ribs, the overall sensation was relaxing. Charlie closed his eyes and savored being prepared for his fast by loving family members. A year before he was all but lost, while now he was where he belonged. His thoughts shifted to Bryan, whose death initiated his transformation.

Was his white brother cheering him on from *Se'han*?

Bryan had not been sympathetic when he failed his first attempt under the direction of his grandfather as a foolish eighteen-year-old. He accused him of having a recto-cranial inversion, some white man expression he still didn't understand. The next time he saw his white brother in a vision he'd have to remember to ask.

Once he was covered as required with black, they added white dots that represented stars to his neck, body, and arms. White Wolf motioned for him to turn around, inspecting their work. He added a few more stars, then nodded, satisfied.

"We paint the person fasting this way," White Wolf explained, "because it ties you to *Maheo's* creations as a child of the universe. One of the Morning Star people. It is a message to the *maiyun* that draws them more quickly. It protects you from evil spirits, which will come to taunt you. We will sing the Grandfather song to invite the grandfather spirits to join us as well."

Charlie smiled, the warmth spreading from his heart to his entire body telling him they already had.

They collected essential items he would need at the fasting site, including man sage, the buffalo skull, sacred red pipe, sweetgrass braid, Eaglefeathers' medicine bundle, and his buffalo robe.

Twilight lit the way as they began their trek up the Sacred Mountain's south side, voices riding the crisp mountain air. They finished the song upon reaching a scree-strewn draw where White Wolf led the way. They took a moment to catch their breath after a few hundred yards where they turned to look back at the view. Sturgis appeared as a sparkling jewel on the darkened plains, town lights fading in day's first light.

"Wow!" Winter Hawk said. "This is even better than Eaglefeathers Butte."

"Later this afternoon we will hike to the summit," White Wolf said. "It is even better."

Charlie smiled, remembering that same hike with Eaglefeathers when White Wolf fasted as a young man. The vast view included four states as well as Bear Butte Lake, which covered over two hundred acres.

They set out again, the path growing steeper while uneven ground slowed their progress. About a quarter mile from camp they arrived at a ridge pocket where the ground leveled out. It provided a clear view to the east so he could see the sunrise, though sunset would be obstructed by the crags looming behind him.

"Consider it sunset and smoke when you are immersed in shadow," White Wolf instructed.

Charlie spread man sage on the ground where he would spend his fast.

"We will smoke together as soon as the sun appears, then Winter Hawk and I will return to camp to make the cloth offerings," White Wolf said.

White Wolf removed the stem to the sacred red pipe from its bag. He handed it to Charlie, who offered it in a circular arc overhead, then from his left over to his right.

As he held out his hand for the bowl, White Wolf hesitated. "Do you know why we do that?" he asked.

Charlie's hand dropped to his lap, mind cycling in vain. "It is what I remember Eaglefeathers doing. He swept it over his head to honor the circle of life, then from left to right to summon his spirit helpers."

"Many of our people do it that way, including Eaglefeathers, but that is not historically correct," White Wolf said. "I have studied our history and found differences. I prefer to do it as Sweet Medicine taught us. It is to honor the *maheyuno*, the Sacred Persons who live at the four corners of the universe. Everything we do has meaning, Littlewolf. Every movement, gesture, and action associated with our ceremonies."

His spirit wilted at his ignorance, then he reminded himself White Wolf was his instructor. It was his duty to teach him these things and make sure he did everything correctly.

He swallowed his pride and responded, "Eaglefeathers spoke often of the Sacred Persons. As if they were close friends. Very close, like I was with Bryan. I am ashamed I do not remember their names."

"You must learn them now. They are very important. *Maheo* created them as special guardians of his creation. We make the food offering, *nivstanivoo*, to them, so they eat with us and bless us. The four Old Man Chiefs represent them here on earth."

"The *maheyuno* are associated with the sacred colors, yes?"

"That is correct. During the cloth healing ceremony, the colors honor, attract, and call upon them for their blessings. The cloth offerings we will make here are intended to do the same— beckon them to join us and those who sent them."

Charlie's soul stirred with the import of such a holy presence, should they accept the invitation.

"Their corners of the Universe are not the same as *Vehoe's* compass. Their directions are sacred and marked each year by the sunrise and sunset on the longest and shortest days of the year."

A pang of guilt struck that he'd mistakenly used compass directions. "I pray they will forgive my mistake. I am grateful to learn the correct way. We make the motions facing east, yes?"

"Yes, we face east. Do not worry about your mistake if it was done with an honest heart. From that position the sacred directions are easily reached, between the compass directions.

"You start above your head, slightly to the right. Then behind your head on the same side over your shoulder. From there, over your head to the left and back to the left front, the motion in a sunwise direction."

He demonstrated, Charlie following the motions.

"Every holy man must know the *maheyuno* as he knows his brothers. He must know which one to call upon when he needs help." White Wolf's eyes drilled into his for a long moment. "This is something you must not only know, but feel."

He patted his chest. "You must hold it in here, as sacred knowledge."

Charlie mirrored the gesture, as if to open his heart to the gravity of his words.

"You must understand that to offer them the pipe means more than going through motions," White Wolf went on. "As you extend it in each direction, think of the Sacred Person who lives there. Invite each one to join you, from your heart. In your mind, call each by name. Ponder what he means. Why or how he might bless the reason you smoke."

Charlie imagined taking several minutes to do so rather than the few seconds it consumed in the past. White Wolf smiled, reading his mind.

"Take your time as you come to know them, Littlewolf. It is worth it. They become sacred allies who are always with you. A rare few have seen them in visions as horned men on horseback. You will know which one by his color."

Again, Charlie's bosom burned with truth.

White Wolf's dark eyes probed his. "I will now introduce you. The first is *Esseneta'he*. He guards the Southeast. His color is white. He rules over life. Light. Morning. Spring, and new life."

"The one healers would call upon most often, yes?" Charlie asked.

White Wolf nodded. "Next is *Sovota*. He guards the Southwest. He brings us warmth in the spring, also rain and thunder. Once again the grass grows. His color is red."

He paused a moment, allowing Charlie to absorb the words.

"*Onxsovon* guards the northwest where the summer sun sets," he continued. "His color is yellow. He brings perfection. Ripeness. Beauty in all its forms." His eyes and voice softened. "*Onxsovon* brought Star into my life."

Charlie's eyes teared up at the reverence and love in his voice when he spoke her name. When the time came to find a proper wife, he would know whom to consult.

When he was a foolish, rebellious teen refusing to complete his first ceremonial fast Eaglefeathers told him that he would marry a *kòhóméháe*, a coyote woman, who would trample his heart and turn on him like a rabid dog.

Which was exactly what happened.

His uncle cleared his throat. He dismissed the sordid memory and met his eyes in full attention.

"Then there is *Notamota* in the Northeast," he continued. "His color is black. He stands for coldness. Being stuck or cowardly. Storms, cold, snow, disease and even death."

Charlie's eyes narrowed, conflicted. "I thought black was the color of victory. Of burned villages and destruction."

"It is. If *Notamota* is properly honored and you fulfill your pledges and other sacrifices, that is what he delivers to your enemy. If you are not worthy, disrespectful, or a coward, then it comes to you."

"Oh."

The past twenty years of hardship imploded his heart. So that was *Notamota*, making his life difficult to beckon him back where he belonged.

Probably at Eaglefeathers' bidding.

Hackles covered Charlie's arms, punctuating another intuitive flash. "*Notamota* was who Black Cloud called upon to curse Dead Horse Canyon, yes?"

White Wolf nodded. "You are learning. That is good. You will know they are there for you when you carry them in your soul and no longer need to think about it. You will not only make offerings and fast for their assistance, but talk to them and seek their guidance as my father did. Their advice will run in the back of your mind in all things."

Which explained more deeply why Eaglefeathers said he'd never be alone if he followed *Maheo.*

"Then you offer the pipe with thoughts in your heart to *Maheo* above and Grandmother Earth, *Esceheman,* where our spirit helpers, the *maiyun,* live. Would you like to offer the pipe to them again?"

Charlie's spirit sagged beneath another heavy blast of humility. So much he didn't know. He felt gratitude for his blessings, but had not acknowledged them to the Sacred Persons as he should. All he'd done was lift the stem, and not even in the proper directions.

"Yes. I would like to do it correctly."

The corner of White Wolf's mouth twitched, as if suppressing a smile. "That is good. Let us make a new start."

"As Chief Morning Star wanted," Winter Hawk added.

"Yes," his father agreed, smile breaking through.

They sat on the man sage cross-legged facing east. Again, White Wolf handed Charlie the stem. He focused his thoughts as he held it aloft, speaking in his mind to each *Maheyuno* as he passed it to each one in the correct directions, then *Maheo* above and Grandmother Earth below.

He attached the bowl.

Loaded tobacco.

Lit the pipe.

Puffed slowly four times to bless the pipe, once for each *maheyuno.*

Blew the eagle bone whistle four times to summon the grandfather spirits.

Sacred vapors swirled upward, delivering his prayer to the Sacred Persons and *Maheo.*

"Great All Father, *Maheo.* It is with much humility that I stand before you here today on *Novavose.* I am most grateful to be here with White Wolf and my brother, Winter Hawk. We are thankful to be in this sacred place where our ancestors called upon you, including Sweet Medicine. I am humbled to be on this Sacred Mountain where he was given the Sacred Arrows.

"I am grateful for White Wolf's knowledge and his patience. For teaching me about your servants, the *maheyuno*. I ask forgiveness from *Esseneta'he, Sovota, Onxsovon* and *Notamota* for my mistakes in not honoring them correctly. I apologize for my ignorance. I meant no disrespect."

Regrets fell heavily upon him for his improper attempts and any offense they may have caused. He swallowed hard and continued, determined to make up for his previous faults.

"The purpose of my fast is to open my mind and spirit that I might learn who I am and how to serve you, the Sacred Persons, and my people.

"I pray that I might take Sweet Medicine's teachings into my heart, honor my ancestors and elders, and help restore my people to where they were before *veheo* robbed us of these sacred ways.

"Help me understand our ceremonies, their meaning, and purpose. I dedicate my life to you and restoring those things that have been taken away from our people."

When the tobacco was spent, he cleaned the pipe in the prescribed manner and replaced it in its bag while White Wolf issued more instructions.

"You will smoke at sunrise, noon, and sunset. Between those times, Littlewolf, you will remain on the man sage facing east. When the spirits come to get you don't be afraid to go with them. Do not question what they teach. Evil spirits will try to convince you to give up. Do not fear them. They cannot hurt you. Smudge yourself with sweetgrass when you need strength to keep going."

"Will I know whether they are good or evil?"

"Yes. By how they make you feel. Sweet Medicine brought us sweetgrass when he brought us the Sacred Arrows. Smudging with it cleanses your body and soul. Evil spirits are repelled by it. Use it generously, especially when you are feeling weak and discouraged."

The ground beneath Charlie rumbled.

A deep voice erupted in his head: *"*Novavose *is 'the hill where the People are taught.' That is why you are here. It is sacred ground, where* Maheo *taught Sweet Medicine how the Cheyennes should live. It was here he was given the sacred arrows wrapped in a kit fox skin quiver."*

White Wolf's eyes remained fixed on his own with no apparent reaction.

Had he not heard the voice?

"Here are Eaglefeathers' buffalo robe, medicine bundle, and a sweetgrass braid," White Wolf said, placing them beside him. "You are in *Maheo's* hands. We will check on you only as the grandfather spirits direct."

Later, I found that old man Thunder is ruler of the universe. He sits at the head of the lodge. He pities nobody. He hasn't any pity in his heart. Yet, out of respect for this ceremony, he must have reconsidered.
—William Tall Bull in "Sweet Medicine" Volume I, p. 381

16. CAPTIVE

WOODLAND PLACE
BOULDER, COLORADO
August 27, Monday
9:50 a.m. MDT

Sara eyed her captor, seated in an armchair across the room. A laptop computer occupied the chair's ottoman, what looked like a nine-millimeter pistol on the table beside him. He wore the hint of a smile, eyes fixed on the screen.

At least he'd been decent enough to let her have her wheelchair back, probably so he wouldn't have to help her to the bathroom. Thank heaven she had enough arm strength to transfer herself to and from the commode.

"Who are you?" she asked, glowering.

He didn't respond, attention fixed on the computer.

She ground her teeth.

Officer Leonard, indeed.

That highway patrolman was a fake, obvious when no report of her I-70 wreck with the eighteen-wheeler showed up. Nothing with the Lakewood police or state troopers. Not a single word, even though it was covered by local news, her car gone, never to be found.

How did he know about that? Did he see the wreck on TV? He wouldn't know about the fake trooper. If it was really him, why would he admit his part in that debacle?

Apparently, he was associated with that bunch who'd tried to kill her. Multiple times. While the others were aggressive, clumsy, and unprofessional, albeit deadly, his calmness suggested he knew exactly what he was doing.

Was he their handler? Finishing the job they botched?

Who was he working for?

What were his intentions?

Worth more dead or alive?

What was *that* supposed to mean?

Whoever it was, other than kidnapping and drugging her, he'd been a gentlemen. She marveled at the irony. It was obvious her abduction had been carefully planned, based on the size and accessibility of the bathroom. The furnishings were high quality, but too sterile for anyone's residence. Probably a condo rented out as a B&B.

All she could see from the window was a pine forested area with a backdrop of mountains. Generic Colorado, possibly even Boulder. Not enough visual information to identify exactly where she might be.

It was quiet. Obviously not a populated area where the rush of traffic or occasional horn added to the ambiance, like her condo. No sounds of car doors slamming, voices, or other noises that indicated the proximity of people, either.

Screaming for help would be to no avail.

While she was in the bathroom he'd ditched the trooper uniform in favor of a pair of designer jeans and a white shirt, sleeves rolled up to the elbows, hair no longer slicked back, but more casual with a touch of curl.

That ploy with the uniform gave her the chills. What was the point? Playing cat and mouse? Some mind game or sick psyop?

Her stomach clenched at the multitude of unknowns. But in truth, only a fraction was directed at her abductor's strange behavior.

Being so vulnerable was the greater part of her anxiety. Rage ignited in her chest at the person who poisoned her, causing her paralysis. The majority, however, was self-directed, trickling inside her mind like a slow leak.

Her entire situation was facilitated by her own foolish mistakes.

What an idiot!

Her father would never let her live it down. All his reminders ignored:

Maintain situational awareness.

Don't be so trusting.

Keep your phone and Glock within reach at all times.

Critical advice ignored as if she were a rebellious teen. If she'd practiced any of them she wouldn't be in this potentially lethal situation.

What was wrong with her?

Being over-confident at regaining some independence had backfired, landing her in that recliner where she'd spent the night, emphasizing her helplessness to the point she had to forcefully restrain the scream clawing at her throat for release.

While her captor was clearly in charge, so far he hadn't been threatening since that "dead or alive" comment. For some reason she wasn't afraid. Like when those obnoxious mercenaries invaded her cabin two months before.

Was it simply a ploy to avoid dealing with an hysterical woman?

Only about money?

Or something else?

She skewered him with an unflinching look. "What do you want from me?"

He closed the laptop and leaned forward, elbows resting on his knees.

"As you're certainly aware, there are people out there who want you dead. I know who they are and they're willing to pay. A lot."

Her eyes narrowed. "So it's about money."

He paused as if he hadn't thought about that before, then eventually nodded. "Pretty much."

"So it doesn't matter where it comes from? Them? Or me?"

He held her gaze. "Yes and no. It's simpler if I kill you and collect on the contract. That way you can't identify me. With a seven-figure bounty on your pretty head, there would be plenty of suspects."

Her breaths came rapid and shallow as a renewed wave of fear fell upon her as a phantom in the dark of night. His cool demeanor was somehow more frightening than when Johannsen and his band of Rambo wannabes rushed her cabin. Then again, at that time she wasn't alone and her legs hadn't abandoned their post.

"What if, uh, what if I promise not to identify you? Pay my own ransom?"

"That's why you're still alive."

The glimmer of hope was short lived, disappearing as sparks spewing from an open fire. "How do I know you won't kill me anyway?"

He leaned back in his chair and laughed. "You'll have to trust me."

"Yeah, right," she said, rolling her eyes. "That's a classic line if I ever heard one."

He took out his phone, swiped the screen a few times, then got up and handed it to her. "Here. Check this out."

Her heart seized up.

A photo of her on the patio at her father's, sitting in her mother's old wheelchair. Taken from an elevated vantage point.

How?

A drone?

He loomed beside her. "Just so you know. I had you in the sights of my .308. I just want the money, Sara. Either from the people who have a price on your head or directly from you."

Her hand shook as she handed it back, any composure she'd displayed so far stolen. She'd been the proverbial sitting duck, blissfully unaware of mortal danger. She swallowed hard, heart racing, defying her best efforts to suppress her reaction.

"Maybe you plan to collect both," she said, voice tremulous.

He exhaled through his nose. "Tempting, true. But too much trouble. I don't even know if they'd pay up."

"Who's *they*? And who are you?"

He pulled over the footrest from his chair and sat beside her. "I can't tell you that."

"Why not? Don't I have the right to know who wants me dead?"

He wore a condescending look that implied she was dumb as a rock. "What would you do if I told you? Call the FBI? You're public enemy number one with just about everyone in D.C. I guarantee absolutely no one there would help you."

"So they hired you?"

"No. They hired Keller. But he didn't finish the job. He's locked up on conspiracy charges. He's heading back to prison real soon."

She cocked her head, confused. "Who's Keller? I thought the guy trying to kill me was Eddie Johannsen."

"He worked for Keller."

"Oh." She exhaled slowly. "So who are you?"

"Right now?" He smiled. "I'm your best friend and worst enemy."

"Haha. Don't you have a name?" She shot him another sour look.

He laughed so hard he snorted. "Several, actually. An entire Rolodex full. Which one would you like?"

"Your real one." Her eyes narrowed. "Are you Keller's handler?"

He paused, eyes steady. "Actually, yes. Helped out a few times. Bunch of over-confident amateurs."

"Huh. Exactly what my father said."

"When they got outside their skill set, I provided the necessary resources."

"Nice. So where'd they get the poison? From what I heard it was pretty exotic stuff."

"Designer poison dated back to the Cold War. Years ago, some KGB agent needed money to defect. Got it cheap. Been sitting in a CIA warehouse in Maryland."

A volatile mix of fury and outrage fired through her like the IEDs Bryan told her about when he was on active duty. Too much to contain, she spat out the words, fingernails impaling the wheelchair's padded armrests.

"*You?* They got it from *you*? *Oh, my God!* You did this to me? You rotten beast!"

He held up his hands. "Listen. I just gave it to Johannsen. Told him how to use it. Apparently, he messed up—again—or you'd be dead."

"Lucky me," she snarled.

"It was nothing personal, Sara."

"Yeah, yeah. Just doing your job." She ground her teeth.

"Exactly."

"What is *wrong* with you, doing this to people?" she yelled, fury accelerating like pure oxygen feeding a fire. "What kind of horrible person does stuff like that? People like you are what's wrong with this planet!"

He stood there a moment before answering. "I don't know, Sara. At some point we get too far down the rabbit hole. It's a tight place to turn around."

His cool reaction reminded her of Bryan. He'd let her rant and vent, waiting until she'd calmed down enough to discuss the issue in a civilized manner. Oddly enough, he often referred to being down the *rabbit hole*, too.

Weird.

In fact, whoever this guy was, he reminded her of Bryan.

A lot.

So much so it gave her the creeps.

Same build, same color hair and eyes.

Similar mannerisms.

Could pass for his brother.

When she'd retrieved Bryan's personal effects at the credit union they said the guy who picked them up claimed to be and looked convincingly like his brother. Then there was the guy they hired to take his place, some obnoxious dude from Maryland whom she suspected was CIA. The same guy, perhaps?

"Oh, my God!" she gasped. "You're, you're Jason LaGrange. Wow!"

His only reaction was a small twitch in the corner of his mouth.

"Very good, Sara. What tipped you off?"

"It doesn't matter." For some strange reason knowing who he was brought an unexpected sense of relief. "Have you contacted my father yet?"

"No."

"You need to. He must be frantic. Let me talk to him. *Please*. Let him know I'm okay. We'll pay you so you can let me go. C'mon, Jason. Let's get this over with."

"I want cash."

"A million dollars in *cash*? I suppose you want it all in unmarked twenty-dollar bills." She met his gaze. "Be serious. I'm sure we can transfer it to your bank."

"Surely you jest." He shook his head. "No."

"How about a postal money order? We'll leave the payee blank."

He doubled over, laughing. "They have a thousand-dollar limit, Sara."

"A certified check then. Made out to whomever you want. Don't you have an account in the Cayman Islands under one of your many pseudonyms? C'mon. Please. Let me call Dad. We'll figure it out."

"Yeah, yeah. I was just messing with you. I have an offshore account. But we don't need to involve your father, do we?"

She nodded. "Actually, we do. He's joint owner on my brokerage account. For this size of a withdrawal both signatures are required. And on top of that, I don't have the information I need to log in."

"Such as?"

"My password. I don't remember what it is. I was still recovering from my first wreck when we set it up."

"There's always a 'forgot password' option," he countered. "And it *is* you."

"True." She sighed with self-recrimination. "But there's a problem."

"What?" His eyes narrowed. "You don't want to?"

"At this point I don't care." She shook her head. "I really don't. I'm talking about two-step verification."

"Why's that a problem?"

She flinched, feeling like an idiot. "I, uh, don't have my phone."

He exhaled through his nose. "So? You've replaced it before. The process should be familiar."

"I was in the hospital. Dad took care of the particulars. And he had quite a time proving the situation without any of my ID."

"All minor problems. Besides, your purse is right here." He picked it up from beside his chair and handed it to her. "But it all takes time. At best, it will take a minimum of three to five business days. If it's in a brokerage account, you'll have to sell some assets, which can take a few days."

His eyes met hers as he exhaled through his nose. "You may as well get comfortable, Sara. I'll let you call your father. But you're not going anywhere until I have my money."

She narrowed her eyes and glared. "Really, Jason? I never would have guessed. How about I just write you an IOU? Or a credit card? I'll have to see about increasing my limit with Discover, though."

He almost smiled. "You're really quite the little spitfire, aren't you, Sara? No wonder you intimidated Johannsen. Pretty gutsy chick, especially from a wheelchair. You probably don't want to piss me off, sweetheart. I might rethink that .308."

NOVAVOSE FASTING SITE (Day 1 - Monday)
BEAR BUTTE STATE PARK
SOUTH DAKOTA
Sacred Mountain Time

CHARLIE SAT CROSS-LEGGED on the man sage, Sun high in the sky. He made the sacred motions, then smoked the sacred red pipe. He set it back against the buffalo skull, then held the eagle bone whistle to his lips and blew four times. High-pitched tones caught the breeze and soared skyward, echoes from surrounding cliffs and bluffs repeating the request.

He poured out his heart again in prayer. For Sara, his two daughters, White Wolf and his family, his people, and that he would learn what *Maheo* wanted him to do.

Sensing a presence, he open his eyes. Four white-tail deer, young does, stood before him. As he tried to discern their message, they transformed into beautiful Cheyenne maidens.

He blinked, confused. It made no sense. He bowed his head and closed his eyes as he resumed praying.

"*Maheo*, I do not understand. I did not come to ask for a companion. I am here to honor my elders, especially my grandfather, Eaglefeathers. I wish to learn from Sweet Medicine spirits. I pray for direction how to help my friend, Sara, as well as my people. Help me know what this vision is telling me."

No answer came, so again, he opened his eyes. The maidens lifted their arms to the sky, morphed into golden eagles and ascended one by one, forming a circle. They soared sun wise as eagles do, climbing higher and higher until they were mere dots that disappeared.

Surprised to have a vision so soon, especially one that made no sense, he resumed praying, this time in Cheyenne. He smoked again at sunset, blew the eagle bone whistle. Prayed until darkness fell, then laid down, covered himself with the buffalo robe, and fell asleep.

Moments later his eyes opened at the thunderous flapping of wings. A man-sized raptor silhouetted against the stars soared toward him, giant talons stretched toward the earth. As it landed the bird became a *Tsistsistas* warrior adorned with a headdress trailing a multitude of eagle feathers.

"Tósa'e nénêxhé'óhtse?" Charlie asked. "Where did you come from?"

"I come from the place of the dead, *Se'han nánêxhé'óhtse*. I am Whistling Elk," he answered. "I am here to teach you. Come, *Okohomoxhaahketa*. Bring Eaglefeathers' medicine bundle and the sacred red pipe. There is much to do."

He'd heard amazing stories about Whistling Elk's legacy. His soul warmed with humble gratitude that this great elder came from the afterlife to instruct him.

Engulfed by the vision, he followed in the dim light across rough terrain spotted with scruffy vegetation for over a mile. They passed looming pillars of rock, then descended a rocky slope to a narrow ridge that hugged a craggy formation overlooking the tarns below.

Heights never bothered Charlie before, but the drop-off far exceeded the three- or more hundred-foot depth of Dead Horse Canyon. Unprecedented fear gripped his chest as he concentrated on the path, watching every step, caution separating him several yards from his mysterious guide. Up ahead the path made a hard left, causing him to lose sight of his escort.

He hastened his steps. Upon making the turn he faced the entrance to a cave.

White Wolf told him nearly a hundred years before a group of Cheyenne tried to find the opening to the cave where Sweet Medicine communed with *Maheo* and received *Mahuts*, the sacred arrows.

Could this be it?

The opening faced west, as tradition stated, but no rock obstructed the entrance.

He stepped inside, heart racing.

As his eyes probed the darkness, three passageways resolved. The first lay straight ahead, others angled off to each side.

The one before him glowed red.

On the left, white.

To the right, yellow.

Impressions came at the speed of thought.

Maheyuno's directions.

Sovota, red.

Esseneta'he, white.

Onxsovon, yellow.

Where was *Notamota's*?

Behind you.

Hackles teased the back of his neck.

Going back brought death, storms, cold, and disease.

Whistling Elk spoke his name from behind. He spun around.

"You are here so we may respond to prayers made in this holy place," the elder said. "Your requests are many. But *Maheo* agrees they are righteous desires that benefit others rather than yourself. *Maiyuns* heard your words and are here to assist."

Charlie's mind tumbled through what those prayers addressed. Everything from Sara's health and safety to helping his people. That they'd been heard wasn't surprising, but being answered so directly was.

"Some take time, some eternity," Whistling Elk explained. "Some bound to *Esceheman,* our Earth Mother. Others stretch beyond. To help your brother's widow, Sara, first you must sacrifice your flesh."

His back straightened as he mustered his courage, ready to do whatever was necessary.

"What must I do?" he asked.

"As others before you, pledge ceremonies."

The sacrifice that came to mind was a Sun Dance. Such would prove his sincerity for walking the red road. A step toward redeeming himself from previous failures and blatant mistakes. A suitable response to dubious looks from the four Society members at the rez who knew he hadn't completed his vow with his grandfather in the past.

He hugged Eaglefeathers' medicine bundle to his chest, love and approval issuing from it, a paternal version of *Amasani's* precious blanket.

"I vow before you and *Maheo* that I will complete a Sun Dance."

Whistling Elk's nod was solemn. "That is good. It need not be done at this time. But if you fail to complete it within a year, consequences are harsh."

The price of failure after walking away from his fast with Eaglefeathers still stung. *Maheo* and his servants, the *Maheyuno* and *Maiyun,* did not tolerate mockery by weak, insincere pledgers.

He nodded understanding.

The elder gestured toward the white light.

He summoned courage from the depths of his soul, then stepped within the passageway's misty depths.

Later they described Sweet Medicine's pilgrimage to the Sacred Mountain. . .Yellow Nose
and the others hunted for the door through which Sweet Medicine had entered the lodge
in the mountain, but they were unable to find it. — Peter John Powell, "Sweet Medicine,"
Volume 1, p. 416

17. IN PLAIN SIGHT

MONTGOMERY RESIDENCE
BOULDER, COLORADO
August 27, Monday
3:15 p.m. MDT

"Dad? This is Sara."

Will nearly dropped the phone, heart slamming into his throat. He didn't recognize the number, in which case he normally wouldn't answer except for anticipating such a call.

"Sara!"

He swung around in his leather office chair, shifting his view from his computer screen to the window over the couch. "Where are you? Are you okay?"

Her response was prefaced by a bitter burst of mirthless humor.

"In a manner of speaking. I've been kidnapped."

"That's what I figured. Okay. So now we know." Questions fought each other to get out that he'd fretted about for days. "What are the demands? What do I need to do? Are you okay? Where are you?"

"One thing at a time, Dad. I have no idea where I am, but I'm safe."

His gut relaxed with momentary relief. At least she was alive. Now to find out what it would take to get her released. "What does he want?"

"He wants a million dollars transferred to his Cayman Islands account," she replied. "When that's confirmed, he'll let me go."

She sounded too calm. Was it really her? Or some fake, computer synthesized voice? What was something a stranger wouldn't know?

"What's your dog's name, Sara?" he asked, unable to think of anything else. "I can't remember."

"Oh, Dad, of course you can. You're just testing me. Yes, it's me. Her name is Blossom. And I miss her. Is she okay?"

"She's fine. Misses you, too. She's been pacing non-stop since we picked her up."

A man's voice in the background said, "Alright. That's enough. Tell him we'll be back in touch."

"Wait! Wait!" Will exclaimed, hoping to hang onto the call long enough to trace it. "What do you want me to do?"

"You're joint owner on my brokerage account. Do whatever's necessary to withdraw a million dollars."

The connection ended.

Will gritted his teeth. The call lasted under a minute. No doubt it was a burner. He brought up the number it came from, then switched to an app that traced its location.

He tapped in 207-555-2839.

Gnawed his lip while it processed.

Damn! rubbed his forehead in denial. No way Sara was in Newport, Maine.

Could she be? *Nah.*

The guy either spoofed the number or it was built into the burner.

So much for that.

He exhaled hard, eyes fixed on a magpie in the tree outside while his mind took off in a marathon race for what he should do.

At least she sounded okay. Of course, being paraplegic, it's not like she could run away. Even if he knew where she was, a rescue would be difficult. And risky. He notified the police the day before, but doubted they'd do anything. It's not like he had any concrete clues, other than confirmation she'd been abducted and ransom demanded.

Connie appeared in the doorway carrying a tray with their mid-afternoon snack. Green eyes searched his.

"What's wrong? Did you hear from Sara?"

He swiveled in her direction and nodded. "She just called. She's okay, but he wants a million dollars. She doesn't know where she is and I'm sure she wouldn't be allowed to tell me if she did. I traced the number, but it was obviously a burner. Came up Newport, Maine."

She came into the room, setting the tray on the coffee table as she dropped down on the couch. "I know it's a long shot, but I wonder if Patrice could figure out where she is?"

He wouldn't have thought of that in a thousand years, yet it made sense. "You know, if you'd suggested that six months ago, woman, I'd think you'd lost your mind. But given her track record with her woo-woo craft, that just might work."

"I'll call her," she said, grabbing her phone from beside their croissants and making the call.

"Oh, no," she said, faced etched with disappointment. "It went to phone mail. She must be with a client." Her voice quivered as she left a message:

"Hi, Patrice. This is Connie. I need a rush horary, please. Sara's been kidnapped. She called to say she's okay, said they want a million dollars, but that's all we know. We're wondering what you can tell us. Where she is, if she's safe, whatever you see. Time is 3:20, today. Monday."

NOVAVOSE (Day 1 - Monday Night)
BEAR BUTTE STATE PARK
SOUTH DAKOTA
Sacred Mountain Time

THE CHAMBER'S ENERGY struck like a lance. Charlie's entire body sensed it, similar to finding the location of that oil deposit months before.

Those instances when he used his gifted eyes to look back in time, the sensation was also similar. Did time even exist for the Creator? Or within the bowels of the Earth Mother?

Is this what *Maheo's* presence felt like?

The aura that surrounded objects linked with time was absent. Instead, prismatic waves danced in a cloud of ethereal fog. Stranger yet, his gut sensed it awaited a command.

Was he in his body or spirit? Was this a dream with his body still on the bed of man sage?

Whistling Elk's eyes locked on his. "*Omotome*, the mortal gift of breath, and your immortal *hematasoomao*, are still as one. But you are not focused on what is most important for our people," he said. "It must be resolved."

The cavern's energy matrix churned, materializing in a vision.

Sara in a wheelchair, captor standing across from her. She appeared unharmed. The guy didn't look familiar.

"Is this what is blocking you from your true purpose, Littlewolf?"

His heart sagged with perceived guilt. "Yes. She occupies my mind. I am concerned we were unable to heal her from her injuries. Then, as we were coming here, I learned she'd been kidnapped. I am very worried. Yes, helping her is of great importance to me."

"Open your grandfather's medicine bundle."

Unsure where this was going, he scowled as he obeyed.

"Have you examined all it contains?"

"No."

"Then do so now."

Chills climbed his spine as he sat cross-legged on the frigid stone. He lifted the medicine bag from the larger bundle and untied its flap, releasing the eclectic scent of multiple remedies. He removed each of the pouches and lined them up beside him.

Bear root.

Bitter root.

Peppermint.

Big medicine.

Several more he couldn't name, purposes unknown.

He set the last one beside the others. No impression or intuitive flash impressed his mind.

Clueless what to do next, questioning eyes connected to Whistling Elk's knowing ones.

"Now search the bundle itself."

He remained mystified as he felt around inside. The bottom didn't feel right. Lumpy, as if something else were inside. Probing deeper, he found a concealed knot beneath a flap. He untied it by touch and plunged probing fingers within.

His hand recoiled, a fearful cry stuck in his chest. Whatever was in there was cold, slick, and scaly. Whistling Elk's nod provided courage to continue. Cautious fingers returned within and carefully removed a snakeskin pouch secured with a leather thong.

He held it up. "What is this?"

"You don't know?" The elder almost looked as if he were about to laugh.

Charlie squinted at the pouch, then back at Whistling Elk. "No," he admitted. "I do not."

"It is medicine to restore your friend's ability to walk."

His mouth opened and closed a few times like a freshly hooked river trout. "How is that possible?" he spit out.

"Eaglefeathers was a prophet. He knew it would be needed at this time, but hid it such that you would have to come to *Novavose* to find it."

"How will I get it to her?"

The elder's chest lifted, then dropped with a long, measured sigh, much as Eaglefeathers used to do. "You have much to learn, Littlewolf. Nothing is impossible for *Maheo* and his *maheyuno*."

MONTGOMERY RESIDENCE

BOULDER, COLORADO
August 27, Monday
5:09 p.m. MDT

CONNIE GRABBED HER ringing cell phone from the kitchen counter, fumbling with nervous anticipation.

"Patrice?"

"Hi, Connie. I apologize for the delay. I was with a client and just got your message. I'm running the chart now."

"Thank you! Hopefully it tells us something useful." She exhaled, hand on her chest.

"Give me a moment to see what it says."

"Of course. I'm putting you on speaker. I'm here with Will." She sat down at the breakfast table and set her phone between them.

What seemed hours later, Patrice was back.

"Okay, here's what it looks like. Sara's significator is in the eighth house, which includes intense potentially dangerous events and situations. That house is ruled by the Moon, which is in the second house of income and possessions, which points toward the kidnapper's demand for ransom. Definitely fits the circumstances."

"Can you tell if she's okay?" Her eyes locked with Will's, as wide as her own.

"I believe so. There's no indication she's hurt or will be. If he were going to hurt her, he probably would have done so already. He just wants the ransom, and may be willing to negotiate. He has plans for the money, something related to his work or ambitions."

"You're sure he won't hurt her?" She bit her lip, hoping.

"I don't think so, but you never know. It appears there will be sudden changes or upsets in the situation before it's resolved. Someone gets hurt or disappointed, physically or emotionally, but I don't think it's Sara."

Connie's fingers flexed into tight balls. "I sure hope you're right!"

"Me, too. The event is heavily fated. Pluto says some strange circumstance links them together, something from the past. Mars rules the fourth of endings. He's retrograde in the second house, which suggests things will return to where they were."

"What do you think that means?" Connie asked, sharing Will's puzzled look.

"I'm not sure. Mars retrograde often brings regret for impulsive actions. You may actually recover the money. He also rules the eleventh house of groups and goals as well as the twelfth of seclusion and hidden enemies. That implies her abductor's plan may not work out as expected. There's a lot going on here, that's for sure. Obviously not a random event."

"No," Will stated. "It bears the signature of an abduction orchestrated by a professional. I suspect he was watching her, caused the flat, and took it from there. She called On*Star to fix it, then cancelled. When we talked to the man who took the call, he said someone showed up to help."

"How convenient," Connie quipped, shaking her head.

"Neptune confirms there was deception involved," Patrice commented.

"Can you tell where she might be?" Connie asked, fingers crossed.

"According to the chart, somewhere toward the southwest. Obviously out of sight, possibly a rural area or a park, somewhere with lots of trees."

"Should we attempt a rescue?" Will asked, straightening in his chair.

A pause. "It's not clear you'd be able to find her. My impression is something unexpected will bring it to conclusion. Does Charlie know?"

"We're not sure," Will replied. "I texted him but haven't heard back."

"What should we do?" Connie asked, wringing her hands.

"Pray," Patrice replied. "Follow your instincts and pray that whatever that unexpected event might be brings her home."

The Cheyennes knew that Thunder was one of the rulers of the universe. They knew how to control nature through the ceremonies.
—Peter John Powell, "Sweet Medicine," Volume 1, p. 375

18. PONDERINGS

WOODLAND PLACE
BOULDER, COLORADO
August 27, Monday
7:50 p.m. MDT

Jason's NSA training was such he knew Sara was telling the truth. At least she believed she was. Which didn't make it any less troubling. Limitations on withdrawals from her brokerage account had not entered his mind. He knew she had the money, but failed to consider how liquid or accessible it was.

How long would it take? Should he lower the ransom? Would it make that much difference? Or was Option One—killing her—what he needed to do? There were a multitude of other means besides his .308. It's not like he'd never taken a life before in a more subtle manner.

He took a pensive sip from his third cup of coffee. She sat gazing out the window from her wheelchair, either watching the sun drop behind the mountains or trying to figure out where she was. Didn't matter if she did.

He chuckled.

It's not like she could run away.

The fact she didn't have her phone was sheer luck. It would be a cinch for them to find her if she did.

He could tell she was miserable and bored with the delays, which were grating on his nerves as well. He wasn't a particularly patient person once he made up his mind, and apparently she was much the same.

He sucked in his upper lip. Even more troubling, he was starting to like her. Most women lacked the ability to display spunk without being an obnoxious bitch. The majority of female operatives he knew had a bigger set of balls than many of their male counterparts and exploited it. A gigantic put-off.

Somehow Sara Reynolds mastered it, better than anyone he'd ever known. She was intelligent, quite pretty, definitely feminine, but quick-witted, sarcastic, amazingly courageous, and seemed to be able to read his mind.

Kind of like that chick in *Tomb Raider*.

An actuator hummed as she shifted the wheelchair slightly so her back was to him. She slumped over, shoulders trembling as she buried her face in her hands.

Was she having a meltdown?

For some unknown reason, it tugged at his heart. "I have no intention of hurting you, Sara," he said gently.

She sniffed hard, back still turned when she responded.

"You already did. You're the reason I'm in this wheelchair. I was just getting a grip on my life, reclaiming some independence. Then there you are again, reminding me how helpless I really am."

Another sob interrupted her soliloquy. She wiped her eyes with her hand, then another hum as she swiveled to confront him.

"If you killed me you'd do me a favor. I'm not afraid to die, Jason. I already have. Twice, actually. Once thanks to you. And this is worse than death."

Something that resembled guilt landed in his solar plexus with a *splat*, making him feel like a totally worthless piece of crap.

She punctuated her statement with a tearful glare, then turned back toward the window.

This was not good. His resolve was crumbling. What should he do? He was counting on that money, one way or another. He needed it.

Or did he?

Did he *really* want to run an operation like Keller? Sure, he had the experience and talent, but was that really what he wanted to do for a living?

This last gig with the NSA exposed the dirty underbelly of too many government agencies. The Alphabet Agencies were always sketchy, worse now than ever before. Intruding on other country's affairs, manipulating elections to suit the powers that be, and killing off political opponents to say nothing of whistleblowers had little if any justification, much less honor.

Actions reminiscent of dictator-run Third World countries. Some dictators were better than a plethora of elected officials, many of whom he could name.

Whether a country or its culture was good or bad was subjective, with a few rare exceptions. A matter of opinion, to say nothing of it being no business of whomever occupied the White House.

He thought back to why he signed up in the first place. Lured by the prospect of the different roles he could play. He had a passion for acting, yet hadn't been able to prove his abilities in high school or college, always losing the good roles to some teacher's pet.

Acting in real life had an element of excitement that gave him a better high than any drug, something he avoided. Having his mind intact was essential. He rarely drank, only when he was alone, and usually when he questioned his life decisions.

Did that Rolodex of personalities imply talent? Or psychosis?

Some days he wasn't even sure who he was anymore. He liked some of those characters he played better than who he actually was. He laughed to himself, having passports for all of them.

He thought back to taking Bryan Reynolds' credit union job. The code that man fabricated was the most innovative he'd ever seen. Clever and effective. He learned so much from it, yet couldn't think of a single job more boring.

Doing that for a living would be like dying and going to hell. One of many careers he could do, and do well, but chose not to. No doubt sheer boredom led Reynolds to hacking for entertainment.

If anything, he was intrigued by his widow's mission to expose the corruption he found and for which he gave his life. How many females, much less those of his gender, would go to the lengths she had, been damn near killed multiple times, wound up a paraplegic, yet kept fighting?

She shouldn't be assassinated.

She should be cloned.

Or elected president.

He grabbed a paper towel from beside the kitchen sink and walked it over to her.

"Here."

She blew her nose and wiped her eyes. "What are you going to do with the money?"

He pursed his lips. "I don't know. Anything I want, I suppose."

"You really don't know?" Her brown eyes were wide, incredulous.

He worked his jaw, somehow feeling on the spot. "Not really. I have a few ideas, just haven't decided."

"Does that mean *maybe* we can negotiate the amount?"

"Maybe."

Now what? Was she laughing or crying?

"Remember that old 80s movie, *Ruthless People*?" she sputtered, confirming humor as opposed to despair.

"The one with Bette Midler and Danny DeVito?"

"That's the one. I used to watch old movies with my mom, after she got too sick to do anything else. We watched her favorites, over and over, and that was one of them. Remember when Sam kept reducing the ransom and Barbara started to cry, 'I've been kidnapped by K-Mart?'"

Jason laughed, remembering. For him the funniest part of that flick was the stupid duck costumes the abductors wore. "Right," he replied. "Is that a hint?"

"Maybe. Would you?"

"Very funny. My answer? *No.* But we're both bored, waiting on your father. Want to see if we can find it online?"

She stared at him, long and hard, wearing a look of stark disbelief.

"Sure. Why not? Doesn't look like I'm going anywhere, any time soon." She dropped the sarcasm and added, "Under one condition."

He studied her a moment. "What's that?"

"Popcorn. The real thing. Not microwave."

Real popcorn? How? What was that other stuff, fake?

"I don't know where I'd send Door Dash to get that," he replied, mystified. "Where do you get that? A movie theater?"

She rolled her eyes.

"No. It's not rocket science, Jason. A grocery store. Like Whole Foods. Ever been in one? Get organic popcorn kernels, avocado oil, and a big covered pan, if you don't have one. I'll teach you. And one more thing."

"Yes?"

"Are you killing me softly, Jason?"

Wow. This chick really can read my mind.

Whistling Elk used to be the man who made the pilgrimages. Now he is gone. Now the people feel it is necessary for someone to go back. They feel that time is an important factor now. Someone is being selected who has a lot of faith.
— Peter John Powell, "Sweet Medicine," Volume 1, p. 428

19. REVELATIONS

MONTGOMERY RESIDENCE
BOULDER, COLORADO
August 28, Tuesday
7:18 a.m. MDT

Connie turned from the stove where she was cooking French toast and sausage, their homey aromas incapable of relieving her stress. "Do you really think it's a good idea to lie about it, Will? We need to get her out of there as soon as possible."

"I agree. But she seems safe and I can't bring myself to sell these stocks while they're in such a slump. This bear market just isn't the time. Telling her there's a limit gives me a few days to optimize them, at least a little."

One hand parked on her hip while the other pointed the spatula. "Are you kidding? C'mon! She's ready to give away a million dollars to come home! What's losing a few thousand?"

His lips compressed to a line. "I know. Hopefully, tomorrow the market will recover a little. Even a few cents will make a difference for so many shares. Friday is usually the worst day to sell anything, so before then. Besides, maybe the delay will convince him to bring down how much he wants. Patrice thought he might negotiate."

Still holding the spatula, she stepped to the table. "Can I ask you something?"

He donned the poker face he used for such inquiries. "Do I have to answer?"

"Well, yes, that's the idea." She scowled, hoping it would evoke an honest answer. "I'd like an explanation for something I've been wondering about."

He folded his hands in his lap. "Okay. What do you want to know?"

Her hands dropped to her sides. "When did you suddenly decide Patrice was the real deal and worth listening to? I remember you rolling your eyes when you first found out about her."

His eyes remained steady as his jaw relaxed and he almost smiled. "She's been correct enough times to establish credibility. I guess she's helped me realize there's more to life than meets the eye."

She tilted her head, suspecting more. "Is that all? When she came to help with the healing ceremony I didn't expect you to give her such a warm welcome."

"Oh." He took a sip of coffee. "It was that obvious?"

"Yes. What was that about?"

He flattened his hands on the table. "Okay. I confess. When we were in New York, before Sara woke up, I called her. You'd mentioned how she helped you when Ellen died. I was hoping maybe she could help me deal with the situation."

"Oh. So I assume whatever she said helped?" He seldom surprised her, usually the epitome of predictability, but he'd always been a master at concealing his emotions.

He nodded. "Yes. She didn't say Sara would get well, but she put it into a different perspective. She was compassionate and understanding. A good person. She deserved my respect, even if I questioned the viability of her profession. Meanwhile, she's shown there's something to this woo-woo stuff, even if it defies logic."

She smiled, almost smugly, then turned back to the stove to load their plates.

"I'm glad you saw that. I never liked consulting her behind your back. So, back to Sara. I really think we should get her out of there as soon as we can. She's got to be very uncomfortable and worried. We don't know for sure he won't hurt her, especially if he gets impatient. I don't think she'd appreciate you delaying her release."

"True." He sipped his coffee, thought lines raking his forehead a good sign she was getting through. "You're probably right."

She set their food on the oak table, retrieved the coffee pot from the counter, and sat down across from him.

"Blossom is getting depressed," she stated, buttering her French toast. "Every time I look at her she whines, staring at me with those soulful eyes. Do you think there's any chance she could find her?"

As if sensing their conversation, the click of canine nails announced the dog's arrival. She butted Will's leg, to which he obediently scratched her head, then she sat down beside him.

Connie she sat up straight, mind cycling. "Patrice mentioned Sara is probably somewhere southwest of here, maybe around one of the parks or a place with lots of trees. That sounds like it could be right here in Boulder, perhaps at the base of the Flagstaffs, out by all those hiking trails."

His eyes met hers, then switched to the canine. "Who knows? Some believe dogs have psychic abilities." He grabbed the coffee pot and topped off his mug. "What do you suggest? Drive around and see if she reacts?"

"What would it hurt? It's driving me crazy sitting around here waiting. I can't even imagine how Sara must feel."

The dog's attention turned from one to the other, as if following the conversation.

"One problem." He worked his jaw. "'Southwest' encompasses the entire city of Boulder. 'Lots of trees' doesn't help much, either. Every street is loaded."

Connie mentally scanned the city she knew well. "Maybe around the University, or out Boulder Canyon. The Greenbelt, or even Green Mountain. There are hundreds of miles of hiking trails and remote areas all over. Eldo, even. Maybe she's not in Boulder. Ned is southwest of here, too," she went on.

He disagreed. "I don't think Eldorado Canyon has that many hotels or B&Bs. Nederland wouldn't be where an abductor would go to blend in. Too small."

"Okay, scratch that. Maybe the old part of town, around Chautauqua? Or out Sunshine Canyon?"

The pit bull's ears perked up, as if still engaged in the discussion.

"No telling," Will said. "Any of them would fit that description. Too vague. Even if, by some miracle, we figure out where she is, what can we do, woman?"

Connie gave him a blank look. "I don't know. Call the police?"

He shook his head. "No. Bad idea. As far as we know, right now she's not in danger. She didn't sound scared, plus what Patrice said. Any action, however, could change that. We have no idea what her abductor's like. He could be a total psycho."

Connie picked at her fingernails, worries demanding they do something, even if it was wrong. "I'd just feel better if we at least try, Will. Know where she is. Maybe keep an eye on the place to see if he leaves or moves her somewhere. Doesn't Mike live here? Maybe he could help or have an idea where to look."

He exhaled through his nose, her nervousness contagious. "Those are good points. I didn't even think of Mike, but he went back to Falcon Ridge to his old job when he moved out of the condo. Let's look at a map to get a bird's eye view. See if anything jumps out."

She picked up her tablet, always within reach. "I'll pull one up."

Blossom stood up, tail wagging for the first time in days.

SCENIC ROUTE
BOULDER, COLORADO
August 28, Tuesday
8:31 a.m. MDT

WEST OF BOULDER, the front range comprised massive slabs of sedimentary stone the locals called the *flatirons*, which rose skyward, dwarfing the buildings below. While often associated with the city, the metro portion was mostly on flat ground, where the Great Plains met the Rockies.

The Montgomery's were long-time residents who weren't exactly Boulderites, but "NoBos," local slang for those who lived on the north side, outside the heart of the city.

Will turned west on Lookout from their subdivision, then right on Sixty-Third for the Diagonal onramp that headed toward town. He stayed on it until he crossed the main part of the city, then eventually exited on West Baseline, one of the main drags in the vicinity of their assumed target.

His mind cycled through his knowledge of the area. If he were to abduct someone, where would he go? Probably a rental unit in a low traffic area. He didn't know where he was going, just cruising around, waiting for any intuitive nudges he was on the right track.

He hadn't used them much since leaving the FBI, where they served him well as an analyst.

Connie sat with Blossom in the Mercedes' backseat, watching her for any response. So far the dog only stared out the partially open window, attentive but unimpressed.

"Do you think she knows what we're doing?" Connie asked.

Will caught his wife's eyes in the rearview mirror. "I wouldn't doubt it. She probably wonders what took us so long. I'm sure she wanted to look for her days ago."

"True. She spent a lot of time by the door, whining, with that pleading look."

Over a dozen blocks of tree-lined streets filled with stately, beautifully landscaped homes defined the area. Not likely where Sara was, unless perchance her abductor lived around there. In which case, what idiot would take his victim to his home?

Usually, it was a remote, anonymous place, like an abandoned warehouse.

Which didn't fit for multiple reasons.

Sara didn't sound stressed, considering her condition necessitated considerable accommodations. That pointed toward a hotel or possibly B&B designed or at least equipped for the disabled.

They passed Chautauqua Park where the Colorado music festival was held, though all that was visible from the road was an ancient rock wall flanked by trees. If there was one thing Boulder had no shortage of, it was rocks, as its name suggested, and trees.

Over-sized rocks accented hilly yards along with flagstone patios and walkways. Neighborhoods boasted an aesthetic mix of majestic evergreens with deciduous oaks, aspens, maples, and box elders bunched together with junipers, ferns, and azaleas, some accented with decorative stone borders or wood privacy fences.

Homes went from elegant in Chautauqua to humbler in the University Hill area.

Still no reaction from the dog.

Will wound through neighborhood after neighborhood, finally arriving at the intersection of Boulder Canyon Drive and Sixth.

He wasn't sure what it was or why, but somehow it felt as if they were on the right track. In back, Connie eyebrows had that pensive crease between them while the pit bull's perked-up ears indicated full attention.

He crossed the main road, passed Pearl Street, and proceeded into the foothills where he continued to case neighborhoods. Homes were fewer, some elegant estates, an occasional country club or B&B obscured by looming trees and thick shrubbery that covered the changing terrain.

As the two-lane road skirted the base of the Flagstaffs he passed a small cluster of relatively new condos. Each was surrounded by generous green space and massive pines which scented the air, as if the contractor made an effort to preserve the privacy afforded by forest-like ambiance.

He let up on the gas, wondering.

Maybe. . .

He drove until he was out of sight of the buildings, then pulled off the pavement and stopped. An overgrown embankment eased down to what looked like a hiking trail that disappeared among the ubiquitous pines.

He jumped when Blossom let out a single bark, then sprang across the console into the front passenger seat, whining and pawing the window.

"Holy crap!" His gaze locked with his wife's. "I think we found her."

"Now what?" Connie asked, eyes wide.

That night the power of Box Elder's sacred wheel lance was proved to be strong. After Reynolds' attack, the blind priest invoked Ox-zem's concealing protection to cover the movements of the Cheyennes as they attempted to recapture their horses.
— Peter John Powell, "Sweet Medicine," Volume I, p. 99

20. DREAMS

WOODLAND PLACE
BOULDER, COLORADO
August 28, Tuesday
9:50 a.m. MDT

Sara had no reason to get up, so indulged herself by sleeping in. They stayed up late, watching *Ruthless People* as well as *The Bourne Identity*, for which Jason provided commentary of what was right and what was wrong with how it portrayed the CIA.

The smell of coffee was enticing, the pot programmed to brew before they retired, but easily ignored as she lay pondering a weird dream that lasted most of the night.

Shortly after she fell asleep, Charlie appeared from nowhere. The next thing she knew, she was in a cave. The chamber was charged with energy such as she'd never felt. It had this eerie, timeless quality, unlike any dream she'd ever had.

So vivid!

All her senses were sharper and more pronounced, where in most dreams they were muted. The fragrance of burning sweetgrass and sage that filled the air remained in memory, as if still on her clothes.

Throughout the night, he and a few elders sang a multitude of songs in their language. While she couldn't understand their words, the sentiment went straight to her heart. Echoes from the swishing rattles still played in her head, their sound as comforting as pouring rain.

The vanilla scent of sweetgrass was refreshed several times, often accompanied by them smoking a pipe, lending a hint of tobacco or some other herb to the air. While the other elders continued singing, he handed her some tea in a wood cup.

It was far more pleasant than bitter root, which wouldn't take much, considering that was the nastiest thing she'd ever consumed. Even its memory made her gag. What he gave her this time had a strong, acidic flavor, similar to vinegar, but sweeter, with herbal undertones. Upon drinking it her skin flushed as her entire body heated up, then broke into a profuse sweat.

Singing and rattling continued as he helped her turn over and lay face down on a buffalo robe. He told her to relax, explaining he was going to extract the remaining poison. His hands applied pressure to her hips, followed by a pinching sensation. It felt as if something tangible were being drawn out through the base of her spine, though it was more creepy than painful.

Her hands flew to her mouth when he came around in front of her and he spit out a writhing, black snake with red eyes, which he held up for her to see before throwing it into the fire.

After that, he rubbed her back, hips and buttocks with warm massage oil that had a strong pungent fragrance she couldn't identify. More singing, they smoked the pipe again, then all was quiet as he helped her to her feet.

The next thing she knew, she was back in bed, there in the condo.

It seemed so real. So much so, the potion's flavor lingered along with the hypnotic shadow of rattles and singing.

She reached around to her lower back, where it felt somewhat oily.

Then again, she'd been in the same clothes for over two days and could sure use a shower. She swore never to wear these clothes again when this was over. Maybe even burn them.

The real question was, what did it mean?

Had Charlie and White Wolf figured out what they needed to do so she could walk again?

She pushed herself to a sitting position with her elbows as she did every morning, then used her hands to lift each leg over the side of the bed. One armrest of the wheelchair was lowered and the brake set, the seat level with the mattress.

She scooted to the edge of the bed, grabbed the far armrest with her right hand and pushed off the bed with her left, sliding into the seat. She lowered the foot rests and lifted her right leg with her hands as she always did.

But something was different. Instead of dead weight, her leg cooperated. She let go, realizing she could lift her leg without assistance.

She froze.

Was that more than a dream? How could it be?

She elevated the footrests out of the way and set her bare feet on the hardwood floor. Used the armrests to brace herself as she rose to a standing position.

So far so good.

She turned toward the bed, hands on the mattress as she moved sideways, step by step.

After nearly a month of inactivity, atrophied muscles left her legs weak and shaky, but responding. She shuffled back to the wheelchair, using it like a walker to further test her legs. They moved as commanded as she stepped around the room, though her knees felt rubbery.

As a physical therapist, her thoughts flew instantly to what exercises she'd do to rebuild their strength.

About then full comprehension struck.

She sat on the bed, buried her face in her hands, and sobbed until her joy evolved to near-hysterical giggles. She covered her mouth with both hands, not wanting to draw attention.

Now what?

Since giving back her wheelchair, Jason hadn't left. When she was confined to the recliner, he knew she couldn't go anywhere, and went out for food a couple times.

How could she convince him to leave, even for a short errand? Just long enough to escape?

Her breath caught in her throat when he called from the next room.

"Sara! Come here!"

She swallowed hard. Was there surveillance in her room? Did he know?

"Sara! What have you done to me?"

Her mind cycled. What on earth was he talking about? She got into the wheelchair and guided it into the living area.

He wasn't there.

"Sara! Where are you?"

She directed the wheelchair to his bedroom and knocked. "What's wrong?"

"I can't see! What have you done? What did you put in that popcorn?"

What on earth was he talking about?

"Be serious. You ordered it and watched me make it. The butter came from the fridge. What could I have possibly put in it to blind you?"

"Get in here!"

Slowly, she opened the door. Morning light streamed through the drapes. He sat on the edge of the bed in his underwear, sightless eyes staring straight ahead, face saturated with panic.

"You really can't see?" she asked. "What do you want me to do? Call an ambulance?"

He shook his head. "I don't know. I had this strange dream. Your Indian friend was there with someone else. He told me I had to let you go. I laughed. Then another Indian was dancing, one foot in front of the other, pointing these arrows at me. Thrusting them in my direction. He kept singing, 'There you lie helpless easily to be wiped out.' Repeated it several times. When I woke up I couldn't see. What the hell is going on? What was in that popcorn?"

"I don't know, Jason. I ate as much as you and I'm fine."

She was fine, alright. She bit back an incredulous laugh, as astounded by his condition as she was by her own.

"I'm getting a cup of coffee. Do you want one?"

"No. I don't want a cup of coffee. I want to know what the hell is going on!"

"I have no idea. If you change your mind on the coffee, let me know."

She sucked in her lips, wondering. Could he hear the grin in her voice? So what if he could? The smile stretched until it hurt.

My, oh, my, how the tables have turned.

In case he was lying, she cruised out of his room in the wheelchair, abandoning it as soon as she closed his door.

While her thoughts rumbled in their quest for an escape plan, she tiptoed back to her room to get her purse. Every inch of the condo was familiar after being confined there for a couple days, bored to tears. There were two exits, the front door in the living room and back door in the kitchen.

The car keys were on a hook by another door in the laundry room that led to the garage. The garage opened to the same side of the condo as the front door.

No point wasting any time, in case his condition was temporary. She tiptoed to the laundry room.

The keys were there.

Her vision tunneled, then blurred, knees threatening to fail.

Panic surged.

Oh, my God!

Was it really the popcorn? Was she next?

You're hyperventilating, stupid! Calm down!

She steadied herself against the washing machine and closed her eyes.

Inhale. Deep and slow. Hold for the count of ten. One, two, three, four. . .. It's okay. You've got this.

Gradually, her adrenaline-fired vitals slowed from panic mode.

Her eyes opened.

Her vision was clear.

Another deep breath, hands over her heart.

Whew.

She grabbed the keys and opened the door. The car beckoned. She flipped the switch next to the door and the garage door hummed upward.

Muffled protests came from down the hall.

"Sara! What are you doing?"

Then he laughed. "Very funny! What are you going to do, drive away? Good luck!"

Surprise! she thought.

It was a different car than before. She got inside and slipped the key in the ignition. The dashboard lit up, including the media center. It contained a keyboard and fingerprint sensor that flashed "CONFIRM IDENTITY/ENTER PASSCODE" while a robotic female voice repeated the message, evoking a cry of exasperation.

Of course. Any former agent from a spy organization would protect his vehicle from would-be thieves.

The screen went dark and silent.

The garage door hummed closed.

A countdown clock appeared, starting at sixty.

She swallowed hard.

Would it lock her inside? *Blow Up?*

She couldn't get out fast enough, no choice but to go back inside.

Shuffling sounds came from down the hall.

"Sara! Where are you? *What do you think you're doing?*"

A racket followed, accompanied by a litany of curses climaxed by a loud thud.

She giggled in spite of the fact finding her abandoned wheelchair meant her secret was out.

To get to the front door she had to go past the hall where he was, blind or not. Heart hammering again, she hustled to the kitchen and slipped outside, easing the door closed behind her.

A cozy flagstone patio enclosed by a six-foot privacy fence awaited awash in pine-scented air.

A boxwood hedge lined the perimeter along with columbines, chrysanthemums, and a young red maple in one corner. Hope soared when she spotted a gate, uttered a silent prayer it wasn't locked.

The smooth stones were cool beneath her bare feet as she stepped over to check, relieved when it opened. It clicked shut behind her, to what she hoped was freedom. A walkway constructed from the same flat rocks extended in both directions.

Which way?

As far away as possible made the most sense, but how far she could go was questionable. Her knees were shaking, panic surfacing again. Where she was, how far from assistance, or means to call for help threw red flags to her sense of freedom.

Maybe she should circle back around front and follow the driveway, which would certainly lead to a road at some point.

A friendly, familiar, yet unexpected sound caught her attention, from beyond the trees.

There'd never been any outside noise. No voices, car doors, ambient neighborhood sounds. Wildlife activity was limited to birds, most notably a woodpecker that hung out in the cottonwood outside the living room window.

Not a single sound that indicated the presence of any neighbors. But there was no mistaking what she heard:

Barking.

Either someone lived nearby who had a dog or was out for a hike.

Perfect!

Or was it Jason's? A guard dog to keep her from getting away? Finding her if she did?

If so, why wouldn't it have been on the patio?

Dismissing the paranoia, she made her way down the path in that direction.

That dog was definitely trying to tell its owner something.

An ancient poplar tree, tall arbor vitaes, and sprawling junipers blocked her view. She walked slowly and cautiously toward the sound, rough surface hurting the soles of her feet.

Past a grove of aspens surrounded by white azaleas sprawled a clearing, beyond which the path disappeared among the evergreens.

To the right, an incline inundated with overgrown weeds led up to what appeared to be a road. Apparently, the unit where she'd been detained was in the far back of the complex's property.

The volume of the barking increased as she plodded a bit farther, trying to see if anything was up there. Walking barefoot through those weeds had less appeal than the pathway, which surely led somewhere.

Then she saw it.

She froze, incredulous.

Her father's silver Mercedes, Blossom barking frantically from the passenger seat, muzzle protruding from the open window.

A familiar figure exited from the back, mouth agape.

Tears gushed from her eyes as her dog bounded over the seat and out the rear door, nearly knocking Connie over. Her bark changed pitch from alarm to a joyful greeting as she plunged through the brush.

Sara crouched down to greet her, but her knees failed. She landed on her butt just as the dog fell upon her with a profusion of sloppy doggie kisses.

She wrapped her hands around her thick canine neck and they bumped foreheads as they'd done since they met. She scratched her behind the ears, the pitty whining and yelping with sheer delight.

Dazed by all that had happened since waking up, she knew only one thing: If this was only a dream, she definitely didn't want to wake up.

◆ ◆ ◆

NOVAVOSE (Day 2 - pre-dawn Tuesday)
BEAR BUTTE STATE PARK
SOUTH DAKOTA
Sacred Mountain Time

"YOUR FRIEND IS NOW healed and back with her family," Whistling Elk said. "Now we can proceed. There is much you must learn to help our people."

Charlie and Whistling Elk sat before the fire in the center of the cave. Dancing flames sent sparks soaring upward toward the chamber's ceiling far above, much as his spirit's elation.

He hadn't realized how much Sara's condition contributed to his anxiety until it was gone. Knowing Sara was safe lifted a heavy burden, especially knowing she was now on the way to being healed. She'd still benefit from a sweat, but the fact she could walk again was a substantial relief.

As he basked in success coupled with the new things he'd learned, what the elder was referring to teased his mind.

What exactly did *Maheo* expect him to do with his abilities?

He knew this fast would be life-changing, but so far it exceeded all expectations to the point of shock. His entire body felt as if it were not his own as he entered a world of which he'd only seen glimpses.

Obtaining instructions and inspiration were expected, but not of the magnitude he experienced so far. He was barely starting to absorb how Sara could be healed in the dream state.

Dreams delivering messages was a given, but being an actual realm of existence had not registered before. Beckoning her spirit to Novavose and administering Eaglefeathers' potion under the direction of Porcupine, a master healer from the past, had been the most exhilarating experience of his life.

Sacred knowledge of how the spirit directed the body followed, as demons present in the poison were removed. Humans were dual beings, spirit and body melded in mortality, each affecting the other. Heal the spirit, which animates the body, and the body follows, and sometimes vice versa. Likewise poison one and the other is affected.

The ceremonies he and White Wolf conducted for her had helped rid her body and spirit of some toxins, but she needed the right medicine. Porcupine's inspired protocol, combined with Eaglefeathers' remedy, made all the difference.

No wonder Ice told him nothing of what needed to be done, only that he needed to go to the Sacred Mountain. Had he seen what was to happen?

Probably.

Did White Wolf know? If not, would he be allowed to share his experiences? Charlie was so surprised that day when he implied at some point he would teach him.

He thought back to that moment when his uncle told him he was a healer. He'd been sitting beneath the bur oak outside the ranch house, testing out his ability to see other times and places. He witnessed his accident and all that transpired while he was unconscious. He opened his eyes to find White Wolf and their dog, *Náhkòhe,* standing there.

His uncle explained how his accident awakened him to his new abilities.

"Healing others is but a small part," he'd said. "I will try to explain. *Maheo* gave you five senses to learn about this world. You see, you hear, you smell, you taste, you touch. There are spiritual senses as well that perceive the spiritual world. The Grandfather Spirits give them only to a privileged few. They are sacred and very powerful.

"Your spiritual eyes have opened. Other gifts will come with time and your worthiness. Continue to ponder what you have learned today. You must understand who you are and what you will become," he'd said. "Then I will teach you more. In time, you will teach me."

Now, more than ever, he understood.

White Wolf knew.

No doubt he could share what he learned with him. He couldn't help looking forward to the day he'd tell him something and not get "I know" in response.

The chamber's energy returned to its ambient level following their two tasks. The second one blinded her captor using the Sacred Arrows so she could escape more easily.

They beckoned *Notamota,* the Sacred Person who dwelt in the northeast, for assistance. It had been a long time since the arrows had been used to blind an enemy. Typically, that was done during actual battle.

For some reason, healing Sara was important enough to exact that fate on her abductor. Whether the affliction would be removed was her decision, to be discussed later.

Now the arrows would need to be renewed in a lengthy, solemn ceremony. One in which Charlie knew he'd participate.

"There is much to be done," Whistling Elk stated, interrupting his thoughts. "It is time for Black Cloud's curse to be fulfilled."

In the Iroquois way, when we make decisions, we consider not only our grandchildren, but also the seven generations to come. We burden ourselves with this responsibility for descendants who won't even know who we are—but that doesn't matter, as it is one of the responsibilities the Creator has charged us with.
—Russell FourEagles

21. VISIONS

NOVAVOSE (Day 2 - Tuesday Sunrise)
BEAR BUTTE STATE PARK
SOUTH DAKOTA
Sacred Mountain Time

Charlie awoke as predawn light breached his consciousness. Had Sara actually been healed as the dream indicated? As the sun rose on the second day, its truth fired his mind. He got situated on the man sage and loaded the pipe. Used the eagle bone whistle to summon the grandfather spirits, then began to pray.

Within moments he was back inside the mountain gazing into the fire. Flames separated, revealing a small, but thriving village. He recognized the terrain as that near his cabin. The surrounding trees wore autumn's hue as warriors prepared for the annual buffalo hunt. A few young warriors were posted as sentries as the others departed. Night fell, snow flurries dancing in the glow of fires within the tipis.

The vision expanded to life-size, placing him inside one of the tipis where he became a young boy, about ten years old. Footsteps pattered outside followed by a familiar whistle.

"Who is it?" Charlie asked.

"It's me. Brennan."

He opened the flap, allowing a white boy about the same age to slip inside.

"They are coming to hurt you," the boy said, talking so fast he could barely understand. "They already killed your sentries. You and your people must leave!"

"What are you talking about?" Charlie asked, mind racing.

"Miners! They are coming! They know your men are away. They are going to kill everyone. They're complaining they're hungry and want a big silver deposit that's nearby. Hurry! We must warn the others and leave. Now!"

Shaking with panic, he slipped on his moccasins, then woke up his mother on the other side of the tipi. She gathered up his baby sister on her cradle board and grabbed a few provisions.

"I will warn the others," she said, eyes wide. "Go find your father!"

"I know where the warriors camp," Charlie said. "Come! We must go!"

They'd barely stepped outside when shouting, gunfire, and thundering hooves exploded from within the darkened forest.

His mother ran for a neighboring tipi while the boys fled toward the corral. Sounds of the approaching mob grew louder. The pair scaled the fence, each mounting the first pony they could catch.

"Follow me!" Charlie yelled, gripping the pony's mane.

A group of men on horseback rushed the enclosure.

"Stop! Or we'll shoot!"

Bullets splintered the air, horses in a frenzy.

Charlie hunkered down on his pony as the herd rumbled past. He dug in his heels, likewise heading toward the far side, fingers clutching its mane as they flew over the split-rail fence, his friend right behind.

The stampeding horses were mostly in front, a few by their sides, midnight mayhem enveloped in a choking cloud of dust.

Shouting, then gunfire. Bullets sizzled past. Horses whinnied and fell, adding to the chaos and obstacles in their path. The dark, moonless night lent no direction, but he knew the area well.

The fastest way to the warriors' camp was along the edge of the canyon, which yielded to a well-worn path to the valley below. Coughing and nearly blinded, he led the way.

The sound of hooves changed from the soft crackle of dry leaves to the rhythmic pounding of solid ground. Last of the stragglers passed, disappearing into the night with the rest of the herd.

As the rumble faded, more yelling, though it sounded far away. Charlie pulled back on his pony's mane and stopped, listening. Brennan pulled up beside him. They turned, looking back toward the village. Screams, an endless volley of shots, then silence as flames crept up the trees spilling sparks to mingle with the stars.

Horrified for his mother and sister, he gulped back a sob, then prodded his horse to a gallop, his friend in close pursuit.

A small band of men on horseback burst from the bushes. Charlie's horse reared, spooked by a blinding burst of light.

Agonizing pain ripped through his shoulder, stealing his awareness from the fact he was airborne. Further assaulted by endless branches and sharp-edged boulders, in one horror filled moment he realized why it was taking so long to reach the ground.

Brennan's screams faded to silence, his own trapped in his throat as his fall ended at the base of the canyon, his lifeless body tumbling down the rocky slope into the icy creek below.

All was dark and deadly silent. Charlie's view shifted back to the village. The sun rose on the next morning. Unsuspecting warriors returned with their winter supply of buffalo meat only to find carnage among their tipis' smoking remains.

They scouted the area, seeking survivors.

There were none.

Their chief and his band traced the beaten path from the corral to the canyon's rim. Face distorted with grief, he looked upon the twisted bodies of his youngest son, his white friend, their mounts, and dozens of the band's horses in the shallow water far below.

They prayed, then sang the Journey Song that the boys might find their way along *seozemeo* to *Se'han*, then returned to the village, mourning the loss of their wives, elders, and children.

A band of heavily armed *Vehoes* awaited their return and ordered them to leave. One of the warriors lunged for his rifle.

The man halted when the chief yelled.

"We cannot win," he declared in Cheyenne. "Enough of our people have died." Then he turned toward the miners.

"We ask only that we give our elders, wives, and children a proper farewell. Then we will go north to join our people."

The miners argued among themselves for a few minutes, then finally agreed. The dejected warriors filed off to complete the sordid task, heads bowed in grief compounded by defeat.

They gathered the dead, built pyres, and set the bodies aflame, singing honor songs as well as the Journey Song that their beloved family members might find peace in spite of their violent deaths.

While the stench of burning flesh still rose from their remains, the warriors mounted up as promised, but made one final stop at the rim of the canyon.

Their chief pronounced a blessing on the dead and a curse upon the area, that it would never benefit those who staged the cowardly attack or those in the future of selfish mind and devoid of heart.

Then he declared he would no longer be known as Grey Hawk, but Black Cloud, in memory of those lost.

Profound grief coupled with blind rage seared Charlie's veins, intensity beyond anything experienced vicariously.

He knew what happened at Dead Horse Canyon for most his life. Being part of it, however, ripped a gaping hole in his heart. Now it was visceral, the tragedy more than something stored in his blood. Understanding burst upon him of why it was sacred ground his grandfather watched over until his death.

As the scene's echoes fell silent he found himself seated once more in the cave. Whistling Elk was gone, replaced by Eaglefeathers.

Déjà-vu triggered hackles across the base of his neck.

The scene before him was identical to a dream he had two months past, before his accident. A circle of elders surrounding the fire. Great warriors, as they were in their prime, might and wisdom gleaming from dark eyes.

His grandfather looked nothing like he remembered. Rather than a wrinkled and aging elder, he was a man of powerful stature in his late thirties, about the age Charlie was now. He wanted to embrace him, apologize for the mistakes of his youth, yet knew this was not the time or place.

His father, Little Bear, was among them. Charlie's eyes filled with tears, having not seen him for over two decades. Seeing him healthy again meant even more after watching him waste away with cancer as a result of exposure to Agent Orange during his military service.

Eaglefeathers waited for his full attention, then introduced the others.

Eaglefeathers' father, Rides the Wind; Rides the Wind's father, Silver Sky; Silver Sky's father, Lone Wolf; and Lone Wolf's father, Black Cloud.

An impressive assembly of great chiefs, warriors, and powerful healers. His spirit took flight, honored and humbled that they were more than his tribe. All were his family, their noble blood mingled with his own.

Eaglefeathers' eyes locked with his.

"Littlewolf, you are the seventh generation. You will lead the Cheyenne people back to who we were before *Vehoe's* destruction fell upon us."

His words carried the weight of truth. Their meaning, however, was unclear. What did being the seventh generation have to do with it?

He thought back to the original vision. At the time he understood, but upon awakening it evaporated, as dreams often do. One thing he did remember.

There was another person there. A powerful but faceless individual.

If his dream two months before was precognition, then who and where was that man?

EN ROUTE MONTGOMERY RESIDENCE
BOULDER, COLORADO
August 28, Tuesday
11:15 a.m. MDT

"THE FIRST THING I want to do is get out of these clothes and take a shower," Sara said. "A proper one, not one of those fake, seated, spray-downs."

Connie looked back from the front passenger seat, wiping her eyes. "I can't believe we found you. What a miracle!"

"Charlie has definitely been busy," Will added as he turned down Pearl Street. "I can't begin to think about how he did all this, but I'm sure glad he did. It's a good thing I didn't pull any money from your account yet. The market is horrible right now. Not the time to sell."

"Speaking of the market, Will, let's go by the farmer's market while we're in the area and pick up some fresh veggies."

"I know this drill, woman," Will replied. "No telling how long you'll be sniffing cantaloupes and tapping watermelons. First, let's go by the police station and have them get over there and arrest Sara's abductor. Lock that bastard up where he belongs."

Sara laughed, then turned serious. "I don't know, Dad. What will we tell them? You told them I was confined to a wheelchair, yet here I am, miraculously healed. He's supposedly now blind, unless it's temporary. Who knows?"

"Assuming it's temporary, you think he'll attempt it again?"

"I don't think so. For one thing, I'm not the easy mark I was before. I was an idiot. I made so many mistakes! Besides, I know this sounds crazy, but I don't think he's really a bad guy."

It gave her the creeps to see that photo he took of her on the patio, but oddly enough, after their first conversation, she hadn't felt threatened.

She debated explaining that kidnapping her was his alternative to killing her, but didn't think it would be well-received. Or, on second thought, maybe it would be.

"He certainly can be," she went on, "but other than kidnapping me, I didn't see that side at all. Actually, his original plan was to kill me. And he could have."

"What? He told you that?"

"Yes, but he couldn't do it. He even showed me a picture he took of me sitting on your patio in Mom's wheelchair."

Will growled. "Standard wet work procedure. Before and after."

She scowled, not sure what that meant. "Well, obviously he didn't. So he kidnapped me instead. He was never abusive. I even yelled at him and he just smiled. If he's now blind, that seems punishment enough."

"Oh, Sara, you can be so damn idealistic. He's clearly an assassin. Or has been. Do you really think he should get away with it?"

Her stomach tightened, remembering Jason was the one who procured the poison. If her father knew *that* he'd kill him for sure. "I don't see how it would do either of us any good to report it." She laughed. "At least he got a fancy wheelchair out of it. But what he'll really need is a good dog, like Blossom." She scratched the pitty's head resting on her lap, canine body sprawled across the backseat.

"What about Blossom? Will you keep her?" Connie asked.

"How could I not?" Sara replied, eyes meeting the dog's. She had no doubts the dog was smiling. "I can always use a good guard dog. Those evil people still have a price on my head. I couldn't possibly let her go, though I feel a little guilty for no longer needing all her training."

"Now you should train her as a true guard dog," Will said, protective as always. "She should pick it up easily. Anyone else threatens you, she'll tear their throat out."

"*Ewww*. The main thing is that now I'm well, so I can get back to work. No more being stuck in a wheelchair with limited mobility. I need to get back in touch with NBC. Davis Jenkins told me I could come back any time. People should be even more sympathetic now."

Her father didn't comment other than slowly shaking his head, no happier with her intentions than he was before.

"The police station is up the next block," he said, slowing down. "Go by or not?"

Sara shrugged. Elated to be free, she really didn't care. "I don't know. What evidence do we have? Nothing I can think of. You'll think I'm crazy, but I'm kind of worried about him. If he's still blind, he can't drive and he's out there in that isolated area."

Will laughed, hard. "C'mon, Sara! If he's with one of the alphabet agencies he'll figure it out. So I take that as a 'No.' Okay, next stop, farmer's market."

"And then Patrice's," Connie said. "This is going to blow her mind."

"Sure blows mine," Will replied. "She nailed it—again."

WOODLAND PLACE
BOULDER, COLORADO
August 28, Tuesday
11:50 a.m. MDT

JASON STAGGERED TO HIS FEET after tripping over the wheelchair, head spinning. Of all the risks he'd ever taken or prepared for, being outsmarted by a civilian woman had never been on his radar. The fact he couldn't see was not only unsettling, but a total enigma.

How could it be? It was only a dream!
How could he be blind?

How in the hell could she have done such a thing? How did she so suddenly get well? Was being confined to a wheelchair a ploy for sympathy? If so, she was a better actor than he was. Usually he could read people.

Not this time.

Wow.

She was good. Really good.

He straightened.

Was it possible she, too, was NSA? Or CIA?

The possibilities were so outrageous, giving them serious thought fried his brain.

His main problem right now was obvious. He felt his way along the wall, back into his bedroom, where he fumbled around on the nightstand for his phone, then sat on the bed.

Whom to call for help, however, was not apparent.

He laughed.

His mother?

She'd no doubt tell him it served him right.

How could he possibly explain his situation to anyone who knew him? They'd die laughing. He couldn't drive, that was for sure. He'd rented the condo for a month, not knowing when he'd be able to abduct her, so at least he didn't have to leave for a while.

Maybe by then it would go away.

He should be angry, livid even, but instead respected and admired her even more. When he carried her unconscious body into the apartment, he felt something he'd never encountered before. A warm feeling deep inside that she was a truly good person the planet needed. Hurting her in any way would beckon the hounds of Hades to her defense.

Was she more than human? His guardian angel, perhaps, sent to straighten him out? That could explain a lot, except for being so unbelievable.

Had he lost his mind as well as his vision?

Was that it?

Or was that Indian friend of hers far more than he appeared? That raid Keller's clowns bungled had some strange circumstances, too. He'd seen some pretty weird stuff, especially in Third World countries. Enough to convince him few things were impossible, the previous night a good case in point.

Technology, especially AI, was capable of a plethora of illusions. Arthur C. Clarke's statement, "Technology sufficiently far advanced is indistinguishable from magic," said it all.

His knowledge far exceeded the average person's regarding what was possible in that regard, including methods to achieve mind control, to say nothing of hypnotism. Either of which could make a person believe they were blind.

Could that be it?

Maybe.

He'd been trained to resist such methods, but being asleep was another story. Meanwhile, more practical matters needed to be addressed. If she could adapt to being paraplegic, even if she was faking—in which case she did a damn good job—then surely he could adapt to being blind. The prospect wasn't pleasant, but what choice was there?

As a last resort he could blow his brains out, but that was the coward's way out. At this point he was more intrigued than intimidated.

Would she go to the police? His gut told him no. Would her father? Maybe. Proof, however, would be her word against his. He doubted anyone would believe any of it.

Hell, he could hardly believe it himself.

At least he had the money from Keller. Setting up an operation like that was out of the question now, but it never hurt to have $1.7 million in the bank.

One asset that remained was his acting ability. Surely he could put that to work somehow. If, perchance, he got comfortable getting around, then his vision came back, it would be another skill in his toolbox. If people believed you were blind there's no telling what they might carelessly reveal.

He definitely needed a dog. Maybe Sara would sell hers.

No. She wouldn't. She was too attached to it, but maybe she'd recommend where to get one.

Yo, Sara, this is Jason. Wondering where you got your service dog. Asking for a friend.

He laughed at the thought.

208

So far this day was definitely not going as planned.

He shook his head, incredulous, deciding to have that cup of coffee after all. And something to eat.

He rolled his sightless eyes one more time at his predicament, then picked up his phone and did the one thing he could, eyes working or not.

"Hey, Google. Call Door Dash."

The red nation shall rise again and it shall be a blessing for a sick world; a world filled with broken promises, selfishness and separations; a world longing for light again. I see a time of seven generations when all the colors of mankind will gather under the sacred tree of life and the whole earth will become one circle again.
– Tȟašúŋke Witkó (Crazy Horse), Oglala Lakota Leader (1840-1877)

22. DIRECTIONS

NOVAVOSE (Day 2 - Tuesday)
BEAR BUTTE STATE PARK
SOUTH DAKOTA
Sacred Mountain Time

Charlie's stomach clenched as Eaglefeathers continued. Exactly what was he supposed to do? It sounded daunting, so much so he wasn't sure he wanted him to go on. No wonder he'd shied away as a youth.

The vision of his ancestors vanished, the flames before them collapsing into a pile of glowing embers. Wood smoke scented the dank air of the cave as they sat beside it, facing one another.

"Over a century ago our Lakota brother, holy man *Heȟáka Sápa* (Black Elk), had a vision," his grandfather stated. "He was but a boy of nine who became very ill and nearly died. While in the space between life and death he saw what the Lakota know as the six grandfathers that represent the four sacred directions as well as earth and sky."

"Like our *maheyuno*, Father Sun, and the Earth Mother," Charlie commented.

"Yes." Eaglefeathers nodded. "We have many similar beliefs. Black Elk saw intense suffering would befall indigenous people in the years to come."

He held out his arms, explaining, "He saw a great tree that represented all life on earth." His eyes softened with pain as he went on. "He saw war, famine, and sickness among his people. Their sacred circle was broken. But he was told after seven generations of darkness, better times would come."

His voice grew stronger. "Not only for his people, the Lakota, but all people on earth. That generation's sacred duty is to stand up for our people and the Earth Mother once again. Take back what culture and rights remain and change things for the better for future generations. Restore everything *Vehoe* took away. Crazy Horse, another Lakota brother, had a similar vision."

Charlie nodded as the seventh-generation designation finally made sense, though no less intimidating.

"When you introduced me to my grandfathers, there was another whose face I could not see. Was that Black Elk?"

"Perhaps. Prophets who foresee great future happenings are often engaged in their fulfillment. Being faceless, it could have represented all Indigenous prophets from many tribes who have seen similar things. Our Hopi brothers saw much of what's to come. It could possibly be someone not yet born."

Sadness darkened Eaglefeathers' eyes as he went on. "Before all native people can be unified, we must unite our own tribe. Restore sacred ceremonies that have been lost. Return to the direction given by holy men that has been ignored or distorted from its original truth."

The truth of his words penetrated Charlie's soul, leaving a profound sadness in their wake as his grandfather continued.

"Too many have strayed. Their belief in our sacred ways was weakened or destroyed when *Vehoe* tried to annihilate our language and culture. Sweet Medicine warned us about many things. He prophesied that loss of *Mahuts*, the Sacred Arrows, or *Is si'wun*, the Sacred Buffalo Hat, would mark the final scattering of the tribe. He was right."

"What happened?" Charlie asked.

Sadness filled his grandfather's dark eyes. "The arrows were captured by the Pawnee in 1830. Why? Because the proper ceremony was not performed prior to the battle. In 1835 they gave back one buffalo arrow. In 1837 the Brulé Sioux battle against them captured back one of the man arrows, which they returned to us."

"Why didn't they do it correctly?" He couldn't imagine being so careless. His father's words, "Do it right or not at all," had always kept him from doing anything in a sloppy manner.

"They were impatient and angry," Eaglefeathers said. "They lost reverence for *Maheo* and our sacred ways. Took them for granted. Before any of the originals were returned, in 1834 new ones were consecrated by Crazy Mule and Box Elder. The Sacred Hat was also desecrated. It was repaired, but lacks its former power. We must renew both, *Mahuts* and *Is si'wun*."

"That makes sense," Charlie agreed. "What else must we do?"

"The last *Massaum* was over a century ago. It is the earth-giving ceremony. It must be held." Eaglefeathers got up to fetch a few more logs for the fire. Embers spit sparks, a trickle of flames greeting the additions.

Charlie was speechless as his mind spun. What was the *Massaum*?

"You, Littlewolf, will restore these ceremonies to their original truth," his grandfather went on as he sat back down.

Charlie smiled, remembering how his bones used to creak as an old man.

"That will unite the Cheyenne people," Eaglefeathers continued. "That alone assures our future." He paused, searching Charlie's face. "What is wrong, grandson?"

"I don't even know what that is," he admitted, feeling stupid.

"Of course we will teach you how. That is why you are here."

Intimidation washed over him at the weight it carried. He had no idea where to start. Fulfilling his destiny would take the rest of his life. No wonder Eaglefeathers attempted to train him at such a young age.

His grandfather continued, "Sweet Medicine Spirits, the *maiyun*, tell me the Earth Mother is impatient. She is tired of being abused and exploited by evil people. Our brothers in other tribes are being given this same message. They, too, must unite. Set aside all foolish contention."

Charlie inhaled sharply as he recognized a connection. "In two moons a *Peace Gathering of Indigenous Leaders* is planned on the Northern Cheyenne Reservation. White Wolf is in charge," he said. "That will be part of this, yes?"

"Yes," Eaglefeathers agreed. "It will be key in uniting the tribes. After it ends in Montana, a special ceremony will be held with the same chiefs and medicine men on the sacred ground at Dead Horse Canyon. If we unite within our tribe and with our indigenous brothers, *Maheo* and the Earth Mother will reward us by restoring all that was promised."

Skepticism rankled his mind at something so idealistic. With all due respect to his grandfather, such unification sounded too good to be true. He knew from his upbringing there were similarities in beliefs between tribes. Similar prophesies along with much that could be considered common ground. The sweat lodge, variations of the Sun Dance, medicine wheel, as well as ceremonial fasting, sometimes referred to by other tribes as a vision quest.

Differences, however, even if minor, were what caused division. Bickering like Christian churches, which likewise strayed from their original teachings. Each tribe believed their way was right, all others wrong. Such as what he witnessed growing up between his *Diné* mother and Cheyenne father.

While he didn't want to be disrespectful and argue, he had serious doubts any such thing could occur.

"How can all tribes come together and agree to anything?" he asked. "Even our own medicine men and forty-four Old Man Chiefs don't always agree."

Eaglefeathers nodded. "You are correct. What all people don't realize, Littlewolf, is that *Maheo* does not expect all our brothers from other nations to agree with one another. Only settle divisions within their own tribe by returning to original ceremonies, then show respect and tolerance for those with different beliefs. Our actions demonstrate our beliefs, but what matters most is our intent. What is in our heart. Arguing and contention must stop."

Charlie's posture reflected his confusion. "I always wondered who was right, my mother or father. So there is not only one way to live that is correct?"

Dark eyes drilled into his own. "That is true, grandson. When Motseyoef, now known as Sweet Medicine, received instructions from *Maheo* how *Tseteshestahese* people should live, other tribes received similar directions from the person who would become their spiritual leader. Each tribe's message was slightly different, though all indigenous peoples have some practices in common. Beliefs are absorbed into each tribe's culture. Differences in interpretation are inevitable."

Fascinated by the concept, he pondered what that might entail. "First, each tribe is to return to what they were originally told?"

"Yes and no." Eaglefeathers eyes assumed a pensive look. "For most ceremonies, yes. In some cases we will share our beliefs and ceremonies that have meaning others may wish to adopt. What is most important is to peacefully agree."

Charlies mind rumbled, conflicting ideas bouncing like arrows missing their mark. "We have been greatly humbled since *Vehoe* stole our land," he said. "It is no wonder our traditions likewise disappeared as we struggled to survive."

Eaglefeathers nodded agreement. "That is why we will invite other tribes to participate in the *Massaum* and teach them the ceremony, if they desire. They may have their own version already."

Charlie blinked, again confused. "I have never heard of the *Massaum*. What is it?"

His grandfather's dark eyes acquired a distant look, as if looking back in time. "It is thousands of years old and, as far as I know, unique to the Cheyenne. But it should draw interest from our indigenous brothers as the earth-giving ceremony. We have had such gatherings for many years and learned from one another."

"Like pow-wows?"

"No. Pow-wows are social events. These gatherings are of a spiritual nature studying our glorious past and future destiny as a people. Not just the Cheyenne, but all tribes. In the beginning, our beliefs were more alike. Over time and with *Vehoe* trying to destroy us, many were lost. We will compare our beliefs with other tribes and seek common ground. Some may have remembered what others lost."

Eaglefeathers shook his head with sadness. "Everything Sweet Medicine said would happen came about. Some of it was our fault. We didn't listen. It is time to unite in peace. Only then will the Earth Mother and *Maheo* restore what was lost."

Charlie likewise stood when Eaglefeathers got up and rose to his full height, slightly taller than Charlie. "There is much to do and little time."

Charlie lost track of what day it was after they healed Sara. Being in the cave, vision or otherwise, distorted all sense of time. Was it Tuesday? Wednesday? If so, he had just over two days to learn everything. If it was Thursday, even less.

Impossible.

His concerns spilled out as an urgent plea.

"But Grandfather, how will I learn all this in two days?"

Eaglefeathers' eyes drilled into his.

"That is why you were told to come to *Novavose*. Have you not noticed, grandson? Sweet Medicine Spirits are the *maiyun* who control 'Indian Time.' Each of the remaining hours of your fast will be as long as required."

While hard to comprehend, his intuition screamed its truth. Like when his spiritual eyes were first opened and White Wolf told him he was seeing the past.

His grandfather's smile was encouraging.

"Be at peace, Littlewolf, be at peace. You have plenty of time."

He crouched down to stoke the fire, igniting new flames that he stared into for a time before continuing.

"Whenever one of us fasts here on *Novavose* it renews the tribe," he said, their eyes once more connected. "They will be ready. You will teach elders on and off the reservation who know our sacred ceremonies what you learn here and any changes that need to be made. Then they will serve as instructors for those who pledge them. Eventually, you will pledge Crossing the Four Ridges as an example to your brothers. You will lead, but you are never alone doing *Maheo's* work."

SARA'S CONDO
DENVER
August 28, Tuesday
3:38 p.m.

SARA STOOD IN HER living room wearing a crooked smile. Everything she'd done to facilitate her independence now needed to be undone.

She laughed.

Patrice was right again. As soon as she accepted the situation she got well.

Was that woman ever wrong?

It was so much fun to go by Cosmic Portals and tell her how everything worked out. The astrologer could hardly believe it, even though she'd predicted that something unexpected would set her free.

"You just can't make this stuff up!" she'd said, grinning as she patted the computer screen that displayed the horary chart, which to their fascination she'd explained in detail.

It felt so good to be back on her feet that she couldn't help shouting a celebratory *"Yes!"* with a little happy dance.

Her knees were still a little weak and legs shaky, but physical therapy would fix that. Just climbing the stairs would tone her legs and buttocks in no time.

She laughed again when Blossom sat up in her bed next to the front door, forehead wrinkled with a doggie, "Are you crazy?" frown.

When was the last time she'd been this elated? She was excited when she and Charlie found Bryan's data stash, but that was different. She hadn't felt *this* good since before becoming a widow.

Probably when Bryan received an honorable discharge from the Air Force, and she expected they'd have a long, happy future together.

Her mood deflated.

She shook it off the best she could and shifted her thoughts to Charlie, whom she'd called numerous times to thank, but they'd all gone to phone mail. Hopefully, he was okay and not having troubles of his own.

Her father called the Buick dealer about returning her outfitted car. They'd pick it up early tomorrow and leave a normal one in its place. Will also offered to get in touch with the contractor who installed the lift about removing it, but she was undecided.

She stepped over to the closet and opened the door, staring at the seat enclosed in the transparent tube. Should she keep it? It was out of the way in both locations. If any more unwelcome visitors showed up it could come in handy. With a passcode, at least they couldn't use it to her detriment like they had with the opening they'd created for Mike to get through from the unit next-door.

While she hoped they'd leave her alone, in reality she knew she was being naïve. Especially since, like Jason said, there was still a price on her head. Plus the fact she planned to make more noise than ever about what Bryan found, fueled further by her own experience with government bullies.

She wandered about, pondering whether to keep other changes to the condo. The new refrigerator and rearranging the cupboards were all she found. There was no reason to change either. That way her dog could still function as her helper, an incredibly awesome roomie. She was also a major deterrent to further attacks.

Anyone who broke in now would be confronted with a very unpleasant surprise. Attacking someone and ripping them to shreds was a nasty thought, particularly the mess it would make, yet she felt much safer. She made a mental note to contact the service dog academy about additional training. Her canine instincts would do a pretty good job in the meantime.

The fact the dog was key to finding her still boggled her mind.

Her eyes wandered to the photo over the couch, one she'd taken of spring wildflowers out by the cabin. It felt like forever since she'd been out there and she longed to return as soon as possible. At least no changes had been made out there that needed to be undone. It would be fun to see her friend, Liz Hudson, maybe even the other *Mah Jongg* ladies.

What would Ida have to say about her insidious nephew? Did she have any idea he was trying to kill her? Or what else he'd done? She paused, wondering if she'd seen the dash cam video aired on National TV.

That would certainly make for an interesting conversation.

On a more cheerful side, maybe she'd get to see Mike, too. Her father told her how upset he was when she'd been poisoned, that he'd blamed himself. Seeing her walk again would certainly help rid him of any residual guilt.

The more she thought about it, the better getting away sounded. Leave the past miserable month behind and get back on track. Get started on her podcasts, think about adding a book, and definitely see about returning to the *Today Show*.

What better promotion than that?

She plopped down on the couch and checked her GoFundMe account on her phone. She'd gotten quite an influx of donations after those first appearances. The last she remembered it was around $147,000. She signed in, finding a jaw dropping $247,209.

Holy crap on a cracker!

Checking the log of individual donations, she saw most were around $20. Then one earlier that day for $100,000, the maximum allowed.

Wow! Where on earth did that come from?

A like-minded group perhaps?

It was up to the donor whether or not to leave their name. This one came from someone called *Touché*. She checked to see if the person left a note, usually a word of encouragement or agreement with her quest.

She clicked.

And there it was:

Check out a DC nonprofit called LOL.
They hired Keller. Good luck, Jason. ;-)

NOVAVOSE
BEAR BUTTE STATE PARK
SOUTH DAKOTA
August 28, Tuesday
7:32 p.m. MDT

WHITE WOLF SPENT THE afternoon building the sweat lodge with his son. The one at the ranch was built long before Winter Hawk was born, its existence something the boy took for granted. This would be an important learning experience.

They tied nineteen choke cherry trees together in the prescribed manner for the structure, the teen doing most of the work. Between instructions, they sang the Badger Song, a tradition for such an activity.

How to line everything up properly was essential, which the boy now understood wasn't simple. The lodge door needed to face east, the stone pit inside lined up with the door as well as the fire pit outside. He emphasized sacred actions done in a sloppy or haphazard way were offensive to *Maheo* because they showed lack of respect.

After dinner that evening they sat outside the tipi and built a fire. White Wolf broke off a piece from a sweetgrass braid and placed it on a hot coal. As its smoke arose, each smudged himself, made the sacred motions, then made a tobacco offering as prelude to prayer.

"*Maheo*, we are grateful to be here at *Novavose* while Littlewolf fulfills his pledge," White Wolf prayed. "We are thankful for the Sweet Medicine Spirits, the *Maheyuno,* and their assistance in our lives."

Gratitude radiated through his entire being as he continued.

"We pray that Star and Risingsun are safe while we are gone and Rufus Littlesun can attend to my duties without any problems. We pray for Littlewolf's friend, Sara, that she will be safe. That Littlewolf can be strong and endure as he completes the second day of his fast. We ask that he will be taught those things that he must know to help our people."

He paused, remembering when Littlewolf first came to the ranch, broken, both physically and spiritually. His eyes burned, joy lightening his heart for being part of his sacred journey. A week or so before, his deceased brother, Little Bear, who was Littlewolf's father, came to him in a dream to express his love and appreciation for what he'd been able to do for his son.

"Littlewolf has grown in strength and wisdom since he began to walk the red road," his prayer continued. "His progress has been rapid. We pray that he can carry any burden he is given and follow instructions from the *Maheyuno*. We pray that we may know what we can do to assist him."

He opened his eyes as Father Sun disappeared behind *Novavose's* summit, then continued to drop invisibly toward the distant horizon, shades of orange and purple sweeping the western sky. A distinct chill captured the air, deeper and more frigid than the previous night.

He shivered, attention drawn to an invisible *maiyun* who'd captured access to his mind. He turned to his son to deliver its message.

"*Maiyun* tells me it would be good for you to fast and sit with your brother tomorrow," White Wolf said. "The third day is often the most difficult. You will give him additional strength to continue."

"I would like that very much," Winter Hawk replied.

They remained before the fire in silent meditation as darkness fell. A short time later the Rutting Moon, known in Cheyenne as *Hémotséeše'he,* rose in the southeast, the late August "sun of the night."

White Wolf squinted at what appeared to be the silhouette of an approaching horseman beside the moon. Details resolved as it increased in size, including the audible pounding of hooves. As it drew closer, he could see everything about the rider was white. *Esseneta'he's* sacred color: robe, buffalo horn hat, even his body.

Mesmerized, he sat perfectly still as the steed reared just beyond the fire.

With a voice that shook the ground the rider declared, "*O'komóxhaahketa É-ma'heóno'eétàhétšéhešètāno. Maheo émonotse'ónanénoto. Ma'heónèstónestòtse Tsèhésepo'èho'e tsèhe'èhéoohe-aé nūm'hāisto. É-né'ta'e É-màheohtseo'o.*

The message stated Littlewolf was to do something sacred that *Maheo* chose him to do. Those attending the upcoming *Gathering* were to move south to another location for another yet to be revealed sacred ceremony.

Without lingering, *Esseneta'he* turned and galloped skyward the way he came, swallowed by darkness.

His chest heaved with a breathless feeling as the import of the directive settled on his mind. As the event's organizer, the logistical challenges were as intimidating as removing a boulder the size of *Tah'Hó-nehe* from blocking a stream.

He turned to Winter Hawk, wondering if he'd seen it, too. His son's eyes provided the answer.

Without a doubt, this would be a *Novavose* fast to remember, its effects more far-reaching than he could begin to imagine.

All these mysteries and ceremonies came to these men from within the earth; and all they learned about them and afterward taught to the tribes was the instruction that they had received from the spirits whom they encountered in the mysterious underground lodges they had entered.
— The Cheyenne Indians: Their History and Ways of Life, Volume II by George Bird Grinnell

23. SWEET MEDICINE

NOVAVOSE (Day 2 - Tuesday night dream)
BEAR BUTTE STATE PARK
SOUTH DAKOTA
Sacred Mountain Time

As Charlie began to dream the second night, he found himself reading a history book. It explained that Sweet Medicine lived with his people for four long, long lives of men. Young people grew up, became old, and died; other young people were born, grew to old age, and died; but still this man lived.

All through the summer he was a young man; and when fall came and the grass dried up, he began to look older; and about the middle of the winter he was like a very old man, and walked bent over and feebly. In spring he became young again.

At last, he died, but before he died he talked a long time to the people and prophesied some of what would come to them; and he told them, as they were gathered in his lodge, a good many things that it made him sad to repeat, and that the people did not understand.

The book vanished from his hands as he found himself in a lodge with many others. Sweet Medicine was there, a tall elegant man with black hair past his shoulders, distinctly sharp cheekbones, and deep-set eyes. One man who sat in the circle spoke to Sweet Medicine, who for a long time had been sitting in silence with his head hanging down, as if discouraged.

222

He said: "Friend, what is your trouble? Why are you sorrowful?"

Sweet Medicine answered: "Yes, it is true I am troubled. Listen to me carefully. Listen to me carefully." He said this four times.

"Our great-grandfather spoke thus to me, repeating it four times. He said to me that he had put people on this earth, all kinds of people. He made us, but also he made others. There are all kinds of people on earth that you will meet some day, toward the sunrise, by a big river. Some are black, but some day you will meet a people who are white—good-looking people, with light hair and white skins."

A man spoke up, and said, "Shall we know them when we meet them?"

Sweet Medicine nodded. "Yes, you will know them, for they will have long hair on their faces, and will look differently from you. They will wear things different from your things—different clothing. It will be something like the green scum that grows on water about springs.

"Those people will wander this way. You will talk with them. They will give you things like isinglass, things that flash or reflect the light, and something that looks like sand that will taste very sweet. But do not take the things they give you. Do not take them.

"They will be looking for a certain stone. They will wear what I have spoken of, but it will be of all colors, pretty. Perhaps they will not listen to what you say to them, but you will listen to what they say to you.

"They will be people who do not get tired, but who will keep pushing forward, going, going all the time. They will keep coming, coming. They will try always to give you things, but do not take them. Do not take them.

"At last I think that you will take the things that they offer you, and this will bring sickness to you. These people do not follow the way of our great-grandfather. They follow another way. They will travel everywhere, looking for this stone which our great-grandfather put on the earth in many places.

"Buffalo and all animals were given you by our great-grandfather; but these people will come in, and will begin to kill off these animals. They will use a different thing to kill animals from what we use—something that makes a noise, and sends a little round stone to kill.

"Then after a while a different animal will come into the country. It will be smaller than a buffalo, have split hooves and a long tail. These animals will smell differently from the buffalo, and at last you will come to eating them. When you skin them, the flesh will jerk, and at last you will get this same disease and die a slow death.

"At last something will be given to you, which, if you drink it, will make you crazy. These people will have something to give to animals to eat which will kill them.

"There will be many of these people, so many that you cannot stand before them. On the rivers you will see things going up and down, and in these things will be these people, and there will be things moving over dry land in which these people will be.

"Another animal will come, but it will not be like the buffalo. It will have long heavy hair on its neck, and a long heavy tail which drags on the ground. It will come from the south.

"When these animals come, you will catch them, and you will get on their backs and they will carry you from place to place. You will become great travelers. If you see a place a long way off, you will want to go to it, so at last you will get on those animals with my arrows.

"From that time you will act very foolishly. You will never be quiet. You will want to go everywhere. You will be very foolish. You will know nothing.

"These people will not listen to what you say; what they are going to do they will do. You people will change; in the end of your life in those days you will not get up early in the morning; you will never know when day comes; you will lie in bed; you will have disease, and will die suddenly; you will all die off.

"At last those people will ask you for your flesh. At last those people will ask you for your flesh. At last those people will ask you for your flesh. At last those people will ask you for your flesh. But you must say 'No.' They will try to teach you their way of living. If you give up to them your flesh [your children], those that they take away will never know anything.

"They will try to change you from your way of living to theirs, and they will persist at what they try to do. They will work with their hands. They will tear up the earth, and at last you will do it with them. When you do, you will become crazy, and will forget all that I am now teaching you.

"Follow these teachings. When you marry your own sisters[1] you will be Cheyenne no more. Keep your blood pure. Speak the sacred Cheyenne language. Do the sacred red pipe ceremonies exactly as I have taught you. Always remember *Maheo* created you from Grandmother Earth."

CHARLIE WEPT. HEARING the words as they came from the prophet himself ignited his soul. How could people have ignored his sacred words?

Sweet Medicine's prophecy explained so much. Truly the people strayed from his teachings. He told them everything to watch for and what not to do, but they did it anyway.

No wonder their prophet was sad about what he saw.

How foolish men could be.

Sadly, he'd been one of them. Deceived, even with his father and grandfather warning and teaching him about Sweet Medicine.

More than ever he understood the necessity of restoring the ceremonies. Truly the people had deviated from their sacred ways and fallen prey to everything Sweet Medicine warned about.

---

[1] In Cheyenne culture those with the same grandfather are considered sisters and brothers while *Vehoes* refer to this relationship as cousins. Cheyennes had a relatively small tribe that was divided into bands. This reference advises marrying another Cheyenne, but from another band to avoid too close of a relative.

But why would they listen to him when they ignored a true prophet? One who performed so many miracles there was no mistaking his connection with *Maheo*?

WITNESSING SWEET MEDICINE'S prophecy imprinted Charlie's soul at a deep level, the culture hero's existence beyond any doubt. Seeing and hearing him branded his soul. Any previous musings that the man was no more than a myth vanished.

His thoughts turned to when the culture hero received *mahuts*. The Sacred Arrows were a gift from *Maheo* to bless the people and one of the Cheyenne's great mysteries.

As he slept, he watched Sweet Medicine and his wife enter that same room in the cave. A *maiyun* in the form of a mysterious man showed him two sets of arrows. One set of four had hawk feathers, the other, eagle feathers. The man asked the prophet which ones he liked.

Sweet Medicine chose eagle feathers.

The *maiyun* then issued instructions on how to care for them.

"These arrows must be wrapped in a piece of the hide of a four-year-old buffalo. The buffalo must be shot once in the side. If the first shot does not kill it, the buffalo is to be let go, and not shot again. No other kind of hide except this must be used to wrap the arrows, and it must be gotten just as has been told you."

Next, they made a quiver from a kit fox hide to keep them in.

The *maiyun* said, "The arrows must never touch the ground. Their tips must always point away from the person holding them. They are more powerful than you can imagine. You will learn how to use them to blind an enemy."

Charlie smiled, having seen how that was accomplished when they healed Sara.

"If they must be set down, place them upon a bed of sacred white sage spread upon five buffalo chips. When they aren't being carried, hang them from a forked branch, tips pointing toward the earth."

The *maiyun* went on to explain that *mahuts* required an Arrow Keeper. His sacred duty was to watch over them in a dedicated tipi, which would become the Cheyenne's spiritual center.

Charlie's mouth twitched upon learning the Keeper had to be full-blooded *Tsistsistas*, which meant he was excluded.

That requirement was another reason it was difficult to find qualified and willing Arrow Keepers, coupled with how many lost reverence for the arrows over the years.

Years of trouble with the U.S. Government, particularly restrictions on practicing sacred ceremonies, weakened their ability to follow the ways taught by Sweet Medicine. Their spiritual center was decimated during the years that the Sun Dance and other ceremonies were forbidden.

The tribal split into the Southern and Northern contingents nearly two centuries before was another challenge. Those in Oklahoma had not suffered in the same way as those who rebelled against government edicts and insisted they return to their homeland. Due to separation, some traditions between them changed, which would be another challenge in unifying the tribe.

"When the tribe deviates from the way they were instructed to live, the Arrows lose power," the *maiyun* explained. "These include serious tribal violations, such as intratribal murder or contention between military societies. Trouble or sickness indicates the Arrows have weakened and should be renewed."

Renewal ceremonies, known as *maxhoetonstov,* were solemn events that took place over four days, which Charlie then witnessed in their entirety.

Part of the ceremony involved cutting sweet grass braids into 444 pieces, then burning them over four days on coals created by a cottonwood fire. By the ceremony's completion the sweet grass ashes formed a replica of *Novavose.*

While he didn't qualify as an Arrow priest, it would be his responsibility to assure that the ceremony was conducted exactly as the *maiyun* instructed Sweet Medicine.

The thought of contradicting an Arrow Priest made Charlie shudder. Any elders old enough to remember Eaglefeathers still gave him critical and often unfriendly looks.

"It concerns me they will not listen," he said to Porcupine, who'd joined his dream. "In the past I was very foolish. Many remain skeptical of my intent."

"This fast will earn sufficient respect as part of completing your pledge of Crossing the Four Ridges, Littlewolf. No such thing will happen. Remain humble. Pray to *Maheo* to touch their spirits. And they will listen to what you tell them without resistance."

Besides the ceremonial side of *Mahuts*, Charlie witnessed a few incidents that bespoke their power. Most memorable was one that involved Long Hair, *a.k.a.* George Armstrong Custer.

In March 1869, after the attack on the Washita, Long Hair showed up at the Cheyenne camp where the Sacred Arrow lodge was located. The Chiefs were gathered there, and allowed him in, placing him directly under the Sacred Arrow bundle.

Stone Forehead, the Arrow Keeper and a powerful medicine man, offered the pipe to the Sacred Persons, to *Maheo*, and finally to the Arrows themselves. Then he handed the pipe to Custer. The two leaders smoked there, under the Sacred Arrows.

When Custer asked the meaning of the ceremony, he was told that smoking before the Arrows bound a man to tell the truth and the obligation to keep his promise.

Custer stated, "I will never harm the Cheyennes again. I will never point my gun at a Cheyenne again."

After the pipe burned out, Stone Forehead used his wooden pipe tamper to scrape the ashes from the pipe's bowl directly onto Custer's boots.

Again, Long Hair asked its meaning. He was told, "If you break your promise, you and your soldiers will go to dust like this."

Custer repeated, "I will never kill another Cheyenne."

Seven years later, at the Battle of the Little Big Horn, his lies decimated both him and his troops.

Charlie recognized Stone Forehead as the one who blinded Sara's captor.

He smiled, knowing from experience that underestimating the power of a medicine man's words was a really, really bad idea.

Of all the Plains tribes, the Cheyennes most completely centered their lives upon the sacred ceremonies. According to their beliefs, supernatural power permeated every phase of Cheyenne being: peace, war, hunting, courtship, art, and music.
— Peter John Powell, "Sweet Medicine," Volume 1, p. xxv

24. CONVERSATIONS

SARA'S CONDO
DENVER
August 29, Wednesday
9:17 a.m.

Sara paced the living room, undecided. Tell her father? Or not? How would he react? The last thing she wanted was another argument. On the other hand, she didn't know what to do and needed his advice. Sleeping on it hadn't helped.

It fried her brain Jason told her who wanted her dead. But like he told her before, what could she do?

Before she talked to Will she needed more information. She went up to her office, Blossom in close pursuit. She got on the computer and did a web search, dog settling in beneath her feet.

LOL was an acronym for the Lobbyist Opportunity League. It's charter claimed its purpose:

To train future lobbyists in ethics and the appropriate way to interact with lawmakers.

She spurned the statement with a sneer. More likely train people how to commit ethics violations and bribe lawmakers under the table using overseas shell companies that only existed on paper. She fumed, incensed, as she pictured their training material entitled, *Money Laundering 101.*

No wonder these people wanted her dead.

Her actions jeopardized PURF and thus their ill-gotten benefits. Each additional construction phase would be financed in a future budget cycle that required Congressional approval. If she succeeded in getting their constituents outraged enough, it could kill it, leaving them out in the cold.

Making that her primary goal: No further construction.

Her ultimate one was to get lobbying itself outlawed, which would make them even more thirsty for her blood, Congressmen and lobbyists alike.

Lobbying wasn't that bad, initially. After all, environmental protection, animal rights, and a plethora of other groups lobbied, too. Expressing to Congress what the people wanted made sense.

But corporate donations to political candidates exploded following the 2010 Supreme Court decision that declared corporations "people," and therefore declaring such donations legal under the First Amendment regarding free speech.

Such had been forbidden, with good cause, for over a hundred years. The corruption that resulted since had entirely silenced the voice of actual *people*.

Her thoughts focused somewhere faraway, remembering. When Sara was growing up the Democrat Party was the one that favored police, firefighters, auto workers, factory workers, and the common people.

Not anymore.

Their policies were now just as bound to corporations as the party across the aisle, often promoting causes that sounded good, but were impractical and more about amassing fortunes for a chosen few than any benefit to the people at large.

It was sad that candidates with the most campaign money often won. And they were the ones who made promises to corporations such as BlackRock, Statestreet, Vanguard, pharmaceutical companies, and the military-industrial complex.

Could she possibly get a SCOTUS decision reversed? It happened occasionally, like with Roe. vs. Wade. Maybe if she got enough people stirred up by educating them, it could happen.

Bryan told her years before that the legalization of corporate money funding elections was further exacerbated in 2012 when H.R. 4310, the National Defense Authorization Act for Fiscal Year

2013, repealed the Smith-Mundt Act. That law prohibited the U.S. government from unleashing propaganda, including blatant lies, on the people.

Not that campaign promises ever meant much, but now overt, deliberate lying on the part of the government was no longer a crime. This carried further implications that allowed true statements to be debunked with false information, by the government, press, and anyone else.

Rendering integrity an outworn, vestige of the past.

Sadly, too many trusted the media and didn't question what they were told, no matter how outrageous the information. Propaganda was a subtle form of mind control, that could steer the people in dangerous directions.

Bryan wanted to get the truth out, a task now on her shoulders. PURF was the tip of the proverbial iceberg. No wonder she was D.C.'s public enemy number one. The FBI was more likely to lock her up than expose LOL. Arrest her as a domestic terrorist, or perhaps eliminate her themselves.

She got up and resumed pacing, Blossom standing up to watch.

It was clear Federal agencies had been weaponized against those considered enemies of the state. By now it was possible the entire FBI was corrupt, even worse than when it drove her father to leave the agency years before. Her former bodyguard, Mike Fernandez, told a similar tale.

Was there at least one federal agent out there with a modicum of decency?

She ground her teeth, pausing in midstep, knowing she had no choice but to call her father. If nothing else, he needed to know who put her on a hit list, just in case something happened to her.

Not that he could do much about it, either.

She returned downstairs and sat on the couch, fingers stroking the silky fabric as if to sooth her racing thoughts. She looked down, distracted by how much softer this one was versus her old one. When she asked what happened to it, her father told her its cushions were sacrificed to a government lab to be tested for poison while she fought for her life in New York City.

She drew up her knees and got settled cross-legged, Blossom snorting out a jowl-flapping editorial as she jumped up beside her to resume her afternoon nap. She patted her big head, then drew in a deep, cleansing breath.

Then another.

And another.

Braced herself for his reaction.

And made the call.

"Hi, Dad."

"What's up, Sara? Are you okay?"

"Yes and no. I found something out and I'm not sure what to do."

She stifled a giggle at his classic paternal *Now what?* sigh.

"So what did you find out?"

She bit her lip, again hunting for the right words. "The, uh, people who hired the guy that tried to kill me."

Silence.

"Dad? Did you hear me?"

"Yes, Sara. So I assume you're wondering how to go after them."

"How or if, I suppose."

"Who is it?"

"A nonprofit called LOL out of D.C. The Lobbyist Opportunity League."

"*Harrumph.* I can see why they wouldn't like their dirty dealings exposed, legal or otherwise. How'd you find out?"

She balked, not knowing how to tell him without poking a hornet's nest. That was the question she knew he'd ask that made calling so hard in the first place. Lying was definitely out.

"Sara? Are you there?"

"Yes, Dad. I'm here. Okay. So. It was, uh, Jason. The guy who, uh, abducted me. And you won't believe this, Dad, but he donated a hundred thousand dollars to my GoFundMe account! A hundred thousand! I now have over $247,000. Can you believe that?"

She gritted her teeth, hoping maybe that would vindicate him, but still braced for her father's response. She pictured his face, probably rolling his eyes.

"Let me get this straight," he said, voice tinged with sarcastic disbelief. "Your kidnapper. You're on a first-name basis with the guy who knocked you out and held you for a million dollars ransom? *Have you lost your mind?*"

In spite of expecting it, she still cringed.

"I know, I know. And he told me there wasn't much I could do, that I'm *persona non grata* as far as Washington is concerned. LOL would probably get the Congressional Medal of Honor for killing me."

"Wouldn't surprise me, that's for sure. So you believe this is accurate? Would he lie to you, point the finger at someone else?"

"I have no idea. I don't think so, but you never know."

"Okay. Let me see what I can find out."

MONTGOMERY RESIDENCE
BOULDER
August 29, Wednesday
9:30 a.m.

HIS AGING OFFICE CHAIR squawked as Will leaned back and deposited his feet on his desk. He gnawed his bottom lip. Was there anyone left at the Bureau he could trust? This was sensitive, far beyond what Sara could comprehend.

There was plenty not to like about lobbyists and crooked members of Congress, but being exposed for ordering a hit on a U.S. citizen, known in the spy world as "wet work," would shake up the system like never before.

At least it should.

Then again, it's unlikely anyone would be surprised, much less outraged. Too many continued to keep their heads in the sand, believing what they were told by the likes of CNN without asking difficult questions.

Either that or flat-out ignoring the corruption.

Those who were vocal about not going along with the narrative usually wound up—*dead*.

Whew.

He really needed to talk to this Jason person.

Dear God, who and what is he? A total psycho? Messing with her? Or converted to her cause? Who the hell is he?

He had only one possibility for getting in touch with him. If, perchance, he still had the phone he had Sara call from, maybe he would answer. Assuming the number wasn't spoofed.

He scrolled through his received calls.

There it was, glaring at him with all the charm of an audit notice from the IRS.

The one from Newport, Maine.

Yeah, right.

Hell, what did he have to lose?

He pressed the callback icon, not expecting a response.

"Hello, Mr. Montgomery."

Momentarily speechless, Will's feet dropped to the carpeted floor with a soft thud. "I'm impressed. I didn't think you'd answer. Figured that phone was in a Dumpster by now."

"I thought about it. Then decided it might come in handy. Apparently it was a good call. No pun intended. So tell me. Why are you calling? Didn't Sara get home alright?"

Will set the phone on *speaker* and leaned back, crossing his arms. "She did. And as interested as I'd be to hear your side of that crazy story, that's not why I called. I guess you could go so far to say I'm calling as one professional to another."

"Indeed. By the way, thanks for not calling the cops."

Will muffled a snort, given he was ready to. "Right. As Sara pointed out, it's unlikely they would have believed it. We don't need to be on record as nut jobs, if you know what I mean."

The man responded with a humorless, knowing laugh. "All too well. So, how can I help you? I'm sure you called for a reason, not just to chat."

"Yes. I'm looking for advice." Will's prevailing impression so far was that this guy was probably *not* a psycho based on his business-like manner and general aplomb. "I'm wondering how to handle that information. Treacherous territory, needless to say. Volatile accusation. You must have been an insider. Was that your last assignment, keep an eye on the entire operation?"

The man hesitated. "Yes. And I don't think any of them were aware. When so many questionable people and companies are involved, we get a call to keep an eye on things. Keep them out of the woods."

"I hear you. Pretty unprofessional bunch."

"Yeah." Jason chuckled. "You have no idea."

Will exhaled through his nose, curious what he might say next. "I'm guessing that somewhere along the line you left the dark side. Is that correct?"

Another long pause. "Pretty much."

"Will you tell me why?"

If there was anything Will didn't expect, it was sniffles.

"Your daughter," he said, sounding all choked up.

Will's throat likewise threatened to close. He gulped it down saying, "She told me about that photo you took. Of her on the patio. Was that it?"

"That started it. I couldn't kill her." The man cleared his throat. "My *Aha!* moment, I suppose. I still wanted the money, though, so came up with Plan B."

"Which came close to succeeding."

"Yeah. I guess she has some friends in high places."

"Right," Will agreed. "So that was a pretty generous donation. What do you expect her to do with it?"

"Hire a top notch security team. I can recommend a few, if you like. Former Secret Service. When they still could be trusted."

"Not a bad idea. Do you think there's any chance of convicting these bastards?"

"It would be tough. For anyone else, I'd say no. But with those friends in high places, who knows? She just might be able to pull it off."

SARA'S CONDO
DENVER
August 29, Wednesday
10:20 a.m.

KNOWING SHE NEEDED A more peaceful environment to work on her podcasts, Sara packed up to head for her cabin. In addition to being there again, she looked forward to driving the new car.

Who didn't savor that new car smell?

She grinned as she packed Blossom's supplies in her doggie backpack. How would her new bestie respond to the backwoods environment? She was very serious about investigating any new locale, canine curiosity at its peak. No doubt part of her training. Situational awareness that Sara sucked at.

How would K-9 training differ from what she'd already been through? Apparently, it involved such things as hand signals rather than verbal commands. Her father suggested it was advisable since the dog's job description had changed dramatically. She laughed out loud at confronting hostile forces with a trained pit bull by her side.

Her thoughts shifted back to returning to her favorite place on the planet. Where Bryan's spirit still resided. Something about being there allowed her to think more clearly. Perceive things she couldn't in the distraction-laden noise and bustle of the city.

She'd missed it horribly the past several weeks, especially worrying if and when she'd ever get out there again.

The last time was six weeks before, when she and Mike were there. They swept for bugs, Mike did some sleuthing, and she checked on Charlie in the hyperbaric clinic after his accident.

Which didn't exactly count as a break.

While there this time she decided she'd get in touch with Liz, maybe even join the *Mah Jongg* ladies for a break.

Since her TV appearances, they'd have lots of questions.

Satisfied she had everything they needed, she and Blossom got settled in the car and drove toward the interstate. As level ground yielded to the Rockies, the majestic, postcard-quality view settled around her like a soft blanket on a cool night. Hints of autumn were starting to appear on upper elevations, deciduous trees painting rugged mountainsides with shades of red, orange, and yellow.

Her energy shifted as Nature's splendor fell upon her, the very reason she decided to leave town. The drive midweek was quiet, giving her just under two hours to start organizing her thoughts. She still fought a panic attack when an eighteen-wheeler flew past, but other than that, Interstate 70 West was familiar enough for her mind to do some planning while her dog snoozed in back.

Her original intent was to flesh out hers and Bryan's story. Her television appearances barely scratched the surface. She made it known the government spent billions of dollars on a survival bunker for lobbyists, then murdered her husband for trying to expose it, but that was about it.

Which reminded her to contact Davis Jenkins.

Using voice commands, she listened to the list she made before she was kidnapped to refresh her memory.

There were three main topics that included a number of subheadings, each likely to raise a ruckus:

1. Expose PURF as a blatant betrayal by elected officials of taxpayer trust. What other unethical expenditures have they done?

2. Corporatism: Government collusion with corporations via lobbyists, thanks to the Supreme Court.

3. Lying and Propaganda legitimized by reversing the Smith-Mundt Act.

That was enough to get started. Hopefully, anyone who'd seen the broadcasts and was sympathetic would want to learn more. Especially donors to her GoFundMe account, whom she could email if they provided their address.

Her ponderings paused as she approached the only place along the route she dreaded.

The Eisenhower Tunnel.

Without fail, it beckoned her claustrophobic tendencies from hibernation. Her fingers tightened on the steering wheel as she entered.

The sound shift woke up Blossom. She bounded into the front passenger seat, eyes fixed on Sara.

Once she was in the open again, both she and the dog relaxed. The canine remained up front and stared out the side window while Sara's thoughts returned to her podcasts.

If there was one concern she didn't have, it was running out of topics. Her current list provided material through the middle of September, maybe longer. With luck, she could get several written and recorded over the next few days.

She'd been delayed long enough, no thanks to that poison.

Thoughts of which dredged up questions. Was part of Jason's donation related to that? Did he feel guilty? How was he coping with being blind? It was so weird, sitting there watching those movies, like they were old friends or something.

Really weird.

She shoved the tangent away, distractions like that something her brain did too often. It drove Bryan crazy. She could just hear him saying, *Get back on track, Sara!*

A sentimental flash tweaked her heart before she forced herself back to topic.

It was high time people recognized how they were being used.

"Government funded" meant "taxpayer funded."

Lying had been legalized.

And what about that sketchy Supreme Court decision? What part of *"a government, of, by, and for the people"* did those justices fail to understand? Corporations were not people! *Had they, too been paid off?*

The Founding Fathers put the word *people* in there for a reason, having experienced the tyranny of the Crown.

A mission statement would be good.

"Wake up, people, your government is a bunch of crooks," came to mind.

When she laughed aloud, Blossom's head whipped around, startled. She reached over and patted her head. "It's okay, girl."

Outrage at government corruption retreated as she pulled up to her rustic A-frame. Tears filled her eyes as she savored the scene, cabin embraced by a mix of evergreen and deciduous trees starting to sport fall colors, though still partially green.

Never had it looked so idyllic. It felt *so* good to be back. Not only an entirely different vibe than her condo, but saturated with precious memories. Living without it was unthinkable.

Of all the photos she'd ever taken, how did she miss this one? Perhaps taking it for granted until missing it so desperately, awash in fears she'd never return.

She dug her phone out of her purse and took several shots. Having a picture of it at the condo would help her never to forget again how dear it was to her heart.

You don't know what you have until you lose it.

Thanks, Mom, she thought, *I get it now.*

She strapped Blossom's backpack on her, then gathered up her laptop and overnight bag.

Inside was stuffy and a little chilly with the onset of Indian Summer's bipolar weather. She turned on the ceiling fan and opened the side windows while her dog checked the place out, sniffing all around.

She laughed when the dog spent considerable time examining the sheepskin rug in front of the fireplace. She walked over to join her, flooded with memories of her and Bryan's antics upon it.

"I wish you could have known him," she whispered, sitting down cross-legged, fingers caressing soft wool.

Remembering. . .

Swamped with melancholy, it wasn't long before unbidden moisture crept from her eyes. Blossom stopped her investigations, came over to lick away her tears, then curled up beside her, head in her lap.

They became Tsistsistas through the gift of an earth-giving ceremony, the Massaum, which required the formation of an ethnic entity closed to outsiders, an entity that had to be maintained over time. This event took place sometime between 500 and 300 B.C.
—The Wolves of Heaven by Karl H. Schlesier, p. xi

25. MASSAUM

NOVAVOSE (Day 3 - Wednesday)
BEAR BUTTE STATE PARK
SOUTH DAKOTA
Sacred Mountain Time

When Charlie awoke, it felt as if he hadn't slept. The dreams, as with the night before, were so vivid it was as if he were awake the entire night. His mind was ready to explode while his body felt so heavy it took considerable effort to move.

He used his elbows to boost himself into a sitting position, rested a moment, then struggled to his feet to rearrange the man sage. He sat down again, a bit short of breath, getting ready to smoke the sacred red pipe. Posture slouched over, he took a few deep breaths, wondering how he'd make it through another day, much less two.

He reached for the pipe.

Then stopped.

Straightened his back.

He had company.

Winter Hawk stood, off to his right. Charlie's smile of welcome was weak, but sincere.

"My father told me I should fast and sit with you today," the teen said.

"*Néá'eše*," he said, so glad to see him he nearly cried. "White Wolf is a very wise man."

Charlie lit the pipe, smoked with his brother, then cleaned it, and returned it to its place against the buffalo skull. He summoned the spirits with the eagle bone whistle, then prayed awhile, but his throat grew dry and his voice gave out.

Remembering, he dug the Big Medicine out from his grandfather's medicine bundle, broke off a piece, and placed it in his mouth. Saliva returned as he chewed, allowing him to continue.

Before long he felt as if his prayers were too repetitive. "Would you like to pray?" he asked his brother.

Winter Hawk nodded. "It would be an honor, brother."

As the boy began to pray, the hair on his arms stood up. A short time later the sky grew dark. The breeze turned cold, black clouds rumbling above. Prefaced by flashes of lightning, thunder snarled and crackled around them, accented by sprinkles of rain.

When the ground shook beneath them, Winter Hawk's eyes opened wide, meeting Charlie's as he kept praying, then he eventually closed them again. It grew darker, thunder so loud and relentless it swallowed the boy's prayers.

Chilled air yielded unexpectedly to warmth.

Charlie opened his eyes.

They were sitting before the fire at the center of the *maheonox*, the now-familiar lodge within *Novavose*.

They were not alone.

He tapped his brother's arm until he opened his eyes.

Charlie smiled at his brother's expression upon seeing their grandfather sitting with them. As before, the man's appearance was as a warrior in his prime, not an old man.

"Winter Hawk," the man said, intonations softened with deep, paternal love. The teen's eyes rimmed with white. "I am Eaglefeathers, your grandfather. I crossed over before you were born. It was I who brought your immortal *hematasoomao* to join with *omotome*, the mortal gift of breath, for this lifetime."

"I remember you now," the boy said, face brightening. "I did not recognize you in the pictures my father showed me of you."

Eaglefeathers laughed. "Yes, I am no longer an old man. I am very pleased you are here with your brother. I will tell you both about a very important sacred ceremony. It is called the *Massaum*."

Charlie never heard of the *Massaum* until Eaglefeathers mentioned it earlier, making it likely his brother never had, either. Its significance gleamed from Eaglefeathers' dark eyes like the sun breached the horizon at dawn.

"Grandsons, the *Massaum* is very ancient. Listen well, grandsons, for it is very important," Eaglefeathers began, then repeated, "It is very important" three more times.

As he explained the importance of the ancient ceremony, images that illustrated his words arose within the flames.

"The *Massaum* required a spiritual leader to whom earth could be given," he told them. "The *maiyun* gave this honor to Motseyoef, whom we call Sweet Medicine, who taught the *Tsistsistas* how to live. *Nonoma,* Thunder*,* and *Escheman*, the Earth Mother, revealed to him the circular earth drawing that shows the land given to us. It is recognized by all spiritual powers of the universe."

"Thunder and the Earth Mother gave us the land?" Charlie asked.

"Yes. The land given to the *Tsistsistas* through Motseyoef was centered right here at *Novavose*, and sanctified by the first *Massaum* ceremony. That is how our history is kept, grandsons. For thousands of years. In ceremonies, songs, prayers, rituals, and the earth itself."

"I knew they were important, but did not realize that was how our history is kept," Winter Hawk said.

"We do not write such things on paper like *Vehoe*," Eaglefeathers replied. "Paper can burn. It can be destroyed. It can be lost. When it is in our hearts as a people it lives forever, *if we honor it!* Our ceremonies embody our culture so it can be retained and passed down. The *Massaum* explains the giving of the earth to us in the four directions around *Novavose*."

Charlie knew his people had been given the land, but not the details. Its importance struck as a lightning bolt. The comparison that sprang to his mind was that of living with someone versus being married. Being bound by covenant made a significant difference.

"I understand that this has been our land for thousands of years," he said. "I did not know it was given to us in a sacred ceremony. *Vehoe* did not understand or respect it, so he stole our land, yes?"

"Yes, but it was partly our fault," Eaglefeathers continued. "The *Massaum* shows the relationship of our people to the spirit world of the grasslands. It explains our sacred connection with animals as expressed through *Ehyophstah*, Yellow-haired Woman, the buffalo spirit who was made human to assist us. The *Massaum* tells the story of how she taught us the proper way to hunt herd animals of the Plains by calling them into camps and pounds."

"Did we always live here as a people?" Winter Hawk asked.

"No. Our ancient homeland was on the shore of great lakes in the far north. Our village was in the shadow of Eagle Mountain."

"You named Eagles Peak in Colorado?" Charlie asked.

Eaglefeathers smiled. "No. My grandfather did. When our people lived in the north it was before bows and arrows. Motseyoef led those who wanted to come across the Missouri River to *Moxtavhohona*, now called the Black Hills. He conducted the first *Massaum* here, at the foot of *Novavose*. The laws explained every year through the ceremony were intended to protect our way of life."

Eaglefeathers' eyes burned as embers as he continued. "Listen to me very closely, grandsons. Listen to me very closely, for this is very important. This is very important. The Black Hills were the first and permanent *Tsistsistas* homeland in the Plains. It is our homeland! Given to us through the *Massaum* earth-giving ceremony. It also gave us the right to expand our hunt in the four directions from *Novavose*."

"We could expand our land when we needed more space?" Charlie asked.

"Yes. When we needed to move our hunting ranges, a *Massaum* was held to grant us the land and we accepted the responsibility to be its guardian."

"That makes it very clear, that the land was ours," Winter Hawk said.

Eaglefeathers nodded. "It was, but it was not that simple. A *Massaum* had to be held every year. Every year! All *Tsistsistas* bands were required to attend. The camp was a spirit camp. All spirits were present. The Creator, *Maheo*. The *maheyuno* and the *maiyun*. The spirits of animals, plants, and rocks, as well as the spirits of the *Tsistsistas*. Each performance renewed the covenant granted by the *maiyun*."

His words carried daggers that stuck in Charlie's gut as he began to understand where things went wrong. "If it wasn't held, what happened? Did we lose our rights?"

Eaglefeathers' pained expression answered his questions before he spoke. "Yes. Sadly, that is true," he said.

"When was the last one?"

"About a hundred years ago. Those held on the reservation protected that land only. The last one was 1927. Medicine Elk was the ceremony's pledger, but it was a shortened version."

Eaglefeathers' presence darkened to one he'd never seen before. "Starting in that same year, the federal government sponsored the carving of four presidents' faces on Mount Rushmore, here in the Black Hills. The very land which had been given to us by *Maheo* centuries before. The plundering of our land by *Vehoe* was complete."

The air left Charlie's lungs as if he'd been punched in the stomach. "Was a *Massaum* held at Dead Horse Canyon, Grandfather?"

"Yes. Eagles Peak is at its center as another sacred mountain."

"Which is why it was sacred land?" Winter Hawk asked.

"Yes. And *ours*."

Generational anger fired through Charlie's veins. He straightened his back and glared. "We must get it back,"

The look in his grandfathers' eyes as they met his own gave him chills.

"Yes, grandson," he declared. "And we will."

SARA'S CABIN
FALCON RIDGE
August 29, Wednesday
1:48 p.m.

"HI, LIZ. THIS IS Sara. How are you today?"

Sara muffled a giggle at the silence on the other end, her red-headed friend rendered speechless was a true anomaly.

"Oh! My goodness! Sara! How are you? Are you back? I've been so worried about you."

"Yes, I'm here. I've been pretty tied up with a variety of things the past month, but I'm finally settling into life again. I needed a break, so came out here. How are the *Mah Jongg* ladies?"

Sara took a sip of green tea, luxuriating in the view she'd missed so much beyond the kitchen window.

"I'm so glad you did! The ladies are fine, for the most part. Tonight's our last night. Angela and Bob are heading back to Texas tomorrow. They're leaving next week for a Caribbean cruise. Ida dropped out, but Rhonda's still playing. Would you like to join us? It's always a better game with four."

Sara smiled. She could always count on Liz for a neighborhood report. "That sounds great! Where is it?"

"Angela's. Would you like me to pick you up?"

"Sure, that would be great. Around 6:20?"

"Yes, same as before. I'm so glad you'll be there! See you soon."

She hung up, scowling when the thought she should drive herself flashed through her mind.

But why?

She felt well enough she doubted she'd need to leave early. It was also unlikely Liz would want to hang around chatting with any of the other women since she was better friends with her than any of them.

Deciding to get some fresh air, she swapped out her shoes for hiking boots. She laced them up, unable to remember when she'd worn them last.

"C'mon, girl," she called to Blossom, heading for the kitchen door. "You're going to love it out there!"

Never had she appreciated her ability to walk so much as when she strolled across the area between the cabin and the hiking trail where Bryan's ashes resided. The earthy scent of autumn teased the air, afternoon sun warm on her bare arms and legs while the pit bull delighted in all the new scents.

How differently might things have played out if she'd had the dog all along?

By the time they got back, fresh air and exercise had taken its toll. She took a nap that lasted far longer than expected, then got up and checked the freezer for something to eat.

She hesitated a moment, wondering if any had been tampered with. The seals were solid and her dog didn't seem concerned, so she heated up some taquitos, then relaxed on the back deck. Tomorrow would be soon enough to get to work. For now, chilling out felt good.

At the appointed time, Liz's white Escalade pulled up in front.

As she started for the door, Blossom tilted her head and gave her a questioning look. She stopped. Angela would have a fit if she brought her along. Yet, the last time she and the dog were separated was traumatic for them both.

Surely Angela wouldn't mind if the dog sat on their porch, or maybe Liz would let her stay in her car. If not, she'd drive herself, no big deal. Maybe that was what that flash to drive herself was about.

She stepped out on the deck, dog beside her, and waved as Liz got out of the car. She looked the same as always, not one of her well-tamed copper locks out of place.

"When did you get a dog?" she asked, coming up the steps. She held out her hand so the canine could check her out.

"I got her for protection and she has serious separation anxiety. Do you think Angela will mind if I leave her on the porch?"

Liz's lips disappeared in a pensive line. "No telling, but you can leave her in the car. She won't chew it up or anything, will she?"

"No. She's better behaved than most people."

"Then just bring her along. She'll be fine," she said as they walked down to her car. "It's so good to see you! You cut your hair. It looks, well, different."

"Right. I had a, well, health issue, that messed it up. I can't wait for it to grow back."

"Oh! Yes, things like thyroid problems can do that. I'm so glad you're doing okay. I was quite worried about you after you got sick on the *Today Show*. I'm glad it was nothing serious. What was it, honey? A touch of the flu?"

Getting into that was definitely not on Sara's agenda. "It was a bit more than that, but now I'm fine," she replied, brushing it off. Sharing the fact someone was trying to kill her invited more drama than she cared to discuss.

Furthermore, the one who'd made the attempt on her life, *i.e.* Eddie Johannsen, was related to former *Mah Jongg* lady, Ida Schwartz. As much as she liked Liz, her propensity for gossip wasn't something she cared to support.

She let Blossom in back, then climbed into the passenger seat. The car rumbled to life and bumped along rut-ridden dirt roads until reaching the asphalt driveway that led to the Bentley's estate. When they arrived at the call box, Angela activated the ornate gate embellished with the wrought-iron *"B"*, allowing them onto their property.

A few moments later, she parked at the far end of the circular drive, leaving plenty of room behind her for Rhonda.

"You sure it's okay if I just leave her in the car?"

Liz laughed. "Yes, it's fine."

When Angela opened the door her face blanched several shades lighter, defying her heavy makeup. The woman's eyes fluttered a moment, mouth hanging open, before resuming her usual composed, albeit stiff, demeanor, then bid them enter the chandelier-graced entry way, which Sara estimated was the size of her kitchen.

"Well, bless your heart! I must say I'm surprised to see you, Sara. I heard that you were, well, quite ill," the woman said.

An alarm went off in Sara's mind. What had she heard and where?

Not many knew the cause of her illness, as indicated by Liz's query. Mike was back in the area, but he wouldn't say anything. After all, he blamed himself for not protecting her adequately enough, plus there was the matter of confidentiality.

"Where did you hear that, Mrs. Bentley? As you can see, I'm just fine."

"She heard it from me."

Bob Bentley joined them in the entry, giving her a look similar to his wife's, except his booming voice bore an unmistakable blast of hostility.

She met his gaze. "Good evening, Mr. Bentley. May I ask where you heard that? I must say, I'm rather curious."

"My sources are none of your business. And as for your curious nature, Mrs. Reynolds, it might be wise for you to confine it to matters that lie within the law."

Her heartrate slammed into overdrive at the veiled threat, but she held her ground.

"Which matters are you referring to, Mr. Bentley? I don't recall breaking the law."

"You're correct. You did not. You and your questionable actions are protected by the First Amendment. Your husband, however, did. He would be behind bars for unlawful access to classified information, to say nothing of trespassing on a Top Secret government site. Fortunately, he received what traitors deserve and saved the courts the trouble."

Annoyance morphed to anger, fingers balling into fists at her sides as she met his hateful look with one of her own.

"My husband was murdered. Whatever he may have done, he was deprived of the constitutional right to be considered innocent until proven guilty by due process in a court of law."

Bentley's grunt of dissent was more of a growl as she went on, fury gathering momentum she couldn't contain.

"This is supposed to be a country of the people, for the people, and by the people. Not corporations, whose only concern is to make a profit for their shareholders, regardless of who might be hurt. Water contamination right in this area, which is probably what killed Edna Parker, is a case in point."

He rose to his full height. "Who do you think you are, telling me what's lawful and what isn't?"

She held his gaze, her retort's temperature rising.

"Too many laws are amoral, Mr. Bentley. They benefit a chosen few who bribe congressmen to pass legislation that has no benefit whatsoever for ordinary citizens. As a judge, you're part of that broken system. I'm not surprised you think my husband was a criminal for exposing the corruption that goes on behind closed doors."

His eyes smoldered, his venomous glare fixed on her as a snake views easy prey. He stepped toward her, looking down on her literally and figuratively.

"You think you know the law? How about castle doctrine. Ever hear of that, Mrs. Reynolds? It allows me to shoot anyone dead who threatens me on my own property, right here and now. *Dead.* Like you should have been weeks ago."

"Really, Mr. Bentley? This isn't Texas. Doing that in Colorado is a criminal offense."

"I'm done listening to your drivel!" he bellowed. "Get to hell out of my house!"

When the echoes of his gravel-encrusted baritone faded, a tense silence remained, harsh words lingering like the stench of rotten meat.

Someone rang the bell, everyone's head jerking in that direction.

Sara exhaled hard through her nose, turned on her heel, and opened the door, finding herself face to face with Rhonda. The woman gasped and stepped back, confusion scrambling her features.

"I'm sorry," Sara muttered, then excused herself as she stomped down the stone steps on shaky knees, then stared helplessly at Liz's car, where Blossom was barking up a fit.

Fists flexed again at her sides, she lambasted herself for not listening to that impression. Moments later Liz was beside her, arm around her waist. "Are you alright, honey?"

She nodded.

"My goodness, you sure hit a nerve! Angela mentioned that Bob can have an ugly temper, but I've never seen anything like that before."

"Yeah. Wasn't exactly Texas friendly, was it?"

Liz laughed. "I'd say not! C'mon, dear. I'll take you home."

"Thank you. I'm sorry I ruined your last *Mah Jongg* night. I sure never expected that. I'd sure like to know why he thought I was dead."

"I know," Liz agreed as they got into her car, Sara assuring her dog that she was okay.

"I've always wondered about those two," Liz went on. "From the first day we met, I had the impression things were not as they seem. Something about them has always given me the creeps. They seem fake in some way."

Sara fastened her seatbelt. "Right. Like faking they're respectable people."

Liz started the car, then drove around the driveway toward the gate. "That was a lot more excitement than I expected, that's for sure. Poor Rhonda, walking in on that mess."

Once back in Sara's driveway Liz gave her a sympathetic look. "Are you sure you're okay?"

She licked her dry lips, heart still racing. "I guess. Still a little rattled. Angrier than anything else." She exhaled hard. "Would you like to come in for a glass of wine? I could sure use one."

The woman laughed. "You and me both."

They got out of the car, Blossom close to Sara's side as they went up the stairs and in through the front door.

Sara retrieved a bottle of Riesling from the refrigerator. Her hands shook as she extracted the cork, then filled two stemmed glasses, the man's threatening words still reverberating inside her head.

Liz held her glass aloft. "*À votre santé.*"

Sara smirked as she repeated the toast and their glasses clinked.

To my health indeed.

Her gut contracted with foreboding. What consequences might follow that ugly confrontation?

26. STARS

NOVAVOSE (Day 3, Wednesday)
BEAR BUTTE STATE PARK
SOUTH DAKOTA
Sacred Mountain Time

harlie and Winter Hawk did not witness all fifty-six days of the original *Massaum*. Most pertained to its extensive preparation with them seeing only the five that comprised the ceremony itself. Eaglefeathers assured them the condensed version would suffice for now, but would be augmented later.

Details included such things as prayers, cycles of songs, ceremonial sign language, ceremonial painting, and ceremonial smoking. How or when that information might be conveyed he wasn't sure, but trusted his grandfather to say the truth.

When the vision closed, the pair found themselves back on the man sage overlooking the prairie far below. The skies were clear, storm clouds long gone.

Winter Hawk wore a puzzled look. "How were we able to see so much in only one day?" he asked.

Charlie smiled, at this point accustomed to the strange phenomenon. "Sweet Medicine Spirits are the *maiyun* who control 'Indian Time.' Information we receive in the spirit is instantaneous, only limited by the speed of thought."

"That makes sense," Winter Hawk agreed. "Sometimes visions come into my head from nowhere and very fast."

They discussed what they'd learned until sunset at which time Charlie loaded the pipe and smoked again with his brother. After that, the teen departed, making his way along the ridge pocket to its abrupt decline, where he turned to lift his hand in farewell. Charlie did likewise, then Winter Hawk disappeared on his trek back down to the campsite.

Charlie uttered a short prayer of gratitude, rejoicing at sharing yet another sacred experience with his brother. As the Sun disappeared, he continued to ponder all they'd learned with its profound importance.

His mind and soul ignited when pieces fit together that solved a sacred mystery. Things he wondered about since beginning his spiritual journey, yet in some cases he didn't even know the questions, much less answers.

One thing he learned unexpectedly filled a void he'd wondered about for many years: Why was there so little mention of the stars in Cheyenne tradition?

His knowledge of astronomy was tied to his *Diné* roots, namely winter stories told by *Amasani*. Bryan taught him *Vehoe's* constellations. The Coyote Star to him, Canopus to Bryan, was shared knowledge that led him and Sara to Bryan's hidden data.

The Cheyenne didn't ignore the sky, just didn't mention constellations, specific stars, or planets, except perhaps Venus as the Morning Star and the Milky Way, called *Seozemeo*. That included *Sexameo*, Road of the Departed, which led to *Se'han*, the place of the dead. A separate path, *Hekozeemeo*, Road of the Hanged Ones, was for those who committed suicide.

One of their revered peace chiefs was named Morning Star, while the Sun, Moon, and stars were part of the paint he wore for his fast. The blue morning star design was painted on his face as well of that of pledgers for certain other ceremonies.

Navajo culture used the heliacal rise of stars to answer questions, which he had done himself. Being familiar with the importance of the last star to rise before the onset of dawn made him appreciate the *Tsistsistas* use of heliacal rising stars as a calendar for the *Massaum*.

The traditional earth renewal ceremony began with the heliacal rise of the red star, Aldebaran, around June 22. It represented the Red Wolf *maiyun*, a manifestation of *Nonoma*, the Thunder Spirit.

The fifth public day of the ceremony was tied to the heliacal rise of the blue star, Rigel, which occurred twenty-eight days later. It represented *Voh'kis*, the kit fox, a manifestation of *Ehyophstah*, Yellow-Haired Woman, who was part of their creation story.

The *Massaum* ended twenty-eight days after that, indicated by the rise of Sirius. It represented the white wolf, a manifestation of *Eseheman*, Grandmother Earth.

His visit to the ninety-foot Bighorn Mountain Medicine Wheel in Wyoming as a child came to mind. The irregular circle had twenty-eight spoke-like lines and six cairns of man-sized rocks. At the time he was told the Cheyenne claimed it, yet no one could explain what it was used for.

Something in his chest ignited: *Now he knew!*

Bighorn Medicine Wheel, Wyoming. Photo By U.S. Forest Service:
https://commons.wikimedia.org/w/index.php?curid=3358774

Cairns aligned with the heliacal rising of those three stars, the stone structure built centuries, perhaps millennia, before.

It had any number of other possibilities, from being the outline for a *Massaum* Wolf Lodge to an actual "circular earth drawing" that marked their territory claimed by conducting the sacred earth-giving ceremony.

Or possibly both, while in modern times other uses for the Medicine Wheel were speculated upon, created, or re-created, based on inspiration.

Some *Vehoe* researchers suggested the *Massaum* was performed annually for at least two millennia, the creation of the *Tsistsistas* occurring in North Dakota around 500 B.C.

Eons later it started to fall apart, exactly the way Sweet Medicine told them it would.

With it becoming clear it was his sacred duty to put it back together.

His heart sank beneath the weight of such a critical cultural responsibility.

Since his virtual arrival at the *maheonox,* tutoring had been nonstop. Even with the support of Sweet Medicine Spirits, his brain felt as if it might explode.

Fortunately, as always, Eaglefeathers, read his mind.

Upon finishing his instruction on the *Massaum*, his grandfather suggested he and Winter Hawk take time to rest, meditate, pray, and absorb what they learned so far.

He didn't say there was far more to come, but Charlie sensed there was. Whatever fast-track he was on increased his anxiety day by Sacred Mountain Time day.

What if he didn't remember?

What if he made a mistake?

What if the people wouldn't listen?

And the biggest question of all, who and what was he to have this unloaded on him? And why did Winter Hawk witness it as well?

Oddly enough, there was something familiar about it. No doubt the reason he ran away from it years before. It wasn't so much that he was rebellious as a teen, as confused and afraid. In his mother's eyes he couldn't do anything right. That haunted him his entire life, making any new endeavor a failure waiting to happen.

It was nothing short of a miracle he graduated from college, probably because Eaglefeathers wouldn't allow him to quit.

Expectations burned through him from the moment they arrived at Bear Butte.

Excitement.

Fear.

Foreboding.

Intimidation.

Waning confidence.

Yes, he needed a break.

Not only to absorb, but accept whatever he was charged to do.

A conversation with White Wolf the previous month came to mind. One of those moments when glimpses of meaning and understanding penetrated his mind.

"Death-like experiences awaken you," his uncle had said. "They open the door to your destiny. You always had these abilities, but they were asleep. Even among our people your gifts are rare. We have been waiting for you for a long time, Littlewolf."

"But I returned to the red road months ago. I planned to come home by summer's end. Did my injuries cause me to see these things I couldn't before?"

"No. Your spirit coming back did. Had your intent to come home been undecided, you would have died and another take your place."

The unexpected response had served up more questions than answers.

Another? I do not understand.

Again that question arose.

If he didn't accept or accomplish what he was being told, would he be replaced by someone else?

Who? Winter Hawk, perhaps?

Which would be worse?
Die on the Sacred Mountain?
Or fail?

LSO NEW WORKSITE
RURAL FALCON RIDGE
August 29, Wednesday
07:50 a.m.

TREY STOOD TALL, his head held high. The sun rising behind well number one's derrick highlighted it in such an awe-inspiring way, he took out his phone to capture it. As always, the picture was disappointing, but what lay before him was not. As far as he was concerned, it was damned close to paradise.

His chest ballooned with pride. It had taken months of hard work, but at long last the site was up and running. Not only running, but kicking ass. Much to his relief, the new petro-geologist was sharp.

Not intuitive like Littlewolf, but good. He scrutinized the seismic survey, made a couple educated guesses, and before they knew it, they had three production rigs in place, wells going full bore.

He pumped his fist and let out a full-blown Texas, *"Yeeehaw!"*

What the oil business was all about.

The basin was no longer recognizable versus when they started drilling with a track-mounted wildcat rig months before. Back in June, it was pristine, albeit barren land surrounded by snowcapped craggy peaks.

Now the Rockies competed with a towering derrick and two wells connected to six-inch pipes attached to a network of high-pressure manifolds.

These, in turn, linked the well's output to a commercial pipeline a few miles to the southeast. They crisscrossed the property like a pipefitter's dream, delivering a combined average total of over 785 BOPD (Barrels of Oil per Day) of black gold to refineries in Wyoming.

LSO's crude was particularly valuable since it had a lower water content, being accessed without the fracking process, which required steaming it out.

The original road had doubled in width and been covered with asphalt. No more stuck or tilting rigs to worry about. While they were at it, they even paved a parking area.

Better access to the site allowed most of the heavy equipment to be delivered through ground transportation. Some components still had to be flown in with heavy-lift choppers when it wouldn't fit around that pain-in-the-ass turn in that friggin' country road.

How many inaccessible deposits lurked below?

What a goddamn waste.

Even seismic surveys were impossible in such terrain. There were possibilities with horizontal drilling. But they'd still need to know where the crude was beforehand.

There were four times as many employees as before, which required three rows of barracks. No longer comprised of trailers, they'd been replaced by prefab metal buildings; likewise, the mess hall, administration building with his office, and the lab.

Support equipment, including ATVs, bulldozers, front loaders, and even a small crane sat clustered between the buildings and rigs.

Nothing short of an oilman's paradise.

So far, there'd been one snow storm worth noting. It would undoubtedly get worse, but he remained optimistic. As long as they had plenty of food on hand, they could hunker down and keep working through just about anything short of a full-blown, zero visibility blizzard.

He spent the past thirty-nine years of his life in this business, and this had always been his dream—locate and supervise the setup of a new production site. He busted his ass along with dozens of others, some of whom lost their lives in that blowout, to achieve it.

He bowed his head, chest aching, as he thought of the men he lost. That was always hard to take. However, he couldn't help but think that losing their lives in this business made more sense than buying the farm in some politically-driven foreign war.

What a waste, defending people in some Third World, shithole country who'd inevitably turn against them.

Oil made the world go round. It kept it running in more ways than he could count. Gasoline was but one of a plethora of petroleum products people counted on every, single day. Without oil, modern civilization would collapse. No transportation alone would stop everything in its tracks.

Boom! No food.

Boom! No electricity.

Boom! No PVC pipe.

Boom! No packaging materials.

Boom! No plastics.

Boom! No heating oil.

He could go on and on.

Yesiree, total freakin' collapse.

The entire world should be kissing oil's ass, not giving them a bunch of tree hugger/environmental green bullshit.

Furthermore, unlike the military, those that stuck it out and retired from this business were well-compensated. His next bonus would be close to, possibly even over, a million dollars. Combined with the money he'd already stashed, plus LSO's generous retirement plan, he could live in style any damn time and place he wanted.

But at this point, he wasn't even close to ready. He thoroughly enjoyed his work and wasn't sure what he'd do instead.

Travel?

Go fishing?

Play golf?

Buy a Ferrari and chase women?

A chuckle rumbled through his chest. Chase women, hell— they'd be chasing him.

He thought back to that first day when he and Littlewolf went up there. What would that Indian think of things now? What he made possible? The jobs he helped create?

Hot damn, where the hell was that Indian, anyway?

He really needed to find him. Take him out for a beer. That accident had been such a bad break. He sincerely prayed his recovery was complete, that he was doing okay.

Maybe someday they'd meet again.

He sincerely hoped so.

Without him, none of this, his life-long dream, would have been possible.

NOVAVOSE (Day 3 Wednesday night)
BEAR BUTTE STATE PARK
SOUTH DAKOTA
Sacred Mountain Time

AS DARKNESS FELL, Charlie lit the sweetgrass braid, smudged, made the sacred motions, smoked, then prayed fervently for assurance. He pulled the buffalo robe around him against the cold, soft fur caressing his painted skin while his heart warmed with the unmistakable essence he knew well.

In his mind's eye he saw himself as a newborn infant, cradled in the arms of *Amasani*. The one person in his life from whom he always felt untarnished, unconditional love.

He paused his prayer.

Opened his eyes.

And there she was.

Except for that feeling, he never would have known who it was. She appeared as a beautiful young woman, not unlike one of the maidens in his first vision. Her braids coal black, eyes filled with soul-touching affection as always, skin flawless as the desert sky. Her dress bore sacred symbols in orange, aqua, and yellow, a heavy turquoise and silver necklace gracing her throat.

The last time he saw her she appeared as he remembered, a wrinkled old woman, back when he was unconscious following his accident. She had just crossed over and came to tell him goodbye, then left him a special gift by instilling her love into every fiber of the special blanket she wove for him as a child.

"*Yá'át'ééh, Naalnish,*" she said, her sweet voice embracing him with the spirit of peace.

Her *Diné* greeting originally meant *Everything upon the surface of the earth and in my life is good.* Modern times downgraded its meaning to their substitute for *Hello.* Yet to her it would always retain the original sentiment.

"You are beautiful, *Amasani,*" he said. "But you have always been beautiful to me."

She smiled. "I was not always an old woman, *Naalnish.* I am here because you are troubled. What is it I can do to help you in this very sacred place?"

His throat clogged, blocking the words. He swallowed hard. "Yes, I am deeply troubled, *Amasani,*" he admitted, a lead weight suspended within his chest. "What I am learning is amazing and wonderful. I am honored and humbled that I am expected to help our people. But I fear the burden is beyond what I can bear. How can I possibly do everything I'm being told?"

She searched his face, eyes locked on his. "*Naalnish.* Do you trust me?"

He held her gaze, puzzled by the odd question. "Of course, *Amasani.*"

"Do you trust your grandfather?"

"Yes."

"Do you trust our Creator?"

"Yes, I trust *Maheo.*"

"They trust you, *Naalnish.* Why do you not trust yourself?"

The weight in his chest increased as lack of confidence brought yet another reason to feel inadequate. "I am overwhelmed. I do not see how I can do all that is expected."

Her hand rested on his arm. "You are questioning the judgment of those you trust. Do you believe any of them, who care deeply about you, would charge you with something important knowing you would fail?"

He swallowed again, attempting to rid his dry throat of the persistent, unwelcome obstruction. "No," he said, his voice hoarse. "They would not."

"Listen carefully, *Naalnish*. I have not told you this before. Every word of it is true. Every word. From the day you were born, I knew you would do something very important. Something great. Something no one else could do but *you*. Are you listening, *Naalnish*?"

"Yes, *Amasani*."

"It was not because you are my grandson. It was not because I love you. It was because I felt your spirit and its strength. It is good you are humble. That does not mean you are weak or cannot do what you are being told. If you cannot trust yourself, then trust those who do. Those who believe in you. Those who know your greatness."

He nodded, duly reprimanded, yet from her it had no sting.

His heart swelled with affection and gratitude for having her in his life. "I will make you proud, *Amasani*."

She smiled. "I know." She hugged him, kissed his cheek, then vanished as smoke within the stars of *Sexameo* on her way home to *Seozemeo*.

Charlie basked in the adoration he always felt from *Amasani*. What a blessing to see her, Eaglefeathers, and his father, plus commune with great Cheyenne leaders from the past.

Novavose was truly a sacred portal to *Se'han*.

How he would accomplish everything he didn't know, neither did it matter. His spirit was calm, filled with peace and love. All was as it was supposed to be.

> *"We are all linked by a fabric of unseen connections. This fabric is constantly changing and evolving. This field is directly structured and influenced by our behavior and by our understanding."*
> *--David Bohm, Physicist*

27. HISTORY

SARA'S CABIN
RURAL FALCON RIDGE
August 30, Thursday
9:12 a.m.

The more Sara thought about it, the more disturbed she became with Bentley's comment. Since he had connections with PURF, he undoubtedly had knowledge of the entire situation, which could easily include attempts on her life.

The next morning she sat with her coffee, gazing out a triangular window to the mountains beyond. Anger smoldered like an abandoned campfire, embers awaiting the breeze that would awaken flames to spawn a raging wildfire. If there was one thing she knew, it was that she'd give blood and pay money to expose that sleaze ball for what he was.

However, now more than ever, she was aware of the consequences of messing with someone in a position of power, further fueling the fury.

After what she'd been through, was it worth the risk?

Maybe Charlie would have some thoughts on the matter.

Where was he, anyway? Did it relate in some way to how she was healed? Surely, he would contact her soon. If nothing else, she needed to thank him other than the phone message, which he may not receive.

Meanwhile, the confrontation with Bentley had her mind in a vise. Her thoughts raced, twisting any hope of rational ideas into a

Gordian knot of righteous indignation. Concentrating on her podcast was impossible.

She needed to escape, at least for a while. Going somewhere, even a short hike, had no appeal. Rather than free her mind, out there she'd continue to obsess, probably gripe to Bryan and get even more riled up. She needed to find something to occupy her mind enough to set it aside so she could think straight.

Coffee in hand, she got up and ambled aimlessly around the cabin, Blossom beside her every step of the way. She paced around the central fireplace between the kitchen and living area in an ambling figure-eight, until she found herself back in the main living area.

Her canine companion sat down beside her with a questioning look. She gave the dog a reassuring pat while her eyes and thoughts drifted toward the guest room.

Following some strange prompting, she entered the room that had once been the original cabin. No telling how old it was. Bryan probably knew, but she had no idea. No doubt suitable distraction lay within that bench seat below the ancient window, where so many other secrets had lurked.

Sun streamed through the single window, glass rippled by time, while dust particles danced in the air. The room's rustic flavor remained, accented by several oval rag rugs reposing upon ancient, hand-hewn planks.

An antique blanket of Native American design graced the wall above the double bed. She stood there a moment, lured back in time.

If log walls could talk, what might they say?

In response to her unspoken query, the hair stood up on the back of her neck.

The walls might be silent, but the bench seat wasn't.

While she'd explored some of its contents earlier, she'd never gone through everything. Perhaps delving into the past was what she needed. Help her forget the present's unknowns and unpleasantries, at least long enough to clear her mind.

She set her mug on the window sill, tossed the needlepoint throw pillows from the bench to the bed, then pulled over one of the rugs to kneel upon.

Blossom's look was one only a dog could achieve, the canine's intent to nap on it clear. Sara laughed, put it back, then retrieved another.

The ancient lid squeaked as she lifted it, then rotated the lid's metal brace to hold it in place. The musty smell of the past rushed free, as if history itself had been awakened.

Old wool blankets on top were slightly moth-eaten, but still soft. She hugged them close, savoring their earthy scent.

Who'd slept beneath them? And when?

Smiling, she set them on the bed behind her with the pillows.

One by one she did the same with cardboard and plastic boxes that contained Bryan's memorabilia and family photos.

Looking at them would invite a sentimental excursion that would deliver a meltdown she didn't need, emotions already in a knot.

She sought a distraction, not a reminder.

She was always fascinated by history. While other kids hated it, she looked forward to it, always imagining what it would have been like to live in different times.

Would what lay buried and forgotten within its confines provide a vicarious adventure? Reveal enticing secrets from the past? Surely her heroine from *Tomb Raider*, Lara Kroft would approve.

After all, what was nestled within was deemed important enough to be retained for decades, maybe longer.

Bryan was a clean freak and well-organized. So much so, at times he drove her nuts. No doubt he'd been through everything at some point and made the decision what to keep.

As a history buff himself, no wonder there was so much, especially since he had a deep appreciation for details and any human actions that drove notable events.

If she came across anything of historical value, she could always donate it to a museum or historical society. Then it would be preserved so others could enjoy it as well.

An old wooden box, darkened and bruised by time, beckoned from the bottom. She lifted it out, then set it on the bed where she released its metal latches.

What rested on top was unexpected—a blue report folder. She opened it, finding a lengthy report Bryan wrote for a college history classes.

Underneath were stacks of yellowed, fragile-looking documents, some in official, embossed sleeves. A few ancient newspapers, a stack of letters held together with cotton string, and a rolled-up map.

No doubt the aged documents represented his research material. His propensity for meticulous substantiation for the truth had obviously originated a long time before.

Going through everything while sitting on the bed was awkward, so she moved everything, including her coffee, to the couch in the living area.

The cover page comprised the original assignment sheet. A take-home final exam that included three sections: 1) Overview of a Specific Time Period; 2) Individual Research into an Event or Situation Not Found in History Books; 3) Personal History and/or Genealogy Associated with the Chosen Area.

She smiled wistfully and began to read, Bryan's voice in her head telling the lengthy tale.

Section I: Overview of a Specific Time Period

White fur traders first came to this part of Colorado early in the 19th century. While the 1851 Treaty of Fort Laramie allowed white settlers to reside there, the United States promised the Cheyenne and Arapaho tribes they could retain control of Colorado's Eastern Plains between the North Platte and Arkansas Rivers, eastward from the Rocky Mountains. The Kansas-

Nebraska Act of 1854 allowed land claims, but ironically, the land remained the property of Native Americans, making those claimants technically no more than illegal squatters.

The Pike's Peak Gold rush from 1858 - 1861 brought an increase in white homesteaders who pressured the U.S. government to deal with the fact title to the land still resided with Native Americans. In 1861, the Treaty of Fort Wise negated the Fort Laramie treaty and land ownership was ceded to the United States.

About that same time, some of the Southern States seceded, preamble to the Civil War. Thus, the Union wanted to secure the area for themselves because it was rich in lead, silver, and gold. Shortly thereafter, President James Buchanan designated Colorado an official territory, including land which had previously been part of Utah, Nebraska, Kansas, and New Mexico territories.

How typical, Sara thought. Exploited by the U.S. Government from Day One. No wonder Bryan was pissed.

From that point on, he concentrated on the Native Americans, which wasn't surprising, due to his relationship with Charlie.

He touched on the highlights of the Colorado War fought between the settlers and different Indian tribes, then concentrated on a small band of Cheyenne led by a chief who dissented from those who signed the Fort Wise Treaty.

Section II: Individual Research into an Event or Situation Not Found in History Books

A small Cheyenne band refused to accept the Treaty of Fort Wise's terms, which included being removed to an Indian reservation along the Arkansas River between the northern boundary of New Mexico and Sand Creek. Moreover, the tribes would be converted from nomadic hunting to a farming lifestyle, to which they said not only "No" but "Hell, no."

Sara laughed out loud. Only Bryan would include such an irreverent statement in a college history paper. She read on:

One of their major objections to white encroachment had been the slicing up of the bison herds, due to increased activity, such as wagon trains, on the westward trails. Thus, this band of Cheyenne, led by a chief named Black Cloud, drove a medium size herd from the Eastern Plains farther west.

They followed a path along the South Platte past Bison Peak, through Wilkerson Pass, then followed the Arkansas River north, until they reached the valley between the Gore and Sawatch Ranges. This migration was started toward the end of summer, during the bison's mating season, when the herd included animals of both sexes; other times of year, the herds separated by gender. (Not a bad idea for humans, actually.)

The bison didn't object to being moved when they found plenty of grass along the way, as well as in their new location. The Cheyenne built a small village, unaware of the ensuing wars between the settlers and their fellow Native Americans.

A few years later, around 1864, miners infiltrated the area and discovered the renegade Indians, who were supposed to have gone to a reservation with the others years before. Settlers who didn't succeed in finding silver or gold began slaughtering bison for their hides. This infuriated the Cheyenne, who managed their resources carefully. Arguments and a few skirmishes ensued, but agreements were reached when silver was eventually found and the settlers went to work in the mines.

A permanent mining camp was established, which took the settlers' interest away from the bison. This pleased the Cheyenne, who then lived peacefully alongside the miners for a few years, trading goods between them with some miners even taking Cheyenne women as wives.

The relationship began to fall apart again when leachings from the mines began to poison the streams that not only watered the buffalo herds, but where the Cheyenne fished, the excess of which they'd been trading to the miners in return for guns and ammunition. When there was no more excess, the Cheyenne refused to sell or trade anything, which caused considerable unrest among the miners.

This ultimately led to a drunken horde of hungry miners going on a rampage and raiding the village, while the braves were away for their seasonal buffalo hunt. The raid resulted in numerous deaths, including that of the chief's son and the son of one of the miners, who had gone to warn them of the raid, as well as a few dozen horses that were driven over a cliff.

With their families dead, there was no longer any reason for the warriors to stay in the area, plus the miners demanded they leave. Thus, they returned to their last known village. When they got there, they found it deserted, its residents slain a few years before in the Sand Creek massacre with the area now populated by white settlers. At first, the incoming Cheyenne were mistaken for another raid, three warriors killed before their intent was determined to be peaceful and directions provided to the reservation.

Every year, until into the late 1990s, a contingent would return during the summer to pray and honor those who had died during the raid, the area surrounding Tomahawk Creek considered sacred ground.

She smiled, recognizing the story of Dead Horse Canyon. But why didn't Bryan mention the curse? Too controversial for a history paper? Or didn't he know?

In *Section III: Personal History Associated with the Area,* a pedigree chart showed Bryan's extensive Colorado heritage spanned seven generations, going all the way back to the original settlers. He mentioned Colonel Joseph Reynolds was a distant uncle, who fought in many Colorado Wars.

In 1876 he led an attack on a Cheyenne encampment in Montana Territory. It had been unsuccessful, other than to drive the Northern Cheyenne and Lakota Sioux together in joint resolve to resist selling the Black Hills to the United States.

She winced. What a slap in the face Mount Rushmore must have represented to its original residents.

Bryan went on to note that Reynolds and Black Cloud were contemporaries, and speculated that they may have encountered one another at some time or another, most likely in an unfriendly manner.

The bibliography was detailed and long, most likely referring to the documents in the box, plus a reference to a local Cheyenne named Charles Littlewolf, his source for the story of Black Cloud.

Sara scowled, considering what she just learned. The history lesson served its purpose as an excellent distraction, giving her plenty to ponder. She kept out the history report to show Charlie. Perhaps he'd like a copy, if he didn't already have one.

She got up from the couch to put the box back. Upon lifting the lid an old manila envelope tucked along the side caught her eye, "Mom and Dad" written across it in Bryan's hand.

She picked it up, unwound the string fastener, and looked inside, finding a sheaf of paper about a half-inch thick held together with a binder clip. She flipped through it, curious. It appeared to be a compilation of reports or documents, some redacted.

He never told her much about his parents. It was clearly a painful subject since both died when he was young, leaving him to be raised by his grandfather, much as Charlie was. Maybe their story was inside.

Mind already saturated, she put it back in the envelope and secured it closed. Something to go through some other time. She set it on top of the box, then returned both to the bench seat.

She closed the lid, wondering at the nagging feeling it evoked, Bentley's glowering specter for now, at least, set aside.

The [Catholic] church holds that the finest in the pre-Christian religions reflected the eternal truth and beauty of God. Thus, these religions were, in their way, preparations for God's revelation of Himself in human flesh as Jesus Christ.
— Peter John Powell, "Sweet Medicine," Volume I, p. xxiii

20. SURPRISES

NOVAVOSE (Day 4 - Thursday)
BEAR BUTTE STATE PARK
SOUTH DAKOTA
Sacred Mountain Time

The next morning Charlie's body drooped even more with fatigue, yet his spirit soared. Movements slow and requiring sustained effort, he got settled on the man sage, smoked at dawn, blew the eagle bone whistle, then offered a heart-felt prayer of gratitude. For seeing his dear ones again, sharing a vision with his brother, and the fire ignited in his breast to do whatever required to help his people.

Truly love was the greatest motivator, while fear brought stagnation and confusion.

As he completed his prayer, he opened his eyes to see Porcupine standing beside him, wearing a red and white striped wool cloak. Their eyes met, Charlie weary but ready for instruction on the final day of his fast.

Porcupine appeared around his age, a bit taller, with silky black hair well past his shoulders. His deep-set, soulful eyes were kind, yet sad, reflecting the horrors and disappointments he'd witnessed. Sculpted cheek bones and other fine features bespoke strong Cheyenne heritage.

Besides his pleasing appearance he projected dignity, confidence, humility, and nearly tangible spirituality. Something about him felt different than Eaglefeathers or other holy men he knew.

"I am the one they say brought the Ghost Dance to the Cheyenne," he said. "That is not exactly the way it was. I will tell you what happened and how its true meaning was lost."

Charlie was aware that the Ghost Dance caused problems in the past, so much so it triggered the massacre at Wounded Knee. Many believed the mysterious dance would bring back dead relatives to help rebel against the whites to get their land back.

"It was originally the *Dance of Peace and Welcome*. Its intent was to unify the tribes and inspire peace with *veheo*," Porcupine explained. "Our Paiute brother, Wovoka, was inspired to teach the dance. He also taught that Native people must be good and love one another, not quarrel, and live in peace with the whites. That we must work, and not lie or steal. That we must put away all old practices that glorified war.

"That if we faithfully obeyed his instructions, we would at last be reunited with our friends in this other world, where there would be no more death or sickness or old age. He taught this to many tribes."

The truth of his words resonated in Charlie's breast. "Do you believe he was a true prophet?"

"Yes," Porcupine replied with conviction. "While he was very sick and unconscious with scarlet fever, he went to Heaven. When he woke up it was during a total eclipse." He smiled. "His tribe believed he stopped a monster from eating the Sun. He saw our Creator many times, who gave him five sacred songs to control the weather to make sure his people and others would believe him."

Fascinated, Charlie asked, "So he became a rainmaker?"

"Yes. He even saved his people from a drought."

"What happened that changed the dance?"

"The promise of the dance was to bring peace and eventually the return of our land and the buffalo. This required being kind, clean, honest, and shunning the ways of *veheo*, especially alcohol. Some, particularly Sitting Bull, were impatient and full of hate for *veheo*. He saw it as a war dance. That was a big mistake."

"Sitting Bull was a great warrior."

"Yes. But he couldn't let it go." Porcupine eyes saddened as he continued. "While some, like Red Cloud and Wovoka, promoted peace, those who wanted to fight gave the dance their own interpretation and stirred up trouble. By calling it a war dance, the government believed it was going to lead to an uprising. So the Ghost Dance was banned."

"You taught it as a dance of peace to the Cheyenne?" Charlie asked.

"I tried, but Standing Elk and Little Chief sensed trouble, even with its intended peaceful purpose. So we did not teach it to our people. Many of the teachings for peace we already knew from Morning Star. Did you know he was only called Dull Knife because he didn't want to fight?"

Charlie shook his head. "No. I always wondered about that. It seemed an inappropriate name for such a great man."

"Not doing the Dance turned out to be a good decision," Porcupine continued. "We were not perceived as starting trouble. That allowed us to return to Lame Deer in 1891."

Porcupine's voice grew soft, as if remembering brought great sorrow. "Confusion and misunderstandings caused the massacre at Wounded Knee. There were 500 soldiers and 350 of our people, with 128 of them innocent women and children. They gathered at the request of Red Cloud, who wanted peace."

He sat down beside him as his story continued. "The soldiers, however, thought they were planning a rebellion. They placed four huge guns around the camp, even though our people surrendered peacefully to the soldiers. They were told to set up camp at Wounded Knee Creek."

Charlie knew the rest of the story, heart heavy as he recalled the tragic tale. In the cold morning of December 29, 1890, soldiers came into their camp to gather firearms. A soldier attempted to take a rifle from one of their deaf brothers in a rough manner. It fired, which caused the soldiers to believe a rebellion had begun so they started shooting, including the artillery.

That night a brutal blizzard closed in. The corpses turned to ice and were buried three days later in a mass grave.

"That massacre never would have happened had the true message of the dance been honored," Porcupine explained. "Perhaps it was divine justice that Sitting Bull died as a result of his incorrect views and changing the dance's purpose. Wovoka told me the Great Spirit Father was not pleased with what Sitting Bull did. He said that is why the Sioux were killed, because the Medicine turned bad."

Porcupine's chest rose and fell with a heavy breath, face laden with sadness. "So, the Great Spirit Father decided that the spirits of our dead, and the elk, antelope, and buffalo, would not return. At least not as soon as expected. With the dance banned, its message died as well."

Remembering Wounded Knee always brought a lump to Charlie's throat. The fact so many women and children, who gathered in good faith, were killed was the ultimate betrayal by *Vehoe*.

"So the dance of peace had the opposite effect."

"Yes and no," Porcupine explained. "That was the end of the wars with *Veheo*, but that was not the peace intended. If it had not been represented as a war dance and become a concern to the government, it would not have ended that way. But the people were not ready to live the way they were told, either."

"Where did the dance come from?" Charlie asked. "Who taught it to us? Wovoka?"

"He taught it to some, but I learned it when members from many different native nations were called to Walker Lake, Nevada in March 1890. Some of us were beckoned there in dreams, some by bearded visitors in white robes, others by runners, or purely by inspiration. But each of us received a personal invitation."

Charlie was stunned. Getting to Nevada back then for a single occasion sounded impossible. "That is a long way from Montana! How did you travel so far?"

Porcupine explained: "I first met with the Paiutes in Winnemucca, then at Wadsworth by traveling on the Central

Pacific Railroad. We took a wagon to the Pyramid Lake Agency, then to Wabuska, then finally to Walker Lake. There was mail service back then. Many of us knew enough English to write or have someone do it for us. I met with Wovoka at least three times."

He licked his lips, amazed by the answer. "I did not know railroads were built so long ago. What happened at the meeting in Nevada?"

"It was a very holy occasion. Our brothers from several tribes—Lakota, Arapahos, Paiutes, Gros-Ventres, Utes, *Diné*, Bannocks, and many others were there. Sixteen or more tribes, some from Canada and Mexico. The Sioux, who changed the Ghost Dance to a war dance, were not even there. They did not witness what happened! Or who taught us the dance and how we should live."

"Perhaps they were not invited because they were so dedicated to fighting," Charlie said.

"That is possible." For the first time Porcupine's face brightened. "I can tell you that our Creator is very real, for he came down to Grandmother Earth to meet with us."

"*Maheo* was there?" Charlie gasped, incredulous.

"Yes. The Great Spirit Father was there. To us, he is *Maheo*. He has a son, who is our Creator. We know him as *Heammawihio,* the White Man Above. To many he is Jesus Christ. The Messiah."

It took Charlie several seconds to absorb the shocking revelation. "There are two? Both are real? *Actual men?* Who came to see *our* people? How is that possible?"

"It is true." Porcupine's aura brightened to that of polished gold as he conveyed his experience. "*Heammawihio* came and taught us many days. I saw him. He told us how to live. That we should not kill men of any kind. He is very fair to look upon. He had no beard, his hair long, like ours. His skin is not white like *Veheo*, nor as dark as ours. But he looks like one of us."

"He does?" Charlie gasped.

"Yes. He is a man. A very powerful one. He is full of love. He took me by the hand and said we were all his children. He made us and everything around us, including Grandmother Earth. Once you see him, you can see him again in your sleep."

His countenance brightened further as he continued. "If you have shaken his hand, you can go to heaven and see your friends who are dead. Short Bull, who's Lakota, said that he went to heaven through a hole in the sky and returned. We all spoke different languages, yet we each heard Jesus speak in our own."

Bombarded by more startling information, Charlie's mind spun. He blinked, long-held beliefs swirling within a vortex of questions.

Vehoe's God, whom they claim as their Father in Heaven, was the same being as *Maheo*? And *Heammawihio* and Jesus were the same? *How could it be?*

"I am to restore our ceremonies, such as the *Massaum*," Charlie said. "The whites told us our ceremonies were wrong and banned them. If our Gods are the same, why are our beliefs so different? Who is right?"

"We are both right and we are both wrong, Littlewolf. Both cultures have strayed from what we were originally taught. Our beliefs should be the same. How we express them is different. God honors and celebrates our differences. They are a result of our free will. How we pray to *Maheo* and honor him through our ceremonies are part of our culture. Such differences do not matter to him. What's important is to honor our Creator, worship him, love each other, and have his peace in our hearts."

Charlie's thoughts tangled into knots, but his bosom burned, telling him Porcupine was telling the truth.

"We are all brothers," Porcupine stated. "Our differences make us part of a great tapestry. Those things taught to our people by the Messiah over a hundred years ago brought his teachings back to us. Small differences, not only with *Vehoe*, but even with other tribes, do not make anyone wrong. We are wrong when we fight each other and have hate behind our actions.

"We must unite in the spirit of peace, filled with love. Live the way we were told. There is one God. He told us all the same thing. Not to kill one another. Be honest, kind, and generous. Do not judge others. Do not drink alcohol or use drugs."

"Yes," Charlie agreed. "But some do not listen."

"Sad, but true. Even as *Vehoes* crucified Christ, evil whites who claimed to believe in him tried to destroy our language and traditions as well as us. They did not understand our ceremonies came to us from the same Creator. Restoring them to their original form is important. Obedience connects us with Heaven's powers."

Porcupine's eyes held his as he then declared, "Straying separated us from our Creator. Losing that connection caused us to lose *Maheo's* protection and fall prey to evil whites, who also strayed from the true message of Christianity. Evil men used it for their own purposes."

"Which allowed them to justify killing us and stealing our land," Charlie added.

"Yes. But it can be restored."

"It can? How?"

"The intent of the *Dance of Welcome and Peace* is to unite native peoples, of all tribes. You will teach it once more to our brothers at the *Gathering* in October. They, in turn, will take it back to their people. In unity, we will have great strength. As it was intended to be. We are getting a second chance."

Again, Charlie's spirit acknowledged the truth as Porcupine continued. It fit perfectly with what Eaglefeathers said he was to achieve for all indigenous people.

"Greedy white men are destroying Grandmother Earth," Porcupine continued. "They are even destroying their own people. Whatever good existed in their culture has become corrupt and is crumbling. Rotting away. Now is the time for us to join with our brothers. With our Creator's help, take back what was ours."

Charlie was speechless. *Maheo* and the multitude of Great Spirit Father and Creator Gods other tribes worshiped were all the same person? An actual *person*? And even more remarkable, the same one Christians worshipped? Their beliefs actually had something in common with *Veheo*?

Porcupine's eyes drilled into his. "I promise you in *Maheo's* and *Heammawihio's* sacred names that my words are true. Come. I will teach you the dance and other things you will need to know."

SARA'S CABIN
RURAL FALCON RIDGE
August 30, Thursday
10:10 a.m. MDT

SARA DRUMMED HER FINGERS on the breakfast bar, waiting for Davis Jenkins to come on the phone. If she could be a guest again, surely it would help her blog reach a lot more people.

"Mrs. Reynolds? Are you still there?"

Her eyes narrowed with disappointment when it was the same person who initially answered the phone.

"Yes. Is he not available?" she asked.

"Well, actually, he is. But talking with you would violate station policy."

And with that, the woman hung up.

Sara's mind exploded.

What? Talking to him would violate station policy? Where on earth did *that* come from?

She turned to her laptop and brought up their website to see if her appearance was still there.

It wasn't.

Jason's statement that she was *persona non grata* in D.C. sprung to mind.

So that was it.

No doubt Bentley was involved.

Bryan always said the government dictated to media outlets what they could broadcast. He believed free speech was a thing of the past.

She didn't believe him then.

She did now.

WHITE WOLF'S RANCH
NORTHERN CHEYENNE RESERVATION
BUSBY, MONTANA
August 30, Thursday
11:02 a.m. MDT

STAR SMILED AT THE array of goods lined up on the dining table. Dried elk meat in a cheesecloth bag. A sack of dried corn. A basket of carrots and potatoes, freshly dug from the giver's garden. A slab of salt pork in a covered pan. A bag of freshly ground coffee beans. Even a ceramic bowl of juniper berry pudding.

The outpouring of caring support warmed her heart. Each member of the tribe who sent an offering cloth to *Novavose* remembered the following day Littlewolf would complete his fast. They knew she would prepare a feast for its conclusion and take it to them the next morning. Their appreciation, love, and prayers were with her family and demonstrated by their considerate actions.

Littlewolf's accomplishment was great cause for celebration. When a tribal member fasted on the Sacred Mountain, it blessed all the Cheyenne people. Similar to a Sun Dance or some of their other ceremonies, it renewed the entire tribe.

But even with their help, there was much work to do. Some of the food was dehydrated. It needed to be soaked, cooked, and ready to go before the next morning when she and Risingsun would leave.

The week had passed quickly with only one troubling incident. At least the washing machine died when nearly everyone was gone. Unfortunately, they'd return with a burgeoning heap of dirty laundry.

When they went to Colorado, the water heater went out. Did such things purposely wait to break down when her husband was somewhere else?

Was some trickster *maiyun* teasing her? One that dared not appear when White Wolf was there?

As she placed the meat in a pot to soak, the corn in another, she wondered when Risingsun would get back from fishing. He wanted to contribute something to tomorrow's feast, so went to Eaglefeathers Creek to see what he could catch. It was a nice gesture she couldn't bring herself to deny, but at this point she could really use his help.

While Winter Hawk was dependable, even as a young boy, Risingsun was a dreamer who lived in his own world. As a result, his version of Indian Time was far more warped than most.

His artistic talent, however was incredible. The past few days he sketched out a design to paint on *Tah-Hó'nehe* when they returned. It had the Cheyenne flag at the center surrounded by Eaglefeathers' Butte, two wolves, a hawk, sunrise, Moon, and stars as well as other sacred symbols that pertained to their family.

A wistful smile appeared. So much talent.

But if he didn't return by noon, on top of everything else, she'd have to hunt him down and make sure he was okay.

Meanwhile, she figured out exactly what to prepare and take, put away what she'd leave behind, then looked for the map they had somewhere that showed Montana, Wyoming, and South Dakota. It had been a very long time since she'd been to the Sacred Mountain.

It was a long drive.

What if she got lost?

Or their old car broke down?

She licked her lips, neck muscles tense.

After looking for the map everywhere she could think of in the house, she went outside to see if it was in the Explorer. It wasn't. Surely they would have one at the Busby Trading Post, or someone there could give her directions. She needed to go by today because she had to leave early the next day, before they opened.

She returned to the house to get her bag, realizing Risingsun still had not made it home. Back in the car, she drove first for the spot on Eaglefeathers Creek where they built a small fishing dock.

The old SUV bumped and rocked its way across the rough terrain. From several yards away she could tell that her son was not on the dock. She parked the car and got out.

"Risingsun! Where are you?" she called.

She walked to the pier.

Littlewolf's canoe wasn't there, either.

A spark of worry tightened her stomach.

Her adolescent son was not supposed to take it out by himself. At least the creek was partially dry this time of year as opposed to a mini-river like it was in spring.

She stepped gingerly along the soggy banks, calling his name, finally hearing a faint reply. There he was, up ahead fifty feet or so, trying to get the canoe unstuck from the mud.

She bowed her head and ran her fingers through her hair, then her hands found their place on her hips. At least he was okay, but a filthy mess, in the last of his clean clothes. She was in a similar position herself, helping him out not an option.

"Risingsun. You know you are not supposed to take the canoe out by yourself. Look at you! What are you going to wear when we go to the Sacred Mountain to celebrate with your father, Littlewolf, and your brother?"

The boy hung his head. "I do not know. Do I have to stay home, Mother?"

She closed her eyes and sighed. "No. But here is what you will do. Take off all your clothes."

He did as he was told, standing there with his jeans, underwear, and shirt in hand, wearing only an expectant look.

"Now you will wash your clothes in the creek. When they are clean, bring them home and hang them to dry. I must go into town. I expect you to be home when I return."

A mixed array of emotions played across his face, reminding her so much of her dear, deceased brother.

"I will, Mother," he replied. "I am sorry. But what about the canoe?"

"It does not look like it is going anywhere. We will talk about this when everyone gets home."

She turned around to return to the car, realizing she'd walked at least a quarter mile. By the time she was halfway back, tears of frustration dampened her cheeks.

She stopped.

Hung her head.

Blessed herself with the earth.

Faced east, and prayed.

"*Maheo*. I am grateful for my brothers and sisters who brought so many generous gifts for me to take to the Sacred Mountain. But so far this day is not going well. Please help me get everything prepared and ready so I can leave on time and do my part to make sure Littlewolf's fast has a joyful conclusion."

29. DESCENT

NOVAVOSE (Day 4 - Thursday)
BEAR BUTTE STATE PARK
SOUTH DAKOTA
Sacred Mountain Time

As Charlie smoked at sunset the final day he prayed for understanding. Bombarded with so much startling information, he needed help. His breathing was rapid and shallow. His weak body begged for nourishment. His head hurt behind his eyes and through the top of his head. It took supreme effort to move, and his brain felt as if it might explode.

How did it fit all together?

How would he accomplish all he'd been charged to do, even in a lifetime?

It had only been four days, yet felt like years.

A lifetime of instruction in a few days.

Panic flared again, doused as the feeling induced by *Amasani's* visit returned.

The additional history he learned was somehow familiar. In his DNA, perhaps, as genetic memory. Seeing Sweet Medicine was inspiring, especially witnessing his prophesy and when he received the Sacred Arrows. The *Massaum* was entirely new knowledge. It made so much sense! They truly were *given* the land. Also, confirmation that their history was preserved in songs, ceremonies, petroglyphs, and the medicine wheel.

No wonder *Vehoe* outlawed their ceremonies as an attempt to erase their culture.

But most shocking of all was that *Maheo,* the Great Spirit Father, had a son who was Jesus. Why different names? Was it a matter of language? Each had different names for animals, food, and locations.

Did being called different names let the Creator know who was praying? A test to see if they'd argue over who's God was greater? Some sort of divine joke that they were actually all the same?

Not having to give up his beliefs, but simply incorporate a few new ones funneled peace into his soul. That alone would help unify his brothers from other tribes. Now it made sense why they had so many things in common.

Over six hundred tribes were recognized by the federal government. There were approximately 6.9 million Native Americans, with around six hundred thousand living on reservations.

Intimidation slammed him again. How could he possibly reach them all? Especially with the majority scattered across the country and not living on reservations?

That they attained that number in spite of *Vehoe* trying to kill them off was a testament to their resilience and strength.

And that *Maheo* truly loved them.

He finished smoking, cleaned the pipe, disassembled it, and placed it in the deerskin bag. He laid down on the man sage, encompassed by its pungent scent as he fell asleep, praying for strength and wisdom to do all he was expected to do.

NOVAVOSE
BEAR BUTTE STATE PARK
SOUTH DAKOTA
August 31, Friday
5:45 a.m. MDT

"WAKE UP, WINTER HAWK. It's time to go up the hill and bring down your brother."

The teen turned over and opened his eyes, features barely visible in the predawn light. He stretched, then got up, feeling around for his moccasins. Pulled on his favorite sweatshirt with the Cheyenne flag on back.

Outside the tipi, they blessed themselves with the earth, then faced the coming dawn while White Wolf said a prayer that all would be safe, especially Star driving from Busby, and that each of them would find joy in the conclusion of this sacred occasion.

Grandmother Moon was low in the western sky, a few days past full, but shedding sufficient light to guide their way.

They plodded up the draw, footsteps crunching on rocky ground, serenaded by the cry of two golden eagles soaring overhead on their morning hunt. White Wolf pointed to them, tiny shadows skimming the stars.

"Look, son. The Grandfather Spirits are watching over us," he said.

The boy grinned.

Littlewolf was still asleep when they arrived, curled up on the man sage beneath the buffalo robe. To awaken him, White Wolf began singing the Grandmother Song to thank the Moon for lighting their way.

Winter Hawk joined in, Littlewolf stirring moments later. He smiled, slowly sat up cross-legged, and tried to join the singing. His throat was too dry, however, so he hummed along until they finished, then broke off a piece of big medicine to chew.

"Winter Hawk, grab some man sage and help me rub him down to remove some of the paint to bring him back from the world of spirits."

His son complied, Littlewolf's eyes closed as they ran the sage along his arms, shoulders, and back.

"Are you able to stand, Littlewolf?"

"I think so," he said, still hoarse as he slowly forced himself to his feet. He wobbled, unsteady.

Winter Hawk set his hands on his waist from behind while White Wolf finished wiping his legs, then placed the buffalo robe around him while his son gathered up the pipe bag and buffalo skull.

"Ready?" White Wolf asked.

Littlewolf exhaled hard, then nodded.

White Wolf placed a protective arm around his pledger's back and gave him an affectionate side hug, pleased he had successfully completed the ceremony. They walked slowly across the ridge pocket, then one cautious step at a time down the steep incline. Halfway they paused to rest, splintered rays from the rising sun greeting them with splashes of fall color on the trees below.

WHITE WOLF'S RANCH
NORTHERN CHEYENNE RESERVATION
BUSBY, MONTANA
August 31, Friday
6:32 a.m. MDT

STAR ASSESSED THE OLD Explorer's cargo area, making sure she hadn't forgotten anything. Big kettle of elk stew with potatoes; corn; salt pork; berry pudding; carrot sticks and dried apples for snacks; coffee; bowls; and utensils. Towels for the sweat; five more gallons of water, but from Eaglefeathers' spring rather than making another stop besides the one already planned.

A smile flickered across her lips as she remembered getting back to the house the day before. Tired and discouraged after hunting for her wandering son, she found four sisters sitting on the front porch, ready to help get everything ready. One made the trip to Bear Butte a month before, so gave directions, making the trip to the trading post unnecessary.

The route's simplicity yielded welcome relief: East on Highway 212, then south on Highway 79. How easy was that?

Not only did the women help get everything prepared, but had a joyful time doing it. They giggled like teens, laughed, and shared sacred stories of *Novavose*, then made plans to get together in the weeks to come to prepare for the *Gathering*. While they all had suitable regalia for local pow-wows, this one demanded special versions to represent and commemorate the important occasion.

Little did they yet know what would be required for the *Massaum*.

Star reached up on tiptoe to close the Explorer's back hatch, then made sure Risingsun in the backseat had his seatbelt fastened. A wry smile emerged at the caked mud on his moccasins, then she got settled in the driver's seat and bumped across the dirt road to pick up their honored guest.

While walking back after her fretful prayer the day before, she felt impressed to invite Ice to join them for the sweat. The elder was delighted, his face aglow as he climbed into the passenger seat.

"White Wolf and Littlewolf will be so pleased to see you," she said.

"*Néá eše* for including me," he replied. "*Maheo* tells me this fast at *Novavose* is one for the history books. I am grateful to be included in its conclusion where I can hear from Littlewolf all that occurred."

The trip would take about three and a half hours. She was grateful to have company, not only her son, but such a highly esteemed member of the medicine man community.

With him along, her worries that some trickster *maiyun* might cause problems along the way joined the car's dusty wake in the rearview mirror.

SARA'S CABIN
RURAL FALCON RIDGE
August 31, Friday
8:22 a.m. MDT

STILL SPUN-UP FROM Bentley's attack and now NBC's blatant dismissal, Sara's heated glower defied the idyllic scene beyond the window. She still hadn't heard back from Charlie, either. She wilted with defeat.

Where was he?

Certainly he was aware of what happened, or should be, since he was there. At least he was in her dream. What a dream! A dream come true, for sure. She'd hardly dared hope she'd ever walk again. Yet, here she was, back at the cabin, able to pace at will.

A spontaneous smile dissipated the bad feelings like sunshine after a thunderstorm. Frustration shifted to reverence as she pronounced a prayer of gratitude, adding a request for advice.

The path ahead was not as clear as she'd hoped. Without media support reaching people would be far more difficult. Informing the public was more important than ever. With censorship looming, it might require some underground platform as opposed to the more popular blog sites.

She'd written a few the past few days, but still needed to record and upload them. So far she hadn't set up an account anywhere to post them.

Her strategy needed review as well as checking other available options.

Usually the cabin was her sanctuary, but since the confrontation with Bentley, it didn't feel right. The possibility she was in danger crossed her mind, confirmed by a rush of goosebumps raising the hair on her arms.

Blossom nudged her hand, reminding her it was walk time.

"Okay, girl, I know. But after that, we're going back to Denver. Something's changed and it doesn't feel right. I need to talk to Dad and find out what's going on with Charlie."

NOVAVOSE
BEAR BUTTE STATE PARK
SOUTH DAKOTA
August 31, Friday
9:53 a.m. MDT

HAVING SO FAR PROCRASTINATED the heavy task, White Wolf and his son had no choice but to retrieve the stones from the truck as soon as they got back to camp with Littlewolf. He should have known better than to put so many in the wagon, which now had two severely bent axels. Small price to pay, however, for fewer trips.

Whether Star would agree remained to be seen.

The fire heating the stones roared, sparks jubilant in the morning air. Buffalo robes covered the choke cherry structure, man sage spread on the ground within. Winter Hawk was out of sight beyond the trees flanking the parking lot, waiting for Star.

White Wolf prayed much of the night that their old vehicle would have enough life left to get there safely. Littlewolf's truck was slightly better, but she would be bringing food items that could be compromised in its open bed, plus its manual transmission made her nervous. It was a long drive, but at least didn't involve any big cities.

She was a careful driver, but got flustered on busy roads outside the reservation. A gentle smile of appreciation formed as he anticipated seeing her, to say nothing of the bounty she was sure to bring. Star was such a good wife.

He prayed Littlewolf would find one like her someday. With the work *Maheo* had for him, he'd need the love, encouragement, and support that a good mate provided. It was no wonder his path was obstructed by that *màsèhá'e* he married before, a crazy woman so much like his mother.

He was more grateful than ever for their home and its many comforts, spending the coming night in a bed more welcome than he dared admit. Camping out in a tipi for the better part of the week was easy, certainly part of his heritage, but living that way would definitely present challenges.

Winter Hawk appeared from within the stand of trees, waving both arms. "She's here!" he yelled.

Warmth captured his heart as Star appeared behind him, helping an older man, but still too far away to recognize. It wouldn't be unusual for other tribal members to join them, his only concern whether the sweat lodge would be big enough.

As they drew closer his smile stretched.

It was Ice! How wonderful for the elder to join them for this joyful occasion!

He rushed down the gentle grade to meet them, elated. With luck he'd be willing to preside over the sweat.

"I'm so glad you joined us," he said, shaking the elder's hand, then relieving his wife of the man's arm. "Let me get you settled in the tipi with Littlewolf while we unload the car."

Star's forehead wrinkled as her eyes met his. Greeting the elder first, while appropriate, was nonetheless not appreciated. He gave her his best apologetic look, then led their guest to the campsite.

Littlewolf's clear exhaustion lightened as Ice ducked inside. He managed a laugh, though clearly depleted from the ordeal. From what he could tell, he'd probably lost around fifteen pounds.

"I understand now why you wouldn't tell me anything," he said, his voice hoarse. "I would not have believed you if you did."

Ice nodded. "I am grateful your experience explained my response. I was surprised by it myself. I will be very happy to hear about what you learned."

White Wolf would have preferred to join them, but knew getting the Explorer unloaded, thanking Star properly for her efforts, then concluding Littlewolf's fast with the sweat was more important.

Winter Hawk entered the tipi carrying a stew pot. It smelled delicious, but would have to wait. Risingsun followed, carrying towels and a bowl of corn. Star was right behind, juggling two more containers.

He followed her back outside.

"*Néá eše*, wife," he said. "It was so kind to bring Ice. And the food smells wonderful."

"You are welcome," she replied, then set her hands on her hips. "What did you do to my wagon, husband? Did Winter Hawk pull you up the mountain in it?"

He didn't answer, arms akimbo.

She folded hers.

White Wolf's gut sank. "Wife, I am certain we can fix it. If not, we will buy you a new one. I am sorry. It helped us very much."

Her frown deepened, but eventually melted.

"When I saw Littlewolf load it in *Tah-Hó'nehe* I had a feeling I would not see it again. I am glad that it died being of service to my dear husband and Littlewolf on *Novavose*."

He gave her a hug and a kiss, then noticed the boys were on their way with the water jugs, so met them halfway to help carry them to the fire to warm up.

As a ceremonial sweat Star would not participate, giving her time to relax after the long drive. The fact she made it safely in their old Ford SUV was yet another blessing to be grateful for.

The stones would be ready by the time they were. Risingsun would be door keeper, a task he fulfilled at home enough times to do well. He was warned of his role before they left and remembered to bring the deer antlers needed to carry the stones, which White Wolf had forgotten.

With everything brought in from the car, Star waited outside the tipi while the men stripped down inside. After the second round she'd start a fire to reheat the meal, then have it ready when they finished

White Wolf anticipated this special sweat would include spirit helpers also celebrating Littlewolf's success. Having his sons there made it even more special, something they'd always remember. An experience that would encourage them to conduct their own ceremonial fast when they were old enough.

Contentment and gratitude washed over him like unexpected summer rain kisses parched earth. So far this pilgrimage exceeded anything he could have imagined.

It was the morning of the fourth day that the vision came. Deafy saw a rider on top of the Sacred Mountain. The rider was facing east. Suddenly he charged. His horse galloped past Deafy at full speed, and on down the side of the mountain. However, nothing happened to either horse or rider.
Soon the horse and rider appeared again. Once more the horse charged down toward the foot of the mountain. As they went by, Deafy noticed that there was a boy sitting behind the rider. Again, they reached the bottom safely. —Peter John Powell, "Sweet Medicine," Volume 1, p. 418

30. SWEAT

NOVAVOSE
BEAR BUTTE STATE PARK
SOUTH DAKOTA
August 31, Friday
10:47 a.m. MDT

When White Wolf offered Ice the sacred red pipe and asked if he'd preside over the sweat, his acceptance brought another wave of gratitude. While he'd officiated himself hundreds of times, it was a blessing not to have those duties. He could meditate upon the past four days without distraction, seek new insights into the vision shared with his son, and rejoice in Littlewolf's accomplishment.

All was ready to begin, pipe resting on a badger hide on the lodge roof. Within the structure, the esteemed elder sat on the south side of the stone pit, Winter Hawk next to Ice, and Littlewolf in back, facing the door. White Wolf was next with door keeper, Risingsun, on his left.

The first five stones smoldered in the pit, red glow casting eerie shadows. Ice filled the dipper from the bucket and handed it to Littlewolf.

"Refresh your face and body," he said.

Littlewolf poured it over himself. Ice repeated the action three more times, then gave him yet another, telling him to drink slowly.

When he finished and handed back the dipper, Ice broke off a piece of sweetgrass and placed it on the center stone. Smudged himself, the rattle, and bucket of water, then waved its fragrant vapors about the lodge. He signaled Risingsun to retrieve the other six stones for the first round.

Water whispered softly as it touched red hot stones, ushering them into another realm. Ice blew the eagle bone whistle, inviting the grandfather spirits. The soothing whoosh of the buffalo rattle joined moisture-laden air as he began singing the Grandfather Song. Everyone followed along, except Littlewolf praying in back.

CHARLIE REMAINED OVERWHELMED by the expectations placed upon him, yet knew he wouldn't trade the experience for anything. Tears filled his eyes as he recalled the past four days. His heart's slow, heavy beats reflected the strength gained from so many great men in his multitude of visions.

Weakened in body yet strengthened in spirit, he prayed as never before, filled with gratitude for all he experienced.

"*Maheo, néá eše*. I am deeply grateful and humbled by the blessings received from this ceremony. Seeing precious family members like my father, grandfather, and *Amasani*, knowing that they still live, brought joy such as I didn't know existed. I miss them so much.

"*Néá eše* for healing Sara and bringing her home. I never imagined that such was possible.

"*Néá eše* for what I learned about the *Tsistsistas* people, how long we have dwelt on this land, and the beauty of the *Massaum*. Learning the *Dance of Peace and Welcome* and its true meaning from Porcupine gave me hope as never before. His witness that you and your son, who we know as *Heammawihio*, both live and love us, fills my soul with great happiness."

"I am honored and greatly humbled to be entrusted with this great work to benefit not only my people but all my indigenous brothers and sisters. I am grateful for *Amasani's* wise words of encouragement, which help me believe that with your help we can accomplish great things for our people."

Risingsun opened the door, admitting a blast of cool air. His prayer paused while water was passed. He took a small drink, then found a man sage branch to use as a switch for the next round.

WHITE WOLF SANG ALONG with the Buffalo Song as the second round began, reflecting on the vision shared with Winter Hawk.

Esseneta'he. Giver of light, spring, and new life. His message imprinted his mind as deeply as scars on his chest witnessed the Sun Dance he completed years before.

"*Maheo, néá eše* for the great blessing of sharing a vision of one of your sacred helpers with my son. He is such a good boy and brings much happiness to me and my dear wife. It is so good that he was here to share this experience as Littlewolf completed his vow.

"Please help me with responsibilities I have for the *Gathering*. I need help for it to succeed. There is much to do and we need many resources. I do not know where they will come from. Many attending are poor. Help us help them. May they feel love and Sweet Medicine Spirits lift them up with hope.

"I am puzzled what we must do in Colorado. As sacred ground it had a strong spirit. Its distance troubles me. Getting to Montana will be a challenge for many, much less Colorado.

"What will we do there?"

He paused, listening, as Sweet Medicine Spirits granted him a response.

Littlewolf knows what is to be done. He will help you. All that is to occur is Maheo's *will for his people.*

Worry misted away as water touching hot stones. Intuition witnessed that he would not only have help but be astounded by its scope.

CHARLIE KEPT PRAYING though the Badger Song stung like air on an open wound. Guilt gripped his soul with regret for being so foolish to name the bore hole *Mahahkoe*. His intent was to call upon the revered *maiyun* to protect the Earth Mother, but clearly it mocked him as an insult.

"*Mahahkoe*, forgive me. I am so very sorry. Please forgive me. I deserved your wrath. Yet I am grateful for the blessings that came from the accident. It brought me home. It brought me the sacred gift of vision. It brought me back to my family. White Wolf's wisdom has taught me much. *Néá eše.*

A vision appeared. Grandmother Earth seething with vengeance, her wrath spewing forth destruction on those who mocked her. Great upheavals and a bottomless gorge gurgled with magma as she unleashed her fury. A giant badger appeared within the turmoil, impressing his soul that the *maiyun* was deeply involved in what was to come.

Yet peace filled his heart. Badger had forgiven him.

BEING AT THE SACRED MOUNTAIN, as well as various other times throughout his young life, Winter Hawk felt as if he were living a dream. It wasn't unusual for someone besides himself to get inside his head.

Strange memories surfaced, ideas and thoughts from another realm. Words came out of his mouth sometimes that baffled him. Were they his own? Escaping from his DNA? Why did he have these weird impressions?

When he mentioned them to his teenage friends, they looked at him as if he were crazy.

Was he?

Thus it was now as he sang along with the Wolf Song. He tried to remember learning it, but the words were always there. He was proud to be *Tsistsistas*. His heritage was strong. His father an honorable and powerful medicine man who taught him *Tseteshestahese* traditions since he was a young child. Everything he was told made sense.

It felt right.

Familiar.

That he was exactly who and where he should be.

"Néá eše, Maheo, for being included in my brother's fast. I was afraid to ask, yet it felt like *maiyun* forced me to speak up. I am so grateful for the vision I shared with my father and the one of the *Massaum* with my brother. *Néá eše* for trusting me with this sacred knowledge."

Oddly enough, much of what occurred the past four days also felt familiar. As if he were recalling something he'd done before.

How could that be?

Yet his spirit said it was true, warming as the rising sun chased the chill on an autumn morning. An instant later it filled with joy and hope as a familiar voice spoke to his mind.

Winter Hawk, you are one of my most valiant spirits. You have already done great things and will yet do many more. You are deeply loved. Cherish these experiences and forever keep them in your heart, especially should difficult times come. I will always be with you.

He smiled as his younger brother opened the door, allowing cool air to deliver a refreshing break. Risingsun fetched the next group of seething stones one by one and stacked them on the others, as Winter Hawk had done many times himself.

The door closed, sweat lodge swaddled in darkness as sweetgrass vapors rode the steam.

THE REVELATIONS FROM the past four days impacted Charlie's soul as an axe on seasoned wood. As profound as each was, two stood out for the responsibility implied. Having Eaglefeathers tell both him and his brother about the *Massaum* infused him with hope, even more so for being shared.

"What will happen when the ceremony is conducted again?" he prayed. "It is exciting, joyful, and terrifying. We have our beautiful reservation. Will we get our other lands back, too? Even *Novavose*, here in the Black Hills, where it all began?"

Equal to the *Massaum* was the impression left by Porcupine's message.

"Teaching me about the meeting at Walker Lake was something I never imagined. So astounding my mind still spins as a tornado crossing the prairie. I am amazed you and *Heammawihio* came down to teach us. I wish I was there. Not because I don't believe, but to meet you, as my brother, Porcupine, did. To learn the *Dance of Peace and Welcome* from you.

"Help me understand its full meaning. Bless my brothers that they believe my words and are as thrilled as I to learn of it and that we may be unified."

Intimidation washed over him again as the import fell upon him, his weakened body barely able to sit up, much less imagine the work ahead. As thrilling as the experience was, as blessed as he felt, the reality of what it meant loomed over him as a mountain he had to move alone, shovelful by shovelful.

"*Maheo. Heammawihio.* Jesus. Please help me. How will I remember all you told me to teach my people?"

A SENSE OF PEACE fell upon White Wolf as he pondered his duties with the *Gathering*. What message were they to convey to his many brothers? Exactly what they were to do was still unclear, but it was a relief to be told Littlewolf knew. He trusted *Maheo* would help them, yet it was strange not to know what was to transpire that required two weeks. He sang along with the Wolf Song, pondering what Littlewolf learned during his fast.

A familiar voice came into his mind.

It is good you recognize Littlewolf's path. For this ceremonial fast you are his instructor. For many to come you will pledge and he will instruct.

He witnessed ceremonies as they were taught by Sweet Medicine. For years many were done incorrectly. They must be restored so the Cheyenne can return to their former greatness.

CHARLIE FELT A SURGE that could only be described as an infusion of divine love.

Okohomoxhaahketa, I hear your prayers. Is not worry fear of what is to come? Do you not know that it is I who heals? Performs miracles? That I do your bidding in righteousness? Have you forgotten your gift to see through time? Return to these visions as often as required until they are etched in your heart and soul. I will never abandon you as you lead your people back to greatness.

He inhaled sharply, feeling foolish, yet relieved.

No wonder he was given such a remarkable spiritual gift. Being able to remember what he'd been taught the past four days could its main purpose.

He continued to pray, spirit overflowing with gratitude.

"Now I understand many things. Why Eaglefeathers wanted me to have this experience when I was young. I pray that you and he forgive me for being such a foolish young man. I am very sorry.

"Néá eše for seeing Eaglefeathers again."

In spite of the oppressive heat, singing, and soft swish of the rattle, Eaglefeathers' voice came into his head as if he stood beside him.

Grandson, I know your heart. Your return to Sweet Medicine's teachings gives me great joy. There are no mistakes, only different paths. There was a reason for your delay in accepting our ways.

Admitting mistakes and coming back is an example of strength. It is never too late. For eternal things, time matters not.

Be at peace, Grandson. When you walk with Maheo *you will never be alone.*

"Ultimately, all moments are really one, therefore now is an eternity."
~ David Bohm, Physicist

31. RETURNING

The midday glare struck as a blow as Charlie stumbled out of the sweat lodge. While his body felt heavy, weak and emaciated, his mind was clear and confidence stronger than when he stepped within its depths.

Ice removed the sacred red pipe from its resting place atop the lodge's roof, filled, and lit it. They sat facing east and smoked, passing the pipe, thanking the Sweet Medicine Spirits for helping him through his fast and the marvelous visions experienced.

As soon as they finished, everyone expressed gratitude to Ice for officiating, then congratulated Charlie. The feast's aroma filled the air, causing other campers to look their way. Star stepped out of the tipi, bidding welcome.

"Come," she said, beckoning them inside. "There is elk stew, potatoes, corn, juniper berry pudding, and coffee."

White Wolf blessed the food, then Risingsun took out the food offering. White Wolf invited Ice to serve himself first. Everyone got settled around the outdoor fire pit where they indulged in generous portions while Charlie had a cup of broth with a small piece of meat, salt pork, and potato that he consumed slowly to reacquaint his body with nourishment.

As they enjoyed the delicious spread, Ice turned to Charlie. "Your fast was attended by powerful spirits. You were given directives and taught much sacred knowledge. Some you may share openly and some only with select individuals." He tapped his chest with his fist. "The Sacred Powers will prompt you here when it is allowed."

Charlie nodded, the elder's words confirming what he'd already discerned. He looked forward to Ice's insights, knowing his discussion with White Wolf would be ongoing.

Star paused, eyeing each of them in turn. "When we leave, why don't the boys ride with me so you men can talk freely on the way back?"

The men exchanged knowing glances and nodded. The only one who looked unhappy was Winter Hawk, but he said nothing. White Wolf noticed and said, "Son, we will talk about your experiences and some of Littlewolf's when we get home."

The youth's disappointed look softened. Charlie caught his eye and nodded. The young man's strong spirit was apparent since his arrival at the ranch over a month before, which led him to suspect little would be withheld.

Before long all the food was consumed, which made clean-up simple. As soon as they finished, White Wolf directed the two boys to prepare the hot stones from the sweat for travel.

"Carefully spread them out on the ground outside, then pour the leftover water on them. Then use the camp shovel to fill the fire pit so we leave the area as we found it. Let them cool until we're almost ready to leave, then wrap them in the buffalo robes and take them down to the parking lot."

"Remember we are leaving three behind," Winter Hawk said.

"Yes," White Wolf agreed. "Then take down the structure. We'll bring the choke cherry trees home and keep them in the barn for when Littlewolf has his own house and builds a sweat lodge."

The boys returned to the site to do as instructed. Meanwhile, they broke camp, Star, Ice and Charlie helping with lighter tasks.

When the rocks cooled enough to wrap, the boys loaded as many as they dared in the sagging wagon, then hauled them down to *Tah-Hó'nehe*, which took several trips.

Before long, both vehicles were ready to go, the bulk of which was in *Tah-Hó'nehe's* more expansive cargo area. Charlie sat in the back of the Explorer beneath its open lift gate with Ice and Star while White Wolf and the boys made one final sweep of the area.

When they returned, the boys were arguing over who would ride up front with their mother.

"I rode in back on the way here," Winter Hawk said.

"So did I," Risingsun replied, hands on his hips. "And the back seat of *Tah-Hó'nehe* is a whole lot nicer!"

Winter Hawk couldn't argue with that, so climbed in back, Risingsun wearing a victorious grin.

White Wolf turned to Star. "Did you have any car problems getting here, wife?"

"No, it drove like new." Star glanced at Ice beside her and smiled. "But that was probably due to our passenger."

White Wolf chuckled. "Yes. And another blessing of our being here. We will follow you on the way back to make sure all is well." He gave Charlie a look. "And assure we do not challenge speed limits along the way." He paused, concern replacing the critique. "Do you feel well enough to drive, Littlewolf?"

Charlie pursed his lips to stifle a smile. Should he refuse, forcing White Wolf to finally drive *Tah-Hó'nehe*? He definitely felt drained, but sleeping was unlikely with so much to talk about with Ice.

"Driving is not difficult. If I get tired we can always switch. We will need to stop for gas somewhere."

"Very well," White Wolf agreed, visibly relieved.

They piled into their respective vehicles and turned north on Highway 79. Traffic was heavier than usual due to the coming Labor Day weekend.

As soon as the vehicle's Wi-Fi connected, a string of text messages from Sara appeared on the media screen along with phone mail notifications.

Charlie grinned. Since healing Sara was the first thing accomplished during his fast, it seemed like ancient history. He hadn't even mentioned it yet to White Wolf or Ice. He laughed to himself as he called up the phone messages.

What better way for them to find out than from her?

He pressed *Play.*

[Message received: Tuesday, August 28 at 12:50 pm] Charlie! Oh my gosh! How did you do that? That was the most incredible experience of my life! Oh, my gosh! And blinding him was brilliant! I was a little wobbly on my feet, but I got away! And would you believe Connie and Dad were out there waiting? I can't wait to talk to you. Thank you thank you thank you! Call me back. [End of message. To save, press 1. To delete, press 7. To listen again, press 3]

He glanced at White Wolf in the rearview mirror, then Ice beside him in the passenger seat. Both of their mouths gaped open in disbelief.

Charlie stifled a laugh.

"Would you like to explain that, Littlewolf?" White Wolf asked, eyes so wide the whites showed.

"Remember when we were leaving the ranch and heard she'd been kidnapped? When you said there was no place we could do her more good than *Novavose*?"

"Yes. Of course."

"Those words were truly prophetic."

Charlie's arms reacted with goosebumps as he absorbed the miracle's scope himself.

"Here's what happened. Whistling Elk told me my concern for her was a distraction that needed to be fixed so I could concentrate on what I needed to do for our people. So Porcupine healed her with medicine that was in Eaglefeathers' medicine bundle all along."

By now Ice was laughing, White Wolf still too shocked to speak, as Charlie provided the details.

"An *e'ehyo'm* is powerful enough to do harm from a distance, so why not heal?" Ice commented. "To say nothing of doing so from *Novavose.*"

After answering all their questions, he called Sara on speaker.

"Charlie! There you are! Where have you been?" she asked.

"In South Dakota. At the Sacred Mountain with White Wolf and Winter Hawk. We're driving back now with Ice, an elder who advised us about helping you get well. When we got in *Tah-Hó'nehe* your messages came up."

"*Tah-Hó'nehe?*"

"That's what we named our Tahoe."

"Got it. How can I ever thank you, Charlie? I'd begun to accept I'd never walk again. I even got a service dog. But now I'm as good as new. How did you do that?"

"You were there, Sara. All credit goes to *Maheo*, Sweet Medicine Spirits, and their assistant, Porcupine."

"Wow. I can hardly believe it. Do I still need a sweat?"

Charlie glanced at his passengers, both nodding. "Yes. That will assure all the poison's effects are reversed with all toxins out of your body."

"Okay. We can figure that out later. Right now I'm picking up some groceries and dog food. Call me when you can so we can talk about it."

"Okay, Sara. I will. We have some important things coming up I want to tell you about, too."

"Okay. And Charlie? Thank you again! If there's anything I can ever do for you or your family let me know. *Anything!*"

"I will. Be safe, Sara."

"I sure hope so. Bye, Charlie."

"*Ne' Stae va'hose vooma'tse.* I will see you again."

SARA'S CONDO
DENVER
August 31, Friday
2:18 p.m. MDT

WHEN SARA GOT HOME from Whole Foods, she set the bags on the floor so Blossom could help put everything away. She giggled as she watched her open cabinets and set cans on the shelf, pushing them in place with her nose.

The most terrific roommate ever. She couldn't wait to introduce her to Charlie.

Talking to him brought a welcome wave of relief. *Finally!* Days had passed since her first call, concern for his well-being increasing each day. Yet, deep inside, she felt he was okay, perhaps simply out of range of a cell tower. Now it made sense, giving her one less thing to worry about.

At this point she was incredibly curious. The Sacred Mountain? What a place that must be. And the sweat. What would it be like? Would she feel even better after that than she did now?

She smiled. Most of all she looked forward to seeing Charlie as well as his wonderful family.

Maybe she should drive up to Montana again, get away for a few days. It was also the perfect place to hide if anyone was stalking her, thanks to Bob Bentley.

Her thoughts shifted to the one thing she was even more determined to do—launch her podcast. The ones she wrote at the cabin were mainly about the Supreme Court decision and how it changed the political climate.

She'd exposed a little during her TV interviews, but not much. Mostly it emphasized what they did to her and Bryan as opposed to what he discovered.

Where did it all begin? Whose bright idea was it in the first place? She'd bet dollars to donuts it was one of those blood-sucking lobbyists. No doubt the Bentleys were involved, too.

Too many people got into politics to get rich. Like Harry Truman said, "Show me a man that gets rich by being a politician, and I'll show you a crook."

Amen, to that.

She laughed. That mission statement she thought of as a joke actually fit too well. Maybe she'd use it, after all.

So was PURF only about protecting lobbyists in case of an apocalypse, which POTUS had justified? Or something else?

Or was it even dirtier than it appeared?

Ours is a government of checks and balances. The Mafia and crooked businessmen make out checks, and the politicians and other compromised officials improve their bank balances.
--Steve Allen

32. SUPURFLUOUS

RANIER OFFICE BUILDING
WASHINGTON, DC
August 31, Friday
10:10 a.m. EDT

Just under eight weeks remained until the big event. Ingrid perused her checklist, noting who hadn't R.S.V.P.'d. She bit her lip and stared out her high rise office window to ant-sized school children filing into the National Air and Space Museum.

It's not like she didn't know what she was getting into when she volunteered. Sometimes the high-minded, arrogant people she worked for got on her last nerve, but she wouldn't trade her job for anything. They weren't the nicest, but they were interesting, powerful, and rich. Maybe one of these day's she'd snag another husband and no longer have to live on a barely adequate $231,730.81 a year.

She admonished herself for daydreaming and turned back to the job at hand.

The guest list stood at six thousand one-hundred-forty-three confirmed and paid. So far two-hundred-eighteen had not R.S.V.P.'d or, of course, paid. It was safe to assume anyone who remitted their fees planned to attend.

Before she provided the final count to the caterers, which she'd promised to do before Labor Day, any additional attendees needed to be confirmed. Sending an email would be easiest, but the most likely response would be the delete key.

With no other choice she opened the Excel spreadsheet, sorted on "Unconfirmed," and began the onerous task.

BENTLEY RESIDENCE
ARLINGTON, TEXAS
August 31, Friday
9:15 a.m. CDT

ANGELA BENTLEY SAT in the breakfast room of their palatial estate northeast of Arlington. Her Texas big-hair reflection stared back in the wrap-around bay window.

Beyond the glass, rain pounded their expansive lawn and flagstone patio as well as the twenty acres that lay beyond, deluge arriving in wind-driven sheets.

Or, as Bob would say, "like a cow pissing on a flat rock."

Hurricane Henry made landfall south of Houston a few days before, then made its way up I-45, inundating them with over eight inches so far. Saturated ground refused to absorb another drop, shiny pools of standing water spreading.

The phone rang. She didn't move, expecting her Hispanic maid to answer. Moments later, she appeared, holding out the receiver.

"Call for you, ma'am." Her accent was soft and pleasant, her command of English better than many Texans.

"Who is it, Lupe?"

"Someone in Washington, D.C., ma'am."

"Who?"

The housekeeper held the phone to her own ear. "May I ask who's calling? Okay, thank you. One moment please." She held it out again. "A Mrs. Thorson, ma'am."

Angela accepted the receiver, unsure who that was, but relieved it wasn't her father-in-law, whom she detested more than breaking a freshly manicured nail. Her Southern Baptist upbringing sensed pure evil emanating from that man.

"This is Angela Bentley."

"Good morning, Mrs. Bentley. This is Ingrid Thorson, calling on behalf of the PURF Open House on October 23. Will you and your husband be attending?"

Angela's brows lowered. "I'm sorry, the *what*?"

"The formal open house and gala to celebrate completion of Phase One of the Pearson Underground Residential Facility in Colorado."

Angela scowled.

"I'm sorry, but I don't recall hearing about it. I guess this relates to something for my husband's position. I'll have to check with him and let y'all know."

"Thank you, Mrs. Bentley. I'm needing a final count for the caterers and would appreciate knowing before the end of the day. And should you choose to attend, there's a charge to help cover expenses."

Her free hand flew to her chest, eyes wide. "There's a charge? Well, isn't that special. And how much might that be?"

"There will be a full spread of *hors d'oeuvres*, a five-course, gourmet dinner, and open bar. It's $1,500 per plate or $2,500 per couple. It's in Colorado so transportation will be provided. Any excess will be donated to LOL. The Lobbyist Opportunity League."

Angela expression darkened. So that very questionable nonprofit Myron founded was involved. Bob was worried about his father's unethical activities biting him since its inception.

"Well, bless your heart for asking. Probably not, Mrs. Thorson. But I'll ask my husband to make sure and call back if we decide to come."

"Thank you. I'd appreciate it. Good-bye, Mrs. Bentley. Have a lovely day."

"Thank you. Same to y'all." She turned off the phone and set it on the glass-topped table.

$2,500 a couple indeed.

The nerve. She could get that diamond pendant she admired for that.

Besides, if any portion was going to LOL, such a donation would look especially bad with Bob a federal district judge.

With a derisive sniff, she dismissed it as not worth mentioning.

Beyond the glass, rain still pounded the ground, hopefully all the hurricane's remnants would deliver. Flooding was bad enough. As far as she was concerned, the Dallas-Fort Worth area had already been slammed by their quota of tornados.

SOUTH PACIFIC DIVISION
U.S. ARMY CORPS OF ENGINEERS
ALBUQUERQUE, NM
August 31, Friday
9:52 a.m. MDT

THOMAS MARTIN STEWED in his fourth-floor office, watching a jack rabbit nibble a cactus, part of the landscaping skirting the parking lot. As director of the South Pacific Division of the U.S. Army Corps of Engineers, he was government construction lead for PURF.

He never played the race card to further his career and found it offensive when others did. Just because he was black didn't mean he got it courtesy of Affirmative Action or some other government edict.

With a Masters in civil engineering from the University of Chicago and fifteen years with the Corps, he knew what he was doing and qualified to handle such a project, as he had multiple times in the past.

It was a massive endeavor that provided a multitude of much-needed jobs. So now Phase I was being dedicated at some D.C. style, on-site wingding.

Pay $2,500 for him and Ella to rub elbows with Washington's elite?

Fat chance.

His teeth clenched. He wouldn't piss on any of them if they were in flames.

He thought back to the negotiating he did to make sure his division got the assignment. Some of the land fell in the Northwest Division, which resulted in a turf battle, from which he emerged as victor.

Which in retrospect, had not been a good thing.

If he knew then what he did now, he never would have fought so hard.

It was one disaster after another, all of which splashed on him as the official government overseer. At first, he was relieved that most of the project management dirty work would be done by Elite Management Partners Incorporated, known as EMPI.

Until he met the person filling the project manager, role.

He thought back to when he first met Virgil Steinbrenner, EMPI's Chief Operations Officer. The man sat on the other side of Thomas' desk to receive his initial contact briefing. It was Steinbrenner's first government contract and he didn't even try to disguise his elation—or his ignorance.

It was obvious the jerk had no clue what was expected of the Project Manager, much less Top Secret project security. Steinbrenner's flippant attitude branded him as an arrogant ass strutting around like the biggest bird at a turkey shoot. The pained look on the NSA guy administering his security oaths indicated a similar impression.

In an open bidding situation the likes of him never would have passed orals. However, some Colorado senator sandbagged EMPI into the job, supposedly based on past performance, which no doubt related to a campaign donation.

The security team, also located out of Albuquerque, was supposedly populated by former Special Forces members. Back then, he hoped they knew enough about sensitive operations not to be dependent on their PM's direction.

As it turned out, both concerns hit the bullseye. If nothing else, this entire experience taught him to pay attention to his gut. A month or so ago, he ran into the agent who'd been both

Steinbrenner's and the security team's handler in Crystal City. When he asked how things were going, the guy spit out an expletive as if it were a rotten piece of meat.

While EMPI installed encryption software to protect the documentation, its decoder sat on their server unprotected. They may as well have named a ReadMe file *Hackers Enter Here*. The average middle schooler could get in, next step posting it on Facebook.

The project was above Top Secret. They didn't mess around with that stuff. The NSA was sick of that "right to know" crap and handled violations in a way that assured it didn't happen again.

He exhaled, hard, remembering how shaken up the team was when Steinbrenner turned up neutralized sniper-style.

If the data had been properly protected that poor sucker, Reynolds, would be alive today. The security team screwed that one up as well, their amateurish tactics eventually broadcast on network TV when the guy's wife went public.

Then there was that issue with the oil company.

USACE work with EPA Superfunds had been a bit rocky, literally and figuratively. Nonetheless, somehow it worked. This time it would be further complicated by an oil company out of Texas.

They, too would be working with the EPA. The idea to use contaminated mine water for the drilling operation necessary for the geothermal system made sense—on paper. In practice, it presented the risk of releasing it instead of containing or eliminating it.

EPA Superfund activity in Colorado was already trying to clean up tons of cyanide, lead, and other pollutants generated by the 19th Century mining industry. The combination of that with fracking sounded too much like striking a match to check the gas tank.

Initially, he hoped LSO was competent and experienced enough to pull it off. If there was one thing they sure as hell didn't need it was another debacle like the 2015 Gold King Mine disaster.

He was relieved when the meeting with Lone Star Operations went well. LSO's Chief Operating Officer, Gerald Bentley, indicated, in his own colorful Texas parlance, that "this ain't our first rodeo" and seemed to know "how the cow ate the cabbage."

Using AMD, or acid mine drainage, for the drilling fluid instead of robbing the local aquifer made sense, was cheaper, and didn't appear to increase the risk.

The only concern was the above-ground infrastructure required during construction, which would stand out like the proverbial sore thumb. On the positive side, it could provide a cover for activity, like transporting heavy equipment into the area.

As it turned out, it was USACE's boring machine that let out their dirty little secret in that Reynolds guy's photos, not the drilling rig.

But LSO didn't come out of it with a clean slate.

The location of the deep injection well for drilling fluids was miscalculated and wound up poisoning the local water supply. The result was at least one death, of which he was aware.

Bentley managed damage control, the particulars of which he didn't know, neither cared to.

Every Herculean endeavor came with hazards.

Construction projects were loaded. Over the years, he lost three employees to workplace accidents. Inevitable, when you build dams and bridges. Safety was his top priority, the only possible thing that could match its importance being a Top Secret classification.

Yet PURF saw twice as many deaths, courtesy of SNAFUs galore. As if the project was cursed from the start.

Then, as if that weren't enough, there was the matter of why the facility was built. In theory, it was an underground condo unit intended to house six thousand families.

What he didn't understand was why they needed another one? Several others already existed to house key government and military officials.

In some cases, they were more like dormitories and not the slightest bit luxurious. This one clearly was. And included some very strange features that made little sense.

A gargantuan deep underground assembly area with a fire pit and altar? What were they going to do? Roast marshmallows?

He hadn't pursued it, more concerned with how many billets he'd need and finding the talent required.

When he found out later who and what the facility was for, he was so incensed on moral grounds, he came close to quitting. Fortunately, his wife reminded him he only had another ten years before he could retire, so he stuck it out.

Bottom line, as the project from hell, perhaps literally, he couldn't put it behind him fast enough.

WASHINGTON, D.C.
RANIER OFFICE BUILDING
August 31, Friday
4:52 p.m. EDT

INGRID'S CHALLENGES CONTINUED as she hung-up from another reminder call. Of those who failed to respond, all but a hundred twenty-nine decided to attend. Most that declined were contractors and a few agency directors who either balked at the cost or being held midweek.

Now that she had a final count of six-thousand-two-hundred-thirty-two, she could notify the caterers, and meet her "Before Labor Day" deadline. Fortunately, the facility had a gymnasium-sized kitchen, an obvious necessity should PURF ever be used for its intended purpose. That way they could prepare all the food there; transporting raw goods was far simpler than thousands of meals to-go.

Tables and chairs as well as linens were on-site, along with plates, glasses, and silverware. Industrial-grade dishwashers were another advantage. She still needed to find out how many each table could seat. Then she could figure out how many would be required and notify the decorators.

They, in turn, would contact the florist and any other vendors.

She smiled as she sent off the email to Silver City Catering that included an attachment of the kitchen layout and other relevant details, such as dining room maps.

A satisfied smile crinkled the crow's feet teasing her eyes as again she gazed out her window to the mall.

This would be a once in a lifetime event to remember.

Was the tightness in her gut because she missed something?

Or another reason?

Little Wolf always considered a situation in advance and planned what should be done. He possessed great foresight, tried to think of and to provide for every contingency, and to leave nothing to chance. — George Bird Grinnell, "The Cheyenne Indians: Their History and Ways of Life" Volume II, p. 51-2

33. PLANS

NORTHERN CHEYENNE RESERVATION
MONTANA
September 5, Wednesday
3:17 p.m. MDT

The first few days since returning from *Novavose* found Charlie helping resolve the problems that arose during their absence. The first thing he did was help Risingsun retrieve the canoe from Eaglefeathers Creek. He reminded the boy that canoes operated best in water, then tasked him to haul enough buckets from the creek to wash *Tah-Hó'nehe* after their trip.

"I want to make sure you understand what water looks like," he explained. Risingsun assured him he wouldn't make that mistake again.

The next issue was the dead washing machine. It was so old parts were no longer available, so he ordered a new one from the appliance store in Colstrip. While he was at it, he added a dryer. Since the house wasn't wired for 220, he bought one that used propane.

That meant contacting the local supplier to install a two-hundred-fifty-gallon tank, with a new stove on its way as well, much to Star's delight.

Enough she forgave the wagon incident, though he replaced that, too.

Trip aftermath on the home front taken care of, every spare moment since was devoted to the *Gathering*. The dining room table was scattered with notes, to-do lists, coffee cups, and receipts with Charlie and White Wolf figuring out what to do next.

If one thing was clear, it was everything happened for a reason, under the wise direction of *Maheo*. Only a fool would believe such things were a coincidence.

The *Gathering* had been scheduled years before, to be held there at this very time. Until now, neither he nor White Wolf understood its true purpose, especially its two week duration.

As many as a thousand Indigenous civic and spiritual leaders would converge on the Northern Cheyenne Reservation in Montana. While some such events were open to the public, this one was by invitation, every tribe included. Truly *Maheo* was its master planner, having foreseen all that would occur.

After talking to Sara during the ride home Charlie described to White Wolf and Ice what else he experienced. While both had a general impression of its importance, as with any ceremonial fast, learning the details stunned them both.

As Charlie told them about each vision and answered their questions it allowed him to see each ceremony's significance more clearly himself, as well as how it all tied together. It felt so good to share, their comments and questions cementing his own understanding.

The visions were not simply teaching Cheyenne history. They were preparation for something Indigenous holy men like Black Elk and Crazy Horse prophesied centuries before, all to be accomplished by the seventh generation.

At long last, after centuries of suffering, it was time.

"Great things always happen at these gatherings," White Wolf said. "But this one will be exceptional."

"Yes. I'm sure you remember that my parents met at a pan nation pow-wow in New Mexico. Otherwise my *Diné* mother and Cheyenne father never would have met."

White Wolf grunted. "Which wasn't exactly a good thing."

"Maybe," Charlie replied. "I grew up torn between two cultures. That drove me to abandon both. But between *Amasani's* and Eaglefeathers' teachings, I saw truth and beauty in each. And their similarities. That gives me an advantage uniting the tribes. I'm not just some Northern Cheyenne telling them what to do, but half *Diné*, with a perspective on their beliefs as one of the largest."

"Yes. I think only the Cherokees have greater numbers."

"I believe so."

"Littlewolf, remember this was never intended to be a pow-wow. They are social occasions. This involves only Native spiritual and civic leaders and has a spiritual purpose."

"Yes, of course."

Their discussion returned to arrangements that needed to be made. It was scheduled three years in advance for the last two weeks of October and into the first of November so other tribes could plan their events around it.

All Cheyenne, men, women, and children, from both the North and South were invited since multitudes of people were needed for the *Massaum*. Leaders from other tribes would be invited to witness the ceremony and learn its purpose, then adopt it, if they chose to do so. The following Monday they'd leave for Colorado where they'd perform the *Dance of Peace and Welcome*.

"How much land do you and Sara have?" White Wolf asked.

"I have fifty acres. I believe she has around four or five hundred."

"You are sure she will not mind? Several hundred, maybe even a thousand of us, can make quite a racket. It could be the First Nation equivalent of Woodstock."

He shook his head. "No, she will not mind. You heard what she said on the phone in *Tah-Hó'nehe*."

"Have you asked her?"

"No. But trust me. She will not mind."

Furthermore, since his fast he sensed all of this related to Bryan's dying plea not to let the government get away with PURF, much less his murder, and tied back to the Curse as well as several ancient prophecies.

"We have transportation issues to work out," White Wolf went on. "It would be best to charter buses. Safer and more efficient to move so many." His lips tightened. "But expensive."

"I agree. We will do that." He smiled. "I am confident I can find a benefactor to help."

White Wolf looked a bit skeptical, yet still nodded. "Good. I will get an estimate. I think it best if those attending pay a small fee, so they do not take it for granted."

"Agreed. Has word gone out about the Dance?"

"Yes. Instructions have been sent to all reservations. They are to assemble their leaders and practice before they arrive. Then they are to teach it to their people, who will perform it on their own land at the same time we do, if possible. Also, the new song. Each will receive a translation so they understand its meaning, but it will be sung here with vocables. That way no one is excluded."

Charlie nodded agreement. "Do they understand the significance?"

"Historically, yes." White Wolf's smile snuck across his face like a badger stalking a rabbit. "This performance, no."

Both chuckled, then Charlie added, "Many memories will be made that day. It will never be forgotten for all future generations. It will be a treasured moment in our collective history. I wish Eaglefeathers were here to witness it."

White Wolf lowered his chin and gave him his signature condescending look. "Do you really believe he will not be there, Littlewolf?"

Charlie's eyes met his. "You are correct. He would not miss it."

"It's safe to assume that many attendees have cell phones. During the trip to Colorado, we could hold an online meeting to provide further instructions."

"That's an excellent idea. We should create a Facebook page for the event, too."

As he pondered what was to come, however, one misgiving crept in. As always, he sensed White Wolf tapping his thoughts. While he was now skilled enough to block the intrusion, there was no justification. Secrets were possible, but pointless.

"You are troubled about someone," his uncle prompted.

"Yes. Actually, at least two. They treated me well. In some ways, they even gave me back my self-respect. It feels wrong to injure them. Would it be inappropriate to warn them?"

"No. Or ask *Maheo* to create a diversion. Some circumstance that directs them somewhere else."

"That is wise. And more subtle. That worked when Winter Hawk and I asked *Maheo* to honor the Curse to take care of the *ok kliwŭs* who killed my white brother."

"Yes. I am sure that something similar will occur."

"Yes. If it is right before *Maheo,* it will."

SARA'S CONDO
DENVER, CO
September 5, Wednesday
5:28 p.m. MDT

SARA'S PHONE CHIRPED a text notification. She picked it up from beside her computer where she was researching one of her planned podcasts. She grinned, heart leaping like a spooked rabbit, when she saw who it was from. She opened it, mystified by the request.

First, Charlie wanted to know how much acreage she had. Second, whether she'd mind if some of his people used it for a conference in about six weeks.

She certainly didn't mind, but her curiosity was tweaked. An unfamiliar sensation in her chest told her it was important and might relate to whatever he alluded to when they spoke about her doing a sweat.

Rather than text she called.

"Hi, Sara. You got my text?"

"Yes, I did. I'm pretty sure I have around 450 acres. What's going on?"

"We have a big *Gathering* coming up, which will mostly be up here. However, we've got some things planned down there, so we're hoping to find a place to set up some tipis for about a week. I promise we'll clean up the mess."

"Sure, no problem. Sounds exciting. How many do you expect?"

He exhaled hard enough she heard it, a somewhat ominous preamble. "Well, uh, quite a few. Several hundred. Maybe even a thousand."

"Holy crap on a cracker, Charlie!" she said, not expecting such a high number. "That's a lot of people! How are they going to get there?"

"We plan to charter enough buses to get them down there. But we, uh, well, we have a bit of a problem."

"Oh? What's that?"

"We don't have enough in our budget to cover it."

She scowled. "How much are you short?"

"Uh, well, if we charge each person $5, somewhere around $43,000. Some of these people are simply too poor for us to charge any more."

"Ouch."

Considering she planned to will her cabin with all its property to him and his people, this really wasn't a big deal. As far as she was concerned, it was already theirs. Especially in view of his role in restoring her health, which was priceless. If she didn't have the money already, she'd have no problem taking out a loan.

"Do you need some help with that, Charlie?"

"I, uh, well. Okay. Yes, I'm afraid we do. And I promise you won't be sorry. At least not if you're still planning a podcast or writing a book."

She laughed, more curious than ever. "Really? Why is that?"

His conspiratorial chuckle made her grin. "What we plan to do down there is, well, historic. And you'll have a front row seat. It could turn out to be the story of the century. In fact, I'm sure you could recover the cost a hundred times over if you make a video."

"Indeed!" She straightened in her chair. "And what exactly is it? Are you going to tell me what you're up to?"

His pause was long and, no doubt, thoughtful. "I can tell you a little. Do you know anything about the Ghost Dance?"

"Never heard of it. Why?"

"Because it's about to draw some serious attention. It would give your podcast a helpful boost. Since it will be on your property, we can keep it private, so you'd be the only reporter. And, believe me, it will enhance your own story more than you can imagine."

Curiosity clawed at her psyche like a mystery novel cliffhanger. "Okay, Charlie. Tell me where to send it. $43,000, right?"

"Yes. You can just send me a check, here at the ranch. Make it out to '*Peace Gathering of Indigenous Leaders.*' You won't be sorry, Sara. I promise."

"No problem, Charlie. I mean it. Text me your address."

"Okay, I will. Meanwhile, find out everything you can about the dance. You'll need that background for your story. It has historical significance, though I'm sure most people today never heard of it. I doubt the government takes it seriously these days. But they did in the past. Enough to outlaw it and slaughter some of our people for practicing it."

Her heartrate jumped, intuition blaring there was far more to this than he was saying. "That's incredible. They killed them for performing a dance?"

"Yes. The massacre at Wounded Knee included women and children as well as elders."

"That's horrible!" she cried. "How could they do such a thing?"

"Just another sordid part of our history, Sara. Check it out, then ask any questions you have. Much of what's recorded about the dance is inaccurate. I have some firsthand information from someone that explains its true origin and purpose."

"Okay."

"Anyway, here's the plan. We're coming down in a week or two to check everything out and make local arrangements. Porta-potties, water trucks, stuff like that, then scope out the property for the best place to set up. I'll tell you more then." He paused. "I really look forward to seeing you again."

"Yes. Same here. See you soon."

Smiling at the prospect, she set aside her current podcast idea for what he told her to check out.

Chills raised the hair on her arms as she read the posts online.

A prophecy that the earth would swallow up the white man, heal the land, restore the buffalo, and return it to indigenous people?

It sounded entirely off-the-wall, too far-fetched to take seriously. Yet, it was easy to see why it concerned the government. The creepy feeling it generated was strong, so much so she could no more dismiss it than her growing feelings for Charlie.

Before the pale-faces came among us, we enjoyed the happiness of unbounded freedom,
and were acquainted with neither riches, wants, nor oppression. How is it now? Wants
and oppressions are our lot; for are we not controlled in everything, and dare we move
without asking, by your leave?
—Tecumseh, 1811

34. GONE

SARA'S CONDO
DENVER, CO
September 6, Thursday
9:18 a.m.

Sara sat in her combination guest room/office the next morning, wrote out a check for $50,000, folded it up in a piece of paper, and slipped it in an envelope addressed according to Charlie's directions. She added a stamp, then decided to transfer some money from her brokerage account, since it took her credit union balance lower than she preferred.

She brought up the website on her laptop and logged in. She scowled.

Incorrect Account Information

Assuming she typed it in wrong, she tried again.

Same result.

What was going on?

A third try was no different, so she scrolled down for the number to call.

After slogging through their horrendous electronic switchboard, she finally got connected to a human. Customer service had apparently been outsourced judging by the woman's accent and unpronounceable name.

With forced patience she explained. "My name is Sara Reynolds and I'm having trouble logging into my account."

"Do you hahve your ahkoont noomber, madam?"

"Yes, I do."

She provided the information, then settled in to what she expected to be a long wait.

She didn't like the heavy feeling brewing in her gut. Blossom, in her usual spot beneath her feet, gave her a concerned look. She bent down to provide a reassuring scratch behind the ears as her mind wandered back to the blog she was working on.

After reading about the Ghost Dance, she decided to set it aside until she finished the current one. She'd finally set up an account on a website that allowed both blogs and podcasts to which she'd already posted a few, calling out the government for its failure to follow the will of the people.

Polls showed people did not approve of sending billions of dollars overseas when so many U.S. citizens needed help. She pointed out how much money corporations spent on lobbying for government favors as well as ridiculous pork barrel projects that cost taxpayers billions of dollars with PURF the star example.

Then there was that Supreme Court decision that exacerbated the problem.

She included that along with other examples, including who voted for it. Each one was substantiated with facts and hard data from government websites. Her intent was to inform her audience what was going on though they undoubtedly sounded like rants.

So what?

Clearly there were a lot of people out there who agreed, based on the response to her GoFundMe account.

The hold music stopped.

"Mizzes Rhaynoolds? Your ahkoont hass been terminhated."

"*What?* By whom?"

Surely her father, the joint owner, would not do any such thing without telling her.

The response was more hold music.

Panic zipped through her like convenience store sushi. There was over two million dollars in that account! The bulk of Bryan's life insurance money in a portfolio her father recommended. The remainder was in the credit union, divided between her checking account and some rolling Certificates of Deposit.

After several minutes the music stopped when the connection ended.

Oh, my God! What is going on?

Her hand trembled as she called Will.

It went to phone mail.

"Dad!" she cried, voice shaking. "Call me! Our brokerage account is gone! Do you know anything about this?"

Knowing he didn't always check his messages, she sent a text.

Took several deep breaths.

It had to be a mistake. *How could it just disappear?* That woman probably didn't have a clue what she was doing.

She jumped when her phone rang.

"Hey, Dad. I don't know what's going on, but for some reason our brokerage account is gone."

"*Gone?* What do you mean, *gone*?" he asked, the surprise in his voice even more disconcerting.

"G-O-N-E. *Gone.* I tried to log in and it said *Incorrect Account information.* I called customer service and was told by some woman with a horrific accent that the account was 'terminated.' I asked how and why, but they cut me off. What should we do?"

"I'll call them."

His tone was grim, fully restoring her panic.

She paced back and forth, finally staring blankly out the window at the parking lot, frantic by the time he called back.

"What did you find out?" she asked, hand over her pounding heart.

He exhaled hard. "Nothing good. I finally got a hold of a supervisor. He claimed he wasn't authorized to provide any information about who ordered it. I got the impression it was some government agency."

"Oh, my God. So my money's gone? What am I going to do?"

"Don't panic yet, Sara. We're going to find out who and why. Do you think there's any chance your kidnapper friend did this? Decided he wanted the ransom after all?"

"I suppose it's possible, but I don't think so. If so, why would he give me that gigantic donation?"

"I don't know, Sara. Let me call him and see if he knows anything. What about your bank account? Is it still intact?"

"I don't know. I need to check my GoFundMe account, too."

"Right. You do that while I call him. His name's Jason, right?"

"Yes. Jason LaGrange."

He hung up, his iffy reassurance insufficient to arrest the panic.

She sat down at her laptop. Her hands trembled as she typed in the URL of The Denver City and County Employees Federal Credit Union website.

Its homepage filled the screen.

The website Bryan designed when he was their system administrator. The very position Jason took over after this death.

A tsunami of nostalgia coupled with another Jason reminder slammed her already agitated state.

She bit her lip, summoning the nerve she needed to find out.

She logged in.

Slowly exhaled, hoping for the best.

She waited, thinking she probably should have removed Bryan from their joint account.

An ominous message flashed across the screen.

Account Restricted. Contact Customer Service for Assistance.

At least in this case she expected answers.

She grabbed her phone and called. When the electronic switchboard came on she opted to talk to a person. The receptionist, new since Bryan was killed, answered.

"Hi. This is Sara Reynolds. I'd like to talk to Mr. Tompkins, please."

Surely the manager remembered her and would provide some answers.

"Good morning, Sara. I assume you're calling about your account."

"Yes, I am, David. Can you please tell me what's going on?"

When he paused, she closed her eyes and prayed.

"Why don't you come into the office, Sara? I'd rather not talk about this on the phone."

"Okay. When's a good time?"

"Whenever you can come in is fine."

"Is it okay if I bring my father?"

"Of course."

"Okay. Thanks, David. See you soon."

Her hand trembled as she called her father, but it went to phone mail. She left a message, then checked her GoFundMe account.

To her relief, it was all still there

Excited, she decided to withdraw it immediately, before it disappeared, too.

Then remembered.

She didn't have direct access. It could only be transferred to her bank.

She buried her face in her hands and sobbed.

With all her money gone she had no choice but to go back to work. That in itself wasn't the end of the world.

But above all else, what would she tell Charlie?

HEWITT IMAGING SERVICES
BOULDER, CO
September 6, Thursday
10:32 a.m. MDT

WILL'S WINDOWLESS OFFICE was connected to a secure area guarded by a retinal scanner, security equal to the satellite control room. Immediately beyond sprawled a four-thousand square foot area filled with mainframe computers and analysis stations, some of which were occupied.

For the second time that day, he closed his office door, ambient noise with it. This would be another conversation he didn't want overheard.

He found the number with the 207 area code and pressed *Call*.

"Hello, Mr. Montgomery. I've been expecting you."

Will straightened, instincts on high alert.

"Indeed. And why is that, Mr. LaGrange? What do you know about Sara's accounts?"

"Quite a bit, actually."

His heartrate took off at a full gallop. "*You did this?*"

"Yes. But hear me out. It's not what you think."

"Indeed. So what exactly is it, then?" He snarled to himself, knowing this guy was some species of nutjob all along.

"Here's the deal. The Feds classified her as a domestic terrorist. Something related to sensitive content on her blog site. Rather than censor the material they were freezing her assets."

"Okay. Where do you fit in?"

"I beat them to it. I cashed out the brokerage account and emptied her credit union funds into a secure account in the Cayman Islands. By the way, there were no restrictions on withdrawals from the brokerage account."

Will flinched, busted, but didn't respond. No longer mattered, other than making himself out a liar. "Why?" he asked, ignoring the last comment. "You want that ransom after all?"

"Close, but not exactly. What I want is my eyes back. If I get that, Sara gets her money. Which you realize would have been gone for good if the Feds got to it first."

Will held his head, incredulous. "How in the hell is she supposed to get your sight back?"

"I don't know, Mr. Montgomery. She clearly had something to do with losing it. Thus, she should be able to figure out how to get it restored."

Will exhaled hard. "Okay. I'll tell her. I hope for both your sakes she can do that."

"Me, too. Thank you."

Will hung up, glowering with suspicion How'd he manage to do all that if he was still blind? Or was he lying? Was her money truly gone with this a ploy to get his sight back?

Not that he blamed him. Being blind would definitely be a bummer.

Fingers massaged his temples while his thoughts longed for the quiet, predictable days before his son-in-law was murdered for hacking classified information.

Damn you, Bryan Reynolds.

He worked his jaw, furious. Forced himself to calm down before picking up his phone to call Sara.

"Hi, Dad. Did you get my message?"

"No. I just hung up with LaGrange."

"Oh. Well, my credit union account is gone, too. But the manager said he'd tell us more if we come into the office."

"We don't need to, Sara. Turns out your abductor is behind this."

"*What*? Why? What did he say?"

"He wants you to do whatever's necessary to restore his vision. Then he'll give back your money. He said the Feds were ready to confiscate it, but he got to it first. Says it's in an account in the Cayman Islands. I don't know whether to believe him or not."

"From what I've seen of him, Dad, he doesn't lie. I actually thought of asking him if he could get it back for me."

He scowled, surprised the strident tones of panic were gone from her voice. Why on God's green earth would she trust that man?

"But I don't know if or how I can do that, Dad," she went on. "Hopefully, Charlie will. I suppose if he could cure me, he should be able to reverse whatever they did to Jason so I could escape."

When you know who you are; when your mission is clear and you burn with the inner fire of unbreakable will; no cold can touch your heart; no deluge can dampen your purpose. You know that you are alive.
—*Chief Seattle*

35. DEALS

SARA'S CONDO
DENVER, CO
September 6, Thursday
10:45 a.m. MDT

Sara brought up Charlie's number, then sat at her desk staring into space. The fact Jason had her money caused her initial panic to evaporate like fog on a spring morning. Surely they could do this. After all, they blinded him in the first place.

Her memory of being healed was fuzzy. Like most dreams, it dimmed with time. Even her escape was unclear, the excitement and surprise so intense her mind raced on an adrenaline high the entire time. Like a video on fast-forward.

Charlie never explained, either. Just acknowledged it happened. He was there, but someone else was, too. Would that person have to fix Jason's eyes?

The only way to find out was to call him. If they couldn't, the consequences would be brutal—for everyone.

He picked up immediately. "Is everything okay?" he asked, before she could speak.

"Hi, Charlie. Actually, no. But I hope you can fix it." She crossed her fingers.

"Why? What's wrong?"

"Well, the Feds were going to take all my money. Jason found out somehow, so he took it before they could."

"He took your money?"

"Yes. *But* I can get it back. He just wants his eyes back. Can you do that?"

"I, uh, don't know."

"If you can't, I'm broke, Charlie!" Panic spiked again, resuming it grip like a relapse of some dreaded disease. "And I won't be able to help you, either. Unless there's some way I can still get to my GoFundMe account. But under the circumstances, I may have to give all that money back to the donors."

"Why? Why did this happen?"

Her response was a derisive snort. "The government didn't like what I posted on my blog. Imagine that. *Ha!* I haven't even posted that much. Mainly about that Supreme Court decision, PURF's legislative history, and who voted for it. Barely got started. I suspect Bob Bentley had something to do with it. He was sure nasty to me the last time I was at the cabin."

"He was? What happened?"

She recoiled at the ugly memory. "I guess he thought I was dead and was pretty shocked when I showed up with Liz to play *Mah Jongg* with his wife. We got into quite a scene when he said Bryan got what he deserved. I let him have it."

He chuckled. "Good for you. You know his father is behind this, right? Including targeting you?"

"Oh! That must be Myron Bentley, right? He's the president of that sketchy lobbyist group that wants me dead. I hadn't put the two together before. Wow. That makes perfect sense."

"Right. They're all in on it. So back to your kidnapper's eyes. I'll see what I can find out. Did he give you a deadline?"

"No. But I suspect he doesn't want to wait. And I need my money back to help you."

"Okay, Sara. Let me see what I can find out and get back to you."

"Thanks, Charlie."

She hung up, crossed the fingers on both hands, and pleaded with all her might for a positive outcome.

Kind of like when she was eleven and wished for a pony, hoping this time would yield better results.

NORTHERN CHEYENNE RESERVATON
BUSBY, MT.
September 6, Thursday
11:15 a.m. MDT

CHARLIE'S SOLEMN EYES connected with White Wolf's, who froze in his tracks. Both men were unloading hay bales from a trailer behind *Tah-Hó'nehe*, then stacking them in the barn for the coming winter. They'd cleared the area a few days before where the *Gathering* would be held, so it would be ready for the camp circle and *Massaum* activities.

"What is wrong, Littlewolf?" he asked, either reading his mind or expression.

"When we healed Sara we blinded her abductor so she could escape," he explained. "He's taken all her money, but will return it in exchange for getting his sight back. Can that be done?"

White Wolf rarely looked as confused as he did now. "Something is not right. Usually, the blinding ceremony is not permanent. When it's used in battle or for protection, it's purpose is for the enemy not to see you. It does not *blind* you. They can see everything else. It's for that situation only. Camouflage. I'm surprised his eyes didn't return when she was safely out of range."

"Well, apparently they didn't. Unless he's lying."

"That should be easy enough to check, Littlewolf."

Charlie laughed. "True. But whatever is going on needs to be fixed or our bus budget is gone."

White Wolf grimaced. "Check with Ice. None of what happened at *Novavose* surprised him. He will know."

"Good idea."

Charlie took out his phone. Then remembered—Ice didn't have one. He'd have to drive out there. And do it properly by laying down tobacco.

He patted the breast pocket of his buffalo plaid shirt, bulge confirming he had some.

"I'm going over there now. Sara sounded frantic."

He unhitched the trailer, still partially loaded with hay, then jumped in *Tah-Hó'nehe,* which he steered across a convoluted shortcut of dirt ranch roads to the elder's cabin.

Ice opened the door and greeted him with a friendly nod. Charlie offered the tobacco, which he accepted and motioned him inside.

"I am surprised to see you, Littlewolf," he said. "By the way, preparing for the *Gathering* is much work. If White Wolf needs me to cover for him let me know. Is that why you're here?"

"*Néá'eše.* We appreciate that. No, I am here because I need advice." He explained the situation to which Ice also looked surprised.

"That means *Maheo* allowed the blindness to continue for a reason."

Charlie's mind opened with an abrupt blast of understanding. "Of course! *Maheo* does not want Sara to lose her money. She pledged to help with *Gathering* expenses, which we desperately need. What must she do for his eyes to return?"

"*É-émanané.* Do a sweat. It will reveal more about the situation."

"*Néá'eše.* That is perfect," Charlie replied. "She needs one anyway, to assure all the toxins are out of her body."

Ice agreed, then added, "It would be best if the person who needs his eyes joins the sweat."

Charlie stiffened. "I do not know if that is possible. But I will tell her."

"If it is meant to be, he will."

As soon as he got back in *Tah-Hó'nehe* he called Sara.

"Hi, Charlie. What did you find out?"

"I asked Ice, a very wise elder. He recommended a sweat. You need one anyway, so that sounds like a good solution. But there's a catch."

"What's that?" Considerable tension colored her voice.

"It would be best if he's also in the sweat."

His intuition felt her discomfort during the ensuing pause.

"I, uh, I don't know if I want to see him again, even if he would. He can be dangerous, Charlie. I think I can trust him, but I'm not sure. No telling what he might do if it doesn't work."

"It will work, Sara. If he wants to be sure, then that is what he needs to do."

She hesitated. "Oh. Okay. I'll tell him. Can we do the sweat here? Or do we all need to go to Montana?"

"It would be better and safer here. But like I told you, White Wolf and I plan to come down in a week or so to make arrangements for the *Gathering*. We could do it then, since I have a sweat lodge at my cabin. Can you wait that long?"

"Probably not. I'm sure he wants his sight as much as I want my money. I'll let you know. Thanks, Charlie. I'm relieved we can reverse it. It would be really bad otherwise."

"Let me know when you'll be here. We'll be ready."

SARA'S CONDO
DENVER, CO
September 6, Thursday
1:52 p.m.

AS MUCH AS SARA dreaded it, it was time to talk directly to Jason. She got his number from her father, who asked her to find out how he did all that if he was blind. She wondered, too, as she spent several minutes trying to figure out what to say.

It was time for Blossom's walk, so she took her on their usual early afternoon stroll around the condo's green space, which was now boasting splashes of autumn colors as well. When they got back, she fixed herself a cup of hibiscus tea, procrastinating some more.

What was going on with Jason, anyway? Why was he looking out for her? Or was it purely selfish? Why did she feel guilty for escaping like that? As if she were the one who did something wrong?

With his background, there was no telling what he was up to. Yet she didn't feel threatened. That night they watched those movies it felt as if they were old friends.

How crazy was that?

He supplied the poison that nearly killed me, for heaven sake!

She snarled at the insanity of it all, then forced herself to make the call.

"You have reached LaGrange Financial Services. How can we help you today?"

Impatience flared. "Very funny, Jason."

"Can I get my sight back?"

"I asked. Yes, you can. But there's something we need to do."

"Oh? And what's that? Contribute ten percent to the Native American Rights Fund?"

She scowled at his sarcasm. "No. I need to do a sweat. And if you really want to make sure it works, you need to do one, too." She ducked her head and arched her back, as if expecting a blow.

"Okay."

She straightened, surprised there was no argument. "You're willing to do that?"

"Of course. What were you willing to do to get your legs back?"

"Gotcha." Her shoulders relaxed as she stifled a sigh. That was easier than expected. "By the way, my father has a question for you."

"What?"

"How did you get to my funds and do all that if you're blind?"

He laughed as if it were the stupidest question ever. "Are you kidding? Ever hear of accessibility options? Voice commands? Talk-backs? You really think I've never had to do anything in the dark? C'mon."

"Oh. Yeah. That makes sense."

"So where do we need to go to do this sweat?"

She braced herself, curious how he'd react. "Montana."

"You're kidding. How are we supposed to get there?"

"You mean you don't have a self-driving car?"

"Correct. Wouldn't trust one if I did. Too easy to hack."

"Well, Jason, if I had my money I'd charter a private jet. Lacking that, I guess we drive."

"Okay. When do we leave? I'll pay for gas."

EN ROUTE INTERSTATE 25 NORTH
BOULDER, CO
September 8, Saturday
8:03 a.m.

SARA CLIMBED INTO THE driver's seat and handed Jason back his credit card. "Thanks," she said.

"You're welcome."

"Who's Biergarten LLC?"

"Shell account of mine. Tax shelter."

In back her father grunted, Connie giggled, and Blossom snorted.

She pushed the ignition button, pulled out of the gas station, and steered toward the I-25 North onramp. The last time she drove this route she had Charlie in back telling her there was someone following them.

Now she had Jason up front because Will didn't want him in back. Her father was carrying, but for all they knew, Jason was, too.

Doubtful, if he was truly blind. Did his pistol have accessibility options? Anything was possible, considering.

The plan was to drive straight through except for stopping for gas and switching drivers. Will would take the wheel when they got to Casper, just past halfway.

Knowing her father's scorn for speed limits, she expected they'd arrive sooner than the predicted six hours and fifty-two minutes.

Introducing him to Jason had been a hoot. As expected, Will had been less than friendly, Jason's humor dry, but undeniably funny. He was still staying where he'd taken her, making it easy to find, though the memories it evoked gave her the creeps. When they pulled into the driveway he must have heard the car because by the time she got out to get him he was out the front door. He looked like a typical blind man, decked out with sunglasses and a white cane, gym bag slung over his shoulder.

"Hello, Sara. Long time no see."

"Haha," she said humorlessly. "Can I help you to the car?"

"No, thanks. I'm good. I navigate with SONAR. Like a bat. Am I riding shotgun?"

"Yes."

He started toward the car, pausing when Will exited from the passenger seat.

Jason took a few more steps and held out his hand. "Jason LaGrange. Mr. Montgomery, I assume."

Will took his hand, but didn't look pleased. "Yes. My wife, Connie's, in back."

Jason leaned inside and held out his hand. "Nice to meet you, ma'am," he said.

Connie took it, making the face she made when trying not to laugh. "Same here."

Will rolled his eyes and joined her in back.

Jason got settled in front and pulled on the seatbelt. "What's your dog's name, Sara?"

Her muscles tensed as she slid behind the wheel.

Blossom didn't make a sound. Is he really blind or lying?

"I can smell her," he added. "Connie's wearing *Coco*, there's a bucket of fried chicken with Cole slaw in back, and yes, Sara, I really am blind."

"Oh. Uh, her name's Blossom. And she's been trained to protect me, too. You should get a service dog. They're very helpful."

"I would, but I don't plan to stay this way. Right?"

"Right."

Not much had been said since, other than stating his zip code as he handed over his credit card when she stopped to fill the tank.

Miles flew by without the distractions and incidents when she'd driven Charlie what seemed eons ago. Will connected his laptop to the Buick's Wi-Fi and was working, Connie doing whatever it was she did on her tablet when she wasn't cooking or shopping, probably that word game she was addicted to.

It was lunch time by the time she pulled into the Flying J Travel Center in Casper. Everyone got out to stretch their legs, Will manning the fuel nozzle at the Sinclair station while Sara took her pit bull off the pavement into the rough so the dog could do what dogs do.

A cluster of restaurants populated the immediate area around the truck stop's gasoline pumps and convenience store. Rusted-out cars were littered about, some integrated into the landscaping. Desolate, dried up prairie surrounded them, Bighorn Mountains barely visible to the west.

"Let's find a place to sit and eat here instead of in the car," Connie suggested.

No one argued, several boulders providing seating beside the webbed feet of a twenty-foot tall Donald Duck. They finished the fried chicken and individual cups of Cole slaw, then washed up and used the bathroom.

Back in the car, Will took the driver's seat.

"Buckle up tight, everyone," Sara teased from the back.

Connie laughed, Will muttered something, then, "Let's get this show on the road."

There were two obvious reasons he was crabby. Whether or not Jason could be trusted was a major concern. Of equal and possibly greater value was the sweat.

Charlie explained that it was best for her entire family to be there. Connie was all for it, always welcoming a new experience. Will, on the other hand, had been skeptical and uncomfortable during her initial healing ceremony.

He couldn't argue the fact that somehow those methods made her mobile again, but participating in a sweat was definitely not on his bucket list.

She smiled to herself as she got comfortable with Connie in back. Her father's long-held paradigms had been shattered unmercifully the past few months.

Poor Dad. First astrology, now this.

He followed the arrows that led to I-25, zoomed up the on-ramp, then gunned it some more, cutting across two lanes of traffic to the inside lane.

"You may want to slow down within city limits with out-of-state plates," Jason advised.

Will backed off the gas and checked the rearview mirror while Sara and Connie stifled giggles.

Once beyond the city limits, he accelerated again. After several miles of silence, he asked Jason, "How hard was it to adapt to being blind?"

"It's been an interesting experience. I'd heard your other senses improve to compensate and that's definitely the case. I had a blind roommate in college and wondered how he did it. Now I have some idea. I could live this way if I had to, but won't mind if it's temporary. When I found out the Feds were after Sara's assets, I felt I owed it to her to intervene. Then I thought maybe we could swing a deal."

"Why did you think you owed her something?"

Sara stiffened, hoping Jason wouldn't mention the poison. She had no idea how her father would react, but it wouldn't be good.

"Maybe I owed it to myself," Jason replied. "I felt bad for what I put her through."

Sara silently exhaled the air she was holding in her lungs. Like she'd told her father, he didn't lie. Was that why she was inclined to trust him, in spite of all he'd done?

"I get the feeling you were still stalking her," Will said.

"No. This time protecting her. I suspected the Feds would pull something like this."

"Do you think her life is still at risk?"

Sara strained to hear his answer, but couldn't over the racket of passing an eighteen-wheeler hauling double trailers.

"They may have decided it was too risky and switched to harassment. Sometimes they just make a person miserable by wielding a show of power rather than eliminating someone."

"Apparently."

The two men continued to chat, Will's hostile tone softening. Connie put away her tablet, closed her eyes, and fell asleep. Sara didn't plan to join her, but soon drifted off.

"Sara? Wake up."

She bolted awake.

"What is it, Dad?"

"We're almost to Sheridan. You said there's a shortcut to the reservation?"

"Yes. Highway 314. There's a big truck stop outside of town called Common Cents. Bring it up on the media screen. We can fill up the car, then check into the motel, since it may be late when we get back."

"I remember that place," Connie said with a yawn. "Great pizza and the cappuccino was delicious."

"Yes, it was great, but I'm sure Charlie's family will have plenty of food for us when we arrive."

After getting those things settled, they followed the back roads. A little over an hour later, they pulled up at White Wolf's ranch.

The entire family came out to greet them, Charlie and his uncle taking full advantage of Jason's blindness as they scoped him out. Their black dog showed considerable interest in Blossom, but the pit bull was unimpressed and stuck by her mistress.

As Sara suspected, Star had prepared a meal fit for royalty. After they finished eating Sara and Connie helped clean up, then joined the others while Charlie and White Wolf told them what to expect from the sweat and answered questions. Charlie emphasized not to eat anything other than a very light breakfast, allowable only because the motel was over an hour away.

Both Sara and Jason were told they would declare their respective purposes when it began. After that, they were instructed to pray or meditate upon what they wanted to achieve for the duration, which would be divided into four rounds of about twenty minutes each.

Charlie and White Wolf shared some personal sweat lodge experiences, warned them visions or visitations were possible, courtesy of the Grandfather Spirits, but not to fear them. The prospect didn't bother Sara, happy to welcome Bryan or her mom. Jason, on the other hand, said nothing, but nearly palpable fear seeped from his body language and sightless eyes.

A few hours later, everyone thanked Star and White Wolf for their hospitality, then returned to the motel, agreeing to be back the next morning by nine.

TAIL LIGHTS VANISHED within the deepening twilight. "What did you think?" Charlie asked.

White Wolf's pensive look bespoke a medley of impressions.

"That man has many demons. Bad ones. It is good that he is here."

Thought creates our world, and then says "I didn't do it."
~ David Bohm, Physicist

36. SWEATING

WHITE WOLF'S SWEAT LODGE
BUSBY, MT
September 9, Sunday
8:52 a.m.

Jason thrived on new experiences. So far this one beat the cake. The humidity was more stifling than the heat, though both bowed to other sensations. The olfactory assault competed with the auditory: Sage, earthy steam, and human sweat mingled with the high-pitched cry of a whistle, rhythmic *swoosh* of a rattle, rustling leaves, and singing in their indigenous language.

Sensory overload, especially without eyes, though not unpleasant. Whatever White Wolf placed on the hot stones each round reminded him of vanilla, its fragrance soothing.

He and Sara sat in back, facing the door, based on the air flow. Leaf-covered branches of some sort cushioned the ground, prickly against his bare legs. He picked one up and smelled it.

Ah. Some sort of sage.

Everyone's placement was discerned by voices. Sara on his right, then White Wolf's wife, Charlie, then White Wolf, who was running things. To his left was White Wolf's older son, Mrs. Montgomery, Mr. Montgomery, then White Wolf's younger son.

He hadn't done much praying in life. A few desperate pleas during chemistry finals and risky ops that went south were about it.

Sara was talking to someone. Whether it was God, herself, or her dead husband he couldn't tell.

Her purpose was to rid herself of any remaining poison that nearly killed her and paralyzed her legs. The statement pummeled his psyche as much as that meltdown she'd had.

His purpose was simple: *Be able to see.*

Sweat dribbled from his temples, over his cheeks to his chin, then dropped on his chest. Unable to evaporate in the moisture laden air, it failed to cool. He wiped his arm across his forehead, hoping none splashed on Sara.

What was it about this woman, anyway? Already she'd changed his life. Whether it was for the better was hard to tell.

He thought he knew who and what he was.

Not anymore.

Not since that moment he couldn't take the shot. It was as if she awakened a part of him he didn't know existed. Yet another persona in his Rolodex of personalities. A good one, perhaps?

The *swooshing* and singing stopped. A cool breeze hit his face, then wafted through the lodge, provoking a medley of sighs. Sara tapped his arm and handed him a bottle of water.

His stomach clenched, remembering when he handed her one.

Another stone clunked into place, the size of a melon, based on the sound, followed by ten more of equal mass. The heat radiating from each was cumulative. Once again the scorched vanilla scent, the whistle, rattle, and singing resumed.

Did he deserve having his eyes restored? Was this his due for what he'd done? Not only to Sara, but others too numerous to mention, many of whom did not fare as well as she had. Were they cursing him from wherever the dead reside?

He heard his name. Held his breath, listening.

"Please help Jason. Restore his sight so I have the money to help Charlie with the *Gathering* as I promised."

His eyes teared up, fortunately disguised by sweat.

Don't worry, Sara. You can have your money whether it comes back or not. I've been blind all my life. It's no wonder this was my fate.

Yet as bad as he was, there were others far worse. Too many in government sold their souls in exchange for power and obscene wealth.

He knew far more about PURF than those awaiting assignment through the bogus lottery system. Only those in the inner-most circle would find placement.

It hadn't taken long for the vilest among them to decide the facility was perfect for their demonic rituals. An apocalyptic Bohemian Grove.

Sick, sick people who made him look like a saint.

What they did to kids was unthinkable.

And unforgivable.

Sweat poured from his head, down his neck and spine, inundating his body, entirely drenched. That vanilla incense masked the odor of human sweat, but not entirely.

His mind wandered, attempts to avoid forbidden paths denied. Another blast of cool air, water, bracing for the next round.

The *clunk* of more seething stones.

Breeze gone, more incense, swooshing, singing....

Thoughts resumed, justification for his actions weak. As part of the enforcement sector he knew, but simply did as he was told. Objecting made you a target.

Don't ask questions.

Just do your job.

Do not judge.

Just the way it is.

With time, his IT skills earned a welcome transfer. Someone who could manage electronic complexities, whether hardware, coding, developing software, or designing firmware, to say nothing of hacking, was harder to find than a good sniper.

Transferring billions of dollars in shady deals was less messy than government sponsored wet jobs.

Paid better, too.

Suspending judgment, likewise morals, still required.

Shut up, do your job.

A blast of cool air, more water.

The now familiar *clunk* of seething stones.

Then another.

Three...four...five...six...seven...eight...nine...ten...eleven.

Breeze gone, more incense, swooshing, singing....

It was as if he were floating when the visions came. Endless tunnels, terrified people.

Especially the children.

Their eyes.

Pleading.

He'd never forget their eyes.

Just do your job.

He looked away.

No wonder they'd taken his.

His chest ached as if to implode, heart creeping into his throat. He'd be sweating even without the stone-sponsored heat.

Forbidden tears, denied release decades before, burst as a dam, now unstoppable.

Gasps arrested by sobs wracked with remorse.

Horrific visions he'd refused to see merciless in their assault.

A near-irresistible urge to throw himself on the radiating stones surged through him.

Would it make them stop? Give him peace?

A firm but gentle voice urged him to pray.

Hail, Mary. Full of grace....the Lord is with thee...

More memories long cloaked in darkness emerged.

A young altar boy.

The children.

Sent away.

He was one of them.

God, if you're there, I'm sorry. I'm sorry! I beg of you, please forgive me. Forgive them. Keep my eyes if they'll stop these memories and pay for what I've done.

I'm sorry. I'm sorry. I'm sorry....

Another sob detonated inside his chest. He buried his face in his hands.

Everything was quiet.

Another cool breeze struck his sweat-soaked body.

No one moved, no more stones.

Was it over?

He lifted his head.

The door was open, the glare of midday visible beyond. Blue sky, smoking remains of the fire, a distant tree.

An arrested sob morphed to a laugh.

He turned toward Sara.

She, too, was drenched, face and arms shimmering like silver. "Well?" she asked. "Did it work? Can you see?"

His laugh had a bitter edge. "A little too much, actually. Yes. I can see."

All eyes were upon him, everyone smiling. "Thank you," he said, different tears emerging, this time in gratitude they couldn't begin to understand. "Thank you."

FOR THE FIRST ROUND Sara spent more time praying for Jason's eyes than for herself. The heat was stifling, but nonetheless felt good. Therapeutic. The scents and sounds were unfamiliar, but soothing. She loved incense, the sweetgrass relaxing. The rattle's hypnotic effects nudged her thoughts to psychology classes, long ago.

Mind and body were definitely connected, something she witnessed as a physical therapist. Patients with a positive attitude healed much faster than those who did nothing but complain. Like Patrice said, when an obstacle was accepted it was mostly surmounted. She visualized any remnants of the poison being swept up and leaving her body as sweat.

She already felt great since getting her legs back. An emotional high fueled by gratitude. Never would she take mobility for granted again. Her compassion for those stuck that way for life expanded until it knew no bounds.

Maybe she should go back to work, perhaps for free, just to help people. Pay it forward, after being so blessed.

But only after she fulfilled Bryan's last request.

Would she?

Or would they get away with it?

I'll keep fighting, Bryan. Help me—help us—win.

With a start she realized it was his birthday.

Happy birthday, Bryan. Sure wish you were here.

She smiled as a loving whisper replied, *I do, too, sweetheart,* settling into her mind as gentle rain on a spring morning.

Which meant it was Charlie's birthday, too. The trip was so sudden, she completely forgot.

The next round, thoughts drifted to her mother's words: "You don't appreciate what you have until you lose it."

Her mom certainly knew about that, having lost all muscle control, including her ability to talk.

Did she know Sara would recover fully? Was that why she told her to go back? Experience a lesson in appreciation and compassion she otherwise might have missed?

Overwhelmed again with gratitude, she thanked God, her Mom, Charlie, White Wolf, Porcupine, and the Sacred Mountain with its Sweet Medicine Spirits for restoring her ability to walk.

By the third round, the growing pile of stones cast everyone in red shadow, but enough to see. Star beside her on one side was singing, her voice sweet.

Jason on her left was mostly quiet, but from what she could see in the dim light, his face was animated.

Praying? Probably not.

Connie appeared to be humming along. No doubt enjoying the new experience. She'd be praying for Jason, too, so Sara would get her money back, and no doubt for her to be entirely healed. Such a good person.

Her father looked lost, or as Bryan would say, "like he woke up on another planet after a cheap drunk." By the second round, he looked more relaxed and appeared to be praying. She smiled. He and Connie were holding hands.

Therapeutic value emanated from every element of the ceremony. Aroma therapy, sound therapy, comradery, and shared love. Precious things only now being rediscovered in the so-called modern world.

To think indigenous people were considered primitive savages when in reality their cultures, which had endured for centuries, maybe even millennia, were more stable and people-centered.

Where did they learn these things? It was odd, the many similarities between tribes. Not likely so many like traditions spontaneously evolved.

Could they?

By the fourth round, the intensity peaked. Heat and humidity near suffocating. Singing more strained, wilting participants saturated with sweat and determination. Her father had his eyes closed. Hopefully, he'd taken his blood pressure meds. Did White Wolf have remedies for cardiac arrest?

Connie looked drained, smile gone.

At first she thought Jason was convulsing. No, sobbing. Muttering. In clear distress. Whatever was going on, hopefully it would bring back his vision.

Sounds grew muffled as her mind drifted. Her mother hovered before her, appearing as a young woman as she had when Sara was comatose on life-support. Her dark hair was long and lustrous, brown eyes bright in a face radiant with joy and contentment.

Tears filled Sara's eyes. "Hi, Mom. Thank you for sending me back. You were so right. Like you always were. Thank you. Oh, Mom. I love and miss you so much."

I know, darling. I love and miss you, too. Know that I will always be with you, even if you can't see me. I'm very proud of you, Sara. You will yet do many great things. Never give up on what's right. All of us here are watching over you. Your heritage is a great one you must learn about someday.

The vision vanished when Risingsun opened the door for the final time. All eyes turned to Jason. He lowered his hands from his face.

"Well?" Sara asked. "Did it work? Can you see?"

SARA FOLLOWED BEHIND Star as White Wolf led the way out of the sweat lodge. She was no sooner outside when her dog appeared, sniffing her like crazy, no doubt stressed while she was out of view.

Everyone stretched, enjoying the mild September air. White Wolf, Charlie, and the two boys strolled for the camping shower behind the sweat lodge while Star invited everyone else inside for a proper one.

"Luckily, we have a new water heater," she said. "But warm may not be what you're looking for right now."

Good-natured murmurs of agreement responded.

Sara went first, then donned a pair of jeans and a hot pink T-shirt and sat on the front porch with Blossom while the others took their turns. The late summer prairie was dry, sparse trees hinting at the changing seasons. She sensed movement, Charlie and White Wolf heading toward the house, boys still up on the rise disassembling the sweat lodge.

The pair stopped at the foot of the steps.

"Happy birthday, Charlie," she said.

"Thank you. How do you feel?" Charlie asked. "Any different?"

She smiled. "Yes. I already felt pretty good, but it's like the emotional burden is gone, too. I feel lighter. Like a new person. And of course relief that Jason can see!"

"Yes. He was unburdened with many toxins as well," White Wolf said. "Both body and spirit. I must talk with him before you leave."

He proceeded into the house, leaving Charlie behind. He came up the steps and sat beside her, Blossom watching him from the other. His eyes met hers, the first they'd been alone since both the Sacred Mountain and her arrival the night before.

They fell into a hug, holding each other tight, her face buried in his shoulder as unexpected tears fell.

He kissed her on the head and tightened his arms around her.

"I really didn't think I'd ever walk again," she stammered through the tears. "That was the craziest experience of my entire life. I was truly afraid it was only a dream within a dream and that I'd wake up, still crippled."

"But you didn't. And here you are," he said. "I must say, I was surprised as well."

They released from the hug, except for his arm which remained snug around her shoulders. He went on to explain about having the remedy in Eaglefeathers' medicine bundle all along and everything else that transpired.

"I think the only one who wasn't surprised was Patrice," she said. "I have no idea how she knew something unexpected would occur."

Their eyes met again. He pulled her close and kissed her softly on the lips.

Just as someone opened the door.

It was Connie, wearing a crooked grin. "Are you two ready to eat?"

They laughed as they got up and followed her into the house, dog taking the lead. Everyone else was already seated around the dining room table.

Star brought in a steaming cast iron pot that included a ladle as the boys passed around bowls and silverware. "It's a fairly simple meal, salt pork and navy beans, but one of our family favorites."

"Yeah," Risingsun said with a boyish snigger. "Later we can have a farting contest. Winter Hawk can make them whistle."

"You made one in the sweat lodge!" Winter Hawk countered, then, *"É-pánestse! É-pánestse!"* taunting him in Cheyenne.

Star admonished her sons with a stern look that was lost in a wave of humor-laden reactions from her guests.

"That should make for an entertaining ride back to the Comfort Inn," Jason said. "I hope my sense of smell is less acute now that I have my eyes back."

Connie laughed so hard she was crying, Will trying to suppress a smile, everyone else snickering.

Risingsun was still chuckling as he took out the food offering, after which everyone was invited to serve themselves. They dug in, ravenous following the sweat. The men all had a second bowl that generated some teasing and a few more good-natured laughs.

"Does anyone want to share their experience?" White Wolf asked. "The first time is often quite intense."

Again, Bryan's voice came into Sara's head: "That's what *she* said."

Shut up, Bryan, she thought, trying not to smile.

"I found it relaxing," Connie volunteered. "I was ready for it to end, though. I'm not used to that much heat and humidity."

Will nodded. "Heat got oppressive near the end. Pretty soothing, otherwise." He hesitated, eyes connecting with Connie's. "I got to see Ellen. She's very happy for us."

Connie's eyes filled with tears. "I saw her, too," she said softly. "I miss my best friend."

"I saw Mom as well," Sara added, likewise tearful. "I thanked her for sending me back. During most of it I visualized what was left of those toxins leaving for good. And realized how modern therapies are replicating what sweats have done for centuries."

Everyone's eyes turned to Jason. He glanced around the table, then exhaled, hard. "I can't say it was pleasant. On the other hand, I got what I asked for. To be able to see. *Ha!* Let's just say I saw a few things through new eyes, some of which I was trying to forget. Wasn't fun. But I had it coming, I suppose."

"Let's go into the living room, where it's more comfortable," Star suggested. Everyone got up, leaving the boys to clear the table.

Beige walls sported a framed art print of *Custer's Last Stand*, known to the Cheyenne as *The Battle of Long Hair*, another of a buffalo hunt, and an enlarged modern photo of Bear Butte, a.k.a., The Sacred Mountain.

Sara walked up to it, fascinated. "Is this where you were when I was healed?" she asked Charlie.

"Yes." He pointed to the general area where his fasting site was, the others joining them as well.

Goosebumps tickled her arms, confirming it was a very special place.

She pointed to what looked like an old black and white formal photo of two traditionally dressed Native Americans. "Who are these men?" she asked.

White Wolf pointed at the one on the left. "That is Littlewolf, a great chief from years past."

"So Charlie was named for him?" she asked.

His uncle nodded. "Yes. My father gave him that name."

"What about the other one?" she asked, pointing to the one on the right.

"That is Morning Star, sometimes called Dull Knife," White Wolf said. "A great peace chief who led us back to the land where we were born."

"Are you related to them?" Connie asked.

Charlie looked thoughtful. "Yes and no. We consider ourselves brothers and sisters throughout the tribe. I'm sure we're tied together somewhere, though."

After that, they assembled on the sagging sectional sofa, scarred by years of active family living. The couch - loveseat combination configured at right angles was sufficient to accommodate everyone. Jason on Sara's right, Blossom at her feet, Will and Connie on her left on the sofa with White Wolf, Star, and Charlie on the loveseat, square table angled between them.

"I'm trying to decide what to do about my blog," Sara directed to Jason beside her. "If they can't get to me financially, what might they do next?"

He scoffed. "No telling, but I made sure their records show they *did* wipe you out. Their finances are such a purposeful mess they'll never know it's not there in their coffers. What I need to do is set up an encrypted website for people like you who are trying to get the truth out. Put it on a server in another country. I can secure it so they can't find, much less touch it."

"That sounds terrific, but might they still come after me?"

"Not if I can help it," he replied. "I've got your back, Sara."

"Really?" she asked. "Why?"

He paused, shifting his gaze a few moments before it landed back on her. "I've done some pretty bad things. It's time to use those same skills to do something good for a change."

"Exactly how do you plan to do that?" Will asked, eyes narrowed.

Jason responded in a matter-of-fact tone, as if discussing the weather or which teams would play in the World Series that season. "Easy," he said. "I know which channels to monitor. If Sara's name or code name shows up, I'll take appropriate remedial action."

"I have a code name?" she asked, giggling. "What is it?"

"Project Kassandra."

Connie dug into her bag and whipped out her tablet. "It says here, 'In Greek mythology she was a Trojan priestess dedicated to the god Apollo and fated by him to utter true prophecies that would never be believed.'"

Sara's laugh lacked humor. "Perfect. The original queen of conspiracy theories, no doubt. It fits. Except I hope people will believe me."

"That's their goal, for people not to believe you," Jason explained. "Debunk everything you say. Their problem, so far, is that it hasn't worked."

"So I should continue with my plans to expose them?"

"Absolutely. Don't give in to their harassment. Like I said, I've got your back. The FBI might show up from time to time, but rest assured I'll have them on a tight leash."

Will's scowl broadcasted disapproval, but he remained quiet.

Jason turned to White Wolf and Charlie. "Thank you for all you've done. How can I repay you? I've heard mention of some *Gathering*. What can I do to help?"

"They're having a conference of Indigenous leaders here in about six weeks," Sara explained. "I was going to pay for transportation, which is when I discovered I had no money."

"You'll have your money as soon as we get back," Jason assured her. "But I can help, too. What can I do?"

White Wolf and Charlie exchanged thoughtful looks.

"Part of the *Gathering* is here on the reservation, the other part on mine and Sara's property in Colorado," Charlie explained. "We have lots of arrangements that need to be made to accommodate hundreds, maybe even a thousand of our people in both locations."

"Porta-potties, water trucks, food trucks. Things like that," White Wolf added.

Jason took out his wallet, flipped it open, and removed a credit card, which he handed to White Wolf. "Here. Use this. As much as you need."

White Wolf scrutinized the card. "Who exactly is Biergarten LLC?"

"It's me. But if you prefer, I can write a check."

White Wolf handed it back. "Thank you, that might be best."

"No problem. I'll be sure to do that before we leave," Jason said. "So part of the event will be here?"

"Yes. On our ranch," White Wolf said. "Come, we will show you around."

WHITE WOLF SILENTLY thanked *Maheo* for the excuse to invite everyone outside for a brief tour, his intent to find an opportunity to take Jason aside. Whenever someone had a difficult experience in his sweat lodge he felt responsible to help them through it. As the original holistic healers, Medicine men looked after their patients, body, mind, and spirit.

Everyone, including the boys, followed out to the barn, where the horses were the center of attention. Winter Hawk showed off Hobo while Risingsun followed with Spring Thunder.

"They're beautiful animals," Sara said, taking time to stroke and admire each one. "My mother won dozens of silver cups at equestrian activities. She competed when she was younger and took me riding many times. I'd really enjoy the chance to go again someday."

"If you don't mind my asking," Will said, "How much land do you have, Joe?"

"I inherited 160 acres from my father, Eaglefeathers," White Wolf said. "That's about a quarter-mile square. The house is toward the north boundary, the road on the west, south is part of the way to Eaglefeathers Butte, then out into the prairie to the east. Rosebud Creek crosses it and Eaglefeathers Creek runs the entire length. Littlewolf's land adjoins mine with the land surrounding us a tribal livestock grazing unit. "

"Where will the event be held?" Jason asked.

"The southeast corner, where we'll have access to the creek and within view of the Butte."

"Will you have trouble finding services out here?"

"No. It's not the first time for such an event. A few local ranchers provide them as side businesses, at least water trucks and toilet facilities. It's not difficult to attract food vendors to such events."

"Would you like to start such a business yourself?" Jason asked.

As the conversation diverted the others looked bored. Star scoped out the situation and asked, "Who wants to see my garden?"

"I definitely do," Connie said. "We have a farmer's market nearby so don't have one of our own, but I prefer fresh produce. I'd love to have one someday, though."

As intended, everyone but White Wolf, Charlie, and Jason walked back toward the house.

"I really don't have time to run a business," White Wolf answered as the others took off.

"I'd be interested," Charlie said. "I have the same amount of land as White Wolf. I plan to build a house next year and will be looking for a source of income."

"Not going back to the oil business, I assume?" Jason asked with a wry smile.

Charlie groaned. "Never. I'd fear for my life if I upset Grandmother Earth or Badger any more than I already have."

Jason exhaled through his nose. "I can definitely understand that. When you decide what you'd like to do, let me know. I'd like to help you out."

"Thank you," Charlie said, shaking his hand. "That's very generous."

"How are you feeling?" White Wolf asked, shifting the conversation to his original intent. "I sensed the sweat was difficult for you."

The man hesitated, emotions locked. He didn't want to talk about it, but was clearly unaware White Wolf could discern his thoughts.

"Shedding past burdens opens up old wounds," White Wolf explained. "Open wounds can be dangerous. They are subject to infection, on a spiritual level."

Jason's eyes held his, pain lurking within like snakes in a woodpile.

"When you remember past trauma, especially any that you buried, you are forced to relive it before you can work through it. That can be very painful," White Wolf continued. "Anything suppressed builds up pressure and eventually resurfaces. You cannot escape confronting what occurred. It can be overwhelming. If you like, I can give you something to help you sleep and for depression, which is very common."

"*Maheo* has forgiven you. Now you must forgive yourself," Charlie added.

"Thank you, I appreciate it," Jason said, avoiding their eyes. "But I don't know if I can."

Money and corruption are ruining the land, crooked politicians betray the working man, pocketing the profits and treating us like sheep, and we're tired of hearing promises that we know they'll never keep.
—Ray Davies

37. VISITORS

IRON SHIRT RESIDENCE
GAITHERSBURG, MARYLAND
September 9, Sunday
11:48 p.m. EDT

Naomi Iron Shirt awoke with a start, breathing hard. She sat up in bed, eyes wide in the darkened room. Her hand reached over to switch on the bedside lamp. Trembling hands hugged the star quilt to her chest that her sisters gave her when she left Montana years before.

What a crazy dream! Was it that spicy Thai food she had for dinner with her executive staff?

Maybe.

It had been awhile, but she'd had such dreams before.

Indeed, a dozen years past a dream forewarned her of being appointed Secretary of the Interior. At the time, she was only in the consideration phase of running for the House of Representatives.

The dream was very clear that she should. Naomi obeyed, and against all odds, was elected.

She did a outstanding job representing her people, speaking up against medical abuse in the past such as forced sterilization and experimentation. That included untested vaccines and implanting indigenous people with chips, supposedly to maintain their medical records. However, they were also capable of draining

360

their bank accounts, even when medical services were not provided.

She spoke up against human trafficking, especially as it involved Missing and Murdered Indigenous Women and Girls (MMIWG). Demanded the FBI stop referring to them as "high risk victims," which implied they didn't matter, making such cases low priority. Using their vast resources to arrest those at the top, not just the patsies at the bottom of the evil operations, was another demand.

They seldom listened, but she did her best.

In addition, over the years she studied every tribal treaty ever written, the U.S. Constitution, and even attained a Master's Degree in Public Administration at George Washington University.

Determination drove every action that when the time came for that dream to be fulfilled, she'd be ready. It occurred a few years later with a change of Administration, when she was indeed appointed Secretary of the Interior, the position she currently held.

Elouise Cobell was her heroine for fighting a class action suit for fifteen years to recoup billions of dollars owed to Native Americans in mineral royalties, grazing fees, and other revenues that were mishandled or lost over the course of more than 100 years. Assuming Native Americans were incapable of handling their own money, the government then proceeded to pilfer away billions of dollars of the funds themselves.

The guilty party was none other than the very Department she now ran, coupled with the equally corrupt Bureau of Indian Affairs.

Still on her agenda was coordinating with the Rep who took her place in the House to fight for reparations for survivors of the boarding schools Indigenous children were forced to attend. Not only were they brutally punished for speaking their native language, their hair cut, and culture demonized, but family ties severed.

Having been raised as orphans and traumatized by forced separation from their parents and culture, their own parenting skills were compromised, affecting their ability to raise successful families. They deserved help as well.

This time, as before, the nocturnal advisor was none other than Grandfather Iron Shirt, a revered warrior and powerful medicine man, which went back six generations. The story was told that his war shirt, painted with red earth paint, had medicine powers that turned it to iron during battle, causing bullets to fall to the ground. He fought beside Chief Little Wolf in numerous important conflicts with the white man.

What he told her was so incredulous she nearly laughed, except it would have been horribly disrespectful. His message was clear and repeated four times, allowing her to memorize the words.

In forty-four days prophesied events will bring great change. Honor will be yours and give you unimaginable power. Your duty is to restore to Indigenous people that which was lost. Do not hesitate. Do not fear. It is Maheo's *will for our people.*

Wishing she'd done so last time, she got up and wrote it down, noting the message contained forty-four words, a sacred number in her culture. Next, she checked the calendar.

At least this time she knew when it would occur.

What would happen on October 23?

SARA'S CONDO
DENVER, CO
September 18, Tuesday
5:18 p.m.

AS PROMISED, WITHIN a few days Jason set up a secure website that was perfect for blogs, podcasts, and videos. He even made Sara the administrator so she'd have total control of its content. She wasted no time closing down her other one, then uploading what she had to his. She included a detailed biography and background, mentioning her TV appearances. It felt good to have that milestone complete so she could set it aside a while to help Charlie and White Wolf with the *Gathering*.

The big event was now a mere five weeks away.

They were expected to arrive in a few hours, spend the night, then all drive out to Falcon Ridge in the morning. Sara offered to handle any services needed, such as the porta-potties, so they could concentrate on site logistics.

They probably wouldn't feel like going out for something to eat, so Sara was making a pot of stew. Depending on how hungry they were, maybe they'd have leftovers for tomorrow.

As she cut up, floured, and browned a four-pound chuck roast with a chopped up onion, her thoughts slipped back to that very nice kiss on White Wolf's front porch. Her feelings for Charlie had bloomed since the healing episode. While he'd been a friend for a long time, now it had a new dimension. Considering that kiss, it appeared he felt the same way.

In a way, it felt as if she were cheating on Bryan. Yet deep inside she knew he'd approve. Kind of like her mom and Connie, being best friends since college.

She looked down at her canine companion, forever nearby. "Charlie will be here soon, girl." Her tail wagged, a canine smile lifting the corners of her mouth.

By now, the potatoes and carrots were peeled, so she added them along with two cans of stewed tomatoes. She turned up the heat until it boiled, then back down to simmer.

While she waited, she took a shower, then changed into a fresh pair of slacks with a white ruffled blouse with a sexy neckline.

She simply couldn't stop thinking about Charlie. Why not let him know, albeit subtly, the feeling was mutual?

A knock came from the door, breaking her reverie.

Cool. They were early.

Blossom growled. "It's okay, it should be Charlie," she said, then fluffed her cropped hair, straightened her blouse, and raced downstairs wearing a grin.

She threw open the door.

The grin flopped.

It wasn't them.

Instead, two ominous looking men in dark suits.

Definitely not Mormon missionaries.

The dog positioned herself between them and snarled, ears back and teeth exposed.

The taller one eyed the dog, then her. "Mrs. Reynolds?"

"Yes. Can I help you?"

"Guy Allison, FBI."

Her back tensed as the man flashed his badge.

Jason's warning came to mind. Did he really 'have her back' or not? At least her money was secured in that anonymous offshore account.

She guessed the 'Guy guy' was probably late forties, though his high forehead made him look older. Thinning brown hair hovered above cold grey eyes, height slightly taller than her five foot seven, a little pudgy around the middle. His partner was younger, perhaps right out of college, mid-twentyish, blond with a crew cut.

"Can we come in?" he asked, eyeing the dog.

For an instant she debated letting her pit bull follow her instincts, but thought better of it and invited them in.

Allison didn't waste any time with pleasantries. "I was surprised to learn you survived your recent illness," he said. "We have a few questions regarding this event you're planning with that group of Indians."

She froze.

How did they find out and why did they care? What was going on? Was the Dance still illegal?

"Do you mind if we sit down?" he prompted.

Adrenaline fired, heart and mind racing. Blossom gave her a questioning look. "Do I have a choice?" Sara asked through tight lips.

The man's icy eyes drilled into hers. "Yes. But if you refuse, we'll have to take you in. If you cooperate, maybe we can get this resolved right here."

Her lips formed a tight line, anger rising. *Good luck with that,* she thought, remembering why she was retraining her dog to K-9 status.

"Fine."

She strode into the living room and pointed to the couch, where the pair sat down. Arms folded, she sat in the chair across from them, still wondering at their source. Tapping her phone, perhaps?

"What do you want?" She reached over and placed her hand on her dog's head, trying not to smile when the men squirmed.

"We have information that the Cheyenne Indians up in Montana are planning a big pow-pow next month. Your property, here in Colorado, is listed as part of the venue. I assume you're aware of that?"

"Of course I am. I gave them permission. What's the problem?"

"Are you aware that some Native American activities are against the law?"

"Against the law?" Her nose wrinkled with unbelief. "I don't know what you're talking about."

"Let me clarify. Some of their weird rituals associated with their religion are illegal, when performed off the reservation. We don't give a damn what they do on their own land. They can eat their young, for all we care. But when they come onto ours, it's another story."

Her eyes narrowed. "Which *weird* rituals are you talking about? Furthermore, it's *my* property, not yours."

"They have something called the Sun Dance. And people have been known to die during their sweats. If they plan to do either, the only way they can do so legally is to have it cleared through the Bureau of Indian Affairs working with the local board of health and the FDA, if they plan to use peyote."

She set her jaw, resisting the temptation to roll her eyes. "As far as I know, they're not doing any of those things. My understanding is that it's a commemorative ceremony for something that occurred over a hundred years ago."

Another knock came from the door, light and friendly. Blossom looked that way, tail wagging.

Would these obnoxious Feds haul them off? Did Jason's protection extend to them, too? If not, it was apparent her dog's did.

Allison's mocking look was smug. "Feel free to get the door, Mrs. Reynolds. If you don't know the answers, I'm sure they will."

She cast them a scathing look as she got up, wondering how they knew. Damn snoops. When she opened the door, Charlie started to give her a hug, then stopped abruptly when he noticed two men in the living room.

She exhaled hard. "We have company."

Charlie stooped down to pet Blossom as he threw some seriously hard looks in their direction. "Who are they?" he asked in a low voice.

"FBI."

Suspicions clouded his dark eyes as he followed her into the room. He and White Wolf managed to be cool nonetheless, shaking hands as everyone introduced themselves.

"So you're the ones in charge of this pow-wow next month?" Allison asked.

"Yes, we are," White Wolf responded, assessing Allison with a gaze that reflected his warrior heritage. "But it's not a pow-wow. It's officially called the *Peace Gathering of Indigenous Leaders*. Is there a problem?"

"Possibly. What exactly do you plan to do on Mrs. Reynolds' property in Belton County?"

White Wolf's eyes darkened as he continued to size-up the agent. "We will be commemorating an historical event that occurred in that area in the late 1800s. It's sacred ground to us. We'll dance, pray, and express our respect to our ancestors who died there. If anything, it could be compared to a peace rally."

"Indeed. Will you be conducting sweats?"

"No."

"What about the Sun Dance? That one where you mutilate yourselves. Whatever you people call it."

"Sun Dances are done in the summer and confined to the reservation. It is a sacred ritual to us, but we know it can be upsetting to you white people."

"Do you have any problem if we attend this event? The one here in Colorado?"

White Wolf narrowed his eyes. "Do you not trust us, Mr. Allison?"

"Never have, never will." The agent laughed, as if he just made a great joke. "Actually, I'm just curious. I'd like to witness one of your ceremonies. I have a son-in-law who's part Crow. He told me about some of them. I find them fascinating, from an anthropological point of view."

"This particular gathering is not open to the public, but you may join us, if you wish. There will be a lot of noise you may find unpleasant. Dress casual. You need to blend in, for your own safety, as well as show proper respect as our guest. Some of our people will not be pleased by your presence."

Me, too, Sara thought, then smiled to herself, thinking how outnumbered he'd be.

"Right," Allison acknowledged. "I hope by casual you don't mean a loin cloth."

White Wolf's mien darkened another notch, warrior heritage of full display. Charlie, likewise, looked downright pissed.

"It may be a bit chilly for that, but it's up to you," White Wolf replied. "Jeans would be fine. Is there anything else you'd like to know?"

"No, I think that should do it. Thank you for clarifying your plans." The two men got up, shook hands with everyone but her, and plodded toward the door. Sara swung it open, unable to return their fake smiles with anything but a scornful look.

Allison paused, matching her expression with one of his own. "By the way, Mrs. Reynolds. Just so you know. Your podcasts and blogs are being watched. The line between freedom of speech and sedition is rather blurry and open to interpretation. You might want to keep that in mind."

His mouth twitched as his steel grey eyes blatantly sized her up, then did the same to Charlie before giving him a lascivious wink. "Enjoy your, uh, *pow-wow*, you two."

Blossom growled, then barked a canine *Good riddance!* as she shoved the door closed behind them with an extra push.

"Can you believe that?" she grumbled, hands on her hips. "I wish Jason could keep them away entirely, not just supposedly *under control*."

Charlie put his arms around her and delivered the postponed hug. "They're gone. Everything's okay. Whatever you're cooking smells delicious."

"Hopefully it didn't burn while those idiots were here. C'mon, let's eat."

Sara's appetite departed with the agents, but her guests ate as if they were starving. When finished, they returned to the living room, where she asked more questions about the *Gathering*.

How many people did they expect? How would they be dressed? What were the other details of the dance? Would there be a fire? A big one? From what she'd seen of their ceremonies, she assumed singing and dancing would be included.

After discussing each of them, their conversation waned. Charlie went out to get their bags while Sara showed White Wolf to the guest room. The elder thanked her, went inside, and closed the door. When she turned back around, she shrieked upon bumping into Charlie, heart taking off in at least two directions.

Her eyes met his with an attempted glare. "Sneaky damn Indian," she hissed, trying not to laugh. "I hate it when you do that."

Her attempt at sternness fell flat when he wrapped his arms around her, pulled her close and silenced her with a kiss, far more sensuous than the last one.

From the doorway behind them White Wolf cleared his throat. "Where's the bathroom?"

It's a fool who looks for logic in the chambers of the human heart.
—Everett McGill (from the movie "O, Brother Where Art Thou?")

38. RIDES

SARA'S CONDO
DENVER, CO
September 19, Wednesday
7:48 a.m.

The next morning, Sara and her two guests lounged around the kitchen table feasting on the breakfast she prepared. Homemade waffles, bacon, sausage, scrambled eggs, and biscuits reposed in their respective containers, mouth-watering vapors infusing the air.

While her first objective was to please her man, she was likewise ravenous and consuming her meal with as must gusto as they were. The aroma of comfort foods, seasoned with heavy overtones of pheromones, inundated the entire condo, the only sound that of eating utensils connecting with plates, then finding salivating palates.

Sara took a long, sensuous sip of coffee, sultry eyes locked with Charlie's on the other side of the table as he mirrored her suggestive pose. Her toes flexed against his as they rubbed each other's bare feet beneath the table. The previous night had included multiple amorous encounters, the last of which had occurred slightly over an hour before—an acrobatic feat in the shower.

Her dreamy interlude shattered when White Wolf cleared his throat and clanked his fork beside his plate with a firm, deliberate motion. She broke her lusty gaze and turned her attention toward him, having nearly forgotten he was there.

Both hers and Charlie's faces shifted from seductive to "busted" as they straightened in their chairs, feet flat on the floor, like two itinerant teenagers.

The medicine man looked from one to the other, glare of silent reproach coming to rest on Charlie like the flaming arrow he'd alluded to the night before.

"No more sex," he stated. "You are not married. That is not the Cheyenne way of life."

It was not a suggestion, but a commandment. Sara bit her lip, face as red as the indigenous men at her table. Charlie's lips pressed together in a line turned down at the corners. Blossom froze in her bed across the room, assessing the situation.

The Cheyenne elder glared. "Look at you! You are both lazy and weak. If you could do anything you wanted today, what would it be?"

He paused for effect, but went on to answer his own question. "You would go back to bed and indulge your appetite for each other with no regard to the world around you or your duty to it."

White Wolf exhaled, hard, through his nose, reminding Sara of a snorting bull. Blossom emitted a short, throaty growl. She dropped her hand beside her thigh and gave the stand-down signal, silencing her.

"If this continues, Littlewolf, you will be unable to fulfill your destiny. Our people and many of our Native brothers and sisters are depending on us. Stop being a foolish man. We need to project strength and wisdom. I just took you through a ceremonial fast at the Sacred Mountain. Did you learn nothing from that?"

Charlie likewise exhaled hard, but his eyes reflected the heat of shame. "I apologize. You are right, of course. We will control ourselves and abstain."

Sara didn't mean to pout, but nonetheless disappointment assumed control. Guilt mingled with increased embarrassment as White Wolf's stern words sunk into her endorphin-saturated brain.

Unable to meet anyone's eyes, she got up, collected their plates, and slinked over to the sink to rinse them off, then load them in the dishwasher, noise reverberating like mini-explosions in the heavy silence.

The two men finished off what was left of the bacon and sausage, then helped clear the table.

Her mind shifted, albeit reluctantly, to what needed to be done before driving out to Falcon Ridge. Fortunately, not much, and it wouldn't take long.

She retrieved an ice chest from the pantry and proceeded to fill it with food for the next day or so. All the stew was gone, but there was hamburger in the freezer, which Blossom helped retrieve, earning a few raised eyebrows from her guests. There were a few things at the cabin, but she wasn't sure what or if it would be enough, considering how these men could put away food.

Maybe they stored it in some DNA-specific organ repository to get through those long fasts.

Considering White Wolf's lecture, the sleeping logistics were clear. Most likely, the men would stay at Charlie's, just to be safe. A moan escaped unbidden as she closed the ice chest's lid, clearly an analogy to her immediate future as far as anything amorous was concerned.

Charlie closed in to pick it up, brushing against her as he muttered, "Sorry," then carried it out to her car, which they would take, with no point in taking both.

Her hopes cratered. *What if White Wolf didn't even want them in the same vehicle?*

Gratefully, so far that had not been said.

She didn't like it, but he was right. If what was to come was as historically significant as implied, they couldn't chance failure. It was barely over a month away and they needed to concentrate on what needed to be done.

When her Buick was loaded, dog in back, she got in the driver's seat. Charlie opened the passenger door and glanced at White Wolf, who glowered, but nodded.

"Behave," he growled, then climbed in back with the dog, who shuffled away from him to the far side of the seat.

Much to her relief, once they got on I-70, the two men started talking logistics with Charlie describing their properties and where the best locations would be for camping, sanitation facilities, campfires, and of course, the dance.

Their conversation slipped into Cheyenne from time to time, but she understood enough from their intonations to discern their commitment and enthusiasm. It was contagious, her own excitement likewise increasing as the mood shifted.

As they talked, she considered the reality of covering hundreds of acres on foot. She and Bryan rented snowmobiles from time to time, but never bothered to get an ATV, since they preferred hiking. However, for the sake of the *Gathering*, maybe they should.

She waited for a pause in their conversation before breaking in. "How do you plan to get around the site to check on things?"

Charlie looked at White Wolf in back, who said nothing, then back at her. "Our feet, I guess."

"That's a lot of walking. How would you feel about getting an ATV? I'll buy it and just keep it. Or you could even take it back to the rez, if you want."

"Sounds like a great idea," Charlie responded. "There's a lot of ground to cover, in both places."

White Wolf grunted, but otherwise said nothing.

"Okay. That settles it," Sara said.

She exited I-70 and pulled into a Walmart parking lot to check her phone for local dealers. They were almost to Lakewood, which had a motor sports place that handled several makes and included a pre-owned inventory.

They arrived in short order and found a great deal on a Polaris model. The salesman asked where she intended to use it and whether that was her permanent residence. When she explained, he recommended outfitting it with a GPS tracker, not only for if it were stolen, but in case she ever ran out of gas or got lost. She promptly agreed, though they had to wait another twenty minutes while they got it installed.

When it was ready and the salesman asked where to load it up, it was apparent that getting it out to her place presented a challenge. While they debated buying a trailer, the dealer offered to deliver for a small charge, if they could wait until Friday. After agreeing, then taking care of the financial arrangements, again they were on their way.

Neither man seemed to mind staying a few days for the added benefit, though White Wolf made a phone call to make sure his backup medicine man could cover the additional days.

She chuckled to herself. Charlie had looked at the compact machine with as much longing as he had her earlier that day. Now he'd have something fun to ride besides her.

As expected, a couple hours later when they got to the road leading to her cabin, they asked to be dropped off at his place. After leaving them with the ice chest (and therefore, most of the food), she drove to her cabin, feeling somehow abandoned.

The landscape was morphing into winter, fall colors fading with the ground dusted with snow, a bit early but not so much at that elevation.

The first thing she did when she got inside was bring up the phone app to sweep for bugs. Sure enough, there were more, all in places she knew beyond a doubt she'd previously cleaned.

If only Jason could stop them entirely. However, when they'd driven back from Montana he'd explained calling them off completely would raise suspicions up the FBI foodchain. That might cause them to look closely enough to find his intervention. Her file was flagged from a "high authority" not to arrest or take her into custody, which was as far as he could go without inviting scrutiny, which wouldn't go well for either of them.

She growled with frustration when she found another listening device behind the picture over the couch. She removed it, making a total of six, then took them outside, and smashed them with a rock. As she kicked the remains into the dirt she wished she'd thought to give them an angry good riddance.

After that, she texted Charlie to let him know, punctuating it with angry emoji's. Once again, her privacy had been blatantly violated. Being declared a domestic terrorist because of her podcasts was outrageous. Everything she said was substantiated by facts, all found buried on government sites, which was undoubtedly the problem.

Project Kassandra, indeed.

Furthermore, the agents implied they thought she was dead—like Bentley. Too bad they didn't still think that. Jason offered that as an option along with a new identity, but she already had a following she didn't want to lose. Furthermore, the complexities of such an extreme action were too much if she wanted to maintain contact with friends and family.

Initially warmed by fury, as she got settled she noticed it was uncomfortably chilly, even with a heavy wool sweater. She tromped outside to retrieve some wood from under the deck. The equinox was a few days away, which meant solar power would be less reliable as the days shortened, especially if it were cloudy or the panels covered with snow.

The A-frame's roof was steep enough, it usually slid off, leaving snow banks that sometimes landed on the wrap-around deck. Unsure, she hesitated to use the heater so she'd have power stored in the batteries for lights and other incidentals, at least.

For dinner she ate crackers and cheese, then spent most the evening staring into the dying flames with her canine companion, feeling more alone than she'd been in a long time.

SARA'S CABIN
RURAL FALCON RIDGE
September 21, Friday
2:14 p.m.

IT HAD BEEN CLOUDY since their arrival two days before, releasing several inches of snow her second night there. That not only contributed to a contemplative mood, but confirmed her decision the solar panels might not generate enough power for the heater. Losing electricity entirely was unacceptable. She and Bryan discussed putting in a generator, which, obviously, hadn't happened. Another thing for her to-do list.

She hadn't been ambitious enough to haul in more wood, the logs too big for Blossom. Thus, she admonished herself that, as an avid skier, a little cold wasn't a big deal. As such, she bundled up with thermal underwear, insulated ski pants, and a wool sweater.

After shivering all night Thursday, for multiple reasons, Friday morning she hauled in some firewood, something Bryan had always done. Covering such tasks together had been seamless, handling them herself like when he was TDY in the Air Force, delivering an unwanted touch of melancholy.

With nothing else to do, Sara again occupied herself going through the bench seat. This time, the activity served as a distraction to keep her mind off Charlie. Resuming her perusal of its contents, this time she checked out that ancient wooden box, finding a journal that belonged to Bryan's great-great-great-grandfather.

At least that was who it was, according to the pedigree chart in the same box. With it chilly in the guest room, she took it to the breakfast bar, closer to the fire.

The handwriting was difficult to decipher, compounded by faded ink on aging paper. It was worth the effort, however, as it gave her a glimpse of the man's life and the tenuous relationship the miners had with Native Americans.

She paused, realizing this was one of the sources of Bryan's history report. The journal down-played it substantially, loaded with self-righteous indignation that it served them right for cutting off their food supply.

She shuddered, knowing the details of what transpired from Charlie. Engrossed in the narrative, she wasn't expecting a knock on the door.

Her heart froze.

Was it those cursed FBI agents again?

She glanced at Blossom, encouraged when she was alert, but silent, as she got up and followed Sara to the window. To her relief, a flat-bed truck was parked in her snow-laden driveway, the Polaris chained in back.

She opened the door, coming face to face with a blast of cold air as well as a man around her age, wearing an orange, down-filled vest. Dark blond hair surrounded his face in an unruly mullet, squashed further by a Broncos baseball cap.

"Hi. Ms. Reynolds?" He glanced down at the dog, whose tail lilted gently back and forth in welcome. "Nice dog. Pitties are awesome."

"Thanks. Yes, they are, and yes, that's me. I see you brought my ATV. Thanks so much! You can park it next to my car."

He mock saluted and slogged through the snow back to the truck. She stepped out on the deck to watch while he lowered the rear ramp, released the restraints, then backed it down and parked as directed. That accomplished, he came back up the steps, two at a time, and held out the key. "Here you go. You should have some serious fun with this baby out here!"

She accepted the key and smiled. "Yes, I'm sure I will. Thanks so much for bringing it out. Much appreciated."

"Gorgeous country! If you ever decide to get a Snowcat or snowmobile, be sure to keep us in mind. Thanks so much, Ms. Reynolds. Be safe!"

She followed him down the steps to checkout her latest purchase, pondering his comment about a Snowcat. Hopefully, that wouldn't be what they'd need when the big day arrived.

As she looked it over, a smile softened her features for the first time since her arrival. It did look like fun. Too bad Bryan wasn't there. Should she text Charlie? Or drive over to surprise him?

After a few seconds deliberation, she went inside to add a down jacket, hat, and gloves to her ensemble. As she locked up the cabin, she noticed Blossom's questioning stare.

Bryan's objections to having a dog blasted through memory.

"I'm sorry, girl, but you're going to have to stay behind. It's too cold out there for you without a proper doggie parka. Don't worry, I'll get you one soon."

She descended the steps, feeling so guilty she back went inside, then upstairs where she dug one of Bryan's wool ski sweaters out of the dresser, dog right behind her, watching.

Blossom balked a moment as she pulled it over her head, then seemed to catch on as she guided her front legs into the arms.

"There. That should work for now," she told her with a pat on the head, then both went outside and climbed onboard.

It started right up, a deep throaty rumble that vibrated the chassis. Her dog sat tall in the passenger seat, panting with excitement for the new adventure.

It had a half-tank of gas, which should be plenty to get there and back. She made a mental note to go into town to fill a five-gallon gas can, maybe two, so she'd have a spare, just in case.

Sara turned it around and slowly descended the hill, impressed by its grip on snow-covered ground. It wasn't deep enough to be a problem, though she suspected the tires' deep-tread could handle quite a bit, especially with four-wheel drive.

It negotiated the hill with ease, so she opened it up a little.

"Hang on, girl!" she said, then accelerated until they zoomed through the snow, the sensation of flying euphoric. The engine's sporty rumble broke the snow-laden landscape's usual silence, adding to the sense of excitement.

Her smile spread so far it hurt, Blossom's usual more-serious nature yielding to Sara's excitement with a few random barks.

This was *definitely* fun. Almost as great for stress relief as the gun range. When she arrived at Charlie's minutes later, it wasn't a surprise to see them waiting out front.

She turned it off and stepped out, grinning.

"That was really fun! Ready to get to work?"

White Wolf watched while Charlie paced around it, grinning ear to ear. "Can I drive?"

She nodded, expecting as much. "I suppose. We need to go back to my place, though. I'm not sure where my property's boundaries are, so I want to write down the coordinates and get my phone to check them. I don't imagine it would go over too well if your *Gathering* strayed onto any neighboring property. Especially since I have no idea who it belongs to."

Charlie nodded agreement. "I think I know where they are, but it won't hurt to check. We'll get our coats."

Moments later, Charlie climbed into the driver's seat, White Wolf on the passenger side, Sara squeezed between them with Blossom on the floor, muzzle resting on her mistress' thigh.

Charlie's driving was cautious at first, then he gradually gave it more gas until they were moving at what seemed a lot faster than it was.

When they got to her cabin they all went inside while she retrieved the survey map. It showed the various elevations, allowing them to estimate the terrain. Charlie's knowledge of the property indicated he and Bryan had roamed all five hundred acres and quite a bit beyond in their youth.

While she wrote down the coordinates of key survey points, the two men conversed in Cheyenne while pointing out certain areas. The intensity conveyed as they conversed in their native tongue brought goosebumps, intuition raging that something extraordinary was going to happen, right there, on her land.

"Do you want to bring the map along?" she asked.

"No. We've got it all up here," Charlie said, tapping his forehead. "We already have it mostly figured out. It's as if your place were designed specifically for what we have planned."

The two men stepped outside and strolled toward the Polaris while she and Blossom stopped while she locked the door with a trembling hand. For some reason, his casual statement triggered more goosebumps accented by an apocalyptic flash of déjà-vu.

It was apparent Charlie was familiar with the property and knew exactly where he was going as they bumped across acres of snow-covered ground. Their progress slowed as the path ascended through forested areas, dodging pines, boulders and nearly-bare aspens, a few yellow heart-shaped leaves still hanging on.

At a certain point, Blossom nixed the floor and climbed into Sara's lap. She wrapped her arms around her, noting the sweater still bore a hint of Bryan's aftershave, its scent now mingled with that of her dog. She smiled to herself, picturing him scandalized by the combination.

When they broke out of the woods, the pine-scented air faded as nothing but snow-dusted brush lay between them and Eagles Peak's craggy summit, stabbing the sky. Charlie veered left for a few hundred feet, then switched off the ignition. Unearthly quiet settled around them, disturbed only by a breath of wind.

Atop a majestic bluff, they trudged through virgin snow halfway to their knees to within a few feet from the drop-off. Sixty or so feet below sprawled a natural amphitheater, a few hundred yards or more across. The view reminded her of what royalty might enjoy from an elevated viewing box in a coliseum.

"Just what I thought," Charlie stated. "That will be perfect. It's not far from an old mining road, where the buses can drop everyone off."

He held out his arm and pointed where the sanitary facilities would be toward the right, the camp circle and food wagons around the perimeter, with central area left for the dance. His description was so detailed it was if he could already see it.

They reverted to Cheyenne again, their conversation ranging from soft reverent tones to rampant enthusiasm.

Sara's stomach tightened.

Was it something she wasn't supposed to hear? Or simply their normal means of communication?

Which was probably the case, but after fidgeting a moment studying her gloved hands, she turned and took a few steps back toward the ATV to stare at Eagles Peak, wishing herself invisible.

She never thought of Charlie as that different from herself until now. She stole a look from the corner of her eye as the indigenous pair continued their animated conversation. He never looked more feral and integral to the rugged setting. Perhaps his ancestors stood on that very spot, looking down on a bison herd.

Her reverie ended when White Wolf exclaimed, "*Átahe!*" and pointed to the far end of the basin.

She walked back toward the ledge, curious. An elk herd, probably a hundred or more strong, ambled out of the surrounding woods into the open area.

Both men laughed, then mimicked shooting bows in their direction. Before long, the entire herd wandered into the arena. Heads crowned with magnificent antlers ducked and tossed as the majestic animals pranced and frolicked in what appeared to be a joyful dance, as if celebrating the conclusion of rut season, which had peaked a few weeks earlier.

Charlie and White Wolf conversed softly in their native tongue, voices hushed and reverent. Sara had no idea what they were saying, but the moment's magic brought tears to her eyes. She brushed the moisture away, intuition declaring they belonged there, but she didn't.

Never had she felt more confident about giving this land back to its rightful owners.

Upon returning to her cabin, Sara was beyond curious what the elk represented. "Seeing that elk herd was pretty impressive," she said. "Did they have some special meaning?"

Charlie deferred to White Wolf.

"Elk represent many qualities," he explained. "Besides grace, strength, and sticking together as brothers, they teach us to secure our boundaries, protect family, be noble, just, and wise. Their presence reminded us who we are and confirmed *Maheo* approves of the location."

"As well as our intent," Charlie added.

Electrified with awe, her mind swung between elation for her involvement and a renewed sense of intrusion.

"Wow," she whispered, otherwise speechless. Not knowing what else she could say, she cleared her throat and switched to more practical matters.

"Would you like to stay for dinner? Nothing fancy, but I'm sure I can whip up some spaghetti or something."

Charlie looked at White Wolf, who nodded.

"Yes, we would like that," Charlie said. "But I'd like to do something else first, before it gets dark. I'll need the Polaris. Is that okay?"

"Of course. When do you think you'll be back?"

"No more than a couple hours. Maybe less."

"Okay." She smiled, wondering if he just wanted to take out the machine and be a bit reckless with her not onboard. "Be safe."

His mystified look told her that wasn't his intent. "Don't worry. I just need to check out one more thing."

"No problem. See you when you get back."

In that day, there will be those among the Lakota who will carry knowledge and understanding of unity among all living things and the young white ones will come to those of my people and ask for this wisdom.
—*Crazy Horse*

39. LSO

RURAL FALCON RIDGE
September 21, Friday
3:34 p.m.

"Where are we going?"

Charlie was surprised White Wolf hadn't read his mind as they descended the steps.

"I want to check out where I used to work. See what changes occurred since I left."

The man's scrutiny was unexpected. "Do you think that is wise?" he asked.

"Why not?"

White Wolf held his eyes a long moment. "You are right. Why not?"

They got in the ATV and took off toward the back of Sara's cabin, followed the hiking path where they'd scattered Bryan's ashes, then Charlie directed their route across a few miles of rough terrain southwest of Eagles Peak. His plan was to make a straight shot, over to the LSO worksite.

Before it came into view, however, a ten-foot chain-link fence topped with razor wire blocked the path.

He stopped, surprised by the expected the barrier. With no other choice, he turned south and followed the fence until he saw a *No Trespassing* notice for what was designated private property. When he reached the road, just north of Dead Horse Canyon, he turned right, staying on the shoulder until there was a wide enough space beside the fence to get off the road entirely.

When they reached the turnoff that led to the LSO worksite, his mind raced. No longer an obscure dirt road, it was not only paved, but widened to two lanes.

"What's wrong?" White Wolf asked.

His neck muscles tensed. "This was not here before. My vision sometime back revealed that, but seeing it is still, well, disturbing."

He followed the road, another surprise awaiting when a guard shack equipped with a yellow-striped road barrier and tire ripper came into view. He pulled up beside it, the person manning it unfamiliar, other than the red and white LSO logo on his hard hat.

The man slid open the window, scrutinizing them with suspicion. "This is private property," he stated coldly. "There's no outlet and absolutely no recreational activity allowed."

Charlie nodded. "I understand. That isn't why I'm here. My name is Charlie Littlewolf. I used to work for LSO, when the site was first developed. I wanted to say hello to my former boss, Trey Maguire. Is he around?"

"Just a moment."

The guard closed the window and got on the radio. Moments later, the bar lifted, tire ripper dropped, and a second guard waved them through.

He followed the road, eventually recognizing the space where they'd parked to pick up his truck when he left the hospital. It was also paved and occupied by several dozen vehicles. He bore to the right, climbing the incline toward the site.

When it leveled out, he stopped.

Chills assaulted his arms and neck, then down his spine. What he'd seen in vision months before lay spread before him, down to every last unsettling detail.

What had been pristine wilderness, surrounded by forests on one side and Eagles Peak on the other, had exploded into an industrial nightmare—an asphalt island within an ocean of virgin snow.

The wellhead at the site he remembered was now topped with a conglomeration of pipes and crank valves known as a Christmas tree. A similar device was located twenty or so yards farther north, the rumble beneath his feet indicating extraction was in progress. Each was flanked by more chain-link fencing and warning signs. Red pipe connected to the Christmas trees slashed the site like arteries.

An exploration rig to his right was flanked by mud and water trucks as well as a huge stack of pipe, roughnecks in hardhats and orange jumpsuits busy drilling, ear pummeled by a familiar roar.

The distinctive odor of drilling mud triggered a memory flash. He flinched involuntarily, heartbeat responding to the adrenaline prompt. He shook his head as he would to dismiss a mosquito, then turned to peruse the rest of the site.

Trailers were gone, replaced by metal buildings. Instead of the wildcat operation he remembered, now it was an established and permanent production site with wells connected to a commercial pipeline.

A deep scowl etched White Wolf's forehead like stratifications on a canyon wall. "This is where you worked?" he asked, intonations loaded with raging disapproval.

His posture slumped. "Yes."

His uncle's eyes darkened. "And *Maheo* approved?"

"That was my impression."

"*Harrumph.* We must assume *Maheo* has a plan."

"Yes," Charlie agreed. "My guilt softened when I prayed."

Someone exited one of the buildings up ahead and hollered his name.

Bracing himself for how this might go, Charlie put the Polaris in gear and proceeded in that direction.

An eerie, surreal quality made the hair on the back of his neck stand up as Maguire walked toward them with a Texas-sized grin, arms flung wide. The man was so happy to see him he flinched at the impression it was probably giving White Wolf.

More than ever, he hoped he could read his heart and mind.

He stepped out of the ATV, bracing for a classic bear hug from the big redneck. As expected, the man grabbed him to his chest and pounded his back.

"Holy shit, Littlewolf! Is it ever good to see y'all! I was just thinkin' of you the other day, hopin' you'd come back to visit. Y'all must've read my mind, 'cause here y'all are! All y'all, actually," he added, nodding a friendly greeting to White Wolf.

Charlie forced a smile. "Good to see you, too, Trey. This is my uncle, Joe White Wolf."

Trey offered his hand and White Wolf accepted it, though his look was far less friendly than the Texan's.

"So are y'all ready to come back to work?"

Charlie's laugh sounded more like cough. "No, I'm afraid not. I'm, uh, going to be in Montana most the time. Just came down for a visit. We're working logistics for a tribal conference we're having here toward the end of the month."

"Great! So maybe y'all will come back then, too? Hey, would y'all like somethin' to eat? We's got a first-class chow hall these days and it's fixin' to be dinner time."

"Thanks, but no. We have other plans. I mainly wanted to say hello and thank you for everything you did for me."

"Y'all's certainly welcome. None o' this woulda been possible without y'all and those Indian talents. You should be proud. Damn proud. We's producing hundreds o' barrels a day with more drillin' planned for spring. We's LSO's primary site these days, makin' the bosses happy to say nothin' of pretty goddamn rich."

A cavernous pit replaced Charlie's stomach. He had a bigger bank account than he ever imagined from it himself. What was going to happen in a few weeks brought a far different feeling than it had when he and White Wolf stood upon that bluff.

Destruction was not something he savored, even though he knew the Earth Mother resented being violated and would respond as she pleased.

Furthermore, senseless loss of life was never good. The workers here were innocent, just making a living. Furthermore, the thought of something happening to Trey impaled his heart with a battle ax. Yet, if he warned him what was to come, the man would never believe him, just think he'd gone crazy since the accident.

Had he?

"C'mon, let me show y'all around," Trey said. "I wanna introduce y'all to the folks running the lab. We got ourselves a good geologist, finally, and a bunch of fancy new equipment. Once we started makin' some cash, they set us up real good."

Trey led them toward one of the other buildings and escorted them inside, where he announced their arrival in his booming voice. "Hey, y'all. Listen up. Get all y'all's asses on over here and meet the guy who made this all possible."

As a half dozen personnel ambled their way, Charlie eyed the suite of equipment, some of which he didn't even recognize.

"This here's Charlie Littlewolf, the Indian I told y'all about, and a relative of his from up in Montana."

The awe and admiration were downright embarrassing, especially in front of White Wolf. Everyone acted as if he were some sort of a demigod, eyes and smiles wide as they shook his hand.

"You're quite the legend around here," one young man in a lab coat said. "You're a damn hard act to follow. It's a pleasure to meet you, sir."

An older man with unruly hair the color of mud was next, whom Trey introduced as the new geologist. "You can say that again," the man stated. "I'd be screwed without technology, and even that can be misleading."

Charlie accepted the man's outstretched hand, wincing slightly at his iron grip; his people's handshakes were typically lighter, such a clench considered aggressive. "Well, it looks as if you've done just fine without me," he said. "I hardly recognized the place."

Trey exhaled through his teeth. "Yeah, we was just gettin' started back then when we had that goddamn mess, after the blowout. He's lucky he survived. If anyone doubts what sour gas'll do, he can tell y'all a thing or two, right, Littlewolf?"

He nodded agreement, shuddering at the memory—the pain, his vision impaired, disorientation, the crazy road trip home. He was no longer the same person, in more ways than one. Yet, now he understood its role in taking him to the threshold of destiny.

After going back outside, Trey explained the Christmas tree. He made a big deal of pointing out the output gauges, then took them around to the rest of the buildings, finally arriving back where the tour began.

The sun's pink glimmer behind persistent clouds was fading to purple. Between the detour and site tour, more than the expected amount of time had passed.

"It's getting late, so we'd better go," Charlie said. "Thanks for showing us around, Trey."

The trio made their way back to the ATV where he climbed into the driver's seat.

Trey pumped his hand one last time. "We'd seriously enjoy having y'all stay for dinner."

"Thanks. We appreciate the offer, but we need to get back." Out of habit, he glanced at the gas gauge. *Uh, oh.* All but empty. "Uh, Trey? There is one favor I need to ask."

"Anything, just name it."

"We're about out of gas. I don't suppose you might have any around here?"

The man laughed, loud and hard, then pointed toward the back, where heavy equipment was parked. "Head on over there, behind the maintenance shed. I'm pretty damn sure we can fix y'all up."

Trey climbed up in the jump-seat in back, providing directions to what looked like a commercial gas pump. As soon as they stopped, he jumped down and proceeded to fill the tank.

As they waited, another thought came to Charlie's mind. "Is Big Dick still around?"

"Nah, he's back in Texas, waiting for his next assignment. His wheelhouse is wildcatting, so once we went into production, he was gone. They'll probably send him up to Wyoming or North Dakota, I reckon."

"Oh. Well, give him my regards, if you're in touch."

"I will. We email back and forth from time to time. He always asks 'bout y'all. Speakin' of which, hold on a sec! I wanna get a picture. May even post it in the lab to keep 'em on their toes."

He took one of Charlie alone, positioning him with the exploration rig in the background, then switched to selfie mode to get one of them both. Charlie smiled the best he could, a final handshake, then they were gone, setting sun casting darkening shades across the hoary landscape.

He drove back much the same way, until they got to where the security fence turned north. Rather than retrace their original, convoluted path, he set off across the terrain toward his own property, which adjoined Sara's.

Once enclosed by pines, it got dark enough he turned on the headlights. He didn't slow down, the path familiar. The temperature dropped with the sun, the vehicle's cab offering minimal protection.

White Wolf said nothing and neither did he. More than ever, he was haunted by the seriousness of what was to come. He offered a silent prayer to *Maheo* to provide protection for those they just left behind.

Other than that, there wasn't much he could do.

SARA'S CABIN
FALCON RIDGE
September 21, Friday
7:10 p.m.

SARA PACED THE KITCHEN, beyond concerned now that it was dark. What if they ran out of gas and were stranded, heaven knows where? Charlie hadn't said where they were going and she didn't ask, not wanting to appear nosey.

Why hadn't she set up that GPS app to track it? *What an idiot!* She gritted her teeth, hoping that wasn't a catastrophic oversight.

Where would she even begin to look? Her eyes met Blossom's, the dog watching her as if picking up on her concern. Could she possibly find them, if it came to that?

Maybe. But how, trudging through the snow in the dark?

As soon as she heard the Polaris growling up the driveway she ran to the window, relieved. She exhaled hard as she turned on the stove to reheat the spaghetti sauce and boil water for the pasta, then waited by the front door.

Whether it was appropriate to ask where they'd been crossed her mind, since he hadn't volunteered that information. Maybe they went back to consecrate the site or something.

At this point, she didn't care, just glad they were back.

Footsteps sounded on the steps, then stomped outside the door; the familiar sound of snow-laden boots. Both were unusually quiet as they stepped inside with a cold blast of air. Her eyes sought Charlie's, worries renewed.

"Is everything okay?" she asked.

His troubled body language escalated her concern. "Sorry we're late. Everything is fine. I went by LSO, to say hello to Trey. It took longer to get there than expected, then he gave us the grand tour."

"Oh. I was getting worried. Dinner will be ready shortly."

His smile looked forced. "Great. I'm starved. Thanks for inviting us. I, uh, don't know what we would have done, otherwise."

She turned to get plates from the cupboard, unable to keep from rolling her eyes. Holy cow! Those were some serious appetites if they'd emptied the ice chest the previous two nights. She set the table, nonetheless relieved their delay wasn't due to anything catastrophic.

"So what do you mean by *grand tour*?" she asked, trying to break the heavy silence.

Charlie shed his coat and hung it on the back of his chair, forehead wrinkled. "I wouldn't have recognized it. It's a full-blown industrial site with two producing wells, plus they're drilling another one. They're even hooked up to a pipeline. I had no idea it would get to that point so quickly."

She relaxed. That certainly explained why he was so morose. "Yuck. Just what we want for neighbors, oil wells."

He winced. "I know. I'm not exactly proud of my part in it. Or its fate, for that matter."

White Wolf was equally somber. "It is in *Maheo's* hands. Our duty is to obey."

After they'd finished eating, they parked the ATV on the back deck near the kitchen door, where it was protected by the eaves and out of sight from the driveway. While it would have been easier to get an early start if they'd all stayed there, she didn't dare suggest it. Rather, she asked if they were ready to go back, car keys in hand.

"We can just take the Polaris," Charlie offered. "We'll bring it back first thing in the morning so we can leave."

"Okay," she agreed, then stood on the porch watching them leave. Again, she pondered the import of what was to come and how isolated she felt. As if she were intruding somewhere she didn't belong, with being there for the *Gathering* a bad idea.

She shivered, partly from an ominous hollow in her chest, and partly because the fire was about to go out. She scowled at both, then donned her parka and exited the kitchen door to bring in more firewood.

SARA'S CONDO
DENVER
September 22, Saturday
11:02 a.m.

THE NEXT MORNING, Sara still couldn't decide what to do. She wanted to talk to Charlie, but not in front of White Wolf. Of course, the elder made sure they didn't have so much as a minute alone, aborting any chance for a private conversation.

After an uncomfortably quiet ride, they arrived in Denver early enough they simply transferred their bags to Charlie's Tahoe, waved, and drove off for Montana.

She hauled the ice chest back inside, deciding to get one with wheels so Blossom could haul the thing, then rummaged in the fridge for something to eat. Finding nothing but leftover Chinese take-out from the week before, she zapped it in the microwave, then grabbed a fork, and munched away on chicken Chow Mein and a dried-up eggroll.

Second thoughts continued their assault. She dipped the eggroll in sweet and sour sauce, deciding one thing for sure: If she went at all, she *definitely* wasn't going alone.

Her plan had been to help with logistics. The Friday before the attendees arrived on Monday, October 22, someone needed to supervise placement of the porta-potties, water truck, and food vendors. After they left the bluff, she'd offered to do that, then once the *Gathering* started, she planned to observe.

Now she wasn't sure.

She'd do what she'd promised for the deliveries, but it was beginning to sound less like a celebration and more like something else, though exactly *what* was elusive, other than those troubling prophecies.

Could they actually come to pass? She shivered, unable to dismiss the possibility.

One last bite of her sorry lunch, then she tossed the containers in the trash under the sink. Blossom gave her a look. She gave her a wry smile.

"Next time, girl. Sorry. Didn't mean to steal your job."

Immersed again in her quandary, thoughts turned to their tryst a few days before. Was it really less than a week? It felt like months. Did it really even happen? Or was it a very vivid dream, like when she was healed?

An unexpected throb of desire confirmed it was real.

Her hands covered her face. She'd never indulged in such a thing in her life. What had gotten into her, anyway? She cringed at the exceptionally bad pun.

The first thing that came to mind was to talk to Patrice. Maybe she could explain it. Perhaps some cosmic alignment out there was to blame.

She got out her phone and started to call when it rang. She nearly dropped it when she saw who it was.

Had he read her thoughts?

On the other hand, the tension the past few days did not bode well for what he might have to say. Braced for the worst, she hit *Connect.*

"Hello."

"Hey, Sara. We just stopped for gas and White Wolf is filling the tank, so I have a few minutes. Are you doing okay?"

She bit her lip, eyes filling with tears. "I, I don't know."

"Listen, I want to apologize. My behavior was inappropriate. I'm really sorry, Sara."

Her throat closed, eyes leaking. So he had regrets. Sadly, she didn't. But she definitely should have done a better job guarding her emotions.

"Are you there, Sara?"

She cleared her throat. "Yes."

"Listen. Things are really intense right now. I should never have gotten you involved like this. You've been so generous and helped so much. We owe you in many ways. We couldn't do this without you. When this is over, I'll make it up to you. I promise."

He paused, as if expecting a response. When she didn't offer one, he continued.

"If you don't want to have anything else to do with this, I understand. We've already imposed enough. It's entirely up to you. If Bryan were here, it would be another story."

That's for sure. The fact the six-month anniversary of his death was coming up around that same time wasn't helping.

She exhaled through her nose, eyes closed. "I need to think about it, Charlie. I planned to be out there anyway on the 17th. In the meantime, I'm considering going up to Boulder for a few days. I can see my family and maybe Patrice."

"That sounds like an excellent idea. You shouldn't be alone right now. I remember that date as well, Sara. Both our lives changed that day. I apologize for making it more difficult."

His perception brought unexpected solace. She wiped her eyes and swallowed hard.

"I'm glad you understand. That's one of the reasons I'm having a hard time, with everything. But I'm fine. You have enough to deal with for the *Gathering*. And, of course, I'll still direct those deliveries, so don't worry about that."

"Yes, we still have a lot left to do. But we've got this. Thank you so much, Sara, for all you've done. We couldn't have done it without your help, financially and otherwise. Go see your family and relax. Be sure to tell Patrice hello for me. And don't worry. I'll call or text when I can. Gotta go, here he comes."

Whenever the white man treats the Indian as they treat each other, then we will have no more wars. We shall all be alike--brothers of one father and one mother, with one sky above us and one country around us, and one government for all. Then the Great Spirit Chief who rules above will smile upon this land, and send rain to wash out the bloody spots made by brothers' hands from the face of the earth. For this time the Indian race are waiting and praying. I hope that no more groans of wounded men and women will ever go to the ear of the Great Spirit Chief above, and that all people may be one people.
--Young Joseph "Chief Joseph", 1879

40. COINCIDENCES

MONTGOMERY RESIDENCE
BOULDER, CO
September 29, Saturday
01:08 p.m.

Connie met Sara at the door with a boob-crushing hug. She didn't realize how badly she needed it until renegade tears spilled from her eyes. What was the matter with her, anyway? Being emotional was unlike her, besides being downright uncomfortable.

Her arms tightened around her stepmom for a moment, then pulled away to meet her caring, green eyes. "It's good to be here. I missed you and Dad. It's been crazy. I needed a break."

Connie gave her another quick hug, then greeted Sara's canine companion. "Have you had lunch? Want to go out for something?"

A weak but sincere smile found her lips. "Oh, yes," Sara agreed. "Definitely. That sounds wonderful. I had some leftover Chinese, but that's it. Is Dad here?"

"Yes. I'm sure he'll be happy to watch Blossom. After all, she was his idea."

"True," Sara said with a laugh. "Go find Dad," she directed the dog, who ran up the stairs without hesitation.

"Italian?" Connie asked.

"No argument here. I can drive. Just tell me where."

Connie grinned. "Let's go to the Villa. We haven't been there in a long time. Let me check and see if Will wants us to bring anything back. I'll tell him it's 'girly time' so he won't want to join us."

She was back in a flash with his to-go order for shrimp alfredo, then they were on their way. As soon as they entered, the aroma of freshly baked sour dough bread combined with spicy marinara sauce made her feel better. While Connie checked in with the hostess, she enjoyed culinary aroma therapy at its best. Since having her taste buds compromised, then healed again, food tasted better than ever before.

The familiar ambiance with its soft accordion music, red and white checkered tablecloths, and dimly lit dining area was relaxing, too. When Connie came back, she gave her another spontaneous hug before they sat down to wait.

"This is a good idea. You always know what I need."

Connie's eyes sparkled as she peered into hers. "So. Tell me. How's it going with you two? Anything interesting?"

Sara's eyelids fluttered, not sure whether to get into that or not. Then again, having someone to talk to was the reason she was there.

"Interesting is probably pretty accurate. I'll see what happens after the *Gathering*. With him moved to the reservation, it's hard to say."

The hostess called, "Montgomery, table for two."

They followed the hostess to their table, then set the menus aside, knowing what they wanted.

"Yeah, long-distance relationships are tough," Connie commented. "It's like they have a built-in clock, ticking away. They can't go on like that forever."

Sara wrinkled her nose. Not what she wanted to hear. "And in less than two weeks it's exactly six months since Bryan died. That isn't helping."

"It's strange," Connie replied. "It feels like ages ago, yet yesterday."

Sara nodded, lines creasing her forehead. "Exactly. It's like the entire world changed. So much has happened, my head's still spinning."

"So what's *interesting* about you and Charlie?"

She hoped the subdued lighting disguised the fact she was blushing. Connie didn't miss it, judging by her mischievous smirk and sparkle in her eyes.

"Alright, Sara. Out with it! What happened?"

She giggled in spite of herself. "I'm really not sure. And I don't think he knows, either."

Their server appeared, a young brunette with a short, bouncy haircut. They gave her their orders, Connie adding a pitcher of Sangria.

"Okay, go on," Connie prompted, not letting her back out.

She stifled a laugh, then told her what happened with the FBI, their arrival, and so forth. "After dinner, White Wolf went to bed early. Charlie and I stayed downstairs, talking." She giggled. "Next thing I knew, *boom!* We were in the sack."

Connie covered her mouth to muffle her giggles.

"I kid you not!" Sara went on, keeping her voice low. "Since I got well, there's this overwhelming attraction." She winced, going on to tell her about White Wolf chewing them out,.

Their server arrived, providing a needed respite. By the time they'd consumed some wine, salad, and steaming hot bread, enough humor dissipated for a more lucid conversation.

Sara took another sip of sangria, then laid her palms flat on the table. "So, long story short, I'd like to see Patrice while I'm up here. Maybe she can explain it. I sure can't."

"I'll text to see if she's busy." Her response came back within seconds. "She says any time after 2:30."

A wave of relief washed over her. Or perhaps it was the sangria. Whatever it was, coming to Boulder was a good idea.

When the rest of their order came, she thoroughly savored every bite of her eggplant parmesan, Connie opting for her usual lasagna. Too full for dessert, they collected Will's order, paid with cash, then took off for Cosmic Portals.

When they arrived, Patrice was sitting at the counter with her mid-afternoon latté. The scent of freshly baked Spiral Galaxies greeted them, followed by Patrice, who got up to give each a hug. The beaded curtain tinkled as they ducked through, prevailing aroma switching from cinnamon rolls to ylang ylang.

The astrologer sat on her side of the multi-colored, silk-covered table, computer in sleep mode behind her. "It's people like you who make me love my work," she said. "So what's on your mind today?"

"For one thing, I plan to keep a better hold on my purse," Sara said, hugging it to her. "It sure is great to be rid of that wheelchair."

"I can imagine," Patrice said. "So what's up?"

Sara giggled. "You have no idea," she said, then dove into an explanation of what occurred earlier that week, particularly her feelings about the *Gathering*. "I just don't know if I belong there or not. I felt like an outsider. Intruder, even. It made me question if I should be there."

"Okay, let's see what's going on."

Patrice scrutinized the horoscope, jotted down a few notes. "Alright. Here's what it's saying. Yes, you should be part of it, but you'll remain behind the scenes. They can really use your help, so don't feel as if you're intruding. The fact you're not part of their culture is okay. They have no problem with you being there, so you shouldn't, either."

Sara nodded, partially relieved. "Okay, that's good. But I have two other things I'm wondering about. First, will this relate to my podcast?"

"Hmmmm." Patrice looked back at the computer. "That's not very clear. Maybe, but things are likely to change. Being immersed in their culture will be intense. You may feel as if you're on a different planet. You're likely to be outside your comfort zone, Sara, but that's okay.

"All this eighth-house stuff indicates this is going to be a potentially earth-shattering event that delivers significant changes," she went on. "It's time for indigenous people to receive the respect they deserve and this will put the spotlight on that. Nothing will be the same afterwards. You, either."

"Really? Wow! So it's going to be something like a giant protest or something? White Wolf told that FBI guy it was like a peace rally. That seemed a rather odd way to describe it, though my research indicates that was the Ghost Dance's original intent."

Patrice wore a faraway, pensive expression for several moments. "In some respects, yes. But it's more than that. There's so much going on here. A lot of fate involved. One of those 'meant to be' events. On a grand scale."

Sara's thoughts shifted to a more personal level and told her what happened with Charlie. The three of them chuckled for a moment, then turned serious. "I've been hopelessly confused about that, since this event is currently his primary focus." She cringed as she told her about White Wolf's edict.

Patrice laughed, hard, muttered, "There's that eighth-house again!" then looked back at the chart, moments later folding her hands on the table.

"Okay. Bear in mind how much Charlie respects him. Culturally, as well as at the personal level. It doesn't mean he doesn't care about you. Not at all! Think of White Wolf as Charlie's superior officer. He has a mission to complete that's important."

Sara nodded, the burden in her chest losing some weight. "Kind of like when Bryan was overseas. He probably would have ignored me in the same way if I were there."

"Exactly." Patrice's long, tapered fingers tapped the table in emphasis. "He needs to give it his full attention. Men can focus like that. Multiplexing is not their forte. Thus, anything between you two is suspended until this *Gathering* thing is over. Don't take it personally. He's just wearing a different hat. Or headdress, if you will, for now."

"That makes sense," Sara agreed, relief settling on her like that beautiful shawl Star sent her.

"Whatever is going on with you two is separate, Sara. Sharing this will strengthen whatever that is. If you stay away, he may think you didn't care. Just give him space to do what he has to do."

Sara's neck muscles relaxed. "Thank you, Patrice. I appreciate your insights so much."

"They aren't mine, sweetie. I'm just reading what the Universe has to say. I can't take the credit."

"Well, without you I'd be clueless. So thank you for translating." She exhaled, releasing the last of the tension. "I feel much better now."

Up until then, Connie was quiet. At this point, she added, "Would be okay if Will and I went with her? To help, at least provide morale support?"

The astrologer nodded. "Absolutely. It will be an incredible experience for all of you. Remember, this involves a culture you've only seen a glimpse of. Be prepared for the unexpected and maintain an open mind. This can either draw you all closer or drive you apart. By the way, when is this going to happen?"

"October 23. On my property, out by Falcon Ridge."

"The 23rd? No kidding?" Patrice sat up straight, emanating curiosity. "What time? Do you know?"

"Some time in the afternoon, I guess. He hasn't said. It'll go on for quite a while, from what I've been able to figure out. Probably around three or four o'clock. Maybe later."

Patrice's eyes widened when the chart appeared. "*Whoa*. Yes, this will be definitely be unforgettable. That's the day the Sun goes into Scorpio."

Sara tilted her head, wondering what difference that made. "What's the deal with Scorpio?"

Patrice's countenance brightened as she explained, "It's an intense, passionate sign that's the eighth-house of the zodiac. It includes things like sex, birth, death, life-changing experiences, debt, other people's money, and transformations. That energy is strong, especially the day it begins, which will reflect on the event."

Chills ran down Sara's arms. "Do you think that's a coincidence?"

Patrice shook her head. "No such thing, sweetie. No such thing."

SARA'S CONDO
DENVER
October 5, Friday
06:08 p.m.

THE NEXT WEEK, as promised, Sara finalized logistics for the *Gathering*. It wasn't as easy as expected since many who provided the needed services only did so within the metropolitan Denver-Boulder area, not distant rural areas lacking the needed infrastructure.

Determination coupled with leads and referrals enabled her to find a small company in Lakewood willing to accommodate the porta-potties. She still needed to find water trucks and enough food vendors willing to go out for the event. With only a few weeks left, it would be a relief when all contracts were in place.

She grinned when the tasks were completed by close of business, grateful it wouldn't hang over her head all weekend. She texted Charlie the good news, wishing they could celebrate the small victory. She didn't feel much like being alone, yet didn't feel like driving to Boulder, either.

As always, Blossom knew someone was at the door before anyone knocked. Sara was in the kitchen, fixing herself a bowl of soup and a salad, when the canine trotted to the door, tail waving softly, back and forth. The inevitable knock sounded.

At least the pit bull didn't seem bothered as she had with those annoying FBI agents. With luck, she wouldn't have to spend the evening alone after all.

Who might it be? Maybe an old friend from work. She got up, hoping, as she peered through the peephole.

She stepped back, puzzled.

Why was Jason there?

It didn't give her a bad feeling, only an odd one. They hadn't had any contact since returning from Montana, other than a few phone calls to give her the information for the blog site he set up and Cayman Islands account.

She opened the door. "I'm surprised to see you, Jason."

"Is it okay if I come in?" He looked almost sheepish, or like he'd just woken up. His usually-slicked-back hair was in disarray, displaying hints of natural curl she hadn't noticed before.

"You're not going to kidnap me again, are you?"

Humorless eyes met hers. "No. I just had a few things I didn't want to discuss on the phone."

"Okay," she said, and beckoned him inside. He squatted down to pet her dog, whose tail continued to swish back and forth.

"Nice place," he commented, looking around as he stood back up. "Much bigger than it appears on camera."

She fidgeted, wondering what he may have seen when the place was infested with cameras and microphones.

"Would you like something to eat?"

"No, thanks. But you go ahead."

She led him into the kitchen and invited him to sit at the table while she finished fixing her meal.

"So what do you want to talk about?" she prompted.

Hazel eyes locked on hers. "First of all, I want to apologize that I couldn't stop the FBI from showing up. I tried, but Allison's boss' superior, the deputy director, insisted. Turns out, there was a different reason than what they may have said behind that visit."

A medley of sour notes went off in her head at mention of the infuriating incident, one hand on her hip. "Oh, really? Like what?"

He held her gaze. "He foolishly assumed you died after you returned from New York and marked your file accordingly. His management instructed him to confirm, in person, whether you were alive or not, after hearing conflicting information." He chuckled. "He's still insisting you have a body double, but his boss isn't buying it."

She growled, incredulous. "What an idiot. Did he get in trouble?"

"Apparently. I doubt he'll make that mistake again."

"He's a total jerk. Really obnoxious. I hope I never see him again."

"I'll do what I can. I can make it permanent if you like."

She wrinkled her nose at the sordid implications. "Thank you, but just staying away from me is good enough."

She opened a jar of tomato basil soup, poured it in a bowl, then placed it in the microwave. "Are you sure you don't want anything to eat?"

"No, I already ate."

"Are your eyes working okay now?"

"Yes, perfectly. Same as before." He shook his head. "Strange, strange experience. I've had some pretty weird ones, all over the world, but that was off the scale."

"Seems to be a lot of that going around lately." She removed the soup from the microwave and set it on the table next to the salad. Hesitated a moment, considering a glass of wine, then decided against it and sat down.

What else did he want, anyway? When he showed no signs of leaving, she picked up her spoon and started to eat.

"This will probably sound strange, Sara, but I really enjoyed that night we watched those old movies."

She nearly choked on her soup.

"I suppose it was kind of fun, all things considered," she sputtered, grabbing a paper towel to wipe her mouth.

What on Earth was he getting at?

She didn't need to wait long for an answer.

"So, I was wondering. Would you like to do that again?"

She set down her spoon and cleared her throat, dumbfounded. "Uh, well...."

"Oh! Okay. I get it. You're, well, involved. With that Cheyenne guy, Charlie. Right?"

She avoided his eyes. "I'm not entirely sure. He and my husband were best friends from the time they were kids. After Bryan died, Charlie understood better than anyone what I was going through. We've become quite close the past few months.

Been through so much together, besides losing Bryan. But I don't know. Maybe, maybe not. Right now he's got a lot going on."

"Okay. I get it."

He stood up, apparently ready to leave, after all. She got up and followed to the door.

"Don't worry, I still have your back, Sara. I owe you that much."

"Thank you," she said.

He opened the door. "Oh, by the way. There's still a live microphone. I believe it's concealed in a heater vent in your bedroom. You may want to remove it."

She tried not to react, but her face nonetheless flushed crimson.

"Th-thank you. I'll be, uh, sure to check."

"If you have any more problems with the Feds, let me know."

"I will."

She waited until he was halfway down the sidewalk, then slowly closed the door, leaned against it, and exhaled a deep and relieved breath.

Oh. My. God.

She buried her face in her hands, not knowing whether to laugh, cry, or scream.

NORTHERN CHEYENNE RESERVATION
MONTANA
October 15, Monday
11:29 a.m.

IT HAD BEEN A BUSY two weeks. Invitations and information for the *Peace Gathering of Indigenous Leaders* were conveyed to nearly a hundred-thousand tribal chiefs, council leaders, and medicine men, mostly via email and video broadcasts.

This would be far different than the usual Pan Nation pow-wow. Rather than food, dancing, and other contests, a *Massaum* would be held. Besides witnessing the ceremony, their brothers and sisters from other tribes would be further schooled in its historical significance, then encouraged to adopt it for their respective tribes as the Earth Giving Ceremony.

In ancient times, the *Tsistsistas* kept it secret, Sweet Medicine teaching the ceremony millennia before to establish the boundaries of their land. Now, as part of unifying all Native Nations, it would be shared.

The invitation was not only well-received but anticipated. As it was in 1890, dreams, visions, and in a few cases visitations prepared the indigenous community for the sacred ceremonies. If there was one thing America's Indigenous people agreed upon it was that they were there first, on land given them by the Creator God.

No one argued that it had been stolen and they wanted it back.

Charlie never expected to be a YouTube star, but views nearing millions brought an unexpected financial benefit as his channel was monetized. *Maheo* had certainly helped the budget, to say nothing of Sara's and Jason's generous contributions.

Of necessity, housing for so many in the sparsely populated area extended as far away as Billings to the west and Sheridan to the south with buses needed for transportation to the reservation as well as later to Dead Horse Canyon.

Most of those driving to the event from around the country would pitch their tipis on the plains in the ceremony's Camp Circle, as they had for thousands of years. The majority would be Northern and Southern Cheyenne, who would participate rather than simply observe.

That morning, a special sweat was held for the main participants in the community sweat lodge in Lame Deer. The sweat's purpose was purification prior to being part of the *Massaum*, which would begin in two days. Hundreds of both sexes and all ages would take part, but in less critical roles.

Charlie, White Wolf, and a dozen others left the sweat to tend to their remaining assignments. It was overcast and chilly, snow flurries dusting the air, though at the moment it felt good. A few days earlier, they'd had a private one, so Star and the boys could attend.

They got in *Tah-Hó'nehe* and drove home to clean up and check last-minute tasks. Charlie turned on the wipers when the flurries shifted to compound flakes. "It will be great if the weather clears up tomorrow, when people begin to arrive," he mused aloud.

White Wolf chuckled. "Weather is but another of the Earth Mother's faces. It is how she reminds us of her moods and power. The Full Moon is the day following the Dance. The ending of one cycle and beginning of the next. It fits well with what is about to happen, does it not?"

"Yes. It does."

When they got to the house they reviewed the itinerary. Invitations for the online meeting were sent out. The caravan of fifteen buses would leave for Colorado before dawn Monday morning, arrival expected approximately twelve hours later.

Longer, if the weather didn't cooperate.

"Should we drive down in *Tah-Hó'nehe* so we have transportation?" Charlie proposed.

White Wolf disagreed. "No. Maintaining solidarity with our brothers by riding together is more important. Demonstrating our unity will help other tribes accept it."

"True. And we can answer any last-minute questions. Sara has everything under control and she has a car. I'm glad she has her family's help. Being so close to the six-month anniversary of Bryan's death makes it difficult."

"Or keeps her mind off it," White Wolf suggested. "And you."

Charlie ignored the comment, wondering if it was a coincidence the *Massaum* began that day?

He suspected Sara still didn't understand how Bryan's death and the *Gathering* were related. Pointing it out crossed his mind, but he didn't want to get her too stirred up, much less distracted.

Or perhaps, as White Wolf had done with him, it would be best for her to figure it out on her own. When it was all over, if he needed to, he'd explain. Then they'd celebrate.

He smiled, anticipating when he could hold her again.

41. MAHEONOX

MASSAUM CEREMONY DAY ONE
NORTHERN CHEYENNE RESERVATION
BUSBY, MT
October 17, Wednesday
7:00 a.m.

Star shivered in the pre-dawn chill as Spica, Virgo's brightest star, kissed the horizon with a brilliant burst of white. The *Tsistsistas* name for that constellation was lost to time, but a *maiyun* told Littlewolf it represented Ehyophstah, and would announce this very special Earth Giving Ceremony.

The heliacal rise of any given star occurred on a specific day, making them useful as ancient calendars. But since the *Massaum* was supposed to be held in the summer, the traditional stars would not work with it well into fall.

Spica vanished, yielding to the glare of the rising Sun, announcing the Massaum's first day. Star smiled as warming rays fell upon thousands of her Cheyenne brothers and sisters, including her grown children and their families as well as special guests from other tribes, all assembled around the camp circle. Her heart filled to overflowing, much as their home was with all their children and grandchildren gathered under the same roof.

Both Northern and Southern Cheyennes arrived the past few days, reunions with extended family not seen for years, sometimes ever, bringing joy and unity to the long-separated tribal units.

What might the restoration of the ancient ceremony bring? The possibilities stirred her soul with hope and gratitude for living in such historic times.

Everyone's expectations were high for the performance of such a meaningful ancient ceremony after a hiatus of nearly a century. Thanks to Littlewolf's and Winter Hawk's vision on *Novavose*, the ceremony could be restored, implying its effects and power would manifest.

Being an integral part of the ceremony, perhaps even the most important role, was so exciting it made her head spin. Unlike others, such as the Sun Dance, renewing the Sacred Arrows or Sacred Buffalo Hat, the *Massaum* preferred a woman pledger. She represented Ehyophstah, or Yellow-haired Woman, the buffalo spirit made human to assist the *Tsistsistas*.

She was humbled as well as brimming with excitement to fulfill that role, heart and mind struggling to comprehend how the original experience may have felt.

She attended every session the past few weeks when the Forty-Four Old Man Chiefs and the tribe's medicine men congregated in the Tribal School auditorium where Littlewolf described the ceremony in detail. For those who would take part from the Southern Cheyenne, the session was streamed live on a private YouTube channel and recorded for later viewing.

Littlewolf emphasized that the reason they got their land back in 1884 when the Northern Cheyenne Reservation was established by Executive Order, it was directly related to the fact they'd laid claim to it through *Massaum* ceremonies many times in the ancient past. *Maheo* would not allow the white man to take away what he had given them through solemn covenant.

It was a lot to absorb, yet Star's soul sang with joy, representing Ehyophstah the epitome of her rich *Tsistsistas* heritage. Ice's wife, Standing Dove, was her friend as well as her instructor. The woman learned the ceremony so easily it was evident her spirit helpers were there to assist.

The main participants were painted red, including Star as the woman pledger; White Wolf as the male pledger as well as her literal and ritual husband; Ice, the chief priest, who represented Motseyoef, known more commonly as Sweet Medicine; Standing Dove and Littlewolf, the instructors. Help with the physical tasks would be provided by many others, including several women as well as her sons.

The crowd grew quiet as the ceremony began. Four main tasks would be completed this first day.

The group left the camp circle with their assigned helpers and walked northwest through prairie grass up to their knees to the grove along Eaglefeathers Creek. Late fall scented the air, fallen leaves crunching welcome beneath their moccasins.

Ice made a prayer to the trees and vegetation:

"Today we are here to do what those two men of ancient times told us we ought to do, and today we ask you for a tree to take part in our ceremony. I beg that all the trees and grass and fruits may thrive and grow strong, and I ask that if we do not perform the ceremony just as it ought to be done, you will pardon us for the mistakes we make." [2]

As pledgers, Star and White Wolf repeated the prayer, then wandered about with Ice until he selected a tree to serve as the ceremony's World Tree, a cottonwood about twenty-five feet high with a base he could enclose with both hands.

He made the sacred motions, then smoked with the tree spirit, pungent vapors scenting the brisk air. Three feigned motions with the axe preceded his striking it with the fourth.

Star and her helpers finished felling the tree as the others sang a solemn song to honor the tree spirit. As part of her role, she selected seven healthy branches at the top, still adorned with golden leaves.

"These branches represent the levels of the universe as well as the celestial spirits of the seven brothers who live in the

---

[2] Grinnell, volume 2, p. 285; Schlesier, Wolves of Heaven, p. 88

Pleiades," she explained. "We will leave these and remove the rest."

She glanced at Standing Dove, whose nod indicated she'd done so correctly. After that, Littlewolf and four women helped her feign lifting it three times before picking it up with the fourth. Together they dragged it back to the camp circle within view of Eaglefeathers Butte.

While Ice made the sacred motions she inhaled deeply a few times to catch her breath. White Wolf's gaze caught her own, the love in his eyes heartwarming. Ice took her hand and joined it with her husband's, directing them to symbolically dig a hole where the tree would be placed. The soil's gritty texture was rough against her palms as they removed a handful, then four more in the sacred directions several inches away.

Winter Hawk stepped in with a crowbar to dig the five holes, each over two feet deep. He started with the center, accompanied by seven men singing. Lodge poles lifted the tree into position, four set in the surrounding holes to secure it in place.

Star stretched her neck and shoulders, ready for the day's second activity, raising the *Maheonox*, or Wolf Lodge. It was twice the size of the typical lodge, the first four poles located in the sacred directions, twenty-four more added for support. Two lodge covers were required, tree extending through the smoke hole, golden leaves rustling in the breeze.

Her excitement escalated as the lodge took form, the ceremony's power charging the air like that before a mighty storm.

The third task entailed removing all living vegetation around the tree to within six feet of the lodge poles. From that location on, grass would remain for the sitting area. Star crawled on her hands and knees, scraping and smoothing with Standing Dove and the other women, until the vast area was cleared. Upon completion, it was noticeably lower than the grassy section by a few inches.

"I remember doing this when we built our sweat lodge, but not that it was so hard," she commented to White Wolf, brushing off her hands when they finished.

"That was many years past, wife," he reminded her. "We were much younger then."

Winter Hawk, Risingsun, and other youth then spread man sage upon the remaining grass, leaving a strip bare where the entrance would be. Her eyes leaked tears of gratitude watching their sons share this rich experience.

SARA'S CABIN
RURAL FALCON RIDGE
COLORADO
October 17, Wednesday
1:20 p.m.

SARA, WILL, AND CONNIE drove out to the cabin the day before the *Gathering* began to commemorate the six-month anniversary of Bryan's death. As if reflecting their collective mood, the weather was overcast, dismal, and cold.

The barren landscape slept beneath several more inches of snow, braced for its winter sojourn. More reminiscent of death than back in May, when she'd pondered spring wildflowers from her perch atop a boulder, hurting too much from her injuries to join them along the steep, uneven path.

Hiking boots sloshed through heavy, wet snow as they traced the path where they'd scattered his ashes, this time leaving chrysanthemum blooms and brightly colored autumn leaves.

"It seems strange without Charlie here," Connie remarked, holding out the basket for Sara to take another fragrant handful.

"I know," Sara agreed. "He's tied up on the Reservation or I'm sure he would be."

Another red maple leaf fluttered toward the ground, one of many Connie collected from Chautauqua Park. Sara's heart ached as she watched it skip across frozen ground, not unlike her life since that fateful day. Renewed grief mingled with outrage that such could occur in a supposedly free society.

Something needed to change.

Which she was more determined than ever to facilitate.

Shivering by the time they got back to the cabin, Will stoked the fire and added another log. She and Connie stood before it, soaking up the warmth with hands extended, while Will retrieved a bottle of chilled Champagne.

"Shall we?" he asked, replicating what they'd done six months before.

Sara wrinkled her nose. Just barely warming up, anything cold, even Champagne, had no appeal.

"I agree," Connie said, taking it from him and putting it back in the fridge. "Hot chocolate, anyone?"

"Yes," Sara said with a nod. "Much better."

Moments later, steaming mugs in hand, they toasted Bryan, then Sara motioned for them to follow to the guest room.

"I want to show you some of the historical stuff I found," she said. She removed the old wooden box from the bench seat, then set it on the bed and opened the lid, releasing the musty smell of old leather-bound documents.

"Look at this old journal." She picked it up carefully, displaying its frayed binding and fragile, yellowed pages. "Did I ever tell you what Charlie told me about the curse on where our accident was?"

"Not that I recall," Connie said.

Will agreed. "Same here."

She repeated what Charlie told her, then read the journal entry of the miner's side of the story.

Connie grimaced. "I guess there are always two sides. Even if one is dead wrong."

"We were uncivilized in a different way back then," Will commented. "But human nature doesn't change."

"No. It doesn't," Sara agreed. "Charlie told me curses were patient. I wonder what happens when it finally runs out?"

MASSAUM CEREMONY DAY ONE
NORTHERN CHEYENNE RESERVATION
BUSBY, MT
October 17, Wednesday
4:28 p.m.

WHILE HER SONS DUG a fire pit between the World Tree and the door, Star and the others gathered rocks for its circumference along with plenty of wood.

While tired from so much exertion, she nonetheless continued to radiate happiness. Goosebumps tickled her arms as intuition's soft nudge intimated many of her ancestors had pledged that same role eons before. Whenever a Cheyenne pledged and completed a ceremony, the entire tribe was strengthened. Already she could feel new life igniting her soul.

It was growing dark by the time it was ready, a reminder why the longer days of summer were more suitable for the labor-intensive ceremony.

Celebratory singing and dancing filled the Wolf Lodge as the fire was lit, flames symbolizing the power of life as a result of *Maheo's* will. Star sang along, tears dampening her cheeks when Ehyophstah's spirit fell upon her, weary body shedding its fatigue as it experienced that very sacred moment at the dawn of time.

LSO NEW WORKSITE
RURAL FALCON RIDGE
October 17, Wednesday
5:42 p.m.

A HEAVY WEIGHT INVADED Trey's chest as he scrutinized a familiar weather signature on his office computer. An ominous squall line, indicated by a blob of green, yellow, and glaring red accented with purple, loomed over the Texas panhandle, west of the Dallas-Fort Worth metroplex.

The worst tornado month was May, but October and November were treacherous, as well. Similar conditions existed when northern cold fronts, such as the one that brought the Rockies' first snow, collided with warm, moist air from the Gulf of Mexico.

His mind raced, slammed with childhood memories. He relit his cigar and leaned back in his chair, reminiscing.

Sirens blaring.

The sharp scent of ozone as a dangerous storm approached, spewing lightning and hail, sometimes the size of baseballs.

Racing for safety, which meant hunkering down in a dank tornado cellar.

Tarantulas, scorpions, snakes, poisonous spiders, mouse-sized roaches, and other nasty critters that hung out in such places, as terrifying as the twisters.

He shivered, remembering how the ground trembled beneath a thunderous roar, ears popping a bad sign the forces of hell had arrived. Visceral fear in his mother's eyes upon emerging, hoping not to find only a chimney or debris trail where the house had once been.

He exhaled hard, summoning adult logic. His townhome was insured for such things, so it really wasn't a big deal. There were a few things with sentimental value—old family pictures and a few heirlooms—but nothing he couldn't live without.

Friends and relatives lived with severe weather all the time. Business as usual. They knew what to do. But the risk and lethal potential was always there.

The worst part about tornados was how quickly they erupted. Folks along the Gulf Coast typically had a day or more of warning when a hurricane headed their way, allowing time to pack up and get out of Dodge. Spending seven years in Houston refineries, he'd been through a few.

He chuckled, remembering commentators joking about the "boat show on the Gulf Freeway," courtesy of a storm surge in

Galveston. He remembered gridlock along evacuation routes, where he spent one such storm in his truck at the traffic loop linking I-45 to I-10, rising water seeping through the floorboards.

He clicked on the screen and dragged the view farther south. He inhaled sharply upon finding a Cat-4 hurricane in the Gulf, multi-colored spaghetti tracks of speculated paths on a beeline to Texas. It was an unusually active year, four hitting his home state so far. Flooding and general mayhem had afflicted several coastal cities including Galveston, Beaumont, and Brownsville. The forecast for this one, Hurricane Isaiah, was to make landfall that night, just north of Corpus Christi, in the Port Aransas area.

He pictured people boarding up windows, then heading inland with fingers crossed their home wouldn't be destroyed or inundated when they returned.

Yeah, he'd take snow over that, any day. Meanwhile, his native state was getting hammered. He took out his phone and set an alert, should severe weather develop in his home region. There was nothing he could do about it, but he stayed informed because several members of his crew had families there.

Blizzards were no picnic, either, but more predictable. When properly prepared, people could survive more easily covered by several feet of snow versus water, as long as the roof didn't collapse. With secure housing, plenty of food, and a means to keep warm, you were fine.

The LSO site was set up with just such facilities. Maintaining operations throughout the year was essential, weather be damned. The entire operation was powered by generators, the mess hall well-stocked. No reason they shouldn't be fine, come what may.

Unlike his fellow Texans, who'd be braced for a rough, soggy ride.

He wished them luck, then went back to check the day's oil prices. Daily production had spiked and was better than ever, their average currently just over 791 BOPD. No doubt the Bentleys were in hog heaven, profits soaring.

He smiled as he got up and wrote the figures on the white board behind his desk. He grunted, making a mental note to remind

Gerald yet again of the part he and his crew played in their current windfall.

Big bonuses had to be approved by the Board of Directors. Maybe it was time his boss called a special meeting.

42. MAHEYUNO

MASSAUM CEREMONY DAY TWO
NORTHERN CHEYENNE RESERVATION
BUSBY, MT
October 18, Thursday
7:02 a.m.

Charlie positioned himself on the west side of the Wolf Lodge, between the World Tree and seating area. The only others present were Ice, Star, Standing Dove, and White Wolf. A few coals remained from the night before, wisps of smoke rising in the frost-laden air.

Charlie closed his eyes and prayed, soul afire with the realization he represented *Maheo* when nothing existed so far in time, for time itself did not yet exist. *Nothing*! An empty, lifeless void, deep in space.

As he crouched down and pressed an indentation in the ground, his hand trembled, dirt cool against his thumb. Four more followed, a few inches away in the sacred directions.

He paused, heart racing as he again absorbed the act's significance. What might the Creator have felt at that sacred moment? Porcupine's recent witness during his fast that the Creator was indeed a man made it even more astounding.

Then, focusing back on the task at hand, he used a stick to excavate a small hole a few inches across in the middle

416

indentation, as wide as it was deep. He removed the earth with four motions, each handful sifted between his fingers on each of the other impressions, creating four little mounds. He took a pinch of red power to cover the two toward the south, then black for the two to the north.

Thus creating the four sacred mountains of the *maheyuno*, *Maheo's* sacred guardians: Esseneta'he, Sovota, Onxsovon, and Notamota.

Using powdered gypsum, he drew four lines from the center hole to the four cardinal directions. He sat back on his heels, awed by its meaning:

Combined with the four mounds, the sand painting represented the universe with *Maheo* at the center.

He got up and retrieved an armful of man sage and tied a few branches to the southeast pole of the Wolf Lodge, then three more to the poles in the other sacred directions. Each represented a *maheyuno,* whom he greeted by name as he aligned a bundle with their respective mounds. A fifth was tied to the western pole, adding *Maheo*.

He stepped outside, momentarily blinded by the rising Sun. He blinked a few times, waiting for his eyes to adjust, though the light of day failed to dissipate the dreamlike quality of his historic actions. Using paint from one of several dishes in each of the sacred colors, he drew *Atovsz*, spirit of the Sun, as a red disk on the lodge's east side. Then to the west, where he painted *Ameonito*, spirit of the Moon, as a blue-black crescent.

He scrutinized his work, pondering the significance of day and night, light and dark, life and death, mortality's many dichotomies, after which he returned inside. On the southwest wall, next to the *maheyuno*, Sovota, he painted a man wearing horns with eagle talon feet, body covered with black dots: Nonoma, the life-giving thunder spirit, who brings the spring rains.

Next came the creation of Esceheman, Grandmother Earth.

He nodded at Star, who left the lodge. Moments later, from outside she called, "I have my hands on it!"

Charlie began singing, Ice and White Wolf joining in. Four songs were sung, their conclusion coinciding with Star's arrival at the door. She made four forward motions holding a buffalo skull, entering with the last. She circled to the left around the tree until opposite the door. With four motions, she placed the skull on the ground, nose facing the tree.

Sacred songs set the mood as she knelt and placed round bundles of grass in the eye sockets and nasal cavity. Charlie painted a black line from the back of the skull down its center to the nasal opening, then outlined it with white, indicating day and night. The remainder was painted red, like the earth, including the grass plugs, which represented earth's vegetation.

A solid blue star of midsummer dawn (Rigel), represented by a cross comprised of four triangles, was added between the horn cores and eyes, then a red Sun on the right jaw and black crescent Moon on the left.

A shallow excavation was prepared facing both the tree and the door, into which the skull was deposited with ceremony, a bundle of man sage in front and a buffalo chip behind.

Esceheman, Grandmother Earth, was now ritually present.

The wolf lodge was now the sacred mountain, Charlie representing Nonoma, the Thunder Spirit, and Standing Dove, Esceheman, Grandmother Earth.

Ice joined them. As Motseyoef, he sat in front of Esseneta'he's bundle, *maheyuno* of the southeast, where he would stay for the remainder of the ceremony.

As Nonoma, Charlie instructed Motseyoef to draw a small spiraling circle in the dirt with his right thumb. This created the *Tsistsistas* with Motseyoef, a.k.a. Sweet Medicine, their spiritual representative.

Their actions thus far symbolized the Thunder Spirit and Grandmother Earth creating the *Tsistsistas* through power granted by *Maheo* within the lodge of the *maiyun,* all accomplished under the watchful eye of the *maheyuno.*

The skins of a male red wolf, a female white wolf, and a female timber fox (because the kit fox was now extinct), were brought in and placed to the right of the buffalo skull.

More men and women entered the lodge, White Wolf sitting next to Ice as Motseyoef's companion.

When night fell, the *maiyun* transformed the structure to a spirit lodge. Eight coals glowed from the east branch of the white cross toward the world tree, sweetgrass upon them blessing the air.

The *maheyuno* then taught Motseyoef and his companion spirit songs and gave instructions how to call the spirits of grassland animals as well as the rules regarding their use.

Charlie's spirit soared with sacred knowledge deep within his soul. The land was created expressly for the *Tsistsistas*. This was *their* land, not only gifted, but created by *Maheo* for his people through the *Massaum* covenant.

LSO NEW WORKSITE
RURAL FALCON RIDGE
October 18, Thursday
10:45 p.m. MDT

SENSITIZED TO KLAXON ALARMS by decades in the oil industry, Trey bolted awake. The strident, pulsing tone that tore him from his slumber could wake the dead. Heart racing, he turned on the light, disoriented.

He relaxed slightly upon finding himself in the camping trailer that served as his onsite apartment, the racket issuing from his phone.

He picked it up with one hand and fumbled with the other for his glasses on the bedside table. He relaxed a notch as he silenced the blaring notification.

What the hell was going on? And where?

Everything at the drilling site was fine.

Any relief was short-lived.

Such was not the case in Texas.

He ground his teeth, earlier fears realized.

A tornado warning coupled with a flashflood advisory. Right, smack in the middle of his home zip code.

Not good.

Warnings were worse than watches. Watches noted conditions could turn ugly; warnings declared they already had.

Doppler radar defined a twisted mosaic of green, yellow, and a preponderance of red that looked like a close-up view of an impressionist painting. The two systems he'd observed earlier were colliding, wreaking havoc on his home turf in a worst-case scenario.

Tropical air from Hurricane Isaiah, since downgraded to a tropical depression, had shifted north. It followed I-35 past Austin into Dallas, bringing stiff sixty-mile-per-hour winds. Driving rain delivered heavy flooding in low-lying areas, ground already saturated by an exceptionally wet autumn.

Invigorated by a cold front encroaching from the west, the squall line was staging a violent rendezvous with Isaiah's remains, creating a severe tornado outbreak. From there, it was predicted to head into Oklahoma and across Arkansas, though for the moment the opposing fronts were in a standoff, stalling the system.

Not good at all.

The one hope that prevailed with bad weather was that it would move on. When it stalled, that was another story—a dangerous one.

A heavy feeling of helplessness in the face of fate invaded his chest. There was absolutely nothing he could do, other than check in the morning. All he could do was hope for the best as he set his phone and glasses back on the table and turned out the light.

Getting comfortable again, he uttered a brief prayer for those in its path, then fell back into a restless sleep.

I-30 WESTBOUND
MILE MARKER 29
GRAND PRAIRIE, TX
October 18, Thursday
11:54 p.m. CDT

BOB BENTLEY'S FOOT RODE the brake, slowing his Lincoln
Navigator to a crawl. Between the late hour and driving rain,
visibility dipped to zero on I-30's westbound lane outside Grand
Prairie. Windshield wipers slashed vainly against the deluge,
heaven's floodgates open. Rain hammered the vehicle, the racket
like being inside a drum at a Led Zeppelin concert.

Rather than an orderly procession of tail lights, Bob's view
comprised a dynamic mix of smeared primary colors, randomly
refracted to dancing, jewel-like patterns. Another blinding flash of
lightning with its explosive blast crackled around them, rocking
the car.

Zeus or some other equally malefic deity was undoubtedly
displeased about something.

"What a crock of shit," Gerald muttered. "Doris told me not
to go out tonight. Now I'll have to listen to her bitch about it the
rest of the goddamn night."

Bob grunted, eyes glued on what little he could see. "If she's
anything like Angela, she's already asleep. And she was right. It
was your bright idea to take the Board out to dinner."

"Yeah, yeah, I know. Now that our Colorado site cracked 800
BOPD, I thought it was worth celebrating."

"Really, Gerald?" Bob knew exactly what it was about and
celebrating was secondary. "As I recall, your point was to rub their
noses in the fact that half of 'em didn't approve of that project from
the git-go."

"So what?" His fist struck the console. "Those stuffy old
bastards needed a reminder. We know what we're doin' and don't
appreciate their whining or nitpickin' when we make a decision. I
didn't hear 'em complainin' 'bout them $125 bacon-wrapped fee-
lay min-yons."

"Or refusing their bonuses."

"Right." Gerald grumbled. "Unappreciative assholes."

"That's for damn sure."

"Speaking of which, are you going to that PURF wing-ding next week?"

Bob glanced over at his brother wearing a scowl. "The what?"

"C'mon, Bob. PURF. Dad's thing. Up by your place in the north country."

"I know what PURF is, Gerald. We leased them the land, for Pete's sake. But I don't know anything about any open house."

"You don't? That's odd. Check with your wife. It's supposed to be some big, high-falootin' D.C. party for its future residents."

Bob spurned the event with a sneer of disdain. "I don't give a rat's ass about that D.C. bunch. Dad's territory, not mine. He sandbagged me into this Federal Judge crap, which I never wanted, either. I was perfectly happy as LSO's corporate attorney."

As if to punctuate his statement, the downpour switched to golf ball-sized hail, impacts drowning their conversation.

"Damn! There goes the paint job!" Bob hollered.

The car trembled, then oscillated back and forth. His fingers tightened around the wheel, efforts fruitless.

"What the bloody hell was that?" Bob roared above the din.

"Hell if I know," his brother yelled back. "Wind, I suppose."

"This goddamn car weighs three tons, Gerald. It should be able to take a little wind!"

The impacts lowered in pitch as gale-driven hail, now the size of tennis balls, pummeled the vehicle. An ominous low frequency vibration seized the SUV, thunder snarling like Dolby wrap-around sound at the IMAX.

"What the hell! My ears just popped!" Gerald exclaimed.

The clamor escalated to a deafening roar, the storm's sub-woofer-range symphony vetoing any attempt at conversation.

Bob's attempts to control the Lincoln failed as the renegade vehicle abruptly slid sideways, paused momentarily, then spun counterclockwise, skidding across four lanes of pavement like a pirouetting, six-thousand-pound ballerina.

The empty feeling in the pit of his stomach that followed reminded him of the rollercoaster at Six Flags, a few miles back. The unmistakable message it conveyed of being airborne, however, was far from entertaining.

The car bucked and tossed, leaving the ground to follow the twister's rotation. Debris of all sizes and descriptions pounded and shrieked against protesting metal.

Gerald clung to the sissy bar with both hands, white-rimmed eyes bulging with terror. Some unwelcome projectile shattered the windshield with a resounding crash. He screamed, expletives lost in the whirlwind's fury.

It seemed like hours—while in fact, only seconds—before the vehicle slammed back to the pavement, nose first. Airbags inflated with an explosive pop. The SUV rocked, all four tires back on solid ground, rebounding on its shock absorbers.

Then, as abruptly as it began, all was still.

Bob coughed, nose bloodied by the air bag.

He wiped it with his hand as he exhaled, hard. *"Whoa!* That was one helluva ride. But I think we're okay, Gerald."

The view through the windshield, however, had shifted from the red flash of brake lights to dual yellow orbs of oncoming traffic.

Bob seized the wheel in a death grip, his life's many decisions flashing before his eyes.

"Then again, maybe not. *Hold on, Gerald!"*

THE POLICE REPORT STATED the tanker driver, likewise recovering from the tornado's grip, tried to brake, but hydroplaned into the Lincoln Navigator facing the wrong way in I-30s eastbound lane. Over fifty accidents were spawned that night, responsible for eight fatalities as two storm systems clashed over the Dallas-Fort Worth metroplex, the most serious damage along the Grand Prairie corridor.

To be a Tsistsistas meant to know the interplay of spiritual and physical forms and to participate in it. The power of the maiyun and hematasoomao over a wide range of manifestations in the universe was empirical knowledge to each Tsistsistas.
"The Wolves of Heaven by Karl H. Schlesier, p. 190

43. EHYOPHSTAH

MASSAUM CEREMONY DAY THREE
NORTHERN CHEYENNE RESERVATION
BUSBY, MT
October 19, Friday
7:19 a.m.

Barely visible in the early morning light within the Wolf Lodge, the ashes of eight coals on which sweet grass burned the night before extended from the white cross to within a few feet of the tree. Sacred motions, songs, and prayers filled the structure as Ehyophstah was ritually created.

Entire body energized with the ceremony's power, Star assimilated the persona of Yellow Haired Woman, the human created from a young buffalo.

She stood straight as Esceheman, portrayed by Standing Dove, painted black rings around her ankles and wrists, a black sun between her breasts, a black crescent moon on her right shoulder blade, and black vertical lines on her face. One reached from her hair down her forehead to the end of her nose with three on each cheek. This paint represented her father, Nonoma.

Littlewolf as Nonoma lit a pipe and passed it to her. She smoked alone, ritually accepting the obligation of service to the *Tsistsistas* as requested by him and Grandmother Earth. As a medicine man's wife, she knew what it meant to serve her tribal sisters and brothers. Her heart swelled recalling the many years of joy it brought. Did Ehyophstah feel that same way?

Next, Littlewolf presented a pipe to White Wolf, as the male pledger. This pipe was shared among the five participants, joining Ehyophstah with a *Tsistsistas* husband witnessed by her parents and Motseyoef, keeper of the *Tsistsistas* earth. Star couldn't restrain the smile when her husband handed her the pipe and their eyes met, the ritual's power cementing their bond as never before.

A woman from the Young Wolves was called into the lodge. She was painted with the design of her society, a red line extending from her hair down to the root of her nose, the lower half of her face solid red. She would serve as messenger during the remainder of the ceremony.

She was instructed to summon the two men selected to prepare the white wolf and timber fox hides. Seven clay bowls were brought in, clear water in one and paint in the others in six colors: blue, black, white, yellow, light red, and dark red.

Littlewolf as Nonoma and Star as Ehyophstah worked on preparing *Maheone honehe*, the red male wolf hide, while the two men prepared *Evevsev honehe,* the female white wolf, and *Voh'kis,* the female timber fox, work that would consume most of the day.

LSO NEW WORKSITE
RURAL FALCON RIDGE
October, 19, Friday
2:03 p.m.

TREY'S HAND TREMBLED AS he hung up the phone, mind numbed by the news. No wonder that bad feeling when that alarm went off. His place in Texas was fine, though the parking lot flooded. Several cars suffered significant hail damage as well. Considering the weather's signature, he expected as much.

But the fact the Bentley brothers were both dead was beyond belief. Not that he was exactly a fan of either. Both were ruthless, slave-driving, money grubbers with questionable morals. He'd known both for over twenty years, yet he had to admit they'd been reasonably good bosses who treated him pretty damn good.

Now they were dead. Both of them.

A wave of guilt struck.

Was it his fault?

He'd been on Gerald like stink on shit about getting the Board to approve those bonuses.

Was that where they were coming from?

He closed his eyes and held his head for a moment before recognizing there was absolutely nothing he could do about it.

What would happen to the company? Not only was its COO and CEO dead, but LSO HQ in Arlington suffered severe damage, including destruction of much of their heavy equipment.

How could a damn rotating column of air pick up a drill rig, much less a crane?

The company's future was now in the hands of its very conservative board of directors.

He buried his face in his hands and groaned at the prospect. It would take a miracle for the company to survive.

The dual funeral would be held in Arlington on the 23rd. Of course, he would attend. In view of the situation, it was probably best to shut down the entire operation. Not only so the workers could go as well, but to learn the company's fate. Those who hailed from Texas wouldn't mind seeing their families for a few days.

His lips pressed together as he composed a list of what needed to be done to secure the site, perhaps permanently.

His neck and shoulders slumped.

So much for his dream job.

MASSAUM CEREMONY DAY THREE
NORTHERN CHEYENNE RESERVATION
BUSBY, MT
October 19, Friday
3:23 p.m.

PREPARING *MAHEONE HONEHE*, the sacred red wolf, entailed far more work than Charlie expected. Since it was only the hide with no bones to support it, the head needed to be modeled by sewing the muzzle skin and throat together, then inserting grass bundles. He was grateful for Star's help in her role as Ehyophstah, her face paint now changed from red to green, representing her mother.

Using sage branches, the hide was moistened with water the day before to soften it, awakening its distinctive scent. He and Star knelt on either side, stretching it into shape. They painted the flesh side white, combed the fur, then, from nose to ears, he painted the face blue-black, brush strokes following the hair's growth.

When dry, a multitude of narrow lines followed, painted horizontally across the muzzle and face using the four sacred colors: white, red, yellow, and black, as well as blue, the color of the Star of Midsummer Dawn.

The paints' earthy scent brought flashes of insight as he carefully traced each line while pondering the *Maheyuno* each color represented. When completed, there were fifty-five, the eleventh repetition of each color emphasized by increased width.

While the lines dried, they used the same blue-black color to paint sacred symbols on the body. These included representations of a man and his heart along the spine, the Sun, Moon, rainbows, and lightning trails on the sides, each representing part of creation.

Four small wheels, *oxzemeo*, were painted red, which represented the *maheyuno*. Star's skilled hands sewed them to the hide at the shoulders and hips. A wheel twice the size of the others, representing *Maheo,* was fastened to the middle of its back above the heart.

As Charlie watched her attach the larger *oxzemeo*, his heart leapt like a wild stag when a startling vision opened up. That of an *oxzem*, or spirit lance, sometimes known as a wheel lance.

Its resemblance to the design along the wolf's spine was striking, the most obvious difference eleven eagle feathers attached to the spirit wheel. Its stone tip was blue, the shaft red on one side, black on the other.

Each *oxzem* was otherwise unique, its design revealed by spirit helpers who inspired its keeper.

He'd nearly forgotten that Eaglefeathers had one, which was buried with him. The fine hairs on his neck stood up as he remembered his grandfather showing it to him when he was a boy, especially his bone-chilling warning to never touch it, for it would anger the spirits, who might harm him.

He stiffened as that old boyhood feeling of dread returned with a vengeance.

They were powerful weapons. It served as a direct line to *Maheo*, who was guaranteed to respond, provided the request was in accordance with his will. If not, the energy was directed to its recalcitrant owner.

Only its creator knew how to care for and use it correctly. It could be dangerous in the hands of anyone else. If its owner abused its power, it could turn on him as well.

You must build one, Okohomoxhaahketa. Build one! Fear not, you will be instructed.

He blinked as the revelation struck his soul as lightning. Trying to absorb the unexpected information, he straightened and peered about the lodge. Everyone looked busy. While the two men worked on *Voh'kis*, White Wolf and Ice worked on *Evevšev honehe*, the female white wolf.

They had just finished molding the head and were attaching a long strip of buffalo fur to it, which would trail the entire length of her body and beyond the tail. Ice reached for the polished buffalo horn tips that would be tied directly behind the wolf's ears. As he did so, he glanced up, catching Charlie's gaze, which delivered a jolt of shared perception.

The *ma'heónéhetane* smiled, nodded once, then returned to his tasks. Directive confirmed by the holy man, Charlie's mind spun.

Where would he find the needed materials?

He tried to relax, reminding himself *maiyun* never gave an order that was impossible to achieve, difficult though it might be.

He shoved his concerns to the back of his mind to address later as work continued on the red and white wolves, which controlled all animals in the four directions of the *Tsistsistas* universe.

At noon, food was brought in that consisted of four categories provided by the Creator: meat, food from plants that grow underground (potatoes), from the ground (corn), and above ground (chokecherries). Five small portions of each were placed at the base of the world tree and under each of the *maheyuno* bundles.

The remainder was passed reverently among those present in the lodge. The five main participants would not eat again until the conclusion of the final day of the ceremony.

Charlie smiled when sounds of construction activity outside indicated the *Hohnuhka* lodge was being erected between the Wolf Lodge and where the animal lodges would be set up the following day. So far everyone was fulfilling their responsibilities as assigned to assure the *Massaum* was conducted correctly.

True to the Contrary principle that dictated everything was done opposite to the norm, its poles were on the outside, lodge cover inside out, and smoke flaps directed the wrong way.

The tipi that contained the sacred arrows was placed southeast of the Wolf Lodge.

As evening settled upon the Camp Circle, again the *Maheonox* transformed to a Spirit Lodge. Eight more coals were laid next to the ashes of the previous row. Sweet grass was placed upon them, their sweet vapors blessing the lodge while sacred songs were taught, including those of the wolf spirits that would bring life to their labors. The veil lifted, ancestral spirits joining the celebration, dancing and rejoicing with their mortal progeny as all that *Maheo* promised was being restored.

AS CHARLIE PRAYED WITHIN the *Maheonox* that night, another vision appeared within the fire.

"Listen well, grandson, and I will direct you in building an *oxzem,*" Eaglefeathers said. "It has a special purpose for what will occur at Dead Horse Canyon."

"I am listening, Grandfather. What must I do?"

"Smoke and pray to Sovota. He will send Nonoma to help you."

Charlie felt everyone's questioning eyes upon him as he picked up the pipe with the sack of tobacco and left the *Maheonox.*

Outside, he turned right, finding the corner post that marked the southwest, Sovota's home. The waxing moon was high in the sky, casting eerie shadows on the ground below. Like his painted skin, Mars in the western sky also glowed red.

He blessed himself with the earth, made the sacred motions, and offered the pipe to the *maheyuno* in the four directions. He loaded and lit it in the prescribed way, then puffed four times to bless it with the smoke. He puffed again, watching the smoke ascend before starting to pray.

"Sovota. Please help me. My grandfather, Eaglefeathers, told me to seek your help. I am instructed to build an *oxzem.*"

He opened his eyes and gazed upon *Seozemeo,* the concentration of stars known to *Veheo* as the Milky Way, Saturn in its midst farther west, soon to set. Smoke spiraled upward in that direction, seeking communion with the stars.

Moments later the heavens opened, releasing a bird-of-prey. It soared high above him, silhouette occulting the stars. Its size expanded as it neared the ground, beating its mighty wings. The earth trembled as the raptor landed, looming over him with its red eyes aglow.

In its beak was a stick about five feet long, which it dropped at Charlie's feet.

"May I touch it?" he asked, shuddering as again his grandfather's admonition rang warning bells in his head.

"Yes," the raptor boomed. "It is not yet endowed with power. You are charged to finish its construction."

Charlie picked it up, gingerly at first, then more confidently. While he sensed its energy potential, at least it didn't zap him into oblivion. One side was red, the other black, colors barely discernible in the moonlight. Its center was already carved with the figure of a man, four branch stubs for arms and legs.

"Construct the rest as *maiyun* directs, then return tomorrow," the raptor instructed.

"I know where to obtain everything but the eagle feathers," Charlie responded. "I have not yet earned enough of my own."

The giant bird's ember-like eyes fixed on him as if he were prey. "If you have not the will to find the materials, how will you endow it with power?"

Before he could answer, the apparition ascended, leaving behind a fiery wake of sparks, drifting lazily toward the ground.

He admonished himself for the foolish comment, then, stick in hand, looked around for the needed resources.

The hoop would be easy. As expected, a young chokecherry bush a few yards outside the camp circle had the branches he needed. He cut off two about four feet long. Finding sinew or leather strips for the woven center, which resembled an oversized dream catcher, wouldn't be a problem with plenty unused after constructing the lodge.

A stone point for the tip shouldn't be difficult, either. The arrowhead he and Winter Hawk found on Eaglefeathers Butte would be perfect, but it was back at the house, over a quarter mile away. Surely there was something nearby.

An impression beckoned him to the grove where they harvested the World Tree. Grateful for the moonlight, he meandered in that direction, watching the ground for suitable rocks.

He made his way through the brush to the grove, halting when a red squirrel blocked his path. It chattered angrily, as if in rebuke for invading its territory. This species was usually not out at night, which in itself was odd, except moonlight could have lured him from his den.

"Hello, little friend," he said, squatting down. "Do you have a message for me?"

The feisty critter scampered a few yards forward, then turned, chattering again.

He smiled. *Thunder sent a squirrel?*

Then again, why not?

He followed, watching for anything he could use. The small animal ran a few yards, then scampered up a nearby cottonwood, one Ice rejected earlier due to its size. It turned around, nose facing the ground, and chattered again.

Moonlight filtered by near-naked branches barely illuminated a small, circular scar in the bark at eye level. He probed the depression with his finger, finding something hard lodged within.

He set down the shaft, got out his knife, and pried it out.

A perfectly formed arrowhead dropped into his palm. He examined it, grinning. Likely a shot gone awry, decades before. In his mind's eye, he saw the wayward arrow, fired at an elk by none other than his grandfather.

"*Néá'eše,*" he said, thanking both the squirrel and Eaglefeathers.

He returned to the *Maheonox*, planning to finish as much of the remaining work he could that night.

44. HESZEPOXSZ

MASSAUM CEREMONY DAY FOUR
NORTHERN CHEYENNE RESERVATION
BUSBY, MT
October 20, Saturday
7:23 a.m.

A busy day lay ahead. As the final day of preparations for its climax the following day, excitement charged the air. A hundred yards beyond the Wolf Lodge, a second camp circle was under construction. It symbolized the *heszepoxsz*, dens below the Sacred Mountain, where all animal spirits resided. When the tipis were set up, the multitudes assigned to impersonate the animals would go inside.

Charlie and the other main performers remained in the Wolf Lodge along with their helpers. Mind abuzz with what yet needed to be done, to say nothing of building his *oxzem*, he explained to two men how to prepare walking sticks from four freshly cut cottonwood branches that would represent the wolves' front legs.

Next, still in his role as Nonoma, he explained to Ehyophstah's husband, *i.e.*, White Wolf, how to prepare the pipe that would be used to call the animals.

He handed him a ball of sinew. "First, close the bottom with this. Then load it with four portions of this," he said, handing him a deerskin bag of smoking material comprised of herbs mixed with buffalo kidney fat. "This symbolizes all plant and animal life. Then seal the opening with a piece of animal fat."

White Wolf nodded understanding and set to work, as instructed.

When the pipe was complete, Star as Ehyophstah moved coals from the fire and placed sweetgrass upon them. She made the sacred motions, then took the pipe from her husband and purified it in the smoke, infusing it with life. Next, she placed it in front of the decorated buffalo skull.

The look Star and White Wolf exchanged as she took the pipe from his hands impaled Charlie's heart like an arrow. The love and devotion between them was solid. White Wolf's words admonishing him at Sara's about not being married blared through memory.

He hung his head. He should have known better. That was not the Cheyenne way. He'd been married, faithfully, even though he wasn't happy. He and Rosina had sexual relations before they were married, yet he noticed a difference once they were legally bound. He owed Sara a serious apology.

Seven Young Wolves came into the lodge, drawing his attention back to the ceremony. They represented wolf spirit helpers charged with constructing the pound. They all made the sacred motions, Charlie purified them with sweetgrass smoke, then focused on describing how and where the pound should be built.

He sketched a drawing on the ground, then explained how to erect a corral, twenty feet away from the Wolf Lodge. A high, crescent-shaped shade would be made using lodge poles and coverings. Its entrance would face the opening in the camp circle and *Novavose*.

The wings of the drive lane would be constructed from freshly cut cottonwood trees and branches, gathered the day before. These would be embedded in the ground, extending from the two sides of the shade in two long lines to just beyond the animals lodges, but before reaching the opening in the *Tsistsistas* camp circle.

After that, the Young Wolves were instructed to raise three tripod frames in the narrow space between the rear of the corral and Wolf Lodge entrance to hold the skins that had been so meticulously prepared.

SARA'S CABIN
RURAL FALCON RIDGE
COLORADO
October 20, Saturday
4:14 p.m.

TWO DOZEN BLUE porta-potties arrived on a flatbed trailer, lined up like so many Tardis units for a Dr. Who convention. Sara wrinkled her nose at the silly comparison, no doubt prompted by science fiction aficionado, Bryan. Such impressions came frequently out there, so much so she considered them normal. She snickered at the crazy possibility of some unsuspecting user getting transported to another time and place.

It was a relief when the tractor miraculously made it up the dirt road to the event site, where they were lined up along the west side. Her original anxiety about helping had settled comfortably to excitement at what might occur.

When that was done, she texted Charlie the toilet facilities were in place, allowing him to scratch one more concern off his list. He hadn't responded to any so far, but she wasn't surprised, assuming he was deep into *Gathering* activities, whatever they might be. He never explained exactly what they were doing, but she sensed its importance.

His people had been conducting such get-togethers for a long time with it unlikely it had been this complicated, back-in-the-day. No doubt they would have simply done their business like the proverbial bear in the woods.

She shuddered. The thought of hundreds or even a thousand Native Americans, or anyone else, for that matter, doing that on her property, however, was definitely less than enchanting.

She gazed about the area, imagining it filled with tipis and hundreds of Charlie's people. Curiosity sparkled through her, the thought of being part of an historical event hard to imagine.

The convergence of energies, however, was palpable. Patrice's words came to mind, and so far she'd never been wrong. Intuition prompted there was definitely some connection with that curse. She shivered chills down her spine, invigorating as well as terrifying.

MASSAUM CEREMONY DAY FOUR
NORTHERN CHEYENNE RESERVATION
BUSBY, MT
October 20, Saturday
4:23 p.m.

AS NONOMA'S SPECIAL HELPER, Winter Hawk instructed the woman from the Young Wolf Society to bring the men into the Wolf Lodge who would impersonate the two wolf spirits. Upon their arrival, Littlewolf as Nonoma purified them with sweetgrass in the usual ceremonial way, then explained to them what to do in their respective roles.

Winter Hawk stood by listening, arms folded, while his brother echoed to the two men what they'd both been told on the Sacred Mountain. He shuffled his feet, humbled, yet at the same time, complimented, that Littlewolf trusted him to paint them as the ones who would wear the wolves' attire later that evening.

His brother said he had something he needed to do and asked if he would mind filling in.

Mind? He was honored by his trust. Having helped paint Littlewolf for his fast bolstered his confidence, to say nothing of witnessing the entire *Massaum* with him at *Novavose*.

Yes, he knew how it should be done.

The first man stripped to a breechclout and moccasins. Winter Hawk carefully and somewhat gingerly began applying the red paint, acutely aware of its earthy scent. Even the man's hair needed to be painted, which was more laborious, taking much longer to assure all the black was covered.

Painting the second man he was just as careful, but more confident, so it went faster. Covering his black hair with white, however, took even longer.

By the time he finished that, the red paint on the first man was dry so he added black rings around his ankles and wrists, a black sun on his chest, and black moon on his right shoulder blade. He then added the same markings to the man painted white.

He had both men turn around so he could inspect his work and make sure he hadn't missed any spots. He bit back a smile at the thought of telling his teenage friends what he'd gotten to do, yet realized that would probably be wrong. As far as he could tell, they had little understanding for sacred things. They already thought he was crazy or even weird, so why share it?

The two men looked fine, but he wasn't done. His parents were next. They, too, were to be painted to ritually prepare them for their roles as Ehyophstah and her husband. Their charge was to bring the animal spirits from the sacred mountain out into the world.

It felt strange, but good, to paint their bodies and hair red, then add the same black designs the wolf impersonators wore.

The look in his father's eyes as he did so brought another homogenized blast of humility and pride. Too solemn of a ritual to smile, his father's eyes said it all. He admired White Wolf more than anyone else on Escheman's earth and his approval meant everything, though he certainly couldn't discount the love he felt emanating from his mother's tearful eyes, which brought moisture to his own as well.

While they waited for the paint to dry before getting dressed again, another Young Wolf came in to report the pound was complete. By this time, Littlewolf was back, just in time to see him finish painting his mother's hair. His brother's nod of approval likewise ignited a fire in his soul.

Littlewolf, back in his role as Nonoma, sent out a crier to inform the camp circle occupants the sacred animals were coming out.

His parents made the sacred motions, then prepared to take out *Maheone honehe*. Hands together, they stood over the red wolf. After reaching toward it three times, with a fourth they touched its back. With four motions they lifted him, then moved him so his head protruded beneath the raised lodge cover for a moment before carrying him out. With four motions, they placed him on the first frame.

Next, *Evevšev honehe* was taken out in the same manner, then *Voh'kis*, the timber fox.

When they returned to the *Maheonox*, the first public part of the ceremony began. People came out of their lodges to gaze upon the three animals from a respectful distance.

Those assigned to portray the rest of the animals on the coming and final day were required to stay in the animal lodges, the actors already considered to be in their respective animal roles.

When the people dispersed, his parents brought the three animals back into Wolf Lodge.

As evening fell, all lodges were closed, fires extinguished, and dogs kept inside. No one was allowed to move within or without the camp circle.

Inside the Wolf Lodge, by the light of the sacred fire, Winter Hawk helped Littlewolf set the red wolf on the man's back, tie it securely, then place the walking sticks in his hands. His fingers caressed the soft fur, imagining what it would be like to pet a live wolf.

Maheone honehe left the lodge accompanied by the *whoosh* of buffalo rattles and a majestic chorus of wolf songs that enlivened the structure. Rapid footfalls sounded outside along the right wing of the drive lane, fading to barely audible as he continued out into the prairie, where he turned right.

Upon reaching the first of the sacred directions, he howled the calling song of the master wolf. Goosebumps tickled Winter Hawk's arms as the eerie sound echoed throughout the lodge.

The red wolf circled the camp, calling from the other three sacred directions while making a small circle at each. The footsteps got louder as he passed back through the camp opening, ran outside the left wing of the brush lane, turned through the corral, then slipped back inside, panting.

Next, Winter Hawk helped put *Evevšev honehe* on the runner's back. More rattles and wolf songs filled the air as the female white wolf left the lodge and ran along the right wing of the brush lane. Footfalls faded beyond the animal lodge camp circle, then turned right within the *Tsistsistas* circle.

Footsteps pattered between the two rings of lodges, stopping at the four sacred directions with calling songs. The runner entered beside the left brush lane and ran inside, just as *Atovsz*, the Sun Spirit, dipped beneath the horizon.

With darkness, again the Wolf Lodge became a spirit lodge. Another line of eight coals topped with sweetgrass glowed beside those from previous evenings. It was the last night of teaching the *Tsistsistas* the calling songs of all animal spirits.

As they sang surrounding the fire, Winter Hawk's eyes connected with those of his brother with whom he'd shared the remarkable experience on *Novavose*.

As spectacular as that was, it was nothing compared to the spiritual fire awakening his soul.

TWILIGHT'S MAGIC SETTLED on the camp, transforming it to the universe. Everything was made holy, inside and out. Beyond the camp circle, time stood still. Animal lodges became *heszepoxsz,* the dens of animal spirits in the deep earth of Escheman's realm.

As Charlie left the *Maheonox* for his rendezvous with Nonoma's raptor representative, he was troubled. He'd found everything he needed for the *oxzem* except the feathers. The rest was relatively easy and in ready supply. Thanks to Winter Hawk's help that afternoon, he had time to put it together as far as he could with what he had.

It was earlier than the night before, but if he had to wait, so be it. It was well into twilight, a rosy pink glow all that remained of the day. He looked up, wondering if the messenger would come from the same place as the night before.

He gasped upon recognizing the rare spectacle greeting him from the heavens above. All planets visible with the naked eye were lined up in the evening sky.

Venus, the original morning star, shone in all her splendor. Just above her, moving west to east, glowed Mercury, then Jupiter. Slightly higher reigned Saturn, then Mars, a sparkling red orb high in the sky. The rising Moon, *Ameonito,* waxed toward full glory, a new phase coming a few days hence.

He marveled, knowing *Maheo* was blessing their efforts with a sign. He returned inside and called the others to witness the rare spectacle. If they had a telescope, they could have seen that all the planets were above the horizon, even Uranus, Neptune, and Pluto, but invisible to the naked eye.

After the others went back inside, he returned to the southwestern pole, made the sacred motions, and sat down cross-legged with the unfinished *oxzem* across his knees. He offered the pipe to the four sacred directions, acknowledging each *Maheyuno*, then loaded and lit it.

As it had the previous night, the smoke floated toward *Seozemeo.* He closed his eyes and prayed, hard, pleading for mercy and forgiveness from the Thunder spirit because he had not found the needed feathers.

He poured out his heart and soul, wondering if Thunder would strike him dead for his failure. No doubt Eaglefeathers was shaking his head, as he had so many times when he was a foolish and rebellious youth.

When something soft touched his right knee, he wondered if the squirrel *maiyun* had returned to help again. He opened his eyes.

All twelve feathers were perfectly attached, eleven to the wheel, and one at the top.

He prayed again to express his gratitude, then asked what must he do to bring it to life?

No answer came.

To be Tsistsistas meant to know the interplay of spiritual and physical forms and to participate in it. The power of the maiyun and hematasoomao over a wide range of manifestations in the universe was empirical knowledge to each Tsistsistas. If this had not been so, this world description would neither have developed nor would it have existed through an enormous number of generations.
"Wolves of Heaven," by Karl H. Schlesier, p. 190

45. NANEOV MEOHOTOXC

MASSAUM CEREMONY DAY FIVE
NORTHERN CHEYENNE RESERVATION
BUSBY, MT
October 21, Sunday
6:18 a.m.

Anticipation filled the Wolf Lodge. As it was the nights before, the only light was from the fire, sunrise over an hour away. Another row of coals topped with sweetgrass crumbled to ashes beside the previous ones.

White Wolf had pledged, instructed, and observed a vast variety of ceremonies during his lifetime. His senses were on full alert, perceiving this one possessed an energy he'd never experienced before.

Was it the sheer complexity?

Its duration?

Number of participants?

He didn't know.

Only that it stirred something within the unseen realm.

While it was still dark, he and the other main performers got ready for the final day. Two painters, as well as the three men who would impersonate the wolves and timber fox, joined them.

Everyone including himself, Littlewolf, Ice, Ice's wife, and Star were again painted red. This time as the paint was applied, its

442

touch lacked the charge he felt when Winter Hawk had done so the day before.

Escheman applied the same black wrist and ankle rings, Sun, and Moon to him and Star as well as the wolf runners. The timber fox runner was painted yellow, black vertical lines under his eyes, blue dots running along his sides from his ankles to his shoulders, as well as along the outside of his arms to his wrists.

He watched as Standing Dove as Escheman painted the blue star on his own precious Star's face. Its four sections spread across her forehead, eyes, and nose. Then White Wolf was painted the same way. Their eyes met, his love for her invigorated by their portrayal of the sacred roles.

Sacred paint delivered the wearer to the world of spirits. The sense of being an observer from another world was real. Like the veil had parted, allowing sights usually hidden from mortal eyes.

The lodge cover rustled as Seven Young Wolves entered, also painted with the blue star.

Littlewolf signaled it was time. White Wolf ducked beneath the lodge cover and proceeded outside. The October morning's frosty touch was cold where the paint had not yet dried. He paused a moment for his eyes to adjust, sky ablaze with stars. He proceeded south of the lodge. Even in the dimmest of light, he could see the bleached buffalo skull he was to deliver to the pound entrance.

He placed it on the ground halfway between the ends of the shade, facing the open space of the drive lane, then returned to the lodge.

As dawn approached, he took Star's hand as they accompanied Littlewolf, Ice, and Standing Dove leaving the lodge first. They faced southeast, awaiting a signal from the sky.

If the ceremony were being performed at its usual time in the summer, Rigel, represented by the blue star on their faces, would appear, shine brightly for a moment, then dim and disappear.

But not in October.

Nonetheless, Littlewolf instructed them to watch. *Maheo* would provide a sign. The sky above was dark except for its multitude of stars, planets from the night before already set, Moon nearing the western horizon.

Abruptly, a brilliant light appeared where Rigel would rise in June. A collective breath escaped, then became a cry of joy when moments later the meteor exploded, celestial fireworks streaking the sky.

The performers entered the corral where they sat in a line with the skull in the middle. Standing Dove and Star on the left, Littlewolf, White Wolf, and Ice on right. The seven women of the Young Wolf Society came out and sat behind them. The red and white wolf and timber fox runners joined them as well, sitting on the other side of Star.

A sacred straight pipe was placed in front of the buffalo skull on a bed of white sage. Inside the left corner of the enclosure, Littlewolf's un-activated lance speared a sheet of dried buffalo meat on the ground.

WINTER HAWK'S EXCITEMENT peaked as the ceremonial hunt began, the most exciting part of the *Massaum*. This was what all those laborious preparations were all about.

He stood with the other helpers outside the Wolf Lodge as the timber fox emerged and followed the same trail as the white wolf the evening before. She howled from the four sacred directions, cry a higher pitch than that of the wolves. Moments later, she entered the drive lane and corral.

Littlewolf removed the timber fox skin from the runner and placed it on the buffalo skull, facing the opening of the drive lane and *Novavose*.

Tipis in the camp circle opened and their occupants looked out. A murmur of excitement rode the predawn breeze. Hackles tickled his arms when a commotion arose from the *heszepoxsz* as costumed, masked, painted impersonators of a multitude of species spilled from their dens.

Electrified with awe, Winter Hawk's mouth hung open at the spectacle such as he'd never seen. Herd animals and those that lived in small groups emerged in bands. The illusion that they were actual buffalo, elk, deer, and antelopes sent his spirit aloft. The costumes themselves were remarkable, their impersonator's actions astounding in how authentic they appeared. Individual gaits, antics, interaction, cries, and behavior left little to the imagination.

He remembered his mother and many tribal sisters working on them, night and day, ever since they returned from *Novavose*. His brother, Risingsun, was out there somewhere, disguised as a young antelope, along with his older siblings who'd come from near and far with their families. For a moment he almost wished he'd chosen to participate rather than help Littlewolf. Upon giving it more thought, however, he realized he wouldn't trade that experience for anything.

Otters, wolves, and cranes followed the herd animals. Coyotes, badgers, beavers, grizzly bears, black bears, cougars, different kinds of foxes, eagles, hawks, ravens, magpies, all paraded in a sun-wise direction between the *Tsistsistas* camp circle and animal lodges, before hordes of enchanted spectators.

The cacophony of sounds was hypnotic, convincing him for a moment these were not impersonators, but live animals.

Then, for an instant, it flashed as memory of a distant time. Witness to the creation itself, including the emergence of *Maheo's* creatures from the Sacred Mountain.

WITHIN THE CORRAL, STAR stood perfectly still as Standing Dove lifted the sacred pipe in a ceremonial way, then placed it in her hands. Followed by the seven Young Wolves, they walked between the wings of the pound. For several moments they stood quietly, praying. Then Star offered the pipe toward the opening and *Novavose*, calling the animals.

"*Naneov meohotoxc*! I am the star of dawn!" she cried out, her own spirit soaring as she announced her sacred position as master spirit of grassland animals given to *Tsistsistas* guardianship.

Maheone honehe, Evevšev honehe, and *Voh'kis* left the enclosure and ran along the stream of animals, forcing them to complete a full circle around the animal camp before entering the drive lane. Calling songs filled the air as the animals came in and surrounded Star, Standing Dove, and the other women.

From the *Hohnunka* lodge, seven contraries portraying thunder spirits ran up, dressed in breechclouts with their body and hair painted white. Their hair was knotted over their forehead where it was impaled with a single eagle feather. Each carried a miniature sky lance painted red.

They mingled with the sacred animals, milling about, ritually killing with stabbing motions. Animals who were struck staggered and fell, feigning injuries.

While the animal impersonators had already done an amazing job, their portrayal of being injured and bleeding was extraordinary. Star shivered as screeching cries and pain-laced wails filled the air, sufficiently real to bring tears to her eyes.

After the animals completed their display around the women, they exited through the brush lane and returned to their dens.

While they were going back, the doctoring portion of the *Massaum* began. Those who were ill, disabled, or wanted a blessing from the animal spirits sat motionless in front of their lodges. When passing, the animals performed brief ceremonial healing or cleansing rituals. *Hohnunka,* who were asked to treat patients in their mysterious contrary way, also did so at this time.

The women returned to their places in the corral while the animals left the pound.

They waited.

When the animal lodges closed, the second hunt began.

Star stood tall, quivering with excitement while Standing Dove placed *Evevšev honehe* on her back with the wolf's head projecting over her forehead. She glanced up at its nose above her own, as the hide touched her back while her instructor tied it in place.

Then, followed by the Young Wolves, they went to the middle of the drive lane and walked in a circle. By wearing the wolf *maiyun,* Star as Ehyophstah proclaimed Nonoma's red master wolf to be her servant.

Again, animals streamed from their lodges and the actions of the preceding hunt were repeated three more times. At the conclusion of the last, Ehyophstah again stood with the sacred pipe.

The group of women stood silently among the dancing, colorful spectacle of animals as they were prodded by *Hohunuka* hunters. Ehyophstah offered the pipe to the animal spirits one last time. This time, the animals did not return to their dens. Instead, they stood by to watch the last acts to be performed in the corral.

By this time it was midday.

Esceheman, Ehyophstah, and the Young Wolves returned to the corral. The sacred pipe rested again on a bed of man sage. Nonoma placed a sheet of dried buffalo meat on the grass in front of the buffalo skull. He handed his medicine lance to Ehyophstah and her husband with ceremony.

With four motions, they drove its tip through the meat, raised the lance, then deposited its blunt end in a hole near the buffalo skull.

CHARLIE, AS NONOMA, placed four buffalo chips marking the four sacred directions on the grass a few yards away from the lance.

The male red wolf runner placed his hands and feet on the buffalo chips, facing the medicine lance, skull, and five performers. By doing so, he declared the master wolf's power over hunting game to the four sacred directions.

A coyote came next, and after three feints, crawled through beneath *Maheone honehe*, symbolizing the dominance of the red wolf over all other predators.

Next, *Voh'kis* made three false motions, then with the fourth ripped dried meat from the lance. This signaled the arrival of hunting time and the end of four successful hunts by making the food of sacred animals available for distribution.

Moments later, *Hohnuhka* snatched the meat from the timber fox and tore it into seven pieces. They ran out in seven directions through the *Tsistsistas* camp where they distributed tiny pieces of meat to everyone to share the animal food blessed by the spirits.

Coyote led the animal groups out into the prairie toward *Novavose*. The joyful mass of animals stopped four times before they reached Eaglefeathers Creek, a *Massaum* song sung at each stop.

After the fourth, a race took place that brought all to the water's edge. Everyone took a drink, ritually ending the fast. On returning, the animals stopped four times to sing another *Massaum* song, then dispersed upon reaching the drive lane.

The *Hohnuhka* returned to their lodge for the brushing off ritual that ended their contrary condition.

All throughout the camp, *Tsistsistas* ended the ceremony using sage for the brushing that returned them to their earthly condition.

ICE TOOK STANDING DOVE'S hand as they returned to the Wolf Lodge with the others. It had been awhile since they shared such a deeply moving and inspiring experience. He knew something notable would come as a result. Whether they would live long enough to see it had been in question.

Not anymore.

What exactly would follow, he wasn't sure, but it would be unforgettable.

Back inside the Wolf Lodge, the five spirits took the positions they had when the earth was made. Ice squeezed his wife's hand before letting go to sit alone on the Southeast side, behind the *Tsistsistas* earth. She sat on the sage, south of the decorated buffalo skull, followed by Nonoma, Ehyophstah, and her husband.

White Wolf's elder son helped remove the wolf and timber fox hides from their runners. Ice couldn't remember when he'd been so impressed by a young man's spirit. His old friend, Eaglefeathers, was deservingly proud to have such strong-spirited progeny as him and Littlewolf.

Ehyophstah brought the sacred pipe to him as Motseyoef. Ice broke the seal and lit it. Passed it to the others, who returned it to him, repeating the sequence until it was smoked completely. Using the pipe stick, he placed the ashes in four motions upon the *Tsistsistas* earth in front of him.

Then he brushed the ashes and earth symbol to the fire pit, leaving no trace on the clean, smooth ground.

Nonoma arose and erased the sand painting of the universe beside the world tree. One by one, he brushed each of the other performers with a small bundle of man sage, touching them lightly along both sides of their bodies from their heads to the earth, bringing them back to their mortal state and concluding the *Massaum*.

ALL LEFT THE LODGE in reverent silence, clinging to the ceremony's magic while taking the animal hides, rattles, pipe, Charlie's lance, and other sacred articles with them.

The next day, the Young Wolves would remove the cover of the Wolf Lodge. Because it served as the Sacred Mountain, it belonged to the spirits. Thus, they would take it to Eaglefeathers Creek where they would place it gently in the waters.

The World Tree, Wolf Lodge, and its twenty-eight-pole frame were left standing.

Before dawn the following day, the camp would break up while the Cheyenne leaders and medicine men, as well as several other tribes who were part of the *Gathering*, departed for Colorado.

In the old days, the various bands would depart to their fall locations, where the impounding of real game in accordance with the *Massaum* law would begin.

And the Great Spirit spoke to us saying: Take this message to my red children and tell it to them as I say it. I have neglected the Indians for many moons, but I will make them my people now if they obey me in this message. The earth is getting old and I will make it new for my chosen people, the Indians, who are to inhabit it, and among them will be all those of their ancestors who have died, their fathers, mothers, brothers, cousins, and wives.
—*Kicking Bear, 1890*

46. DEPARTING

NORTHERN CHEYENNE RESERVATION
MONTANA
October 22, Monday
5:02 a.m.

Before dawn the next morning, Charlie stood outside the first coach of five leaving from Busby. Its interior lights were on, the purr of diesel engines teasing the still, cold air. A multitude of stars blazed overhead, Grandmother Moon skimming the horizon as she prepared to set, last of the planetary parade he'd witnessed two nights before.

His mind and soul still floated, swamped in the afterglow of the *Massaum*. Ideally, he would have preferred some time to absorb it before delving into the next phase of the *Gathering*, but the schedule demanded otherwise. Two weeks was a long time for this many leaders to be away from their people and tribal responsibilities.

He glanced down the long line of brothers and sisters waiting to get onboard. He and White Wolf were assisting each one with a flashlight as they dropped off their bags in the cargo bins, then climbed onboard for the trip to Colorado.

Another ten buses were picking up *Gathering* guests at their hotels in Billings, Sheridan, and Lame Deer. The plan was to rendezvous at 8:00 a.m. at the Common Cents Travel Plaza, also in Sheridan, where they would become a fifteen-coach caravan, at least for a while. It would eventually break up again as each made meal stops in different locations, due to being such a lengthy procession.

While White Wolf knew all the Cheyenne leaders and healers, whom he introduced to Charlie, they were mostly meeting those from other tribes for the first time, other than the few who arrived early for the *Massaum*.

While the next passenger searched for a place in the bins for his bags amid the others, to say nothing of the multitude of Cheyenne tipis to house everyone, Charlie turned to White Wolf.

"Do you think it would be safe in there?" he asked, nodding toward his lance.

White Wolf's look was pensive. "If anything shifts, it could break. But if it's not yet active, it won't hurt anything else."

Charlie's muscles tensed, that not being his concern. He licked his lips. "I, uh, don't want to appear arrogant, having it onboard."

White Wolf didn't agree. "If Thunder spirits directed you to build one, then it is rightfully yours. It will bring respect. Do you have instructions to activate it?"

"Not yet. If I'm to use it at Dead Horse Canyon, I'm sure the spirits will speak."

White Wolf's eyes gleamed. "Indeed, they will."

The next passenger was ready, a Lakota healer, probably in his early sixties. The man paused prior to stepping onboard, scrutinizing Charlie with noticeable intensity. He felt a resonance as well, curious where the connection originated. With a respectful nod, he noted his observation.

"I feel as if I know you, my brother. But I do not recognize your face, only your presence."

The elder's chiseled features, reminiscent of Red Cloud, arranged into one of recognition.

"You were not aware when we last met. You were in a hospital bed in Belton. I am Leaping Elk. A few months ago, I was called to perform a healing for you. It is good to see how well you have recovered."

452

His heart warmed with gratitude. "No wonder I feel I know you. Your energy has mingled with mine in a most memorable way. Thank you. I remembered hearing Lakota, but I was so out of it, I thought it another hallucination. It is a great privilege to meet you. Without your help, I might not have been here today. Thank you again."

The elder waved him off. "Not true. It was not your time. But I am grateful to have assisted."

"I, too, am very grateful. It is an honor to meet you."

The two shook hands, White Wolf holding his out as well. "We spoke on the phone," he said, introducing himself. "I had a dream he was coming home, which your call confirmed. I thank you as well."

"You're welcome. I'm glad I could help and we could finally meet."

Leaping Elk stepped onto the bus while Charlie and White Wolf continued the loading and boarding processes.

So much time was spent explaining the *Massaum* and its meaning as the "Earth-Giving Ceremony" that little was spent during their in-person and online presentations about the promise contained in the *Dance of Peace and Welcome*.

Some were aware of it as the Ghost Dance, but most of what they knew was inaccurate and left out the most important part. Furthermore, the skepticism and unbelief instilled by the white man's culture compromised many, rendering their beliefs and prophecies to the ranks of superstition and folklore.

Charlie knew that syndrome, having been its victim for many years.

Even now, he was ashamed he still harbored a smidgen of doubt, in spite of all he'd seen. While his spirit soared with hope, he had yet to see any tangible results, other than Sara's miraculous healing and his visions. He performed a few routine healings on his own, but it took master healer, Porcupine, to summon *Maheo* to bring her back to full health.

Nonetheless, what could seven hundred forty-four tribal leaders and healers accomplish? Especially when almost half were medicine men at least as skilled as White Wolf, a few like Ice, even more. If the likes of Eaglefeathers returned in spirit along with his other progenitors going back seven generations, no telling what they could accomplish.

When that bus was full, they moved to the next, the end of the boarding line mere silhouettes partially immersed in the coaches" boarding lights, Moon having set and Sun still hiding.

Nonetheless, the atmosphere was one of joy, as it always was when Indigenous people gathered, living evidence their cultures survived attempted annihilation.

When the last person finally boarded, White Wolf gave him a questioning look. Charlie directed the flashlight to his clipboard.

"Three are unaccounted for," he replied.

"I will see if they boarded other buses while we were loading." He exited their bus and took off down the row of coaches.

Charlie stepped onboard to set his wheel lance between the seat and the window, then back outside until White Wolf returned moments later.

"They were beckoned onboard other buses by brothers they hadn't seen in years, not realizing we were counting heads," he explained.

Charlie nodded, satisfied. Moments later, began their journey. It was just after seven with a little over an hour ride to Sheridan. He said a silent prayer the coordinators for the other buses did their job and all would also arrive fairly close to eight.

Charlie and White Wolf occupied the front seat as the coach bumped and swayed along the rough road to the highway. The ride smoothed out when they got to Highway 212, the group immersed in casual conversation until they reached Interstate 90.

The route was purposeful, not the shortest.

The reason was obvious when they came within range of the Little Bighorn Battlefield, bathed in the light of early dawn. They couldn't afford the time for everyone to disembark, but stopped for a few minutes, allowing everyone to meditate on the scene and pray for their success in Colorado.

After that, they sang, whooped, and rejoiced at will.

All except their black driver, whose stiff posture suggested concern for his personal safety.

RANIER OFFICE BUILDING
WASHINGTON, D.C.
October 22, Monday
10:21 a.m. EDT

MYRON BENTLEY SAT IN his expansive corner office on the ninth-floor, overlooking the Washington Mall. While he'd heard the news two days before, it had yet to sink in.

How could both his sons be dead?

The timing couldn't be worse. He was master of ceremonies at the PURF Open House the following day.

The day of his son's double funeral.

He asked both those bitches his boys married to put it off a day or two, but they refused.

They hated him and the feeling was mutual. Of course, they wouldn't do him any favors. If they were aware of the inconvenience it caused, it would have given them even more satisfaction.

The previous Friday he had Ingrid check, after which she confirmed that neither Bob nor Gerald, much less their respective spouses, were on the confirmed guest list. Yes, they were invited, and yes, she made personal contact.

He snarled with derision. So that was how it was. They wouldn't even support him in his moment of glory. After all he'd done for them.

Including sandbagging LSO into the geothermal contract. His financial interests in the company were signed over to them as soon as he accepted the job in D.C. Every dime of those profits went straight into their burgeoning bank accounts. Their ungrateful wives sure didn't have a problem with their luxurious life-styles, courtesy of him.

Not that his resignation from LSO was much of a sacrifice. His new lobbying career assured continued profits for the company he founded, which would wind up in his sons' hands eventually, anyway. Essentially, it worked as intended to expand the family fortune.

A fortune that began over a century before, when his ancestors made the westward trek, right into what would ultimately become PURF's neighborhood. Previously, it had been part of the land grant claimed by Bentley Silver and Lead Mining Associates in the mid-1800s. Leasing the property to the government instead of selling it guaranteed the family a tidy annual income as well.

His sons slapped him in the face by refusing to come to the open house, then, as the *coup de grace*, got their sorry asses killed in a wreck with a Texaco oil tanker.

A competitor, no less, where he originally got his start as an oilman.

Now he had a dilemma. If he didn't show up for their funerals, he'd look like a total asshole.

He glared out his window. So what?

He could piss on their graves any time. It didn't have to be when the dirt was still fresh.

He couldn't think of a single reason why he needed to go. Bob and Gerald certainly wouldn't care. It might be entertaining to taunt their wives, but that had questionable value as well.

Screw it.

His fellows appreciated the time and effort he invested that made PURF a reality. They recognized his role and honored him for it. His sons barely said "Thanks, Dad" when he signed the company over to them.

Rotten ingrates.

Dilemma, hell. There wasn't one. If the situation were reversed, he had no doubts what they'd do.

No, the following day he'd be where he belonged.

And it sure as hell wasn't Texas.

COACH CARAVAN
EN ROUTE DENVER
October 22, Monday
9:22 a.m.

FOLLOWING THEIR RENDEZVOUS in Sheridan, Charlie texted leaders in the other buses it was time for another online session. If all those with cell phones tuned in, everyone would hear what he had to say.

Charlie stood next to his front seat and whistled for attention. White Wolf manned his phone to keep him in view for the video broadcast.

"I want to give you further information regarding why we are going to Colorado to perform the *Dance of Welcome and Peace* instead of staying in Montana," he said.

He started by telling them the story of the Dead Horse Canyon massacre and Black Cloud's curse, followed by what happened to Bryan, then Sara, when she went public about PURF.

"It was built for corporate lobbyists, not government leaders," he explained. "There are some who believe its purpose is even more evil that originally thought."

Charlie took a drink from his water bottle and waited while murmurs rippled among the passengers, then continued when silence resumed.

"As some of you are probably aware, the promise of the *Dance of Welcome and Peace* is to get both our land *and* the buffalo back. But that depends upon us. We must live the way we were taught by the Creator. We must make peace with all men. These conditions were stated when it was introduced in 1890."

He paused, remembering how shocked he was when Porcupine told him the story. He could hardly believe it. If those

457

heading for Colorado didn't believe him, then what? All he could do was pray that the spirits would convince them if he couldn't.

"Its original peaceful message was corrupted when it became a war dance," he continued. "There was still too much hate and contention with the whites. Then it evolved to become what was known as the Ghost Dance, which alarmed the government and caused the massacre at Wounded Knee."

A warm, peaceful glow settled upon him as he recalled his visit with Porcupine. Should he share that? Or was it too sacred? A *maiyun* whispered, *Yes.*

"I recently fasted four days and four nights on our Sacred Mountain in South Dakota," he explained, lowering his voice. "I had a marvelous vision. I learned the dance's true origin from one of my tribal brothers, named Porcupine."

While everyone had been mostly attentive, now they were even more so. The shuffling about earlier as passengers got settled and comfortable for the long haul ceased, all now perfectly still with their faces trained on his in full attention.

He continued, determined to convey what he learned in the same spirit with which he'd received it. "At least sixteen different tribes attended a very special meeting at Walker Lake in Nevada. Short Bull and Kicking Bear were there as well, and of course Wovoka, who helped spread the dance. But most important, the Creator himself was there! He's the one who taught the dance and explained how we should live."

He paused as a wave of gasps and skeptical looks came his way. Whispers buzzed as he sent another silent prayer to *Maheo* that they'd believe him.

"Those who changed it to a war dance were not there, did not see our Creator, and changed its meaning to one of hate and revenge," he declared, its truth again bonding with his soul.

Another wave of subdued comments circulated among the passengers, some simply responding with a smile or nod.

"Now, over a hundred years later," Charlie went on, "the white man's government is hopelessly corrupt. Evil people filled with greed, hate, and lust for power and control use laws and an out-of-control bureaucracy to get rich. They make wars, tell lies, and cause great suffering."

Heads throughout the coach bobbed with agreement.

Charlie straightened, riding the unified wave. "It is not 'one nation under God' as it was supposed to be. In truth, it never was, because evil contaminated it from the beginning, the moment they tried to eliminate our people."

Anger melding with his own brought murmurs that filled the coach's interior. Panic smoldered. These bad feelings needed to be redirected. No matter how justified, this was *not* the spirit needed for success.

He held up his hand. "We are all angry at how we've been treated. It was wrong. But responding in kind is not the answer. It is time for us to be the ones to set an example by living as the Creator told us to. When we perform the dance with peace and love in our hearts, he will listen to our plea. If it is his will, he will help us take our country back, as promised."

A collective chorus of agreement punctuated with nods followed.

"So the reason we're dancing here is to activate Dead Horse Canyon's curse upon PURF's evil," he explained. "The Creator has given us the collective power to fight back. If our hearts are right we can reclaim our land. First, with the *Massaum* covenant, and second, with the *Dance,* which when done with pure love for our Creator and our fellow man, as it was intended, brings the promised blessings."

Stunned silence followed his conclusion, then several individuals asked questions. After that, he taught them the nine songs Wovoka wrote for the *Dance of Welcome and Peace,* which they sang until their arrival in Casper.

Wovoka asserted his power to control the weather, claiming that during his visit to heaven he had been given "control over the elements so that he could make it rain or snow or be dry at will."
—Louis S. Warren, "God's Red Son," p. 105

47. STORMS

INTERSTATE 25
EN ROUTE
CASPER, WYOMING
October 22, Monday
10:45 a.m. CDT

Everyone onboard had their box lunch and was chowing down, including Charlie and White Wolf. Feeding over seven hundred people was far from simple, especially on the road. So they wouldn't overwhelm any town along the way with an unexpected influx of ravenous Native Americans, Sara made arrangements with a caterer in Casper, where each bus picked up box lunches, another stop in Denver planned for a similar dinner.

Charlie took a bite from his barbeque sandwich, then looked at the time on his phone versus the itinerary. Those two stops plus one for fuel were as close as they could get to driving straight through, which would bring them into Falcon Ridge around sunset.

Their only hope for setting up tipis in another camp circle after dark would be the waxing moon.

If the weather cooperated.

Which so far wasn't the case. He gazed out the windshield, scowling. A storm front with the potential for a few feet of snow was closing in. That time of year, whether in Montana or Colorado, was far from ideal for an outdoor gathering.

Whomever set the date years before was either crazy or inspired.

All they could do was pray and trust *Maheo* to lead the way.

PURF FACILITY
RURAL FALCON RIDGE
October 22, Monday
02:47 p.m. EDT

TEARS GLAZED INGRID'S EYES as she viewed the immensity of the dining room, one of ten. One hand covered her breast as she turned, taking in every detail.

While the residential portions were being completed in stages, the central hub was complete. Each food service area could accommodate six hundred guests, ten to a table. Fresh flowers that would grace each one would be added in the morning. When that was accomplished, its appearance would be worthy of a royal wedding.

She pranced about the kitchen as if to take full credit as rows of chefs staged preparations for a gourmet meal for over six thousand guests the following day. Choices included prime rib, squab, Mahi Mahi, or, of course, a gourmet vegan dish for those of the meatless persuasion.

The guests would start to arrive the next morning, at which time they'd enjoy refreshments and a high-tech 3D holographic presentation in the many lounge areas about the facility. Prior to dinner, they'd assemble in the auditorium for an official welcome.

But who would deliver it?

She paused, her pensive look replicated a hundredfold upon stainless steel walls.

It was supposed to be Myron, but due to the tragic deaths of his two sons, she wasn't sure whether he'd perform the task or not. Worse yet, their funerals were to be held that day, which for some reason had been unnegotiable. Probably the next logical person to emcee would be Calvin Nielsen, the original brainchild behind the project.

461

As it was, he was scheduled as keynote speaker, so she was confident he could easily step up, if required.

So far, everything was proceeding without a hitch. Her planning, as always, paid off. She beamed at the prospect of being one who'd be seated on the dais with other dignitaries for the welcome, keynote, and dedication/ribbon cutting ceremony.

That portion was scheduled to last for an hour and a half, beginning at 8:00 p.m. At its conclusion, they'd adjourn to their assigned dining rooms for cocktails and *hors d'oeuvres* with dinner to be served at 9:00 EDT. With an underground facility, there was no reason to change time zones from that of the majority of attendees.

After that, guests could leave at will or remain for a series of dances with live music and other entertainment, provided by a variety of politically-connected celebrities. The event would conclude with a brief closing ceremony that would present awards to those who'd made the facility possible.

She rubbed her hands together and tittered at what praise she might receive for her efforts.

While PURF had not remained the secret it was intended to be, its specific location had not been revealed. The event would be covered by both the Washington Post and the Times. She grinned as she envisioned seeing her efforts acknowledged on the society pages beside others in the high echelons of the Foggy Bottom social register.

If this didn't make her one of them, absolutely nothing would.

I-70 WEST OF DENVER
EN ROUTE FALCON RIDGE
October 22, Monday
05:49 p.m.

THE COACH CARAVAN TOOK up the entire length of the parking area at a rest stop along I-70 West, lined up like a gigantic silver snake. Wind and snow whistled around them. The Interstate, a mere hundred feet away, was invisible. For all the times weathermen were wrong, why were they always right when predicting a nasty storm? It quickly evolved to a white-out, winds high enough to buffet high profile vehicles.

Thus, the drivers pulled off the Interstate until conditions improved.

Based on their solemn looks and hushed conversations, it wasn't hard to figure out what the waylaid passengers were thinking. No matter how primitive their home lodging may be, in most cases it was better than a tipi in a blizzard.

Charlie exhaled through his nose as he turned to White Wolf beside him. "*Ohohyaa!* What do you think?" he asked in Cheyenne. "Is this a bad omen?"

"Think again, Littlewolf. This is not a bad omen." He tucked in his chin and chuckled. "It is an opportunity."

He scrutinized him, not sure if he was being sarcastic. "How is that?"

White Wolf looked at him as if he'd just said something incredibly stupid. "Think, Littlewolf, *think*. Have you learned nothing? What is it we intend to do?"

Charlie paused, thinking. Quite literally, to move mountains. To convince the Earth Mother to combine her forces with their collective nudging.

He ducked his head into his hand and laughed.

"As always, you are correct. Of course it is an opportunity." Even better, something Porcupine taught him on the Sacred Mountain jumped from memory.

He closed his eyes and took himself back to that moment. Fortunately, the song was a simple two phrases that were repeated five times, followed by prayer.

Charlie tried to text the other buses, but there was no signal. That group would have to do. He stood up and called for attention. "As you can see, the Earth Mother is amused by our plans. I believe our Paiute brother, Wovoka, who brought us together to learn the dance, is also smiling.

"He knew how to bring rain, snow, and make it clear again. I will teach you the song, which is in the Numu language. We will repeat it five times. Then we must pray to the Creator. Would anyone like to lead us in that prayer after we sing?"

Leaping Elk stood up. "I would very much like to do so."

Charlie motioned for him to come to the front and take his seat while he taught them yet another song.

He had them repeat it a couple times, to make sure they had it, then launched into singing, directing their intent toward the blizzard raging from above.

He sensed the change as soon as singing began, then intensified when Leaping Elk closed his eyes and started to pray, all onboard repeating the words. Intuition told him a similar scenario, at least of prayer, was occurring on the other buses as well.

Seven minutes later, the blizzard diminished from an impenetrable white wall to random flakes drifting gently to the ground. Three minutes after that, the clouds directly above them cleared on a brilliant blue sky and Father Sun showed his face, glare against the virgin snowscape nearly blinding.

While everyone watched, the foot of snow covering the roadway collapsed until it was no more than a few inches of slush. Moments later, it, too, melted away, puddles evaporating until the westbound interstate was not only clear, but dry.

Their driver's eyes were wide, whites showing all around, accented by his cinnamon-colored face.

The Department of Transportation attributed it to stored heat in the pavement. However, they couldn't explain why it started adjacent to a certain rest stop just past the Eisenhower Tunnel, then proceeded west as far as a small community known as Falcon Ridge, where the phenomenon abruptly ended.

Those onboard the caravan knew otherwise.

As the bus once again pulled onto the Interstate, Charlie stood, arms folded with satisfaction as he declared, "And that, my brothers, is how it's done."

40. PRELUDE

PEACE GATHERING
RURAL FALCON RIDGE
October 22, Monday
7:30 p.m.

The storm disappeared, waxing gibbous Moon lighting the way as Charlie trudged up the incline to check out the encampment area. A warm breeze arose from the south, elevating temperatures above freezing.

The unnatural formation of several box-like structures topped with snow along one side, then the dark silhouette of a vehicle shaped like an oil tanker caught his eye.

Why was that there?

He looked closer.

Tilted back his head and laughed.

Porta-potties flanked by a water truck. Two, actually.

A gigantic, lumpy snow-covered pile at least ten feet high off to the side puzzled him as well. Closer inspection revealed it to be firewood.

He grinned, amazed. Sara had taken care of details he'd failed to mention or even think of. He thought back to his vision months before of Bryan and the dove. What a gift she was. Without her, none of this could have happened.

Filled with gratitude, he took his phone out of his jacket pocket to send her a quick text.

We are here and safe. Thank you for all you've done! Especially the firewood! Feel free to join us if you like. I hope to see you before we leave.

Satisfied all was in order, he went back to tell everyone to disembark.

Cargo compartments opened, allowing everyone to gather their belongings, then tote them onsite and set up in an organized manner. Eighty-eight Cheyennes tipis were erected by the light of Grandmother Moon, doors all facing east. Four marked the cardinal directions, another four the sacred directions, reflecting the *Massaum* earth drawing.

Everyone distributed themselves among the tipis, fires soon kindled within.

Seeing their people getting settled in with joyful enthusiasm, Charlie, White Wolf, Ice, and a handful of other medicine men from other tribes including Leaping Elk, stood in the center of the arena, enjoying the activity. Grandmother Moon cast her light from among the stars, tipis aglow.

"It has gone well," Charlie stated. "Our Creator approves and is with us."

White Wolf nodded agreement. "Yes. We must show our appreciation for his help and humbly request continued assistance."

"Yes, that is important," Ice said. "We should take nothing for granted."

"I know the perfect place," Charlie said. White Wolf caught his eye and smiled, nodding toward the bluff. He nodded back.

"How much of a hike is it?" Ice asked.

Charlie pointed to the bluff on the north side of the arena.

"I believe that's a bit much for me," Ice said, a few others likewise bowing out.

"I understand," Charlie said. "Those who wish to, follow me."

He set off toward the right. Praying there would assure their petition would be heard. It would also allow them to look upon the *Gathering* as a soaring eagle.

Any thought of contacting Sara to bring the Polaris was quickly dismissed. Seven remained of their original group, which would not have fit, plus its feisty engine would present an irreverent distraction to the otherwise peaceful setting.

He treaded northeast, toward Eagles Peak, others following. The moonlit landscape lent an other-worldly atmosphere for their trek, surrounding mountains clearly visible beneath their cloak of newly fallen snow.

The climb was moderately stiff, snow wet and heavy as it succumbed to rising temperatures. The exertion, however, was invigorating, in no way dampening either their progress or determination. When they reached the top, the ground beyond covered in a cloak of white, he turned and beheld a familiar sight.

Beyond stretched a god's eye view of their people in the encampment below, illuminated by Grandmother Moon.

Exactly as he'd seen it when they were there with Sara.

All had been relatively quiet in the camp circle when they left, as if the participants were tired after their long ride and were getting settled for the evening. Since leaving on their hike, however, the people below were decked out in ceremonial garb, including feathers, beads, headdresses and other regalia, ready to celebrate.

After being cooped up on buses for close to twelve hours, the seven-hundred-plus participants were not ready to sleep. Joyful sounds of celebration, song, and dance ascended, circled by tipis aglow. Again, he smiled, that Sara thought of everything.

"Do you know if the dance coordinators planned this?" Leaping Elk asked.

White Wolf shook his head. "If they did, I was unaware. But dance is their responsibility and it was wise for them to plan something for this evening. Much energy built up while confined to those buses. If we'd known everything would go so smoothly, we could have started the Dance tonight."

"There is always a reason," Leaping Elk said.

Whether or not it had been choreographed or spontaneously inspired, the effects were awe-inspiring. The drummers were hard at work as each group sang and danced, turning like wheels beside one of the eight fires marking the cardinal and sacred directions. Praises sung to the Creator in a multitude of indigenous languages echoed toward heaven, rebounding from the towering bluff's face.

Gatherings were always joyful events. Yet, this unusual and unexpected demonstration had a sacred feel that indicated this occasion was unlike any other. Charlie's memory drifted to when they'd seen the elks, the herd's antics presaging the scene.

After a time, the familiar four count drum beat encoded in their collective DNA switched to the seven concussions that announced completion. Each of the groups filed toward the next fire, then the drum prompted them to form another circle. This continued until each visited all eight fires and arrived back to their original location.

They danced there until the drums announced the end of the celebratory spectacle. Silence prevailed for a few seconds, then a collective roar of praise echoed across the snow and through the canyons.

After the grand finale, the participants sat around the fires where they continued singing in small groups until gradually diminishing to conversations. Words were not discernible. The comradery, however, was.

Eventually, Charlie, White Wolf, Leaping Elk, and the others gathered in a line facing east to pray. Each offered a prayer, then spent some additional time meditating. Upon returning to camp they smudged with sweetgrass, then smoked together to thank the Creator for all that occurred so far.

They prayed for the safety of their people and that all would transpire according to the Creator's sacred will.

SARA'S CABIN
RURAL FALCON RIDGE
October 22, Monday
8:25 p.m.

SARA SAT SEMI-RECLINED on the back deck in one of three Adirondack chairs, Will occupying one of the others. The nearly-full Moon overruled the usual spread of stars, sparing the brighter ones that defined the constellations and a smear of Milky Way. Mars, a reddish orange dot, and Saturn, a golden speck, were discernible leaning toward the west. Her vision blurred, stargazing with Bryan something she'd miss. Such a peaceful, awe-inspiring activity.

Tonight, however, different impressions occupied her mind. The usual autumn silence at that elevation, when insects had retired until spring, was absent. Rather, the distant rhythmic pounding of drums accented with Native voices awakened something she couldn't quite identify.

While tempted to go check it out, she didn't want to make a big noisy entrance with the Polaris. Just listening gave her a warm sense of satisfaction that Charlie was nearby and the Gathering going as planned.

She looked up when the kitchen door opened, allowing a cloud laden with a familiar spicy aroma to escape. Connie exited, carrying a tray that contained an insulated pitcher and three steaming mugs. She held it out so Sara and Will could each take one, then set the tray with its payload on the glass-topped patio table.

Sara closed her eyes as her olfactory senses examined her drink. "Is this what I think it is?"

The woman gave her a sassy look as she settled into the third chair. "I'll never tell." Her smile faded to seriousness as she noticed the distant sounds.

"Is it just me, or do they actually sound kind of creepy?"

Sara laughed. "No, it's not just you. Even knowing its source, I find it eerie. Can you imagine what the early settlers would have thought? Such a racket would have scared them to death."

Will chuckled. "That's for sure. It's hard to tell whether they're happy and celebrating or on the warpath. There's such a primitive, uninhibited energy to it." He tapped his chest a few times with his hand. "It's so visceral. Yet, there's something familiar and relaxing about the drums and rhythm, too. As if it's calling you, at some fundamental level."

Sara nodded, then took a sip from her mug. "*Mmmmmm.* Oh, Connie! This gluhwein is delicious. Thanks so much. It reminds me of the last real vacation I had with Bryan, in Vienna."

"My pleasure, honey. Good stuff. I learned about mulled wine at the German Christmas markets during our honeymoon. One of the best things ever about cold weather."

"I'll say. No argument there." She took another sip, savoring the fragrant blend of red wine, cloves, allspice, cinnamon, orange, and a touch of Brandy.

"Charlie texted that they'd arrived safely and we were welcome to join them," she said, then shrugged. "But it just didn't seem right. This is their time. I didn't want to serve as a reminder of how the whites treated them, way back when. It's hard to imagine how they must have felt, being run off land they occupied for centuries. Even millennia."

Will grunted, then took a sip from his mug.

"The Western European culture was definitely unfriendly," he said. "Not that the Far East was any better. It was all about expansion, conquest for more land, resources, the resulting wealth, and room to grow. The end justified the means. They weren't content with what they had and went after it, with no regard for anything other than being strong enough to take what they wanted."

Sara scowled and took another sip. "Not exactly what I would call the spirit of 'One Nation Under God.'"

"Which they took a bit too far in the Nineteenth Century with their obsession with assimilation. Too many were alarmed by the influx of immigrants," Will went on. "Expecting assimilation from those coming here from Europe was one thing, since there was a fair amount of similarity between them. Building a new nation required a certain degree of unity. But demanding it of people from entirely different cultures who were already here was quite another."

Sara nodded agreement. "I suppose it depends on how you look at it, but I'm inclined to think that, in many ways, Native American culture was and still is superior. It's been around as long or longer than many European traditions. How many early western civilizations disappeared?"

Will huffed. "All of them. Usually due to corruption. Or defeated, for the same reason."

"True," she agreed. "There were hundreds, maybe thousands of indigenous tribes, each a little different. Many formed confederacies. They fought each other sometimes, some more aggressively than others, but then they established boundaries and treaties that were documented on wampum belts of seashell beads."

"I'm impressed how much you've learned," Connie added. "They don't teach that in school, that's for sure."

Sara nodded. "True. The past is based on fact, while history is subjective, recorded by those who prevail. The ruling authority tells you what they want you to know and defines supposed *Truth*. Indigenous people established trade with one another in a rather complex manner. They even contributed much to European culture. Can you imagine the Irish without potatoes or Italians without tomatoes? On the other hand, Spain introduced them to horses."

"No kidding?" Connie said. "I had no idea. Are these things you've covered in your podcasts?"

"Either have or I plan to," Sara replied, then took another sip before going on. "People need to appreciate the contribution of indigenous people and what an advanced society they were. Are, actually. They were intimately connected with nature and the Earth. More spiritual, too. Look at what their healing methods did for me. If I was dependent on western medicine, I'd probably be dead, at best, paralyzed."

Connie passed the pitcher around for welcome refills. "It's just a shame that people can't learn to get along. To tolerate other beliefs and cultures without expecting the entire world to think the same way. The world right now is such an intolerant, egocentric, easily offended mess."

Sara nodded. "Can you even imagine Native Americans coming up with an idea like PURF? It's nothing short of ludicrous. Their leaders look out for their people. Ours exploit us. It epitomizes the cultural differences. Virtues honored by the Cheyenne, Lakota, Navajo, and various others were bravery, generosity, fortitude, and wisdom. They looked after each other. Their cultures punished such selfishness. Anyone with such an idea would be ostracized."

Maybe it was the soothing, nostalgic effects of the gluhwein, allowing her to relax in spite of the electric anticipation, but in a fractured moment, all the shards of seemingly random events the past six months slammed together, punctuated by Charlie and Patrice's favorite saying:

There are no coincidences.

Dead Horse Canyon's Curse. PURF. The location of Bryan's death, Charlie's job and transformation. Nineteenth century prophecies. All she'd read about the *Dance*.

All converged, pointing to a culmination that's time had come.

"Oh, my God," she breathed, electrified by the possibilities.

Will turned her way, puzzled expression awash in moonlight. "What is it, Sara?"

"I'm not sure exactly what's going to happen over the next few days, Dad. But I think we might get more than we expect."

HUDSON RESIDENCE
RURAL FALCON RIDGE
October 22, Monday
10:30 p.m.

SOMETHING WASN'T RIGHT and Jim Hudson could feel it as he sat in his recliner, watching the tail end of Fox31's ten o'clock news. Normally, he couldn't care less about what was going on in Washington D.C., but that report about something big going on, albeit on the social calendar, gave him an odd, uneasy feeling.

It reminded him of when he was on active duty and his intuition, survival instinct, or whatever it was, went on high alert. It made no sense, yet he learned the hard way not to ignore it.

He hadn't heard of anything going on from his old Air Force service buddies, some of which were now big shots in the Pentagon. Now that he was officially retired, however, it wasn't surprising to be out of the loop.

He thought of his three-star friend, Fred O'Reilly, whom he asked about that secret facility months before. He chuckled, remembering how Liz's friend exposed it on network television a few months later.

He frowned, wondering. Could that be involved? Since its full exposure in those few TV gigs, it had gone entirely off the media's radar. Totally quiet.

Perhaps too much so.

He decided he'd call Fred again in the morning, see if anything was going on. Not a damn thing he could do about it tonight.

Tomorrow either, for that matter.

Liz already hit the rack, so he decided to go outside for a smoke. He opened the drawer in the end table next to his chair and retrieved his pack of Sky Dancers from where he stashed them, way in the back.

His wife never approved of his smoking, so he seldom did, other than when he was on active duty or quiet, pensive moments like this. When she was around, he was better off sucking a lit road flare.

The landscape through the living room's picture window was nearly as light as day, moon so bright it cast eerie shadows. Nights like this were perfect for flying VFR, back when he had his Cessna. He preferred flying Visual Flight Rules, mainly because it was so much fun watching Liz juggle those cumbersome sectional charts in the small cockpit. She'd get so frustrated he could hardly keep from laughing.

Ah, those were the days.

Freshly fallen snow created a pristine, peaceful, quiet world, like manna to the soul. The mountain air always felt and smelled so good. Perfect for clearing his head. Compared to Eielson in Alaska, where he'd completed a tour decades before, Colorado weather was far from cold.

There was enough of a bite in the air he grabbed a light jacket from a nearby hook, donning it as he opened the sliding glass door. He stepped outside onto their covered patio, then pulled it closed behind him.

Chills ran across his neck and down his arms, not from cold, but some odd, otherworldly, somehow wild sound. His mind rumbled pensively as he retrieved a book of matches from his pocket.

If he didn't know better, he'd think it was an Indian attack. He tapped a cigarette out of the pack, lit up, then took a long, thoughtful drag.

He tuned his ears more closely.

That was no small gathering.

He exhaled, smoke and condensation billowing into the night.

Was he dreaming? Stepped into a time-warp? What the hell was going on? There had to be a rational explanation.

He finished his smoke, doused it in the snow, then went back inside to toss the butt in the kitchen trash, making sure it was buried and covered with potato peels to mask any smell.

Most likely all the racket was just another wild bunch at that RV park up the road. A Native American wedding or something.

He made a mental note to have Liz do her thing with the neighbors and find out in the morning.

That would also get her out of his hair long enough to check in with Fred.

49. CHANGES

WASHINGTON, D.C.
RANIER OFFICE BUILDING
October 23, Tuesday
8:04 a.m. EDT

Ingrid's mouth hung open as she read the inexcusably tardy R.S.V.P. that popped up in her email. Of course they invited the POTUS and VP with their respective wives, but hadn't expected them to attend. Not responding was expected as well, considering they received thousands of invitations. Apparently, for some crazy, unknown reason, they decided to join them, after all.

Absorbing four more people into the meal plans at the last minute was not a problem. In most cases, such contingencies were covered by no-shows. *However*, it had to be assumed that they would arrive with their usual entourage of Secret Service personnel.

Informing the head chef was essential. She buried her face in her hands. That bit of news would not be well-received.

At this point, the catering team couldn't be busier. Refreshments for when guests started arriving, *hors d'oeuvres,* and the entire evening meal were each in some stage of preparation, Antoine overseeing the entire operation.

Oh, well. It was what it was and certainly not her fault.

Bracing herself and forcing a smile, she picked up the phone and dialed the secure government number for the PURF facility manager, crossing her fingers he was in his office. He could hunt down Antoine and bring him to the phone. While it rang, she stared out her window to the mall, knowing from experience that Antoine would be downright testy about it.

She straightened when the man answered. "Yes, hello, Reuben. This is Ingrid. I need to speak with Antoine. Would you be a dear and find him for me, please?"

The man's reply was a snort, then he put her on hold. He was probably pretty busy himself and she was lucky to catch him. The hold music was classical, which was pleasant, at least. While she waited, she pondered how many high-ranking government officials she'd get to meet that day. If she could have her picture taken with the president, that would make all her efforts even more worthwhile.

She sat up straight, teeth holding her lower lip, as the head chef came on the line.

"Hello, Antoine? Yes, this is Ingrid. Sorry, but a few last-minute additions. Yes, I realize it's late. Yes, I know. This isn't my fault. I agree, but we're talking about the President, Vice President, their wives, and of course, their usual cortege of Secret Service people."

She closed her eyes, faced scrunched up while the expected rant, most of which was in French, went on and on. She didn't understand a word, except for a few instances of *merde*. No telling what else he'd said, though the expletives did a pretty good job of saying it all.

"I understand your frustration, Antoine, but they *must* be accommodated. We're talking about the president here. Will there be enough food or do I need to bring additional provisions?"

After another bilingual tirade, some of which she understood this time, he stated that there would be sufficient food, only the inconvenience of setting up additional seating, for which she needed to contact the set-up crew.

Feeling very clever, she read her response from her phone's language app: *"Très bon, Antoine. Merci. Je vous verrai bientôt."*

She giggled when he grunted, then hung up with no further ado. Or *adieu*, as the case may be.

So the President would be there along with other members of Congress, cabinet members, and—of course—the honored guests: The lobbyists.

Again she grinned at being included as she looked up the number for the set-up lead. After conveying her message, received with enthusiasm not unlike Antoine's, an ominous shadow arose in her solar plexus, similar to heartburn from too much rich food.

It was indeed rare to have so many high-ranking government officials congregated in one location.

She dismissed it. If they thought it was okay, why should she disagree? What could possibly go wrong? It was a secure facility built to withstand a nuclear blast. They were probably safer there than in their offices in D.C.

HUDSON RESIDENCE
RURAL FALCON RIDGE
October 23, Tuesday
8:29 a.m.

"THIS IS O'REILLY. I'M BUSY. What the hell do you want?"

Jim always had to laugh at his three-star buddy's greeting, whether live or phone mail. Some things never changed.

"Good morning, Fred. Jim Hudson. Got a minute?"

"Hey, Jim. Sure. I just got word I have a briefing at eleven-hundred, but I'm clear for now. What's up?"

"I was hoping you could tell me."

"Why? What makes you think that?"

He got up from his living room recliner and walked to the patio door, shuddering at the memory of the previous night. "I don't know. Just a funny feeling, I guess. Watching the news last night, they alluded to some big upcoming D.C. wingding. Something about it didn't set right. Put me on alert, if you know what I mean."

"*Harrumph.* You know I don't run in those circles, Jim. I'm not aware of anything. Sounds like Secret Service territory, if anything. You don't know anything specific, other than something tickled your warrior button?"

"Exactly." He pursed his lips, wishing he had a more definitive answer. "And speaking of warriors, I doubt it's connected, but within a few minutes of that newscast, I went outside for a smoke."

O'Reilly chuckled. "Still sneaking around behind Liz's back, eh?"

"Heh-heh. Right. Anyway, we had our first snow and it was a beautiful, moonlit night. So, I'm out there on the patio lightin' up, when I hear this weird, eerie chanting. I swear, it sounded like a bunch of wild Indians on the warpath. Gives me the willies, just thinking about it."

O'Reilly's laugh was uproarious, lasting several seconds before he managed to respond. "What do you think they're gonna do, Jim? Attack Cheyenne Mountain?" He paused to snigger some more. "Because maybe—heh, heh, heh—they're offended by the name?"

He bit his lip, feeling like a fool for mentioning it. It did sound ludicrous, to say the least. "Yeah, yeah, I know," he said, trying to laugh it off. "It was just that feeling. Something's going on, I can feel it. You know how it gets too quiet, that charge in the air? Like right before a thunderstorm, when you're waiting for the first lightning strike."

"Right. Same thing as before an earthquake. I remember having that feeling during basic at Fort Ord, back in the late 70s."

Jim examined his fingernails, hoping he understood. Experience taught him not to ignore such impressions. Fred wouldn't have gotten where he was today if he ignored his intuition.

"Well, whatever it is, Colonel Hudson, it hasn't gotten here yet. If it does, I'll let you know. If you hear anything else or get some specifics, give me a holler. Meanwhile I'll put scrambling the F-117s on hold."

He chuckled. "Roger that. Have a great day, General. I think I'll brew up another cup of Joe and see if there's anything else on the news this morning. *Ciao.*"

"*Ciao.*"

As he stepped into the kitchen, he ran into Liz, bright-eyed and bushy-tailed as she usually was in the morning. "Good morning, Jim. Would you like some breakfast?"

He wrinkled his nose as he considered the offer. "No. Just coffee for now." He stepped over to the Keurig where he dropped in a K-cup of Folger's dark roast. "By the way, I was wondering if you could check something with your network of friends."

She turned to face him, eyes wide. "Oh? What's that?"

"Last night I heard what sounded like a big gathering of some sort. I'm curious what it may have been, because it seemed rather unusual."

Her eyes narrowed into her best suspicious look, used when he was too vague to satisfy her curiosity. "Unusual? In what way?"

"Well, for one thing, it was a week night. Another, it sounded like, well, a bunch of wild Indians."

She burst out laughing. "Seriously? What exactly did you have to drink after I went to bed? Or did you stop by one of those dispensaries the last time we were in Denver and pick up a few joints?"

His smile was forced. "Nothing. I swear. I was stone-cold sober. But it sounded like a bunch of whoops, drums, and such. You know, like you see in the movies."

"I can't imagine, Jim. It's a little early, but I'll make some calls in an hour or so, if that'll make you feel better. I'm sure it was nothing to worry about." The look in her blue eyes shifted from amused to concerned. "It really upset you, though, didn't it?"

He exhaled hard. "I suppose. It just seemed odd, out of place somehow. It gave me this weird feeling. That it meant something. Just don't know what."

She stepped over and kissed his cheek. "I'm sure it has a rational explanation. Why don't you let me fix you some scrambled eggs and bacon?"

The offer made him smile. Why was it women always thought food could fix anything?

And were usually right.

"Okay. Sounds good."

An hour later, he was sitting in his recliner watching CNN, wondering if anything else would turn up. Liz's hand on his shoulder hauled him back to the present.

"I talked to Sara Reynolds. Her Indian friend and a bunch of others are having a gathering of some sort on her property. That must be what you heard last night. She said they'll be there for a few more days. Thus, nothing to worry about."

He nodded. "Oh. Okay. That makes sense. Thanks for checking."

He almost smiled when a line from his favorite movie bolted from memory—*There's been a disturbance in* The Force.

Oddly enough, the ominous feeling didn't go away.

WASHINGTON, D.C.
CAPITOL MAGLEV SUBWAY STATION
October 23, Tuesday
5:52 p.m. EDT

THE LINE AWAITING THE maglev to PURF was far longer than Ingrid expected. The waiting area was well-lit, but far from fancy, essentially a wider space in the tunnel, similar to the Metro that served the D.C. area.

Why couldn't people follow simple directions? Each of the guests had been provided a boarding schedule. Yet, she knew that the class of people she was dealing with did not take directions well.

Nonetheless, much to her surprise, everyone was in a festive mood, as if waiting in line at the Kennedy Center to see *The Nutcracker* at Christmastime. The excitement at visiting the long-awaited facility and what it represented, to say nothing of the gala to follow, were apparently sufficient to generate patience.

From the conversations around her, it was perceived as nothing short of a grand adventure of stellar proportions. One they would share with their grandchildren for years to come.

She smiled, her own impatience ebbing to the jovial chatter coupled with a strong sense of personal pride.

None of this would have been possible without her party planning prowess and organizational skills. While she would put on a guise of humility when acknowledged and thanked (which she truly deserved), she would nonetheless bask in the ensuing applause. These people had no foggy idea what it took to put on such an event.

No telling whom she might meet and connect with as a result.

If all went according to plan, this would be her final trip. There'd been several the past few days in preparation, but this was it. She had her bag, which contained multiple changes of clothes, some redundant in case of a catastrophic spill of pinot noir or gravy upon the striking white formal she purchased for the occasion.

It was a simple matter to return the duplicate if all went well. If there was one thing she understood, it was to be prepared for anything.

The line shuffled forward as the bullet train arrived. Its doors slid open and passengers anticipating the event of a lifetime shuffled onboard. The doors closed before she got there, so she'd have to wait for the next one.

Actually, at this point she didn't mind. The joyful atmosphere fed her soul, none of this possible if it weren't for her.

COSMIC PORTALS
BOULDER
October 23, Tuesday
10:42 p.m.

IF PATRICE AND JIM HUDSON were to compare notes, they'd discover they both sensed a "disturbance in *The Force.*" Patrice already had some idea what it could be, or at least what precipitated it. As an astrologer, however, she longed to know how it could have been predicted.

So far, the afternoon was quiet, as it usually was early in the week. That granted her the luxury of contemplating what was afoot based on its cosmological indicators.

If there was one astrological event that tended to presage important occurrences, it was a total solar eclipse. Their effects could last a long time, often reflected in subsequent events such as battles and treaties. She was always impressed by what mundane astrologers discovered by studying history, world events, and tying them into relevant astrological influences.

Decades before, astrologer Lorne Edward Johndro stated eclipses represented an idea or development that influenced the times. In particular, the area beneath its path of totality was highly susceptible to major events and situations. Areas outside the path were influenced as well, often related to where the planets were directly overhead when the eclipse was at totality. If it was Mars, some form of violence could be expected.

Curious what might be going on, she brought up the map that showed the path for one the previous year. It missed most of Colorado, but had done quite a number on Wyoming, including the Wind River Indian Reservation northwest of Riverton.

Native cultures placed high value on messages from the Heavens. Theoretically, that would have had an effect on Indigenous people there, perhaps nudging them toward some sort of action or triggering a significant event. Some tribes, such as the Navajos, stayed inside during an eclipse, considering it bad luck.

She kept checking eclipse paths until she found one that passed over Falcon Ridge on July 29, 1878. Another one, eleven years later on January 1, 1889, crossed directly over the Northern Cheyenne reservation in Montana as well as other Native American lands, including North Dakota, Colorado, Idaho, Nevada and California.

Bingo.

Those years saw serious contention between the white man and Indigenous populations. She felt particularly drawn to the second one, so she ran the chart to see if anything stood out.

The eclipse occurred in Capricorn which, at the time of the eclipse, was the eighth-house of death and transformations. Mercury, as well as two asteroids, Icarus and Phaethon, were in that sign as well, both archetypal icons of crashing and burning.

She cupped her chin in her hand, thinking. For the sake of speculation, one thing that could make that eclipse hang around like a wrecking ball awaiting its next target would be the anniversary of something special. A treaty or some other agreement, perhaps.

Assuming it to be an event, she ran the transit chart for the present day and compared the two, to see how the current planetary positions interacted.

Ka-bam! Conflicting aspects screamed between the two.

Saturn and Venus connected with the eclipse chart's Pluto to form a pattern known as a Finger of God. Shaped like an arrowhead, it indicated a fate-driven force. In this case, both transformational and potentially earth-shattering energy.

Saturn was often associated with karma, which everyone knew could be a bitch. Venus was presently retrograde in Taurus, which was a biggie. Moving backwards flipped the Love Goddess' friendly vibes to something far different, one in which she donned her armor and became Goddess of War.

In another week, her relative position to Earth would make her the morning star. In that condition, she joined the Valkyries, presenting the cosmic signal for ancient cultures across the ages to go to war.

Far different from the more loving and romantic nature she displayed as an evening star.

The fact Venus was in Scorpio brought a chuckle. That sign's energy pushed Venus' bitch button even harder. As if being retrograde wasn't bad enough, in that sign she was passionate and aggressive. Enough to demand what she wanted, in no uncertain terms.

When she saw Phaethon, Mr. Crash 'n' Burn himself, parked on the eclipse's Pluto like a packet of C-4 explosives, Patrice didn't know whether to laugh or worry.

That arrow-like configuration, known as a yod, was loaded with karmic, self-righteous, war-like overtones related to unresolved past events, its signature message simple:

Paybacks are hell.

Saturn and Pluto in both charts were connected. Reciprocal aspects were powerful indicators something big related to their combined meaning was primed to occur.

Saturn related to authority, such as government, as well as tradition, while Pluto's auspices were power and control.

After all, he was god of the Underworld.

He also excelled at exposing and eliminating corruption, which he had certainly done since going into Capricorn, the sign that ruled such things as corporate entities and governments.

The Aries Moon, another less than friendly influence, was opposing Uranus. Oppositions called for balance, in this case between emotional energy of an aggressive nature, and Uranus' domain of explosions, rebellions, freedom, disturbances, breakthroughs, upsets, disturbances, and sudden change.

Yes, there was definitely a volatile connection between the 1889 eclipse and the current day.

She had no idea what was about to happen, but whatever it was would be epic.

When spirit lances were prominent, no oxzem was like any other in detail because each exemplified secret knowledge and power and was made according to the instructions of the spirits. Each represented a dangerous gift from the spirit world to its shaman keeper who alone mastered the required ritual and care
.—"Wolves of Heaven," by Karl H. Schlesier, p. 17

50. DANCING

PURF FACILITY
RURAL FALCON RIDGE
October 23, Tuesday
4:17 p.m. MDT/6:17 p.m. EDT

Ingrid couldn't believe she forgot the award trophies. She paced the maglev platform at PURF's lowest level, lambasting herself. How could she be so careless? She *never* made mistakes like this. When Myron asked for them, she'd nearly fainted. Her face burned again with humiliation at her gargantuan *faux pas.*

Her only choice was to go back to get them, hopefully returning in time for the ceremony.

The trip each way took a little under a half- hour. The event was based on Eastern Time, not local, which would have been too confusing for all concerned. Furthermore, the attendees, for the most part, had no idea whatsoever where the facility was located. It could be Antarctica, for all they knew.

Of course, she had to get a taxi from the Capitol station to her office and back, which would hopefully only take an hour. With luck, one of the high-speed trains would be available to return. Under the circumstances, she was confident she could demand such a favor.

Everyone of any importance was at the facility—who could possibly complain?

485

However, she needed someone to put in the request, either for one to wait or be sure one was available. She retrieved her cell phone from her purse to call Myron, only to roll her eyes with additional frustration when there was no signal, either for the cell itself or from the facility's Wi-Fi.

If she left to go back up there now, she might miss the one already on its way.

The best laid plans of mice and men.

She fidgeted, doing her best to assure herself it would work out just fine.

Everything else seemed to be coming together perfectly. The food smelled scrumptious. The tables looked amazing, bedecked with bouquets of red, white, and navy-blue roses accented with delicate ferns and baby's breath. It was apparent the guests were enjoying their virtual presentations and guided tours.

An experienced planner, she flinched as she thought through the itinerary. Getting back in time was unlikely, the awards scheduled to follow Myron's eight o'clock welcoming speech. They needed to postpone the awards until after dinner, which began at nine. That would give her plenty of time.

Yes, that would work. All she had to do was call when she got to her office. Surely they'd cooperate. Having the award ceremony without the elegant crystal trophies she ordered would be like having a wedding without the bride. Her hand covered her heart as she assured herself it would all work out.

The ground vibrated beneath her feet.

She sighed with relief.

Good. The train is almost here.

PEACE GATHERING
RURAL FALCON RIDGE
October 23, Tuesday
5:50 p.m. MDT

486

IF THERE WAS ONE thing Charlie knew, it was to follow his instincts. Failing to do so in the past resulted in a multitude of regrets and hard lessons. Thus, he left White Wolf in charge of the ongoing activities and followed the impression, which led him to a wooded area a few hundred yards west of the camp circle. Brighter light up ahead coupled with intimate knowledge of the area told him exactly where he was.

Slushy snow saturated a thick layer of leaves that squished beneath his feet as he stepped through the brush. He halted upon finding himself overlooking Dead Horse Canyon, its depths cloaked in shadow by the late afternoon Sun.

He kept the *oxzem* handy at all times, not knowing when inspiration to activate its powers might arrive. For now, it functioned as a walking stick as he leaned over the edge. The hairpin turn where Bryan's accident occurred six months before sprawled a hundred feet below.

His heart ached as a tapestry of memories unfurled.

Across the road was where he conducted his first four-day fast. The aspen *maiyun* that told him to check Bryan's truck for evidence stood bare, shed leaves splashes of yellow that carpeted the ground and ledge where Bryan's truck first landed.

The canyon itself yawned beyond, time's veil parting to reveal the many spirits that encountered a bad death within its gaping gorge.

Upon recognizing that he stood where the small band's horses and two boys, one white, one *Tsistsistas*, plunged to their deaths over a century before, a chill captured his spine.

Hooves thundered around him, followed by horses galloping past in panic. Whinnies and snorts of terror accented by human cries joined the stampede, the familiar scene from his vision searing his soul as tears filled his eyes.

The ill-fated herd vanished in the mists of time, except one steed that stopped, then turned his way. A majestic white stallion, his lengthy mane billowing softly like the autumn mists lilting skyward from Tomahawk Creek far below.

The animal loped toward him, eyes fixed upon his own, still suspended in the air before him. In the blink of an eye, he was astride its back, *oxzem* in hand, soaring between the canyon's looming walls, then up into the clouds and back, eventually soaring above the camp circle.

Those below were occupied preparing the eight fires at the sacred and cardinal points to illuminate and provide warmth for what was to come. White Wolf and Ice stood beside their tipi, logs in hand. Both looked up as he flew past, their mouths agape.

He sensed a presence beside him. None other than his Paiute brother, Wovoka, on a similar steed. The prophet's signature black Stetson perched above heavy eyebrows, strong jaw flanking a mysterious, knowing smile. Charlie acknowledged him with a nod as their aerial journey continued above the sacred area.

Lake Wilson gleamed fiery pink, reflecting a glorious sunset. Eagles Peak loomed up ahead, snowcap likewise colored by *Atovsz's* daily demise.

Both riders soared upward, alighting on the mountain's craggy summit with the grace of giant birds. The magnificent vista before him filled his heart with love and reverence for all creation. To the east, Sara's cabin nestled in the snow. LSO's worksite huddled to the south. To the southeast sprawled the camp circle, smoke belching from an octet of hospitable flames.

Wovoka turned his way, words spoken in *Numu,* yet understood. They seared his mind and soul as liquid fire, after which the healer turned with his mount and ascended back to his home among the stars.

With the prophet's departure, Thunder rumbled overhead, followed by a voice that quickened his every cell, clear to the bone:

Do you accept responsibility for the powers given you?

Black clouds roiled overhead, awaiting his response.

Questions pummeled his mind, yet the knot in his gut bespoke restraint.

"Yes," he replied, chest afire with foreboding.

You may use your weapon only as directed. Do you understand?

"Yes. I understand."

Lightning sizzled from above. His hair stood on end as it found its mark, entering the *oxzem's* crown, then crackling around every component of its woven wheel. Heartbeats later, it shot out through its stone point, sparks lingering in the frigid air.

The next thing Charlie knew, he was back on his feet, overlooking Dead Horse Canyon. Tendrils of smoke surrounded the ancient weapon, lingering like afterthoughts of Wovoka's powerful words:

It is time.

PURF FACILITY
MAIN AUDITORIUM
October 23, Tuesday
8:00 p.m. EDT/6:00 MDT

MYRON BENTLEY STOOD at the dais, back straight and chin raised, ready to deliver his welcome speech. A sea of faces in the thousands lay beyond. The view included the most powerful and elite members of Washington society. Even the President, Vice President, and their wives decided to join them, not wanting to miss out on the gala occasion.

Men were in tuxes, women in formal gowns that represented the entire spectrum of color, though red, white, and blue dominated. Jewelry that seldom saw the light of day outside safe deposit boxes sent tiny flashes from necks, wrists, and fingers. Indeed, their appearance was resplendent, reminiscent of a royal gathering.

While they could never claim a regal title, nonetheless they held that role and wielded like power. Like true royalty, the proletariat, a.k.a. U.S. taxpayer, was their servant. The peasants worked, paid their taxes, and thus allowed the likes of him—his corporate cronies, and federal government leaders—to enjoy the elegant life of their dreams. Oil barons like himself were the true monarchy, without whom the country couldn't operate.

The price was steep and included his soul, but deemed worth it for moments like this.

His thoughts wandered unbidden to his sons' dual funeral earlier that day in Arlington. The twinge of something that resembled guilt was quickly doused. He was where he belonged, with those of his own kind.

The time on the man-sized digital clock on the far side of the auditorium flashed to 8:00. He cleared his throat.

"If I can have your attention please."

His words reverberated throughout the auditorium from strategically placed speakers. Chatter faded to respectful silence. "It is my privilege to welcome you here today to celebrate the completion of phase one of this marvelous facility."

He paused, awaiting the ripple of applause to die down.

"It is a testimonial and memorial, if you will, to corporate partnerships with our great government system. A place where those of us who are the backbone of the United States of America are at long-last honored for our contribution to our country's greatness. Without our input to Congress, corporations would not be properly represented, their needs unknown."

From the audience one of his fellow's hollered, "Hear, hear!"

He went on, stifling a grin. "Without favorable legislation, our economy would be unfairly encumbered by regulations and restrictions, which would strangle our profitability, eliminate jobs, and force us back to the dark ages."

His back straightened, chest expanding with pride. "Today we honor our system and those that make it work. We show our respect to those who are an inherent cog in the wheel of government, of which I am proud to be a part."

He paused, mind engulfed with salacious thoughts.

And later tonight, while many of you make merry, some of us will descend below to our newest temple to praise Lucifer, the one who really made this possible.

"This country was made great by men like the Rockefellers, J.P. Morgan, Westinghouse, Carnegie, and a host of others in the years since, many of whom are present here today."

Who all got here through the same rituals and sacrifices I did.

"While we abhor the thought, it is a comfort to know that those of us who have continued to build this great land would be around to rebuild, should the need arise."

Again he paused for the ripple of applause. "We welcome you today and thank our Congressmen for valuing our contribution enough to assure our survival, should the worst case scenario befall our great country, either at the hands of Mother Nature or our enemies, domestic or foreign."

He inhaled, nearing the end of his soliloquy. "If you have not already enjoyed either a virtual or guided tour, we invite you to do so. Cocktails and *hors d'oeuvres* will be available immediately following this brief assembly with dinner served in your assigned dining rooms at nine o'clock. After dessert, we will return here for a short awards ceremony while the dining rooms are reconfigured for us to enjoy more drinks and refreshments at multiple grand balls.

He spread his arms in welcome as he concluded.

"Feel free to wander between the ballrooms, interact with your peers, and bask in the reality of your success and value to the millions of American taxpayers who made this all possible. We hope you enjoy this historic evening."

Many believed it was the ensuing roar of applause that caused the ground to tremble.

They were wrong.

SARA'S CABIN
October 23, Tuesday
6:16 p.m. MDT

AFTER FEEDING BLOSSOM, Sara helped the dog don her new doggie parka, then zipped up her own ski jacket. She went outside, joining Connie and Will sitting on her back patio. Charlie didn't give her a time when they'd start, so the only way she'd know was to hear it, which she wouldn't inside. She sat up straight, wondering if a distant sound was only her imagination. Her eyes closed, ears straining to hear.

"Listen," she announced, chills on a slalom run down her arms. "It's starting."

Connie paused mid-sip of her steaming decaf while Will mirrored her pensive stance.

Sara got up and ran inside for the Polaris' key as well as a blanket and a pair of binoculars. Outside again, she motioned to the others to follow as she hustled for the ATV.

"C'mon! This is it. Day one. Let's go!"

While she didn't want to cause a disturbance the night before, she hoped that the noise from the *Gathering* would cover the racket from the Polaris. If not, Charlie and White Wolf would know and could assure the others it was nothing to be concerned about.

She climbed into the driver's seat, her father on the passenger side with Connie squeezed between them. Blossom occupied the floor, flanked by Will's knees. The vehicle rumbled to life. The Sun had set, but enough twilight remained not to need headlights. They sped off over the snow-covered hill behind the cabin. The ensuing ride was cold and bumpy, all-terrain tires defying the slippery surface below.

When they arrived at the bluff, she turned off the engine. The windshield muffled the drums and singing, reflections from multiple fire obscuring the view. Wanting to see clearly, especially for photos, she and the others got out and leaned against the front bumper, eventually sitting on the hood.

"Why don't we get up in the jump seat?" Will suggested.

It overlooked the roof and provided a padded seat with back support. Leaving the dog in the cab, they climbed up and snuggled together, blanket around their backs against the wind sweeping down the mountains behind them.

The basin amplified the drum beats like a gigantic megaphone, their cadence familiar and hypnotic, though slightly different from the night before.

Animated rings of dancers holding hands with interlocked fingers moved in time with the drums with grace and enthusiasm. A step, then a half-step, in a clockwise direction. Surrounded by multiple dance circles, Charlie stood singing at the center, holding some sort of staff. Curious what it was, she raised the binoculars to look more closely.

Was it only her imagination, or was it actually aglow?

Shifting to the dancers, each wore traditional native clothing embellished with fringe, beadwork, and feathers. She handed the binoculars to Connie.

"Wow! That's quite a spectacle, isn't it?" the woman commented.

"Yes, it is," Sara agreed. "With quite a history behind it."

She went on to explain what she'd read about the dance's history, augmented with what Charlie told her.

"It was more than a dance. There was a great gathering in Nevada reported in local newspapers that Jesus appeared to a group of Native Americans, where he taught them the dance and told them how to live. The beautiful part is how it was integrated with their culture, through dance and song. They were not expected to change who and what they were."

"I've seen such combinations in tiny, rural chapels in southern Arizona," Will commented. "They're not only a fascinating blend of native culture with Christian beliefs, but quite beautiful."

Sara nodded, having seen similar examples herself. "Wovoka was a prophet and seer who first learned the dance. His vision wasn't something taught by missionaries from some supposed religion who previously slaughtered them as heathens. Neither were they expected to live as the white man."

"Why did they stop?" Connie asked.

"The original meaning got lost and the government outlawed it, thinking it was a war dance. Which for some, it was." She went on to explain how it facilitated the massacre at Wounded Knee.

They kept passing the binoculars as the dancing continued and skies darkened to night.

"Well, duh," Sara muttered, taking her cell phone out of her jacket pocket. "I can't believe I forgot my camera."

She snapped a few shots, then switched to video. Connie followed suit with her tablet, Will using his phone. They remained engrossed for several minutes until Will broke the silence.

"You know what's a bit troubling?" he said, again using the binoculars. "The ground is vibrating, even up here. The dance rhythm, the drums, and all those people dancing. Remember the Bible story, Joshua and the Walls of Jericho? Some think it was caused by their marching, which created the resonant frequency to destroy the walls, though divine intervention via the Ark of the Covenant was certainly implied."

Again, the kaleidoscope of facts swirling in Sara's mind collided. "I suspect we may be seeing something very, very similar," she said grimly. "Maybe being this close, much less this high up, isn't such a good idea."

Without further discussion, they climbed down and piled back into the cab where Blossom resumed her place between Will's knees. Sara started it up, turning around before switching on the headlights so as not to distract the dancers, then made their way back to the cabin as quickly as she dared, mind abuzz.

What was about to happen?

We had no wish to make trouble, nor did we cause it of ourselves...We had no thought of fighting...We went unarmed to the dance. How could we have held weapons? For thus we danced, in a circle, hand in hand, each man's fingers linked in those of his neighbor...The message that I brought was peace.
—Short Bull

51. RETRIBUTION

PEACE GATHERING
RURAL FALCON RIDGE
NIGHT ONE
October 23, Tuesday
6:20 p.m. MDT

A trance-like state fell upon the dancers. Little space separated the circles, yet it didn't feel crowded. There were no collisions, despite the tight proximity.

Charlie's spirit soared with breathless euphoria.

Unity.

Love.

Maheo's *will being enacted.*

He danced and sang the prayer of praise Porcupine taught him, awareness heightened. He ascended in spirit toward the stars and surveyed what lay below. His mind's eye shifted to Eagles Peak, then LSO. His perception dove beneath the ground to the slip fault, under which lay the reservoir of oil.

Intuition nudged him away.

He shifted back to the surface and soared northwest. The terrain Bryan photographed during his and Sara's fateful excursion spread before him, illuminated by the rising Full Moon.

Even in the darkness, an unearthly haze was visible gathering above the location of the government facility. Not a thundercloud, but a spiritual void, colder than the reaches of space.

Divinely-inspired righteous indignation raged.
Land given his people by Maheo.
Secured by Massaum covenant.
Stolen and polluted.
Broken treaties.
Dance's promise cancelled, corrupted by hate.
A country founded on godly principles sullied by greed.
Innocent lives lost at the hands of evil, selfish men.
Wounded Knee.
Sand Creek.
Dead Horse Canyon.

He shuddered as the spirits' unrest seared his soul. Ethereal threads of righteous indignation churned, swirling above those that represented the epitome of evil.

Without a doubt, PURF, not LSO, was the intended target.

His soul leapt as he assimilated the dancers' will with his own. Through their shared connection, he concentrated their faith on the locus of their quest. A jolt of collective understanding responded.

Knowledge gained from the Sacred Mountain gripped his mind and soul. He raised the *oxzem* and summoned *Notamota, Maheyuno* of the Northeast. Invisible forces merged.

At first, it swirled as a benign force circling a drain. It accelerated, little by little, evolving to a frenzied whirlwind. It culminated in an etheric vortex of spiritual warfare that dove beneath the ground

Use your powers, Littlewolf. Assure Maheo's *will is fulfilled.*

Charlie followed within its eye, *oxzem* shedding sparks before him as his mind's eye descended beneath Grandmother Earth's crust, diving within her geological structure: Past the thin layer of soil, stratified layers, bedrock, then faults that defined the surface topology.

The reinforced concrete foundation of the facility's eastern border rushed past. A thousand feet below, his descent ended where two tectonic plates argued for dominance. Forces that, billions of years before, buckled the earth into the surrounding mountains, valleys, and basins.

In the company of thousands of spirits wronged centuries before, their combined forces melded with that of divine retribution. Charlie's arm muscles jerked as the *oxzem* blasted a searing bolt into the fault, boosting the Earth Mother's mighty wrath.

Grandmother Earth groaned, her fury linked with the rage of her Creator and legions of her martyred children. She twisted and convulsed, faults bursting apart. Magma oozed from her core and oozed between the tectonic plates.

No longer a perk for evil men, PURF transformed instead to their crypt. First the facility trembled, then sank. Slowly at first, then more rapidly, as it yielded to the subterranean magma's seething flow. Its foundation liquefied, delivering those within who exploited their fellow man, the planet, and the indigenous people who honored her, to geological hell, consumed by the molten mass that constituted Grandmother Earth's raging blood.

While carried away to the planet's molten core, its ten-foot-thick walls crumbled, releasing the oxygen therein. It ignited in a mighty blast, energy equal to an underground nuclear explosion. Shock waves tore through the ground at the speed of sound for hundreds of miles from the epicenter.

Fully destabilized by the disturbance at its tectonic base, Eagles Peak trembled. Its weather-eroded crest broke free and toppled over. Like a giant arrowhead, it careened down the side of the mountain upon which it reigned for billions of years. As it reached the tree line, it blasted through forests, leaving acres of splintered timber in its wake, finally slamming into the depression PURF occupied moments before.

Retribution's arrow found its mark.

The subterranean river of lava followed the path of least resistance, forming a tributary along a secondary fault that ran perpendicular to the first. It seeped south along its cleft, until it reached the oil deposit violated four months before. In the anaerobic environment it didn't burn, but the crude yielded to thermal expansion. The ground screamed as it ruptured, spraying a geyser of sludge as dark and polluted as those it so recently consumed.

Upon reaching the surface, oxygen combined with the super-heated fuel. The ensuing explosion carried more of Grandmother Earth's fury, announced with a deafening blast. Annihilated derricks, drills, pumps, pipes, buildings, and vehicles rocketed a thousand feet into the air like terrestrial confetti, then rained back to the ground as a pile of rubble.

All that remained of LSO's premier site was a gaping hole from which the "excrement of the devil" spewed upward, feeding a raging inferno. Skyward it surged, a thousand feet into the sky, blowout flare months before a birthday candle by comparison.

SARA'S CABIN
October 23, Tuesday
6:41 p.m. MDT

BY THE TIME SARA and the others got back to the cabin, the ground convulsed in nauseating waves. Earth's fury rose to a deafening roar, making conversation impossible. She parked the ATV behind the rear deck where they tumbled out, staggering like skid-row drunks toward the back door, multiple phone-sponsored flashlights leading the way.

Sara stopped short of reaching the deck. Darkened windows rattled, motion revealed by reflected moonlight, exterior walls creaking as the cabin swayed on its piered foundation.

Definitely not the safe-haven she'd hoped for.

The trio linked arms, Will in the middle, all undecided what to do, other than the obvious of maintaining their balance as the ground swelled beneath their feet.

Behind the cabin, pine trees lashed as if caught in a whirlwind, roots clinging to the convulsing earth. Lights turned to follow Blossom as she barked, then trotted toward the hiking path a safe distance from both the house and trees. Everyone trusted her lead and slogged along behind through slushy snow.

The three of them hunkered down behind the two-foot boulder where Sara sat when they'd scattered Bryan's ashes months before. One hand on it for leverage, Sara stood up, light slashing the dark. Vibrations indicated it wasn't any more secure than they were. It shook as if alive, Sara pulling back her hand as it lost its purchase and tumbled down the incline, directly toward her car.

"No!" Sara screamed.

Hands flew to her mouth at it crashed into the rear driver-side door with an ear-splitting crash. Traumatized metal shrieked in protest as the force rotated the vehicle sideways, door and quarter-panel annihilated. Unfazed, the boulder continued down the incline to disappear among the trees, their death-defying dance tracing its destructive path.

Motion to Sara's right snagged her peripheral vision. She turned, watching as moonlight revealed snow-crowned Eagles Peak shaking precariously as a low-frequency rumble joined the din, as if the Earth Mother were playing a bass guitar. Illuminated by the Moon, tons of ejected snow billowed into the air, partially obscuring the traumatized peak until it resettled on the ground below.

Suspecting something remarkable was about to happen, Sara fumbled in her pocket for her phone to start a video. The ground grumbled beneath her in rolling, seismic waves, making it impossible to keep her balance. Giving up on standing, Sara knelt in the hole left behind when the boulder abandoned its post. She started recording, struggling to keep the summit in view between her own stability coupled with the mountain's.

The planet's deafening roar crescendoed when a ripping sound echoed across snow-covered ground. Barely keeping the mountain top in view, she gasped when its crown tumbled over completely. Connie screamed while her father's comment was a string of expletives Sara never heard him say before.

The liberated peak rebounded when it hit the ground, then tore completely free with an explosive *crack*. It scraped down what was left of its mighty perch, gathering momentum as what was once literally Eagles Peak disappeared upon reaching the tree line.

Sara stopped recording, mind numb. Thinking it was over, she yelped when another angry tremor rumbled beneath her. Whatever toppled Eagles Peak was not giving up. Moments later, the wrath of a violated planet exploded, spewing a pillar of fire and black smoke that cloaked the snow-covered ground in unearthly hues of orange.

The ensuing shock wave took her breath away, ears ringing. Windows rattled as the shock wave blew past, echoes growling through the canyons. The ground trembled awhile longer, but less violently. Gradually, trees grew still until the inferno's fearsome roar was the dominant sound.

Was the planet's temper tantrum over at last?

Her thoughts turned to Charlie and his people, much closer to Eagles Peak.

Could they have survived what just happened?

Or had his entire entourage become martyrs with the *Dance's* previous performers over a century before? Would the Earth Mother swallow them up? It didn't make sense—they were defending the planet—but Sara's logical side was less optimistic.

"We should check on the *Gathering*," she said, their faces conveying shared unspoken fears.

Her father took Connie by the hand and followed Sara and the dog to the Polaris, where everyone climbed onboard and buckled up, Blossom in Will's lap. She started the engine, turned on the headlights, then drove cautiously down to the road, no way of knowing what lay ahead.

The vehicle bucked and rocked across rough terrain, its surface further disturbed by the quake. She dodged a few fallen trees, eventually reaching the road. It appeared intact, at least as far as the headlights revealed. She proceeded at a cautious pace, encountering a few more toppled trees, eventually reaching the dirt road that led up to the *Gathering*.

Her foot compressed the brake, bringing them to a stop.

The ground beneath them was still, the raging inferno's roar competing with the ATV's noisy engine.

Terrified by what they might find, she set her jaw, turned right, and proceeded, avoiding deep ruts left by the semi's that delivered everything as well as Charlie's buses.

Upon reaching the top, she could only stare.

The scene had changed little from what they'd observed from the bluff. Dancing and singing continued, as if the participants were enclosed within a protective bubble. The ground beneath them was still, dancers smiling as if unaware of any unfolding drama.

An aftershock twisted the ground, lasting for several seconds. Blossom huddled across their laps as Sara and the others clung to the sissy bars until it passed.

Meanwhile, in the space before them, dancing continued, undisturbed.

From what Sara could tell, their feet were not touching the ground.

MAGLEV VEHICLE #47
EAST OF FT. LEAVENWORTH, KS.
October 23, Tuesday
8:05 p.m. EDT

INGRID AND A HANDFUL of fellow passengers, all of whom were running late, exchanged startled glances when the train decelerated abruptly, slamming them against their safety harnesses. The train eventually stopped, which from the maglev's average speed of over three-thousand miles-per-hour, took several minutes.

Stowed items beneath their seats remained confined, but emitted a medley of thumps and crashes, not to mention the tinkling of shattered glass, as everything shifted forward.

"What do you think is wrong?" asked the bearded man across from her.

She and the others onboard shared mystified looks.

Hers turned horrified as she realized what that sound probably represented. Ditching her harness, she stepped to the front of the car, crouched down, and unlatched the door to the stowage area.

The blue soft-sided suitcase that contained the trophies was right there. She reached in and dragged it out, the high-pitched crunching sound confirming her fears. She opened it carefully, wondering if any survived, which was not the case.

She buried her face in her hands and sobbed.

The train had an onboard engineer, but his function was to monitor their arrival time and make sure the automated system turned at the route's appropriate intersections, which it had never failed to do. Troubleshooting any problems along the way also fell in his job description, as well as reporting any incidents back to the control hub.

She and the others waited, expecting someone to show up any moment and explain what went wrong.

Seconds later, the lights went out, plunging them into darkness only possible within the depths of the earth. Panic still didn't ensue, such a reaction undignified for people of their social standing.

Everyone retrieved their cell phones. With no hope for a signal, at least they had flashlights. Some laughed, others made comments about lowest bidders.

A low frequency rumble greeted them moments later.

"Oh, good. That must be another train," Ingrid said. She wiped her eyes. Maybe she'd at least get there in time for the photo-ops. She could always order more trophies.

She gripped her purse as the rumble's amplitude increased to explosive proportions as a blast of super-heated magma swallowed the train.

The vehicle melted along with its dumbfounded passengers before anyone had the slightest inkling what aborted their arrival to the gala event of the century.

The Great Spirit is angry with our enemies; he speaks in thunder, and the earth swallows up villages, and drinks up the Mississippi. The great waters will cover their lowlands; their corn cannot grow; and the Great spirit will sweep those who escape to the hills from the earth with his terrible breath.
—*Tecumseh, Winter 1811*

52. AFTERMATH

PEACE GATHERING
NIGHT ONE
October 23, Tuesday
6:48 p.m. MDT

As the dancers stopped, the ground grew quiet. Sara climbed up into the jump seat to see if she could see Charlie. Illuminated by an octet of flickering campfires and kissed by moonlight, the entire site appeared to be floating. At last, she spotted him toward the center of the arena, engrossed in conversation with White Wolf.

She climbed down. "I see him. I'll be right back."

"We'll be right here," Will stated.

She made her way through the dissipating crowd, hoping he wouldn't take off in the opposite direction. The crowd continued to disperse to tipis, many faces wearing shocked expressions.

After centuries of vain hopes, many had given up. The fact they just effected such a literally earthshaking event was still sinking in, many staring at the severed remains of Eagles Peak in awe. Some laughed, others wept.

She caught Charlie's eye. He waved and made his way toward her, grinning. He wrapped his arms around her in a warm embrace, then his lips found hers. Those in the vicinity watched, some smiling, others confused, no doubt wondering what he was doing with this white woman who'd suddenly appeared in their midst.

"I'm relieved you're okay. I assume your family is, too?" he asked.

"Yes. We're fine. They're right over there, in the ATV," she replied, pointing. "We're a little shaken, to say the least. I'm still in shock. I know you inferred it would be spectacular, but I had no idea."

He grinned. "Yes, the Earth Mother did her part, as promised. Did you get it on video?"

"Yes! Most of it, anyway. I don't know how good it is, though, because things were shaking pretty badly. And it's not like there were any chances for a retake." She got out her phone to show him.

White Wolf joined them, watching as she brought it up.

"Wow! So that's what it looked like on the surface," Charlie said. "My view was of what lies within the Earth Mother. I saw her power and rage as never before. That is what she can do when her patience with her greedy, disrespectful children runs out."

Sara slipped her phone back in her pocket, wondering what occurred besides the earthquake and another blowout at LSO.

"You don't know what else happened, do you?" Charlie asked, as if reading her mind.

"You mean there's more? Like what? What we saw was quite spectacular."

"Do you know where Eagles Peak landed?"

She scowled. "No. We couldn't see that. Somewhere down the slope, I assume."

The same anger she saw in his eyes a few times before returned, but this time tinged with dark satisfaction. "It penetrated the ground directly over PURF."

Her mind stalled, incredulous, mouth gaping. "So it was destroyed?"

"Yes. It sank until it was entirely consumed by a very angry Earth Mother. Eagles Peak landing there to mark the spot was the final blow."

"Wow! That's incredible!" She smiled, eyes still wide. "So it's gone! Bryan is *definitely* celebrating."

"Yes. And it gets better," he went on. "It wasn't empty. People were there. There was some sort of event going on."

"What? People were there? *Really?*"

He nodded, his triumphant smile giving her chills.

"How many?"

"Thousands."

Her heart raced. "So now, all of them are. . ." Her hand shifted from her chest to her mouth. "*Dead?*"

"Swallowed by the Earth Mother. Just like the Creator and many Native prophets promised."

Speechless, it took a few moments before she asked, "Who do you think was there?"

His entire being broadcasted indifference. "Those involved with it in some way. Congressmen, probably. Lobbyists, who it was built for. I suppose we'll find out more on the news."

"Maybe," White Wolf interjected. "They may not admit it, if many of high rank were lost. It's likely to cause a great disturbance."

"Definitely. If enough were killed to disrupt government operations, possibly anarchy," she added.

Both men nodded agreement, their smiles disconcerting.

"Are you going to keep dancing for the other three nights?"

"Absolutely," Charlie replied. "We debated whether we should continue until midnight, but felt as if what was intended was accomplished. However, the Earth Mother may not be finished. We will dance as the Creator taught us. Not doing so would offend him."

Hackles raised the hair on the back of her neck.

"What's going on?" her father asked, stepping up beside her.

"You have no idea," she said, voice shaking. "The earthquake was nothing, compared to what it destroyed."

"That oil well that blew?" Will asked.

"No. It destroyed PURF," she said. "And apparently, it was filled with government dignitaries and lobbyists."

It took a lot to rattle him, but that hit the mark. He gaped at her for several seconds, then a few more working his jaw. "That's not good," he said grimly. "This country is headed for some serious trouble."

Her eyes locked on his. "Yeah."

SARA'S CABIN
RURAL FALCON RIDGE
October 23, Tuesday
9:38 p.m. MDT

WHEN THEY GOT BACK to the cabin, Sara couldn't believe her eyes. Not only were the lights on, but the ATV's headlights revealed a black Suburban behind her Buick.

Her heart and mind hadn't stopped racing since learning about PURF.

Now this.

She ground her teeth. *Nice job, Jason. Why didn't you stop them?*

"Why don't you let me handle this, Sara?" Will suggested, hand on her arm.

"Thanks, Dad, but this is my house. These jerks have been harassing me for months. I'm sick of it."

A smile played with his lips, but his eyes remained concerned. "Okay, whatever you say."

Connie, however, gave her a thumbs-up.

They parked in back as before and came in through the kitchen door. The dog raced for the living area, nearly knocking Sara over.

"Blossom!" she yelled.

The barking stopped. Will started to follow the dog, but Sara waved him back. He scowled disapproval, but took Connie by the hand and stayed out of sight.

The kitchen was in total disarray, cabinet contents strewn across the counters and floor. Sara tiptoed through broken glass to the open staircase to peek into the living area. As expected, Allison was there, sitting on the couch with a different partner. Some scruffy looking guy with a beard.

Sara's pit bull stood a few yards before them in battle position, snarling with her teeth exposed while her tail defied her stance by swaying softly back and forth.

Sara continued into view, stepping around scattered CDs and DVDs shed from the media center. "What are you doing in my house? Do you have a warrant?" she demanded.

"No, but we can certainly get one, if you aren't interested in cooperating," Allison stated, standing up.

The dog's tail froze as a deep, throaty growl rumbled past bared teeth.

"Cooperating? With what?" Sara replied. "I've done nothing wrong."

"First of all, call off your dog or I'll have to shoot her."

"That would be a really bad idea, Mr. Allison," she said, a razor's edge in her voice. "C'mon, girl," she said.

When the dog looked her way, she gave her the signal to back off. Blossom looked between her and the men a few times, then came over beside her and sat down.

"Okay," Allison said. "To be clear. We'll decide whether or not you've done anything wrong. That was quite a seismic disturbance. It seems more than coincidence that it occurred simultaneously with that Indian wing-ding held on your property."

Her eyes burned into his. "Right. So you're saying they caused it? *Are you out of your mind?* If anything, I'd investigate that oil company. The fact fracking can cause quakes seems to be a detail that many, including the EPA, conveniently overlook. Why don't you have a talk with them? Or perhaps one of the owners. Bob Bentley lives not far from here."

"Mr. Bentley has full immunity for anything that occurs in this area. You, however, do not."

"Indeed." She set her hands on her hips, favoring him with a decimating glare. "Why don't you start by telling me what I'm charged with so we can have an intelligent conversation? If you don't know, get out."

The man didn't move, presence darkening. "You've been treading on seditious territory, Mrs. Reynolds. Your involvement with this event further sheds serious questions on your intent. Rest assured, there will be an investigation."

Her glare likewise intensified. "Is that so?"

"You can bet on it. However, if you'll tell us where to find the ones in charge or how they managed to blow the top off that mountain, perhaps we can negotiate a deal. Maybe even forget you're an accessory. Or arrange a plea bargain."

Her laugh was short and bitter. "Sure. I'll be happy to answer the second part. They have a special agreement with the Earth Mother. They speak, she listens. Do the math."

His eyes narrowed, lowered brows increasing the span between them and his receding hairline. "Interesting. We have a warrant accusing them of domestic terrorism. And it wouldn't take much to add you. Let's see if the Earth Mother can protect them from that. "

She laughed again. "Are you really willing to take that chance, Mr. Allison?"

"If those Indians want war, we're ready. I think our military's a bit stronger."

"Have at it," she said, waving her arms. "I'm sure Custer thought so, too. Now, if that's all you've got, *get out*! I'm done with you people."

His laugh was ugly. "Given your cheerful and cooperative demeanor, Mrs. Reynolds, it's clear why someone might want to kill you."

"Alright, that's enough," Will stated, joining them from the kitchen. "She told you to get out."

Sara stepped over and opened the door. The man gave them one final leer, then stomped out, other man right behind him.

Her eyes flashed with additional fury.

Was that her imagination? Or did his seedy partner actually wink at her on his way out?

Even more furious, she slammed the door behind them.

Stuttering with rage, she turned to Will, hand on her chest. "D-do you th-think they were s-serious? A-about arresting them? F-for domestic terrorism?" she spit out. "How could they *possibly* prove the dance caused that earthquake?"

Will chuckled. "I'm sure any number of Indigenous participants would be happy to corroborate that was the case."

Her breath caught in her throat. "So you think they're in trouble?"

"Possibly. But I doubt that even the U.S. Military can outgun Mother Nature, Sara. They've been trying to harness or manipulate her energy for years with limited success. If the Earth is forced to take sides, I think we know how that will turn out. Furthermore, if our government is about to collapse, it's unlikely anything will come of it. They'll have bigger fish to fry than this."

"What's this?" Connie questioned from the living area. She held up a man's billfold. "I think one of your visitors lost his wallet." She giggled.

"Let me see," Sara said, holding out her hand. "Where was it?"

"On the couch."

Without warning, the windows trembled with the concussion of another blast.

"What the hell was that?" Will said. "Another aftershock?"

Sara dropped the wallet in her jacket pocket and dashed to the front window. Surrounded by darkness, another inky column of smoke teased with flickering flames wafted skyward in the direction of the highway.

They scrambled outside and started to pile into the car.

"No good, Sara," Will called as she climbed inside. "That boulder did a number on the quarter panel, which is jammed into the rear tire. You're not going anywhere like this."

Grateful for the ATV, they scrambled back up the incline for that instead, Sara behind the wheel.

Upon reaching the highway, she stopped. A hundred or so yards down the road, the black SUV was engulfed in flames.

"Oh, my God!" she cried. "What should we do?"

"Call 9-1-1," Will replied.

She pulled her phone from her pocket.

Dialed the number.

Groaned upon realizing it would go to Denver.

"Denver Central 911 Dispatch. What's your emergency?"

Sara explained the location discrepancy and what happened.

"I'll redirect your call to the local PD," the woman said.

A click, a few rings, then a familiar voice answered, "Falcon Ridge Police."

"Mike? Is that you?"

"Hey, Sara. Yeah, it's me. What's wrong?"

Grateful the third surprise for the day was a pleasant one, she explained.

"Okay, we'll get someone out there. How are you doing?"

"Really well. I'm as good as new again! Come by anytime so we can catch up."

"I will. We're pretty busy right now with all the commotion, but I'll definitely come by as soon as I can."

She laughed. "I can imagine."

"Gotta go. Bye, Sara."

"Bye, Mike." She put the phone back in her jacket. "So guess who's back?"

"Who?" Connie asked.

"Mike Fernandez!"

She cranked the wheel hard left and drove back to the house, tires spewing slush and gravel. They filed back inside where she took off her coat. Noting the weight in the pocket, she removed her phone as well as the wallet, setting both on the counter.

Connie picked up the billfold and opened it up. "Oh, my! Guess what? This wallet belongs to that guy, Jason!" she exclaimed. "Why would it be here? Was he here before?"

Sara blinked, confused, as Connie handed it over.

Without a doubt, the Maryland driver's license was Jason's. She dug through the billfold, finding another one. From Illinois, some guy named Paul McCullough. The picture matched the scruffy guy with Allison.

The cash compartment was loaded with a hefty wad of hundred-dollar bills. Nestled between them was a note. Her hands trembled as she took it out and eased it open.

Sara. This is the best I could do. He shouldn't bother you any further. Good luck with the Indian guy. Check your mail back in Denver for something I left for him. Jason.

Unable to speak, her hand trembled as she handed the note to Connie, Will right beside her.

"I'll be damned," Will muttered. "But if they already have you listed as a domestic terrorist, this is not good."

Sara collapsed on a stool, elbows on the breakfast bar with her face in her hands.

"Oh, honey," Connie said, massaging her shoulders. "I'm so sorry."

"Why would he do that?" she whimpered, sobbing.

"We'll worry about that later, Sara," Will said. "C'mon. Let's see if there's anything on the news about the earthquake. It's after ten."

Sara sniffed back a sob, wiped her eyes with her sleeve, and followed to the living room where she turned on the TV. Nothing came through. Connie's tablet brought up the CNN website, courtesy of a surviving cell tower somewhere.

All they said was an earthquake estimated at 7.6 on the Richter scale caused a seismic shift in the Rocky Mountains west of Denver. A map of the state appeared, epicenter marked with pulsing concentric circles.

No loss of life was reported and, due to the rural nature of the area, damage was expected to be limited. There was also no mention of the oil well fire, even though its black smoke would be visible by satellite and no doubt head east with prevailing winds.

"Should I send them my video of Eagles Peak? They didn't say a thing about that, either," Sara said, still sniffling.

"If you do, they'll want exclusive rights and you won't be able to use it on your blog," Will stated. "You might want to post it yourself first. I'm sure it won't take long to go viral."

"Right. But you know, now that I think about it, Dad, I'm not sure that's a good idea. If I post what I planned about the Dance's history and so forth, it might be considered evidence against them and make things worse, for both of us. In the past, the dance intimidated the military so much they not only murdered innocent participants, but outlawed it. This could validate their past fears were well-founded. And it's probably still technically illegal!"

She stiffened as another thought struck. "You don't think they'll arrest them, do you? If PURF was actually destroyed and thousands killed, it really does look like domestic terrorism."

"It was an earthquake, Sara. How could they have done such a thing? And who would believe it, if they did? If anyone was responsible, it was that drilling operation."

"I don't know, Dad. Based on my research, Native Americans aren't assumed innocent until proven guilty. Depending on which old laws might be on the books, they might be considered *hostiles* for being off the reservation. No telling what the government might do."

"Depending on what's left," Will said grimly.

When our young men grow angry at some real or imaginary wrong and disfigure their faces with black paint, their hearts also are disfigured and turn black, and then their cruelty is relentless and knows no bounds, and our old men are not able to restrain them.
—Seath'tl, "Seattle", 1854

53. CONSPIRACIES

HUDSON RESIDENCE
RURAL FALCON RIDGE
October 24, Wednesday
9:19 a.m. MDT

Jim Hudson wasn't surprised when his computer wouldn't connect to the internet. He sat at the hutch in the corner of their bedroom staring at Firefox's blank tabs and the "No Internet" message blaring from the screen. No doubt the satellite dish was out of whack, same as the one for the TV. He picked up his phone, activated the hot spot, and succeeded, surprised cell towers hadn't been annihilated as well.

Once he got online, he was surprised by the abbreviated report on every news source. Toppled mountain peaks and burning oil wells were major, yet nary a word.

Absolutely nothing.

His gut tightened. Such silence implied things were bad. Nothing new for media outlets, much less the government, to lie.

But in some cases, justified to avoid mass panic.

His phone rang.

The Pentagon.

"Hey, Fred. You're up early. Something's up, isn't it?"

"Sure as hell is. Is this a secure line?"

"It can be, but I'll have to call you back."

"Do it."

Jim brought up the encrypted app and returned the call. "Okay, Fred. What's going on?"

"You know that facility out your way? The one you asked about a while back?"

"The one that Reynolds woman went public about?"

"That's the one. Well, that 'minimal damage' in the news ignored its total annihilation. From near as we can tell, it's completely gone. Obliterated. Sunk into the depths of the planet. Took out thousands of miles of maglev line, too. That's what tipped us off. But that's only the tip of the iceberg."

"What else, other than covert transportation issues?"

"Well, the good news, I suppose, is that the Secretary of Defense survived. But only because he wasn't invited. The real problem is everyone that *was* there is dead."

"People were there?"

"Yes. Thousands. Including the President, Vice President, Secretary of State, all but four senators, and fifteen House members."

"What?"

Jim's mind imploded. His gut told him something was up, but the actual scope was beyond comprehension. "Why were they all in the same location like that? I thought that was forbidden, for this very reason."

O'Reilly scoffed. "Generally, that's true. But this was assumed to be a secure site. The place was being dedicated, which included a fancy D.C. style gala, when the quake occurred."

Jim's heart sank the rest of the way into his stomach.

"Needless to say this will have unprecedented impact," O'Reilly went on. "We're advising every state's governor to put their National Guard on full alert while succession takes place. No telling how far down the line they'll have to go to find someone qualified to be acting president."

"Do you suspect domestic terrorism?"

"Possibly. Domestic or foreign, it's of epic proportions. The same technology that manipulates the weather can cause earthquakes. We're not the only ones who have it. Our enemies do, too. When you called the other day, you mentioned some Indian ceremony out there. Do you know any more about that?"

"Not really. Supposedly, it was commemorating something that occurred back in the 1800s. Do you think they were involved?"

"It's hard to say. We have satellite video footage that shows some sort of ceremony concurrent with the earthquake. Many believe Native Americans have been in contact with aliens all along. Or, as they call them, the Star People. If that's true, then it's possible they managed to pull this off with ET assistance."

His jaw fell slack even as his shoulder muscles tightened, mind likewise in left field that Fred would suggest such a crazy alliance.

"You can't be serious," he sputtered. "Other than the video showing the two events were concurrent, what evidence is there?"

"None. Which is what makes it even more unsettling."

"I suppose it could have been some advanced technology, though a small nuclear device could have triggered it, if set off between tectonic plates."

"True. Could have been delivered by the oil drilling operation. Maybe set off with a timer from the geothermal system powering the facility. Whatever caused it, Jim, the general consensus among the Joint Chiefs is that it was purposeful and strategic sabotage. We've been controlling weather and trying to harness geophysical energy for decades. It's credible some alien race more advanced in terraforming could manage such a feat."

Jim's mouth hung open again, mind effectively blown. "You actually think that's possible, don't you?" His head started to pound, in sync with their generator grinding away outside the window.

"It's no secret Native Americans want their land back, Jim. It's not much of a stretch that they're prepared to do anything to make that happen. They're pissed we've been violating treaties and impinging on their land for centuries. Can't say I blame them, actually. But if they're in cahoots with aliens, that's of far greater concern than what we were dealing with in the 1800s."

"So what's the plan?" Jim asked.

"There isn't one. Yet. At least not a definitive one. Just options, depending on what we're dealing with. The Bureau of Indian Affairs claims all the tribal leaders they've been able to get in touch with deny any such conspiracy. They admit they had a multi-nation gathering at that location, but that was it. Since it wasn't held on reservation land and was in close proximity to PURF, it seems a very suspicious coincidence."

Jim agreed, knowing the military always questioned suspicious simultaneous events.

"The FBI was supposed to question the land owner, who happens to be that Mrs. Reynolds, who blew the whistle on PURF, back in June," Fred went on. "We haven't heard back. The first concern is getting the government stabilized. Find out who the acting president will be. Considering some of those cabinet secretaries, no telling. Other than that, we wait to see if any further disturbances occur that can be irrefutably connected to Native Americans."

"Makes sense, Fred. But there's one other thing that bothers me. Taking down the government has been the wet dream of various hostile factions for decades. And I'm not just talking about foreign powers. I'm talking domestic. It sounds like a good share of the swamp was drained into the bowels of the planet. But it's naïve to think there aren't any others who'd exploit the situation."

The silence that followed confirmed the threat was real. About the time he wondered if they'd been disconnected, Fred started to laugh.

"Stand by to be reactivated, Jim. Personally, I think it's going to be a helluva good time."

The call disconnected, leaving him staring open-mouthed at his phone.

"Who were you talking to, dear? Is everything okay?"

His eyes shifted to Liz, standing in the doorway. Based on her unruffled persona, she apparently believed the most serious repercussion of the quake was the fact their dishes needed to be replaced.

He groaned, knowing she'd absolutely flip out if he got called up again. Especially since, unlike other wars, this one would be on U.S. soil.

SARA'S CABIN
RURAL FALCON RIDGE
October 24, Wednesday
10:20 a.m. MDT

EVERY DISH WAS BROKEN, the only glasses that survived made of Lexan. At least they had power, thanks to the solar panels. Most of the debris had been swept up the night before, but to make sure all the shards were gone, Sara mopped, then wiped down the cupboards and counters while Connie reorganized the CDs and DVDs in the living area.

The mindless task allowed her thoughts to wander, the distant wail of sirens reminders of the wreck the night before. Eagles Peak with its top sheared off was even more startling in the light of day.

She paused, curious. Would they rename it? Eagles Butte, perhaps?

That Jason had taken such drastic means to rid her of that obnoxious agent left her more rattled than grateful. Especially, since the Feds might accuse her of the deed.

What was he thinking?

Her father telling her that he could tell from the start that he "wasn't wrapped too tight" wasn't much help. An empty, sick feeling persisted that he deliberately gave his life, supposedly while looking out for her.

There was a good chance Mike could tell her more, at least about the wreck, so she decided to invite him for dinner. She could fill him in as well, since she left out the details the night before of who they were and that they'd just left her house.

The call went to voice mail so she left a message.

What would happen, if anything, when the dancing resumed?

Would each repetition bring more catastrophes? Possibly even worse?

National news reports continued with the same toned-down narrative throughout the day. All they showed of the Denver area were a few photos of road damage and grocery shelves askew. What if the Eisenhower Tunnel was compromised or even collapsed? She made a mental note to check for alternative routes home, just in case.

Her thoughts drifted back to Jason.

Why?

That picture he took of her, then kidnapped her instead, but that plan failed, thanks to Charlie. Jason was always so calm, strangely so. How did he go from assassin to protector? Like he flipped a switch.

He even admitted to "an entire Rolodex of personalities."

Was he schizophrenic? Actual split personalities?

Did rejecting his request to watch movies again cause him to go over the edge?

"Are you okay, Sara? You look troubled?"

She looked up from the counter, eyes connecting with her father's. She inhaled deeply, held it a moment before blowing it out.

"I can't stop thinking about Jason, Dad. I can't understand why anyone would do that. You said he 'wasn't wrapped too tight.' Why?"

Will worked his jaw. "His background. He might have been a victim of a psyops program. It ran officially during the 50s and 60s, but was so controversial it shut down in the 70s. Or so they claim."

"Why?"

"Among other things, they brainwashed kids from a young age, hoping to create super-spies and super-soldiers."

Her mind cycled at the concept's familiarity. "The night before I escaped, we watched a few old movies together. That was the plot of one of them. *Ha!* The character's name was even Jason!

He gave me a running commentary on what was inaccurate about it. Would he remember being part of that?"

"Possibly. Or maybe after the sweat. He had a very strong reaction to that. Several of that program's victims committed suicide."

Chills ran down her spine. "Are they still doing it?"

"They insist it stopped, but that's a lie. It continued under a variety of different names. It included hospitals, universities, private foundations, and so forth. In some cases, they claimed to be treating children with autism using all sorts of torture from electric shock treatments to LSD. Some of them died."

"That's horrible!" she said, gaping at him with her hand on her chest. "Our government's been corrupt for so long it boggles my mind."

"Mine, too, Sara. Since before I was born. Seeing it first hand was why I left. Couldn't fix it and sure didn't want any part of it. On top of that, you'd be shocked how many high-level government officials and celebrities are into really sick, ritualistic child abuse."

"Wow. Unbelievable what some people do. What was that program called?"

"Originally, MK-Ultra. No telling what it's called now."

Her phone rang. She smiled when she saw who it was.

"Hi, Mike."

"Hi, Sara," he said. "It's so great to hear your voice. The last time I saw you I didn't know if you'd survive. I'd love to come for dinner. My place is a total wreck. I've been working through the night, making sure everyone is accounted for, doing damage reports for utility companies, and so forth. Power's still out and will be for a while. You're lucky you have those solar panels."

"I know. Bryan did a great job making this place self-sufficient. Does six o'clock work?"

"Perfect! I can catch a nap."

"Okay. See you then."

PEACE GATHERING
RURAL FALCON RIDGE
October 24, Wednesday
11:48 a.m. MDT

THE PARTICIPANTS WERE STUNNED when Charlie explained all that occurred the previous night. Three more performances remained. What might they accomplish? Charlie didn't know specifically, but suspected, as did the others, that it would be no less impressive.

Fortunately, food wagons came in the day before, loaded with a variety of choices for the hungry hoards. After enjoying a bulging burrito with White Wolf, Ice, and Leaping Elk, he wandered about the camp circle, looking for someone from New Mexico who might have word of his kids.

With over a quarter million living in *Diné Bikéyah*, there was no guarantee anyone from where he grew up made it there, but it was worth a try.

He drifted among the tipis, greeting participants, ears tuned for *Diné* conversations. Many years had passed since he'd lived there. When he visited his daughters, it was usually in Gallup, where he rented a motel room. When he returned the girls to their mother, it was usually in a parking lot there in town, other than a few times when he stopped by the rez to say hello to *Amasani*.

He smiled as memories fell upon him as gentle rain. She always insisted that he also go see his mother, though he counted it a plus when she wasn't around and he had an excuse to leave, like a flight to catch.

He searched those milling about for someone familiar, surprised when he didn't have to look far. A serious looking elder, long, grey hair in a pony tail, approached, eyes locked on him with obvious purpose.

The man held out his hand. "Do you remember me, Charlie?" he asked in *Diné*. He took the man's extended hand, scouring memory.

"I am sorry. You look familiar, but I do not remember from where," he responded in the same tongue.

"I am Johnny Wiletto. I married you and Rosina many years past."

"Oh! Yes, of course. Do you know of my daughters? Are they well? I have had a difficult few months and did not get to see them yet, but plan to before the end of the year."

The man smiled. "Yes. They are well. Growing up into beautiful young ladies. Your mother is well, but showing her age as we all do."

"Is my brother, Jacob, still on the rez?"

"No. I'm sorry. Last I heard he was in jail in Albuquerque."

Charlie sucked in his lips. "I'm not surprised. He was on an even worse path than I was."

"Sadly, that is true. Did you know your girls' mother is no longer married?"

Charlie's gut tightened, sensing where this was going. "No, I did not." *Neither do I care.*

"They all asked me to tell you they would very much like you back in their life. It is good for children to have both parents to guide them."

His stomach clenched harder as he sought a respectful answer that lacked commitment.

"I appreciate your message," he replied. "Thank you. I will be sure to call my daughters when the *Gathering* concludes."

The elder's eyes drilled into his several moments before he nodded and walked away.

Charlie gnawed his lower lip, having discovered far more than he set out to find.

SARA'S CABIN
RURAL FALCON RIDGE
October 24, Wednesday
6:20 p.m. MDT

THERE WASN'T A DRY EYE among them when Mike arrived. He was barely inside the door when he wrapped his arms around Sara and give her a sustained, emotion-laden hug.

She hadn't expected the reunion to be so emotional, but awakened memories left no choice. While he was her bodyguard they'd become close friends. The last she'd seen him was before she passed out on the *Today Show* sound stage from the poison.

"It is such a relief to see you," he said, wiping his eyes. "I can't tell you how worried I've been or how guilty I felt."

"No reason for that," Will said, shaking his hand. "She probably would have died for sure if you hadn't been there. Both of us missed finding the poison in her condo."

"Yeah," he agreed. "I'm so grateful you recovered. What treatments did the trick?"

She stared at him blankly, not knowing where to start. "All the credit goes to Charlie. You literally wouldn't believe what it took. But I'm here and that's what counts."

"Indeed. So the culprit wound up in the bottom of Dead Horse Canyon, right? Pretty fitting, if you ask me."

"Well, sort of," she said, leading him to the kitchen table where Connie set down a steaming dish of lasagna along with garlic bread and a green salad. All sat down and loaded their plates.

"What do you mean, *sort of?*" Mike asked, questions animating his round, Hispanic face.

"I actually found out where the poison itself came from. And is there ever a story behind that!"

She went on to tell him about being abducted, an abbreviated version of being healed, and her escape, then wrapping it up with the wreck the night before.

"Hold on a minute, Sara," Will interrupted. "Jason was the one who came up with the poison that nearly killed you?"

Oops.

Sara bit her lip, forgetting he didn't know. "Uh, yeah. That's what he said. But he gave it to Johannsen."

Her father exhaled, hard. "As if he didn't know exactly where it would be used. Good thing he's dead or I'd kill him myself."

"Me, too," Mike added. "So he was the other victim in that wreck?"

"Yes. Hold on," she said, getting up to retrieve the wallet.

"Wow," he said, flipping through the contents. "The Denver field office said the guy who was supposed to go with Allison couldn't make it. Got sick all of a sudden or something. As far as they knew, he came out alone. They were pretty surprised when I told them there were two victims."

"Really? No telling how Jason pulled that one off," Sara mused.

"It was a very sophisticated explosive. Military grade. Not much left of anything. Victims or otherwise."

"Listen," Connie said. "It sounds like the dancing has started again."

"It's not over?" Mike asked, eyes wide. Sara shook her head. "How many nights does it go on?"

"Three more, then through the night on the last one until morning. Did you know that PURF was destroyed last night?"

"I didn't. Probably a good thing. It had some seriously bad vibes."

"Yes. Especially considering who was inside."

"What? It was *occupied*?"

Sara watched him closely, familiar with his ability to hide his emotions, much like her father. "Supposedly, it was being dedicated. A bunch of Congressmen, lobbyists, and even the President were there."

He didn't even try to mask his surprise. "*Whoa*! Do you think each night something else will be destroyed?"

"I believe it's very possible," she said, sharing his apprehensive look.

In 1874, Colonel (Brevet General) George A. Custer led an expedition into the Black Hills, part of the Great Sioux Reservation. Gold was discovered, and the government attempted to purchase the lands. The Indians refused to sell. Meanwhile, miners invaded the area, arousing public sentiment in favor of taking the hills away from the Indians. Now the Sioux and Northern Cheyennes accused the whites of bad faith and of violating the Laramie Treaty.
— Peter John Powell, "Sweet Medicine," Volume I, p. 91

54. RECLAMATION

PEACE GATHERING
NIGHT TWO
October 24, Wednesday
7:48 p.m. MDT

During the day, while brotherhood proliferated among them, those at the *Gathering* discussed old wars. In particular, those fought against each other. Such division had weakened their stand against the whites. Had they been united, they could have prevailed.

In some cases, their Native brothers allied with the whites against other tribes. Now was the time to resolve old battles, resentments, differences, and hate to be unified as the Creator's people. As such, they could invite his blessings.

That night as Charlie sang praises to their Creator surrounded by dancers, his mind's eye opened on Mount Rushmore, the ultimate insult, given its location in the Black Hills, known to them as *Moxtavhohona.*

That area belonged to the Cheyenne for millennia and was under their control until around 1850. As he knew now, it was once secured by the *Massaum* covenant. The U.S. Government originally agreed it would remain theirs—

—until gold was discovered in 1874.

524

The Sioux gained control of the area through treaties with the whites, the Cheyenne eventually forced to leave the area.

Wars raged from 1876-1877. At Powder River, Montana in March 1876, Oglala and Northern Cheyenne warriors under Crazy Horse repelled a cavalry attack led by Colonel Joseph Reynolds.

Tonight Charlie sensed less energy than the night before when his efforts were magnified by an angry Earth Mother. Now his faith and that of the dancers was more important than ever, with much work remaining. All he needed was authority to use the *oxzem*.

His view panned from Rushmore, across the Black Hills to the Sacred Mountain, and then to the imposing Crazy Horse monument, which received scant attention by comparison.

He prayed, the response energizing him such that his hair stood on end. Lacking any doubts, he raised the spirit lance to the sky, angled northeast toward the Sacred Mountain.

"By authority given me by my brother, Porcupine, who was so endowed by the Messiah, I declare *Moxtavhohona* be cleansed and returned to my people!"

PEACE GATHERING
NIGHT THREE
October 25, Thursday
9:34 p.m. MDT

AS CHARLIE DANCED and sang the third night, his spiritual eyes were drawn to parcels of land the government had given back, then proceeded to use as they pleased or reclaim, no doubt the origins of the term "Indian giver."

Instances of desecrating sacred land with oil wells and pipelines as well as compromising its intended use such that it would no longer sustain life as it had in the past was profuse.

Another means of destruction was the existence of dams, which upset the natural balance. That threatened indigenous people's livelihoods and ability to live off the land as they'd done for thousands of years, much less being driven to desolate areas to which they'd been sent by government decree.

Set with determination, his mind's eye did the grand tour of twenty-three water retention structures on or near Native lands. This affected areas occupied by approximately two dozen tribes, spread from Pennsylvania and Tennessee in the east, across multiple states in the Great Plains, west through Arizona and New Mexico to California, then up the Pacific Coast to Oregon and Washington.

His college education in environmental management taught him dams were not all bad. In many cases, they provided flood control and allowed some areas to sustain life that previously could not. His time at LSO brought new insights to the oil industry, also not necessarily all bad.

The key was to be in the hands of those who honored the Earth Mother so they could be properly managed to benefit as many as possible without damage to people's livelihoods or environment.

And thus he petitioned the Messiah, his request delivered through the power of the *oxzem* magnifying his prayers as he held it aloft and offered it to the four sacred persons.

**SARA'S CABIN
RURAL FALCON RIDGE
October 26, Friday
8:21 a.m. MDT**

AS SOON AS THEY finished breakfast, Sara shooed Connie away and cleaned up the kitchen. By the time she finished, she made up her mind she needed a distraction. The day before she spent in a funk, taking a long walk with Blossom, then going on a much-needed cleaning frenzy. Maybe today the others would want to play a game or something.

Bridge, Monopoly, Scrabble, Uno, whatever.
Anything.

A subtle survey of her family revealed her father at the breakfast bar on his laptop, telecommuting. His eyes were fixed on the screen, forehead corrugated with wrinkles.

She knew that look.

Disturbing him was a bad idea.

He was supposed to be on leave, but for some reason was called back. How much related to what occurred at Eagles Peak he didn't know and no one would give him a straight answer. So, if nothing else, he was snooping around online to see what he could find.

Connie was in the living room, sprawled out on the couch with her tablet. Probably playing her favorite word game. She, too, looked fully engaged, so she continued to the guest room.

With nothing better to do, her mind gravitated to what further secrets might be stashed in the bench seat. She opened the lid, first thing that met her eyes the manila envelope labeled "Mom and Dad." Bryan told her they died when he was young, but refused to discuss the details, which clearly upset him, even as an adult.

Curiosity ignited, she unwound the string, lifted the flap, and pulled out the stack of paper.

A small card monogrammed with a gold embossed "*R*" reposed in the bottom. She opened it, finding a handwritten note.

> *Bryan,*
>
> *If anything happens to us, this is what you need to know when you grow up. We refused to get you involved, but we know too much, so it's likely our lives are in danger.*
>
> *We love you,*
> *Mom and Dad*

Goosebumps tickled her arms.

She sat on the bed, removed the binder clip, and flipped through it, page by page. Miscellaneous communications and correspondence, most before email became the norm. Many had handwritten notes in the margin, multiple names redacted. The bulk of the package comprised a government document. Dates indicated Bryan would have been around seven at the time.

A government logo dominated the photocopied cover. An eagle atop a shield that bore a compass rose.

The Central Intelligence Agency.

Her hands shook, mind awash with ominous speculations.

Its summary page described an experiment protocol. She skipped to the end, an unsigned signature page that granted parental permission for a child to be a participant in a study classified TS/SCI. Familiar because that was what her father had, *i.e.*, a Top Secret/Sensitive Compartmented Information clearance.

Following that was a photocopy of two government badges with the CIA logo for his parents, Christine and James Reynolds.

She went back to the beginning and flipped through the document, finding it loaded with unfamiliar medical terms.

Something jumped off the page, causing her to go back and see if she saw correctly.

She did.

Reference to a precursor program:

MK-Ultra.

Air escaped her lungs in a horrified moment of understanding.

No wonder Bryan hated the government.

PEACE GATHERING
NIGHT FOUR/DAY FIVE
October 26, Friday
9:01 p.m. MST

CHARLIE KNEW THAT whatever resulted from tonight's dance, which would continue until dawn, would be the *coup de grace*. The previous nights he'd alternated between the nine different dance songs Wovoka composed. Tonight he sang the special prayer Porcupine taught him in the Sacred Mountain like he had the first night.

Its words filled the camp with renewed passion, his dancing more energetic. Smiling dancers glowed with joy, hope, and brotherhood as they shuffled around their dance circles taking the usual step, then half-step, fingers intertwined.

After a few hours, his mind opened on a view of the entire nation as seen after dark via satellite. City lights embellished the land, bright clusters for the highly populated ones, smaller ones scattered about, then random dots in rural areas.

An invisible line extended from the middle of Texas northward, dividing east from west, where it darkened entirely, indicating less populated regions. Denver, Phoenix, and Salt Lake City stood out, then darkness across the Rockies and Sierra Nevada's to the far west where California, Oregon, and Washington had glaring city-center lights, especially along the coast.

He wasn't as sure of the objective as in previous nights. Why this view of the entire country?

As they danced past midnight, lights started going out. Not due to encroaching dawn, cause unknown.

It started with Saint Louis. Spread radially, consuming Indianapolis, Chicago, Cincinnati, and Detroit. Continued outward to Pittsburgh, Atlanta, Dallas and Houston, which darkened about the same time as New York City, Washington D.C., then Montreal.

As cities went black, the *oxzem's* shaft grew hotter. Sparks flew from its center wheel, increasing in frequency and intensity.

Denver, Salt Lake City, and Phoenix darkened next. Then Los Angeles, San Francisco, Portland, and Seattle.

The entire country was dark, a mere shadow between oceans, dawn crawling across the Atlantic.

Was the darkness symbolic? Or literal?

For the first time since they began, a ominous feeling of death and doom settled upon him. He prayed harder, singing its words with passion.

As dawn's blush reached Colorado's sky, the end of their vigil neared completion. When the Sun's rays shot through jagged mountain tops he stopped singing and signaled the drummers to finish.

Exhausted dancers stood still. Fingers interlocked for hours released and flexed, arms fell to their sides, expectant eyes pleading to know the result of the longest dance of the ceremony.

This time Charlie didn't know, the odd vision haunting, more so with its meaning unknown. He stood tall, elevated the *oxzem* overhead and prayed so all could hear and repeat his words.

"Great Spirit Father, please hear my plea! We have danced in praise and worship to you and your creation for five days as instructed by the Messiah. We are aware miracles occurred, for which we are grateful. We ask now, is there more? My eyes beheld strange visions as we danced past the dark of night into the dawn of a new day. What are we to know of its message?"

Hundreds of repetitions rumbled from the crowd toward the heavens. Within moments the answer came on the voice of thunder. It echoed through the canyons, coming to everyone at the *Gathering* in their own language, repeated four times.

The Earth Mother has spoken to her wrath and will continue to do so. The demise of the corrupt government of the United States will soon unfold. There will be chaos. Soon the wicked shall be destroyed. The time has come when all that was spoken by my holy prophets will come to pass.

Stunned silence enveloped the dancers as meaning penetrated fatigue-laden minds and bodies. A buzz of subdued private conversations followed.

Charlie waved for attention. "First, we pray to express our gratitude for this sacred moment. Next, we pray for our families and our safe return home. Then, we cleanse ourselves symbolically to complete the ceremony. After that, we celebrate with a special feast!"

Murmurs among the crowd prevailed, coupled with puzzled faces. The food wagons had been depleted. From where might so many enjoy a feast?

PEACE GATHERING
October 27, Saturday
3:23 p.m. MDT

AFTER NAPPING A FEW hours, Charlie and the others cheered as the Earth Mother provided their celebratory feast. It was still within the deer/elk season and Running Elk brought along a rifle for safety reasons, in case anything like a grizzly bear showed up.

Charlie expressed no concerns in that regard, assuming that bears were transitioning into hibernation and would avoid such a group, anyway. However, having the weapon along was another inspired addition to their supplies.

Thus, everyone was well-fed, courtesy of a couple bull elks harvested from the herd they saw when they scoped out the site the month before.

Weary, but elated from the long night, they broke camp, then waited, wondering if the coaches might be delayed. His phone rang. He smiled, knowing it was Sara.

"How'd it go?" she asked.

"We did as we were told," he replied. "Now we wait."

"What do you think happened the other nights?"

He drew a sharp breath, previous visions tumbling through his mind. "It is in *Maheo's* hands. It is not yet over. There will be much unrest. Chaos. The Earth Mother has more to say."

"Wow," she said, followed by a long pause. "Is it safe for us to go home? Or should we stay here?"

"The worst damage will be farther east. Shortages are likely everywhere, though. You would be safer with your family. If we see any problems when we go through Denver I'll let you know."

"Thanks. I'll ask the drivers when they come to pick things up, too. If they don't show, I'll assume the worst. Maybe then we'll stay here, but there's not much in the freezer."

They chatted awhile longer, Charlie ending the call when the purr-like rumble of approaching diesel engines confirmed their on-time arrival, intruding on the serenity of the new sacred site.

Everyone gathered their possessions and reported to the boarding area.

Once everything was loaded up, all fifteen coaches pulled out, heading for I-70. Charlie and White Wolf occupied the same seat as before, right behind the driver.

"How are the roads?" Charlie asked him. "Are there any closures we need to go around?"

"There's a small detour before we get there, but the Interstate is clear," the driver replied. "It may add twenty minutes or so to the trip."

Charlie was somewhat surprised the FBI hadn't shown up. In reality, what could they do? What could they prove? But hundreds of years of mistreatment to the point of attempted genocide residing in genetic memory couldn't be silenced.

To say nothing of the encounter at Sara's condo.

He leaned back in his seat, closed his eyes, and consciously shifted his thoughts to their successes, though some impressions remained troubling. Whatever they'd accomplished was not expected to go down easily.

The soft hum of the coach's engine and gentle rocking sensation had barely lulled him to sleep when brakes squeaked and they bolted to an abrupt halt.

His eyes flew open.

He stood up and stared out the windshield to what lay ahead.

A roadblock. Including a half-dozen black SUVs and armed National Guardsmen.

"Another opportunity, Littlewolf," White Wolf said softly. "Would you like me to handle it? You look tired and it may not be wise to use the *oxzem* in this confined area."

He chuckled, thinking otherwise, but agreed. "Yes. Thank you."

White Wolf closed his eyes.

The bus edged forward as each of the half-dozen cars in front was waved through. They pulled up beside the Highway Patrolman issuing the questions. The driver slid open his window.

"Is this the excursion group heading for Denver?" the trooper asked.

The driver nodded. "Yes, sir."

"How many buses in your caravan?"

"Fifteen."

"Okay, you're free to go."

The trooper waved them through.

White Wolf chuckled.

"Was the roadblock not for us?" Charlie asked, momentarily confused.

White Wolf's laugh increased in volume. "No, Littlewolf. It was very much for us. I realize it came out before you were born, but did you ever see the movie, *Star Wars*?"

"Of course. Many times. It was Bryan's favorite. I rather liked it, too."

"Do you recall the Jedi mind trick? Where Obi Wan said, *These are not the droids you're looking for*?"

Charlie's eyes locked on his uncle's, astounded the man had seen that movie, too. "Are you kidding?"

"Not at all. Who do you think invented it, Littlewolf? Certainly not the white man. In this case, these weak-minded individuals were coerced in a similar manner. They believe our caravan contains high school students heading to a band competition."

Charlie chuckled. "What will they do when they figure it out?"

"Not our problem. If and when they do, we'll be safely home."

NORTHERN CHEYENNE RESERVATION
MONTANA
October 28, Sunday
2:17 a.m. MDT

LIKE A SMOLDERING SMUDGE bundle of multiple herbs, a complex mixture of emotions consumed Charlie as what was left of the caravan departed into the dark of night. The majority disembarked in Denver to catch buses or planes home to their respective destinations. The remainder consolidated, reducing their number back to five, like when they started.

Within the dissipating diesel fumes swirled profound memories of the preceding days. They accomplished what they'd set out to do, but now the future was cloudy, much as the dust in the coaches' wake obscured their tail lights.

Now what?

Anticipation drove his energy for weeks, the *Gathering's* completion both euphoric and terrifying. His passion no longer had direction, finding only a void.

He turned to White Wolf beside him, who reflected far more peace than he felt himself. "Again I am overwhelmed with the enormity of what we have done," he said. "What do we do now?"

White Wolf stood tall, head held high.

"We wait. *Maheo* will guide us. We did not know his intent, only followed his promptings. As with healing, we were his servants. This battle will be the same. When our brothers return to their reservations they will conduct *Massaum's* and start holding dances. The Earth Mother will work with them as she did with us."

"Yes," Charlie agreed. "Together with *Maheo* we have destroyed much of their corrupt foundation. They are now as a pack of wolves without an alpha. Each will fight for dominance. But with greed and power their goal, they will destroy each other from within."

"True. When they lie dead on the ground covered with maggots, we will create a land that is truly *of, for, and by the people* and provides *liberty and justice for all.*"

"Yes. Bryan once told me that Thomas Jefferson designed the U.S. Constitution based on the Iroquois confederacy. Yet, they yielded to the white man's drive for dominance and conquest. *Maheo* always intended this land to be one of freedom. In time, it will be again."

55. TECTONICS

MONTGOMERY RESIDENCE
BOULDER
October 30, Tuesday
2:39 p.m.

When Sara finally left the cabin with her family, no new information had surfaced, at least in the media. Her father and Mike managed to bend the quarter-panel far enough away from the tire to drive safely. She could just imagine explaining the damage to the insurance company, especially if the quake had been deemed inconsequential

When the personnel who picked up the water trucks and porta-potties arrived, she asked about conditions in Denver. As far as they were aware, everything was fine, giving her a strange look when she asked.

When she dropped off her father and Connie, conditions appeared normal in Boulder. Her condo was undamaged, but a trip to the grocery store to pick up a few things, including more dog food, revealed many shelves alarmingly empty. She sensed trouble was on the way and decided to pack up and join her family.

As soon as she merged onto Highway 36 she encountered a caravan of army vehicles over a half-mile long. Troop trucks, jeeps, even a few eighteen-wheelers hauling flatbeds with unseen cargo beneath heavy tarps.

She hadn't seen such a convoy in quite a while, especially this time of year. It was more common when the National Guard had their annual "summer camp."

The persistent knot in her gut tightened as she passed the slower moving throng. Knowing what she did, she suspected the government, or what was left of it, was preparing for trouble.

If there was no food would people take to the streets, rioting? Be able to continue their normal lives? Would the stock market crash?

If, as Charlie said, thousands lost their lives—many of which would be considered assassinations—they'd toppled the better part of the government along with Eagles Peak.

Her mind flashed with understanding as its unsettling symbolism struck.

Destruction of the underground facility would be considered an act of war. A war Indigenous Americans could not win, if fought as a conventional battle. She shuddered at the thought of hundreds of tanks, to say nothing of B-52s, ordered in their direction. Another equally horrifying thought questioned:

Where were these going?

Indian reservations were sovereign, independent nations. This would be seen as the ultimate act of rebellion, which could easily be squashed by the U.S. Military. Such a deed was the epitome of treason, to say nothing of open sedition.

As far as she was aware, Charlie *et al* did not intentionally set out to destroy PURF. While he knew it was in the neighborhood, he had no idea it would be directly involved, much less the fact thousands of government dignitaries and their lobbyist cohorts would be present at that time.

Or did he?

Was it the Curse that took out PURF? Did Bryan's death activate it?

If Charlie and his people were found guilty, the result would be more catastrophic than when Columbus "discovered" the New World.

She gripped the wheel with another terrifying thought. Would those viral videos on social media taken by several food vendors of the earthquake serve as damning evidence? All of them included the dancers and even Charlie at the center, some in the same frame as when Eagles Peak collapsed.

When she arrived in Boulder, Blossom was the first one to find Connie, who was up in Will's den surfing the internet for news reports instead of her usual place in the kitchen. Sara hauled over a chair and sat beside her, eventually discovering speculative leaks on blogs, podcasts, and YouTube. Astute, independent journalists uncontrolled by the powers-that-be were asking hard questions.

Why had so many high-ranking government officials, including the President, Vice President, and Secretary of State, not been seen or heard from since October 23?

A week had passed. That many high-profile individuals simply didn't disappear, even during a Congressional recess. One post declared that the Cannon, Longworth, and Rayburn House Office Buildings had been unoccupied for days.

One podcast claimed they'd been kidnapped by aliens.

While they were laughing at that, the kitchen door closed downstairs, announcing Will was home early from work. Blossom barked a quick welcome and bounded down to greet him.

"Hello?" he called from below. "Whatever you two are doing, c'mon down. I have good news and bad news."

The two exchanged a look, then directed their steps toward the stairs.

Connie gave him a welcoming kiss and Sara provided a hug. "So what's the news, Dad?"

"Good or bad?"

Her back straightened. "Uh, how about something good?"

"Okay. Check this out." He set his briefcase on the kitchen table, opened it, and removed two pieces of paper. "First, this one."

It was a color printout of what looked like a satellite shot of some mountains.

"What is it?" Connie asked.

"Look closer. Do you see anything strange? Like a face?"

Sara wrinkled her nose, mystified. "Oh! I see it! It looks just like a Native American." She pointed it out for Connie. "What is this, anyway?"

"It's in Alberta. Saskatchewan, Canada. That formation is known as the Badlands Guardian. A woman discovered it years ago, when she was looking at satellite images. Since then, experts can't decide whether it was created by indigenous people thousands of years ago or Mother Nature. It's nearly a half-mile long, so would have been a colossal undertaking."

The Badlands Guardian

"Okay. Pretty cool. But why is it important now?" Connie asked.

Will grinned and set down another shot of the same area. It took Sara a moment to see the difference.

"That's insane!" she exclaimed, hand on her chest. "Now it looks as if he's smiling! Maybe even laughing. He looks entirely different."

"Exactly," Will stated. "There was some serious tectonic activity up there, right around the same time as the second dance. When the dust settled, this was the result. And it gets better. Remember Mount Rushmore?"

Sara nodded. "Of course. Up there in South Dakota. It became a revered American icon, but was a major insult to Native Americans who possessed that land for millennia."

"Not anymore," Will declared, as he put down another printout.

The entire side of the mountain on which the four Founding Fathers had been carved had, like Eagles Peak, fallen face-down to the ground below. Shattered stone was all that was visible, above and below where the monument reigned for nearly a century.

Goosebumps marched along her arms and the back of her neck. "Are you kidding, Dad? Are these real? Or Photoshopped?"

He gave her a conspiratorial smile. "They're real. Straight off one of our satellites. They're also classified, both areas now restricted. Mount Rushmore is a national memorial, but it's been closed to visitors. This will be devastating to many and very volatile if Native Americans are found to be the perpetrators."

Her mind spun like bald tires on icy roads. *Was that even possible?*

"Do you think Charlie's *Gathering* had anything to do with these? Or were they were independent events?"

Will scowled, rubbing his chin. "Timing indicates he and his cohorts get the credit. Or blame, as the case may be."

"So what's the bad news?" Connie asked, crease between her brows showing guarded concern.

Will exhaled through his nose, formerly elated mood turning grim. "They pulled my security clearance. I no longer have a job. I suspect the FBI complained about my involvement in 'suspicious activities.' Fortunately, these were already in the printer tray when I got notified, so I grabbed them on my way out the door."

ONEIDA INDIAN RESERVATION
VERONA, NEW YORK
October 31, Wednesday

CHILDREN ON THE Oneida Indian Reservation in Central New York State were giddy with excitement. With it Halloween, dressing up and taking part in a ceremony with neighboring tribes, including the Onondaga, Cayuga, Seneca, Mohawk and Tuscarora, was the greatest thing since the *Diné* taught them how to make fry bread.

True, they didn't get to play those roles for a few days, but how much fun would it be when they did? Practice today would be so much fun with a party to follow!

A special dance would be held for another five days, following the *Massaum*. That was supposed to be something their elders said would always be remembered as well.

What fun to be part of history!

They heard mention of the seventh and even eighth generation many times, which they didn't understand, only that they were part of something very special.

MONTGOMERY RESIDENCE
BOULDER
October 31, Wednesday
9:39 a.m.

Sara, Connie and Will sat in the den, transfixed. Whether their journalistic suspicions had been aroused or the mass media were responding to public demand wasn't clear. Nonetheless, pictures of Mount Rushmore taken from a private plane went viral, further fueling the fire. Soon after, networks were abuzz, talking heads speculating on an explanation.

Sara as well as the others suspected a ploy. The most likely scenario was that the media were under orders: Distract your viewers and suppress the ominous indicators until the government gives the go-ahead.

Or what was left of it.

"Why do you think it's taking so long?" Connie mused aloud.

"They're probably trying to decide who should make the announcement," Will stated. "The fact we haven't heard from the President is especially telling. If he was at PURF, it's even more serious than if only Congress Critters were involved."

"Right," Sara agreed. "Who would be in charge? The military? Heaven forbid if it's the 'alphabet agencies' like the CIA, FBI, or NSA. Ugh."

Will grunted. "No telling. It depends on who's still alive. I think everyone knows the first in line for succession is the Vice

President. After that, the Speaker of the House and President Pro-Tempore of the Senate. Then the Secretary of State, Secretary of Defense, Attorney General, Secretary of the Interior, on down the line of the agency secretaries in the chronological order the agencies were created."

"Wow," Sara said. "That shows how critical cabinet appointments are. It's a scary thought for some of them to become president. For example, the Secretary of Defense would probably not even blink before starting a war. Would they serve a full term?"

"No. Only until a new election can be held, which will probably be March. Consider what a big to-do election years are and how long that process takes. They probably won't bother with primaries."

"The country's already divided. Will this bring it together, or create a permanent split? Does a person in the succession list need to be confirmed by Congress?" Connie asked.

"No. They're in until an election is held. The only caveat is they have to qualify for the presidency. Natural born, at least thirty-five years old, live in the U.S. at least 14 years."

"Seems like most would qualify," Sara said.

Will shook his head. "Not really. Quite a few are foreign born of immigrant parents and a handful too young. As far as these disasters are concerned, Eagles Peak's demise could easily be the fault (no pun intended) of the earthquake." Will scowled as he continued. "However, the *Gathering* was recorded on satellite footage along with the geological drama, connecting the two. The time stamps on those photos are within moments of the quake."

"Both Patrice and Charlie claim there's no such thing as a coincidence," Sara mused.

"I wonder what Patrice thinks of all this?" Connie added. "We should go see her. I'm sure she'd be all ears to find out what went on."

"That's a great idea." Sara grabbed her phone. "Patrice! Hi, it's Sara. Connie and I are wondering what your take is on all this."

The woman's hearty laugh brought a smile.

"Sara! You little devil, you! I suspect there's plenty you could tell *me.* Things are pretty quiet here at the shop. Why don't you two come down and fill me in, especially what they're not telling us on the news?"

"Sounds like a plan. We'll be there shortly." She turned to her father. "Do you mind, Dad? Or would you like to join us?"

He chuckled. "You go ahead. I'll stay here and keep track of the networks. I'll text if anything comes up."

With that, the two women grabbed the printouts and left, arriving at Cosmic Portals a few minutes later. Patrice was waiting and beckoned them through the beaded curtain greeted by the usual fragrant scent of ylang ylang.

The astrologer's fingers folded together and rested on the silk-covered table, eyes fired with curiosity.

"I'd been looking at charts and saw some connections, but didn't know exactly what they meant. Maybe you can fill in the blanks. What went on with Charlie's *Gathering*?"

"You have no idea," Sara replied, shaking her head.

Patrice laughed. "I've certainly never heard of one causing an earthquake before. Eclipses, well, maybe."

"Have you ever heard of the Ghost Dance?" Sara asked.

Patrice's eyes fired with curiosity. "No, not that I recall."

Sara filled her in about Wovoka's vision, prophecy, and the *Dance of Peace.* "That's what they did. Hundreds of them, from tribes across the country. It was a very sacred time. And time may be right for its original promise to be fulfilled."

Sara took out her phone and showed her the videos.

"That gives me goosebumps," Patrice said, rubbing her arms.

"The prophecy stated the white men would be swallowed up by the Earth. Considering PURF was consumed by the earthquake that seems spot-on, don't you think?"

Patrice's response was an open-mouth. "That facility you blew the whistle on?"

"Yes," Sara nodded. "And according to Charlie, it was loaded with government officials. We're holding our breath, waiting for the official announcement. But it sounds like it's tied in with the prophecy."

Patrice leaned back in her chair and nodded agreement. "I would definitely agree! And that explains the silence and missing dignitaries." She leaned forward, eyes alive with curiosity. "Do you by any chance happen to know when Wovoka had this vision?"

Sara's eye's connected with hers. By now she knew enough about astrology to realize the woman's mischievous smile was saying she'd give blood and pay money to know the date, time, and place.

Fortunately, she knew.

"From what I've read," she answered, trying unsuccessfully to suppress a grin, "It was during a total eclipse of the Sun. I'm pretty sure it was New Years Day in 1889, somewhere in Nevada."

"Great benefics!" Patrice exclaimed, starting to laugh. "I knew it! I just *knew* something happened then!"

Sara's back straightened, wondering what tipped her off. "You did?"

"Yes! Eclipses are notorious for triggering major events. The ancients recognized them as omens. People today know the celestial mechanics, but ignore their meaning. I was looking for those that crossed Charlie's reservation. The one in 1889 went *right over it,"* she said tapping the silk-covered table.

"I didn't know about Wovoka or his prophecy, much less that it occurred at that time," she continued. "You remember the one back in 2017 that crossed the United States?"

Sara nodded. "Yes, of course. Bryan insisted on seeing it, so we all drove up to Wyoming to watch. It was pretty impressive. Kind of creepy, actually."

"Well, there was another one in 2024 that also crossed the country," Patrice explained. "The fact it was a seven year cycle could be significant. And what's really creepy is the path of those two made a giant "X" across the country."

"What do you think that means?" Connie asked.

"It's hard to say, but it doesn't look good. It's as if God is saying 'I'm done with you people.' There's a town in southern Illinois that's ground zero, crossed over by both. Which happens to be right in the middle of the New Madrid fault."

"Did anything happen?" Sara asked.

"It's hard to say. There were some severe weather events and a lot of political drama, but no earthquakes. But their effects aren't always immediate. Furthermore, another eclipse around the same time formed an 'X' in southern Texas. If that eclipse clear back in 1889 came home to roost now, no telling. That energy can just sit there, waiting to be triggered."

The heavy, dark feeling made a comeback as Patrice validated Sara's impression that prophecies were about to be fulfilled. The conversation shifted the mood from one of discovery to its ominous possibilities.

"Do you think those eclipses started this cycle?" Connie asked.

"That's possible," Patrice replied. "Prediction is difficult. Astrologers who presume to do so get in trouble all the time when they turn out to be wrong. They see what they want to see rather than look at the chart objectively. Makes us all look like frauds. We can discern the general tone, but specifics are difficult. Timing is especially tough. There's a timeless element to this cosmic stuff, even though we need exact times to run an accurate chart. Did you have a kaleidoscope when you were a child?"

Sara nodded. "Yes. I was fascinated by it, how the colors changed, never the same."

"That's similar to how cosmic energy works. It changes, day by day, with the different planetary cycles."

"I can see that. Especially if it takes decades or more to manifest," Sara commented.

"The Moon tends to be a big trigger," she went on. "Lunations, what we call New and Full Moons, typically bring something. Eclipses, even more so. They're the ultimate manifestation of each. Solar eclipses always occur during a New Moon, lunar eclipses during a Full Moon."

Patrice's conspiratorial smile sent more chills down her spine. "However," she continued, "when you combine it with prophecy, especially when it's tied with other eclipses, it's a pretty good bet something will occur, even if it doesn't make the news. Many important events happen in shadows."

"Do you think they're celebrating on reservations across the country?" Sara asked, wrinkling her nose. "I'm concerned they're going to get blamed for this and be in even more trouble than ever before."

Patrice shook her head. "Native Americans are seldom given to frivolity. Their medicine men understand the gravity of the situation. If Mother Earth is behind them, no telling. She certainly seemed to be on their side for this."

Sara nodded agreement. "She's on their side, alright. Look at these satellite images Dad brought home." Patrice covered her mouth as she saw the changes to the Badlands Guardian.

"Considering how Mother Earth has been treated, that's not surprising," she said. "As far as being able to blame indigenous people, that's a bit of a stretch." She held out her hands. "What rational person would believe a peaceful *Gathering* caused such devastation?"

"Furthermore, since when has the press reported supernatural forces associated with catastrophic events?" Connie commented.

"Not since the movie, *Ghostbusters*," Sara said, generating a much-needed touch of humor. "On the other hand, a lot of religious people out there believe the end is near. What if they're right?"

SOUTHERN CHEYENNE - ARAPAHOE RESERVATION OKLAHOMA
+
MATTAPONI and PAMUNKEY RESERVATIONS VIRGINIA
+
CATAWBA RESERVATION

ROCK HILL, SOUTH CAROLINA
+
THIRTY-TWO TRIBES (INCLUDING SOUTHERN CHEYENNE)
INDIAN TERRITORY
OKLAHOMA
+
POTAWATOMI, CHIPPEWA, OTTOWA TRIBES
MICHIGAN
+
CHIPPEWA, STOCKBRIDGE MUNSEE, WINNEBAGO, ONEIDA TRIBES
WISCONSIN
+
CHIPPEWA AND SIOUX TRIBES
MINNESOTA
October 31 - November 5, Wednesday - Monday

PREPARATIONS BEGAN AMONG nearly five dozen tribes to perform the *Massaum*. The concept was one that resonated at the soul level as if stored in genetic memory for thousands of years. The ceremonies would begin the following day.

While the performances may not be quite as elaborate or precise as they'd witnessed in Montana, their hearts were fully engaged and prayers lifted to the heavens that their best efforts be accepted.

Camp circles were defined, World Trees set up, and the creation ceremonially replicated. Names of their own deities were substituted, but the spirit of consecrating the land to the Great Spirit Father and accepting their stewardship of it were maintained.

Littlewolf, the Northern Cheyenne who taught the ceremony, instructed them that if they had a sacred mountain in their culture, they could connect to that. If not, they should direct a connection to a point located in Southern Illinois that was roughly the center of a circle that, when transcribed on a map, enclosed them all.

Many miracles were witnessed upon the *Massaum's* completion five days later. New bison, elk, and even antelope herds were reported that hadn't been seen for decades, likewise smaller game, including *Voh'kis*, the kit fox. Plant species that had disappeared due to over-harvesting, herbicides and other factors would delight many with their return the following spring.

NATIVE TRIBES AND NATIONS
EASTERN HALF OF NORTH AMERICA
November 6 - 10, Tuesday - Saturday
6:23 a.m.

FIVE DAYS THAT COMPRISED the *Dance of Welcome and Peace* followed the *Massaum*. Love and brotherhood flowed among the participants as never before, especially between tribes who gathered together, most dramatically those who had once been bitter enemies.

As the Sun rose on the fifth day, each felt a disturbance similar to what they'd witnessed in Colorado. A swarm of earthquakes of varying magnitudes were reported, the strongest at the point on which they'd been told to focus.

That included the New Madrid Seismic Zone, which touched parts of Illinois, Kentucky, Tennessee, Missouri, Ohio, Mississippi, and Arkansas. Power outages were profuse, but spotty, crews doing their best to get it restored.

An earthquake in that area in 1812 was strong enough to cause the Mississippi River to flow backwards due to historic upheavals of the ground along its shores. These tremors brought a similar effect, damage far more severe due to how much the population had increased over a span of two hundred years.

Cities enclosed by the circle Charlie saw in his vision were heavily damaged. Streets buckled like cardboard, bridges collapsed, power lines severed, whether above or below ground, leaving dark desolation behind.

Areas between New York and Virginia reported catastrophic damage and loss of life. Washington D.C.'s majestic stone buildings designed to mimic ancient Roman structures were shaken on their foundations, but mostly spared.

Their contents, however, were reduced to piles of rubble. These included records retained in the Capitol building and Supreme Court. The National Museums of Art and Natural History, as well as much of the Smithsonian were partially demolished while, oddly enough, the Museum of the American Indian was unscathed.

Courtesy of fortification activities conducted over the years, the White House survived, awaiting its next resident, who would be handed the monumental challenge of putting things back together.

Office buildings surrounding the Mall were mostly flattened, likewise exclusive residential areas such as Georgetown. The Pentagon in Arlington, Virginia along with Crystal City, and Silver Spring, Maryland across the Potomac were heavily damaged as well.

Damage assessments were being conducted and victims either rescued or bodies recovered. Having occurred early on a Saturday morning, most public and commercial buildings were vacant, reducing loss of life, residential areas less severely damaged.

New York City, Baltimore, Philadelphia, Atlanta, Memphis, Boston, Cleveland, Pittsburgh, Omaha, Minneapolis, Milwaukee, Des Moines, St. Louis, and Chicago likewise reported catastrophic damage along with power outages. The worst was in downtown areas, suburbs somewhat spared.

Unprecedented destruction brought mayhem and violence to several cities in the eastern half of the nation as people scrambled for shelter, food, and water. High-rise buildings that still stood were severely affected, having no elevator service or water. Emergency shelters, some of which had auxiliary power, were overcrowded, food scarce with deliveries delayed indefinitely.

First responders and emergency management personnel confronted their worst nightmare as they did their best to maintain order.

MONTGOMERY RESIDENCE
BOULDER
November 12, Monday
10:03 a.m. MST

AFTERSHOCKS IN COLORADO following the *Gathering* continued for weeks. Rolling blackouts began as functional power grids shared electricity with less fortunate areas. Cable television was still out, but satellite internet, as expected, still worked after adjusting the antenna.

With electrical service currently out, Sara, Connie and Will sat around the big screen of his desktop computer, power courtesy of their generator chugging away outside. Whether they'd find gasoline for it as long as the situation persisted was questionable.

Sara held her breath as the President's press conference went live. Due to extensive damage in and around Washington, it was being held in a high school gymnasium in Gaithersburg, Maryland, which had sustained minimal damage with the building considered structurally sound enough to assure safety. Cameras panned flatbed trucks loaded with emergency generators brought in to assure uninterrupted power for the event.

The President's Asian press secretary stood at the podium, much as any other time. Rather than the President, however, the person she introduced was Naomi Iron Shirt, Secretary of the Interior.

Sara, Connie, and Will exchanged wide-eyed glances while everyone present at the briefing did the same. A wave of hushed conversations grew silent as the woman stepped to the dais.

In addition to her name, long black hair and facial features bespoke unmistakable Native American heritage. Sara and her family wore beaming smiles.

"It pains me greatly to announce that the President, Vice President, Secretary of State, and all but four senators and fifteen members of the House of Representatives, have perished in a tragic disaster," she said. "The Speaker of the House and President Pro-Tempore of the Senate were also among the victims, which numbered in the thousands.

"They were touring a newly constructed underground facility when it was destroyed by the earthquake that occurred west of Denver nearly three weeks ago. According to the Presidential Succession Act of 1792, the mantle of the presidency has therefore fallen to me."

She paused until another round of murmurs likewise faded to silence.

"Those that precede my position in succession are either deceased, unable to meet the necessary qualifications, or deferred to me, which was done by the Secretary of Defense." she stated.

"His justification was a deep concern for National Security in light of the dire situation in which we find our country. He believed he could serve our country best by remaining in his current position.

"You may have noticed National Guard personnel in your area," she went on. "They have been deployed by governors of your respective states to assure order is maintained. Authority to institute martial law rests also with state governors. They can assess their situations more accurately than we can at the Federal level.

"Needless to say, what we are dealing with across the country far exceeds FEMA resources. Any relief efforts will be concentrated on major cities, where the need is greatest.

"Due to the lack of a Congressional quorum I will issue Executive Orders under the Emergency Powers Act over the coming weeks, but rest assured I will consult with the remaining members of Congress in doing so.

"Emergency elections are planned for March to replace those who have been so unexpectedly taken from us. It is important to band together to help one another during this difficult time. I pray that God will be with us as we rebuild and encourage you to do the same."

When her speech ended, questions from the press corps included restoration of electrical power; who would provide emergency provisions in the absence of FEMA; national security; financial transactions with undependable power; fuel reserves; and a plethora of others.

The broadcast switched to local stations where governors and, in some cases, mayors, conducted similar news conferences.

"The United States has been skirting the brink of civil war for years," Sara stated. "No telling what states will do. She didn't come right out and say that the federal government is in a state of collapse, but anyone with half a brain should be able to figure that out."

"Reuniting the states under a central government won't be easy," Will said. "Red and blue states have widely polarized ideologies with no compromises in sight. No telling what will happen now."

"Exactly," Connie stated. "Secession by some is likely. The entire union could fall apart. It's a good thing the Secretary of Defense survived. I'm sure our enemies will do what they can to exploit the situation."

"It provides an opportunity to get back to our Constitutional roots and what we were intended to be," Will added. "Often major disasters help people realign their values to where they belong, political leanings or differences losing importance."

"We can always hope, Dad. I think it's beyond interesting that Ms. Iron Shirt is Native American. I wonder how privy she might be to what was going on?"

Her mind raced with the implications.

Just over six months had elapsed since her world was shattered by Bryan's death. Now the United States was in a state of upheaval as well.

Had she and Charlie fulfilled his dying plea?

Could it be said that, after all was said and done, those benefited by PURF did not "get away with it?"

The majority of Executive and Congressional leaders were dead, a Native American woman Acting President of the United States.

Her grin stretched from ear to ear.

It would appear so.

EPILOGUE

SARA'S CONDO
DENVER
November 13, Tuesday
11:22 a.m. MST

Sara sat cross-legged on the living room couch, dog curled up beside her. While the circumstances that brought the canine into her life were dire, the dog was a blessing she wouldn't trade for anything.

Blackouts continued, but were on a schedule so she just 'rolled' with them, rather than stay in Boulder. It was time to go home and figure out what to do.

Noting the date, thoughts turned to Charlie. His near-fatal accident four months before on Friday the 13th made it easy to remember. They'd been through so much together. During the nearly seven months since Bryan's murder, they, too, had come close to joining him. Their mutual support created emotional bonds she struggled to understand.

She didn't hear from him until he got back to Montana following the *Gathering*. He apologized for the delay, explaining his phone died after they broke camp and he didn't have his charger. He thanked her for all her help and confirmed they accomplished what they set out to do.

But that was it.

553

Watching crises unfold across the nation kept her distracted enough not to dwell on it. Understanding why he didn't call earlier satisfied her mind.

Her heart, not so much.

Did any reason to be together expire since fulfilling Bryan's dying plea? Fated connections between Charlie, Bryan, and Dead Horse Canyon spanned generations that still boggled her mind.

Where did she fit in, other than as Bryan's widow?

Except for that impulsive amorous encounter that got Charlie in trouble with White Wolf.

She'd never indulged in anything like that in her entire life. *Never.*

Was that all it was?

She forced her thoughts away from Charlie, finding herself in equally dismal territory. Her podcast and book plans collapsed with PURF and the subsequent upheaval of the entire nation. She had money in her GoFundMe Account with no clue what to do with it. Or if she could even access it, for multiple reasons. The organization's website was down, which bespoke an ominous message.

Should she go back to work as a physical therapist?

She enjoyed her job, compassion stronger than ever since being a paraplegic herself. But resuming her prior vocation lacked enthusiasm, much less passion. It would be satisfying, no doubt, to help people, but going back to her old life without Bryan delivered a strong dose of melancholy.

She didn't need money, thanks to Jason placing it in that Cayman Islands account in a more stable currency than the U.S. dollar. With so much destruction nationwide and the majority of her wealth previously invested in the stock market, if it weren't for Jason she'd probably be broke.

Her phone rang, yanking her from her disheartening reverie.

Her heart skipped a beat. *Had he sensed her thoughts?*

"Hi, Charlie," she answered, unsure what to expect.

"How are you doing, Sara?"

"Okay, I guess. It all seems so anticlimactic. I'm trying to figure out what to do. By the way, I have something for you from Jason."

"You do? How is he? I guess he doesn't need to protect you anymore, right?"

"Actually, Charlie, Jason is dead." She explained what happened, leaving him less shocked than expected."

"White Wolf and I were afraid that might happen. We talked to him after the sweat, but he refused any help we offered for anxiety or depression."

"Well, he went out with a bang. Literally. And he sent something for you and White Wolf to my address. Do you want me to forward it to you?"

"I have a better suggestion."

"Oh? What's that?"

"Why don't you and your family join us for Native American Heritage Day? If you come, just bring it then."

"When is that?"

"The day after Thanksgiving. What you know as Black Friday."

"Oh! That makes sense, given your people's involvement in the first Thanksgiving."

"Yes. But things went downhill after that."

"True," she agreed. "That sounds great. I have no plans. We always have a big dinner at Dad and Connie's. I don't like crowds so don't shop the next day, though sometimes Connie drags Dad out for any deals too good to pass up. But things are so chaotic, I doubt shopping will even be an option. Let me check with them and let you know."

"We always have a big feast on Thanksgiving, too," he said. "Of course we'd want you there for that. Then the next day we have a traditional Cheyenne meal."

"That sounds wonderful. Hopefully we can find enough gas along the way to get there."

"As Bryan used to say, 'Where there's a will, there's a way.' And we will pray for your safe arrival. We have so much to talk about," he went on. "So much happened that I've never had a chance to tell you."

"Does that mean everything that's happened the past few days ties back to your *Gathering*?"

He laughed. "I'm not sure whether I should admit to that or not. I suppose they can't arrest us all. And it's difficult to prove."

"Definitely."

"Well, I have a tribal council meeting I need to go to. Let me know if you can join us. We have a lot to celebrate, which we haven't had a chance to do."

"Okay. I'll let you know."

"Bye, Sara. Hope to see you soon."

"Bye, Charlie."

She smiled as she hung up, though puzzled by what he meant by *celebrate*. Dismissing it, she called Connie to convey the invitation.

"That sounds like fun," Connie said, onboard immediately. "I adore his family. Hold on while I ask your father. Will? Want to go to Montana for Thanksgiving?"

Sara smiled when he replied, "Do I have a choice?"

"It's up to you. Sara and I are going, whether you do or not."

"Okay," he said. "It'll be interesting to learn more of what happened from his perspective, other than the obvious."

"We're in, Sara," Connie said.

"Great! I'll let them know. Have you heard of Native American Heritage Day?" Sara asked.

"No. Hold on, I'll look it up. Okay, here we go: 'The holiday created by Congress in 2008 when they passed a law signed by President George W. Bush that made the Friday after Thanksgiving, unofficially known as 'Black Friday,' National Native American Heritage Day. As the first nationally appointed day dedicated to Native Americans, it represented a welcome and much delayed acknowledgement of their culture.'"

"That's really nice and certainly past-due," Sara commented.

"I thought so," Connie replied. "Too bad it's not publicized more."

Sara laughed. "With our new president, it will be now!"

NORTHERN CHEYENNE RESERVATION
MONTANA
November 16, Friday
9:39 a.m. MST

"I WANT TO MARRY HER."

White Wolf's expression was unreadable as Charlie awaited a reaction, his uncle acting as if he hadn't heard him. Rather, his attention remained on the elk he'd shot a week before. Since then, the carcass had hung in the barn, curing, with it time to remove the hide and prepare the meat for storage.

"Why?" White Wolf replied at last, wiping his hands on a towel. "Guilt? Or something else?"

Charlie's shoulders sagged at the painful reminder. "I am sorry for what happened, but that is not the reason. She is a good woman. Look at all she has done for us. She has never let me down. We have known each other a long time."

"Is that all, Littlewolf?" The man's eyes bore into his.

"No," he said, licking his lips. "I love her. As a friend and as a woman. I miss her and want to be with her." He debated telling him about the vision of the dove, which might convince him. It wasn't like he needed his approval, but he did want his blessings. He knew he had Bryan's.

"I agree she is a good person who has helped us. But she is not Cheyenne. You have much work ahead with the powers *Maheo* entrusted to you. You need a *mésèhée*, a righteous Northern Cheyenne wife, who understands and appreciates those gifts. One who supports what you will be called to do."

His laugh escaped, unbidden. "She is well aware of *Maheo's* gifts, White Wolf. Because of them she can walk again. She has been in the sweat lodge with her family. She is not Cheyenne, but she is one of us."

White Wolf grunted and turned back to the job at hand. "You are a grown man, Littlewolf. That is an important life decision that deserves fasting and much prayer."

"I agree. I have and I will."

WHITE HOUSE OVAL OFFICE
1600 PENNSYLVANIA AVENUE
WASHINGTON, D.C.
November 19, Monday
8:16 a.m. EST

NAOMI SAT BEHIND the massive desk in the Oval Office, mind lilting between joy and apprehension. It still felt like a dream, yet here she was, a week since being declared President of the United States. The work that lay ahead was incomprehensible. Far more important than remodeling the Oval Office, though she was determined to fit the Cheyenne flag in there somewhere.

Her back straightened as thoughts shifted back to her long list of Executive Orders related to Grandfather Iron's Shirt's admonition. The note scrawled that fateful night to preserve his prophetic words reposed on the desk before her:

In forty-four days prophesied events will bring great change. Honor will be yours and give you unimaginable power. Your duty is to restore to indigenous people that which was lost. Do not hesitate. Do not fear. It is Maheo's *will for our people.*

In obedience to his directive, her first EO remanded all Federally owned lands, including National Parks, to the stewardship of the Native people to which they originally belonged. States would be encouraged to do the same. Those that refused would lose federal funding.

That covered lost land.

Culture was another story. Some immigrants fought to retain their practices and beliefs, often in an ugly way. Her people were the First Americans, yet denied theirs.

Anger leaked from her DNA as centuries of offenses paraded through her mind. She closed her eyes and inhaled, then released it slowly through pursed lips, attempting to dispel the generational fury lurking in her blood. Tempting as it was to forge ahead ruthlessly with Iron Shirt's directive, above all else, she committed herself to being fair.

That was all Indigenous people ever wanted, yet didn't receive. She would do what she could to rectify that, but most would simply involve extending benefits other groups already received to include her people. Too many lived in Third World conditions, a National disgrace that broke her heart.

Upheavals coast to coast created shortages from supply chain and transportation issues, forcing most of the country to experience conditions common to reservations. Her lopsided smile upon being asked about that at the press conference bespoke the irony that reservations were mostly oblivious to the country's woes, lack and need their usual conditions. Divine retribution reeked from the fact wealthier areas were harder hit that more humble ones.

Objectives tumbled from her mind faster than chokecherries from an upended basket, though one that demanded immediate attention was the host of treaty violations. She'd studied them extensively for her Master's thesis and knew every one of them by heart. These would be addressed immediately. If what remained of the Congressional representatives wouldn't act upon it, though, she would issue another EO.

Enough was enough.

It was encouraging that the main reason those reps survived was because they didn't attend the PURF dedication. That alone indicated they were more trustworthy than others for shunning the ostentatious event and corrupt people involved.

Senators she'd work with included one from her home state of Montana, whom she knew personally from when she served in the House. The others were from Oklahoma, New Mexico, and South Dakota.

She grinned, not expecting much resistance, as those were all states with a large population of Native Americans among their constituents. Furthermore, she suspected a few of them had some indigenous blood.

Surviving members of the House included representatives for Alaska, Arizona, California, Michigan, Minnesota, Montana, New Mexico, New York, Oklahoma, Oregon, South Dakota, Texas, Washington, Wisconsin, and Utah. Likewise, states with a large number of Native Americans, all of whom she worked with before and often co-sponsored bills.

Grateful tears fell with the realization *Maheo* had orchestrated the situation, right down to those details. Gratitude filled her soul to overflowing. While she started every day with prayer, they came far more frequently since acquiring this incredible responsibility.

Having seen how damaging partisan politics could be, besides taking care of her people she wanted to unify the country as never before. The efforts among her people to bring peace and brotherhood between all Native tribes needed to be extended nationwide to all races and ethnicities.

She extended her arms above her head, swung them wide, then toward the back, trying to convince the muscles to relax. Mind racing again, she pushed back the heavy chair and got up, then walked to the east-facing windows. The Rose Garden lay beyond, prepared for winter as opposed to abloom with color, a dusting of snow on the ground.

Was she being selfish, putting her people first? In response, Grandfather Iron Shirt's words echoed through her mind:

Do not hesitate. Do not fear. It is Maheo's *will for our people.*

The fine hairs on her neck stood up.

Doing the right thing, she made the sacred motions and bowed her head.

"Maheo, I am humbled by the honor as well as the burden placed upon my shoulders. I ask for your help and inspiration at this critical time for our country. Grant me wisdom, fairness, and compassion for all people. Help me be a worthy example of my

heritage as a Northern Cheyenne as well as a citizen of this country. May my actions reflect your will."

SARA'S CONDO
DENVER
November 23, Friday
9:31 a.m. MST

SARA HAD LITTLE TOLERANCE for boredom. Such was never a problem when Bryan was around. Now, however, with her *raison d'etre* accomplished, she sought something engaging to occupy her mind and time.

What did she want to learn that she previously had no time for?

Her thoughts rumbled through her options as she took Blossom on her morning walk around the condo complex. About eight inches of snow covered the ground, but the sidewalks were clear and free of ice. Her bestie wore a quilted red doggie parka and boots to protect her feet that both matched Sara's, protecting them from the frosty bite in the dry winter air.

Her active mind was interested in a variety of topics, which she now had time to pursue. Working with Blossom and teaching her even more skills was a daily task, one they both looked forward to. The K-9 training was a challenge that included various tricky physical maneuvers that got her heart pumping, which felt so good.

Having her body back after nearly losing it had to be the greatest gift she'd ever received. She grinned, quickening her steps and adding something to her gait that almost resembled a skip.

No wonder Mom sent me back. Thanks, Mom!

Thoughts continued to wander among the possibilities. Astrology topped her list. Patrice could certainly tell her how to go about that. Learning herbal medicine was beckoning, too, as was pursuing her fascination with photography.

In view of what she learned about Bryan's past and heritage, a desire to learn more about her own was another one. How his roots tied in with Colonel Joseph Reynolds, who was involved in some of the Indian Wars, fascinated her.

Was it possible that her husband's death was karmic, that in some strange, cosmic way it atoned for his uncle's evil deeds that impacted Native Americans?

There are no coincidences!

Her thoughts took off at what came to mind next: *What if her progenitors had a bearing on her life?*

As far as she knew, the only one who ever did any genealogy was her mother, back when Sara was young. She remembered her explaining a pedigree chart, which seemed odd. To her ten-year-old mind, that was something dogs had, not people.

Where might those old records be? No doubt somewhere in her father's house, where she grew up. Curiosity sparked, she made up her mind to find those old charts and learn more about the period of history her ancestors experienced and where.

Enthusiastic about her new quest, Sara hustled through the remainder of their usual route, dog thoroughly enjoying the increased pace. When they got back inside a short time later, she bounded up the stairs, two at a time, to grab her laptop and a notebook, then got her canine companion settled in the car, and followed the familiar route toward Boulder.

Before leaving Denver she glanced down, noting she needed gas. Fortunately, there was at least one open gas station along the way. Fuel was being rationed, but she didn't go out enough for it to be an issue. Due to power shortages, most businesses were closed, including those that did body work, so the car's smashed-in side remained as a souvenir of what they'd been through.

As always, Connie gave her a hug when she arrived. Will was there, too, since joining the ranks of the unemployed, not that many had jobs these days. The house was a little chilly, thermostats turned down by decree, a few logs burning their last in the fireplace.

"To what do we owe your visit?" Connie asked, crouching down to greet Blossom. "Is everything okay?"

"Yes," she replied. "They're good. I have a new project."

Connie's eyes sparkled. "Nothing like the last one, I hope. Your father will have a fit."

Sara laughed. "No. Nothing like that. I got to thinking how Bryan's life connected with his ancestors and wondered what I might find about mine. People uncover some pretty interesting stories that they share on those genealogy websites. I remember Mom did some research, so I want to see if I can find what she did, as a starter."

"That sounds like fun!" Connie agreed. "Will probably knows where that would be. He's in the den watching the stock market, or what's left of it after the big crash. He figures now's the time to get in on the ground floor of something related to rebuilding the country. I suggested drywall, like U.S. Gypsum, if they're still around."

"That sounds like a good idea. What did he say?"

Sara walked toward the stairs, Connie right behind.

"He agreed, but was looking for something more technological. Hordes of corrupt corporations have been wiped out. So he's looking for a start-up in the communications or media industries."

"It's definitely going to be interesting how this goes, once we get past the stark disaster stage. The price of gas is sure a shocker. Those empty shelves in the supermarket are pretty concerning as well. I'm glad I stocked up on dog food. At least we have the cabin, if things get really bad. Plenty of deer and elk, if nothing else."

"True. As long as we could get there, short of walking."

"Right!"

As expected, Will was on the computer in his den.

"Hi, Dad."

He spun around wearing a frown. "Sara! What are you doing here? Is everything alright?"

"I'm okay, just bored. I was wondering if you know where the genealogy Mom did might be?"

"Should be in the bedroom closet," he said, pointing in that direction. "As I recall, it's in one of those blue archive boxes."

"Great!"

She headed that way, not taking long to find it. She took it to the den and sat down on the well-worn leather couch. A wave of excitement charged through her, as if she might find something important. A new adventure of sorts.

Conveniently, there was a pedigree chart with Sara at the top, showing names for both parents and their respective progenitors. She looked them over, surprised when two names jumped out.

"Dad? Did you know your maternal grandmother?"

Will turned from his computer. "No. She died when I was a baby."

"Do you know if she was Native American?"

His look turned pensive. "Actually, I don't. What makes you think she was?"

"Her maiden name was Elizabeth Whitehorse. That sounds like it could be."

He leaned back in his chair, arms folded. "Interesting. That would mean my mother was half-Indian. Huh. I don't recall it ever being mentioned."

"Here's a picture of her when she married your father. Her appearance suggests she could be. Check out those high cheekbones and almond eyes. I kind of look like her, don't I?"

He put on his glasses and scrutinized the photo. "Well, I'll be. You actually do. I always thought you looked like Ellen. I think her mother was, actually. People back then didn't talk about it much. Too much stigma attached."

Sara's eyebrows lifted, already discovering things she didn't know before. "No kidding? If your grandmother was and Mom's mother was, that means I would have almost a third Native American blood."

She turned to the pedigree chart to see what her maternal grandmother's name was.

"Mom's mother's maiden name was Mary Starving Elk. That *definitely* sounds Native American, too. That's so cool! I can't wait to tell Charlie!"

The archive box was loaded with research material. Sara dug through it for any further information or documentation related to both progenitors.

What she found left her grinning like she'd found the Motherlode.

NORTHERN CHEYENNE RESERVATION
MONTANA
November 29, Thanksgiving Thursday
5:39 p.m. MST

A BLIZZARD BLEW IN late the night before, dumping over a foot of snow across Montana and the Dakota's. Early that morning, Littlewolf tried out *Tah-Hó'nehe's* snowplow, trudging through deep drifts to the barn to get it all set up. After that, he cleared their road all the way to Busby and most the front yard, mounds of snow stacked along the fenced area. White Wolf smiled, forced to admit the vehicle's utility.

Most of the reservation was not so fortunate, however.

Sara and her family's arrival beat the storm, though now they were essentially snowed in. Getting to their hotel in Sheridan that night wasn't going to happen.

Both his and Sara's families lounged around on the sectional couch like most did on Thanksgiving, having eaten too much. He was also acutely aware of how lucky they were, compared to millions following the catastrophes triggered by the *Gathering*.

"It seems like yesterday when our families were together for that sweat," White Wolf commented. "Yet it's been well over two months. So much has happened. We have much to be grateful for."

Murmurs of agreement filled the room.

"Those who lost everything, or much of it, are hopefully enjoying a reasonably good meal in whatever shelter or FEMA camp where they were assigned," Will said.

"So much has happened this past year," Sara said.

"That's for sure," Will agreed. "An entirely different world out there now. What do you think of our new president, Joe?"

White Wolf didn't even try to hide how elated he was. "We couldn't be happier. Did you know Naomi is one of us? A Northern Cheyenne. Born right here, over in Ashland."

"No kidding?" Sara exclaimed. "That's incredible! And guess what? I think I'm part Cheyenne, too. Turns out my mother's mother and my great-grandmother on Dad's side were both Northern Cheyenne."

White Wolf glanced at Littlewolf, whose wide-eyes matched his own and revealed they were equally stunned.

"How did you find that out?" Littlewolf asked.

Sara grinned. "My mother was into genealogy. After seeing all the fascinating connections in Bryan's family, I wondered if there might be something interesting in mine as well. And as it turned out, there it was!"

"Was there any documentation to back it up?" White Wolf asked, eyes locked on hers.

She nodded. "Some. Both of them were living on the Northern Cheyenne reservation for the 1920 census, but not the one in 1930."

"My grandmother's journal indicated the 1920s were rough for Montana," Will said. "Its population fell during that time, so that must be when and why they left. She wound up in Colorado, where she married."

"My grandmother, too," Sara said.

"So we are truly sisters," Star stated, beaming with joy. "That's wonderful! Welcome to the family, Sara!"

Littlewolf's stare felt as if it were burning a hole in the back of White Wolf's head. Their eyes met, his question obvious, even without tuning into his thoughts. He gave a subtle nod, not expecting him to act on it as quickly as he did.

"How would you like to *really* be a member of the family?" Littlewolf asked her. All eyes went from him to Sara, puzzled, while White Wolf knew exactly where this was going.

"What do you mean?" she asked, words and posture drifting to caution, her eyes locked on his.

"If you agree, I'd really like to marry you."

She looked shocked for a moment, giggled, then a broad smile illuminated her entire being. "I'd really like that, too," she replied.

It took a few seconds for what just happened to sink in, then everyone cheered, showing unanimous approval.

A conversation followed of how a Cheyenne man courted a woman in the traditional way, which could take as long as five years.

"Five years?" Sara's horrified look dissolved when Charlie shook his head.

"Not anymore," he said, chuckling.

"You have known each other a respectable amount of time," White Wolf confirmed. "It used to be that the man gave the girl's father as many horses as he could afford as well as other gifts." He couldn't help taunting Littlewolf with an expectant look.

"I like that," Will said. "Great practice. In modern times does that translate to a car? I quite like your Tahoe."

Littlewolf's dumbfounded look indicated he didn't know whether or not his uncle, much less his future father-in-law, was joking. "Uh, well, *Tah-Hó'nehe* belongs to White Wolf. But you're very welcome to my old pickup."

"That would be terrific," Will said, rubbing his hands together. "I could use a truck."

Winter Hawk's expression fell as he responded with an exaggerated groan.

"I'm sorry, brother," Charlie consoled him. "But tradition is tradition."

Star started to giggle, knowing her husband well enough to know it was a joke, prompting everyone else to follow with hearty laughter. "This calls for celebration," she said. "Are you ready for dessert?"

Another chorus of positive replies responded.

White Wolf got up and beckoned Littlewolf to follow to his medicine room. He quietly closed the door.

"That is indeed good news. If she can prove she's over a third Northern Cheyenne and marries you, she can qualify for adoption into the tribe. She just has to live here four years and meet other standards, which shouldn't be difficult."

"So I have your blessings?" Littlewolf asked, efforts to suppress his smile failing miserably.

White Wolf smiled. "Yes, you do."

Relief washed over Littlewolf's face. He licked his lips. "During a fast many months ago, I saw my white brother," he said. "He gave me a dove. I knew it was Sara. At first I thought maybe he just meant for me to look after her. But it didn't take long to realize it meant far more and that he approved."

White Wolf grunted. "You should have told me that before, Littlewolf. I would have never questioned it."

When they returned to the living room, Sara held out an envelope. Littlewolf took it from her hand with a questioning look.

"What is this?" he asked.

"I don't know," she said with a shrug. "It's what Jason sent for you."

Puzzled, he ripped it open and removed a single piece of paper. He scowled as he looked it over, then handed it to White Wolf.

"I don't understand what this is," he said.

White Wolf had the same reaction. As far as he could tell it was a printout of account information listing them as co-owners. The balance at the bottom was a mysterious 379 TOZ.

"What is it?" Sara asked.

He handed it to her, likewise mystified.

She looked it over, frowning at first, then slowly lighting up like lights at a Christmas pow-wow.

"Oh! This is for PAX gold. It's digital and unscathed by what's going on with the dollar. You own 379 troy ounces of actual gold that's stored in London."

"How much is that in dollars?" White Wolf asked.

Will pulled out his phone and did the calculations. "Somewhere around a million bucks."

Littlewolf's color drained as he staggered to a chair, face as white as his guests.

"This is great!" Sara doubled over, laughing. "Now no one can accuse you of marrying for money!"

NORTHERN CHEYENNE RESERVATION
MONTANA
November 30, Friday
Native American Heritage Day
10:03 a.m. MST

EVERYONE, ESPECIALLY SARA, agreed there was no better way to celebrate Native American Heritage Day. With both families present and White Wolf having authority to perform the ceremony, there was no reason to wait. They'd get a license in Lame Deer along with the required testing the following week, those services closed for the holiday.

Services on the reservation were mostly the same as they'd always been. The President had assured Indigenous people were taken care of, mandating that food and gas deliveries be prioritized, claiming they'd suffered enough.

Star's fringed and beaded white deerskin dress handed down from her great-grandmother fit Sara perfectly for her wedding gown. As she explained the tradition, they both marveled that Star's great-grandmother's name was also Starving Elk, apparently a sister of Sara's grandmother.

Her bouquet consisted of man sage, dried yellowweed, sweetgrass, and other dried flowers with special *Tsistsistas* significance.

She and Charlie stood before the picture of *Novavose* and pledged their love and devotion, then enjoyed a traditional Cheyenne feast.

"Where are you going to live?" Connie asked, concern lurking in her eyes.

"We'll stay in Colorado for now to sell my condo, then live in the cabin until spring," Sara said. She smiled as her step-mother relaxed, at least a little.

Until Charlie added, "Then we'll come back here. We'll build us a new home on my land that adjoins White Wolf's."

Sara knew for certain why she couldn't figure out before what to do with her time or money.

Now she knew.

"I want to set up a foundation to help those in need on the reservation," she said. "I also want to set up a school to teach and preserve the Cheyenne language. Especially since I need to learn it myself!"

The only ones who weren't deliriously happy were Will and Connie, their only consolation the couple would be in Colorado for several months.

"If you're twenty-five percent Cheyenne, Will," Charlie said. "You could apply for tribal membership, too. You'd have to live here, though."

"Not a bad idea," he replied. "Do you agree, woman?"

"No argument here," Connie agreed.

He grinned. "I'll even have a truck waiting for me."

THE END

ABOUT THE AUTHORS

Marcha Fox earned a bachelor's degree in physics from Utah State University in 1987, which facilitated a 21-year career at NASA's Johnson Space Center in Houston, Texas. Her positions there included that of a technical writer, engineer, lead, and manager.

Her previous fiction work includes five novels in the hard science fiction genre. Her epic Star Trails Tetralogy series has been highly acclaimed for its family-oriented plot as well as its science content. Directed primarily to young readers with an interest in science or engineering, more information can be found on StarTrailsSaga.com.

Forever fascinated by the heavens, when her attempt to debunk astrology backfired, she pursued knowledge in that field as well. She graduated from the International Academy of Astrology's professional development program in 2012 and created ValkyrieAstrology.com. Much of the popular website's informational content can be found in her book, "Whobeda's Guide to Basic Astrology."

Born in Peekskill, New York, she has lived in California, Utah, and Texas in the course of raising her family that comprises six grown children and several grandchildren and great-grandchildren. She pampers her two indoor cats, provides readings for her astrology clients, keeps up with her home, friends, and family, and of course, writes. She currently makes her home in the Finger Lakes Region of New York State.

Pete Risingsun is a full-blooded Northern Cheyenne and an enrolled member of that Tribe. He is well-versed in their ceremonies and traditions, having served as a spirit helper to medicine men in ceremonial sweat lodges where traditional procedures are meticulously followed. Born the eighth child of ten in 1950, he was raised on a small ranch east of Busby on the Northern Cheyenne reservation in southeastern Montana.

Pete wears his grandfather's Cheyenne name, *Mo'öhtáveaénohe* (Black Hawk), who was a member of the Council of Forty-Four Chiefs.

In addition, he's a proud fifth generation descendant of Iron Shirt, a ceremonial medicine man warrior who fought beside Chief Littlewolf. The story is told that his buckskin Cheyenne war shirt had powerful medicine that made him fearless. The buckskin would turn to iron during battle and the soldiers' bullets would fall to the ground.

After graduating high school in 1968, he attended Montana State University for four years. When offered a position with Exxon as an employee relations director overseas, he turned it down, instead completing a three-year apprenticeship in plant operations in Billings, Montana. He worked in that capacity for one additional year until he accepted a job as adult education director for the Northern Cheyenne Tribe back home in Lame Deer, Montana, thus bidding farewell to the refinery.

Back on the reservation, Pete raised black Angus cattle and bred championship Quarter horses. He served as a Tribal Council member for six years and was the first Northern Cheyenne elected as a Rosebud County Commissioner, a position he held from January 1, 2007 to December 31, 2012.

He's the proud father of one daughter, Echo Raine, who blessed him with two grandchildren, Sierra Star and Skyler Seven. Pete is currently retired, but has stayed busy co-writing *The Curse of Dead Horse Canyon* trilogy the past few years as well as compiling an accurate history of his tribe from the Northern Cheyenne point of view.

Learn more about the authors, how to contact them on social media, watch book trailers, and read related blogs on the trilogy website:

Dead-Horse-Canyon.com

A good leader takes a little more than his share of the blame, and a little less than his share of the credit.
—Arnold H. Glasgow

ACKNOWLEDGEMENTS

This book would not have been possible if it weren't for Pete's intimate knowledge of Northern Cheyenne culture as a ceremonial man. This was augmented by substantial research found in the great works by several renowned anthropologists and historians, some of which are noted in the Bibliography.

Too many tragic, immoral actions were rationalized by a culture that had no reverence for life or indigenous people. Christian churches should be ashamed of their attempt at cultural if not literal genocide since *Veheo's* arrival on the shores of the "New World." I suspect mistranslations of the Bible contributed, perhaps as simple as one word found in the King James Version: *Dominion.*

What else would you expect from a translation commissioned by a king? Why "dominion" instead of "stewardship?" Where does it say that the white man was entitled to that versus those of a different color? It doesn't! And there you have it.

The history scattered throughout this story was heavily researched and implemented as accurately as possible, including the story of Walker Lake. Obvious exceptions are the fictitious Dead Horse Canyon massacre and much of Bryan's history report.

I am grateful for editorial assistance provided by my cosmic sister and fellow author, Dawn Greenfield Ireland of Artistic Origins. You can find her at https://degreefield.com/Services.

Thank you as well to our readers who have been waiting far too long for this final book to be published. We hope you enjoy the story's conclusion and find it worth the wait.

574

I have asked some of the great white chiefs where they get their authority to say to the Indian that he shall stay in one place, while he sees white men going where they please. They can not tell me.
— *Young Joseph "Chief Joseph", 1879*

BIBLIOGRAPHY

Powell, Peter John; Sweet Medicine Volumes 1 and 2; University of Oklahoma Press, Norman, Oklahoma; 1969.

Grinnell, George Bird; The Cheyenne Indians: Their History and Way of Life Volume I and II; University of Nebraska Press; Lincoln, Nebraska; 1972. (Reproduction of 1st Edition published by Yale University Press; 1923.)

Maryboy, Nancy C. and Begay, David; Sharing the Skies: Navajo Astronomy; Rio Nuevo Publishers, Tucson, Arizona; 2010.

Schlesier, Karl H.; The Wolves of Heaven: Cheyenne Shamanism, Ceremonies, and Prehistoric Origins; 1985

Waldman, Carl; Encyclopedia of Native American Tribes 3rd Edition; Checkmark Books; 2006.

Waldman, Carl; Atlas of The North American Indian 3rd Edition; Checkmark Books; 2009.

Hittman, Michael; Wovoka and the Ghost Dance; University of Nebraska Press; 1990

Stands In Timber, John and Liberty, Margot; Cheyenne Memories; Yale University Press; 1967

Warren, Louis S.; God's Red Son: The Ghost Dance Religion and the Making of Modern American; Basic Books; 2017

Brinkerhoff, Val; The Remnant Awakens; Createspace; 2018

And many others, including websites too numerous to mention....

The most beautiful and most profound emotion we can experience is the sensation of the mystical. It is the source of all art and science. So to whom this emotion is a stranger, who can no longer wonder and stand rapt in awe, is as good as dead; his eyes are closed.
—Albert Einstein

ABOUT ASTROLOGY

While Patrice Renard is a fictitious character, the astrology in this story is real. I kid you not. No one is more astounded than I am. The birthdates of the characters were made up and used with places close to those invented for the sake of the story. How the astrological influences on fictitious characters for the timeframe chosen could tie in perfectly with the plot is beyond my comprehension.

At times when I wasn't sure what would happen next, all I had to do was refer to the astrological influences of that moment to find out. Conveniently, I'm also a professional astrologer, so this was easily done. I'll post blogs to the series website on the details some time in the future. It's too fascinating not to share.

The information noted about eclipses is mostly true, though worked into the fictitious storyline.

If you think astrology is weird, I suggest you study quantum theory, or the newly emerging ontological physics, which to any rational person, is even farther out. I'm a physicist and I personally think the concept of parallel dimensions where we exist in all of them is ridiculous.

I'm really excited about ontology since it incorporates psychic and supernatural phenomena as well as a role for consciousness, which easily suggests a place for astrology to say nothing of all the phenomena represented in this book.

Time will tell.